Changeling

Moon

by Christine Morgan

Published by:

Sabledrake Enterprises
PO Box 30751
Seattle, WA 98113
http://www.sabledrake.com
sabledrake@sabledrake.com

This book is dedicated to the Jericho Fan Club.
You sick, sick, twisted people . . .
How I love you all!

Prologue

The car with the dying girl in the back seat screamed down the black ribbon of road, headlights cutting a swath through the night. The glow of the dashboard cast eerie shadows onto the driver's tense face. He leaned forward, hunched over the wheel upon which his hands were white-knuckled clamps.

His gaze stuttered from the road ahead to the rectangular murky darkness of the rearview mirror, passing briefly over the reflection of his own worried face, which was haggard and looked much older than his years. He searched for the pursuit he knew would be coming.

He wanted to turn on the radio, fill the car with music to drown out the girl. Her breathing, a series of harsh barking gasps. Her low, helpless cries whenever the tires thudded over an uneven patch of asphalt.

A single white eye opened in the mirror, growing rapidly. As fast as they were going, so fast that the lines down the center of the two-lane blacktop were a pale streak like stars seen from a spaceship accelerating into hyperspace, their pursuer was gaining.

The driver muttered a curse and pressed the gas pedal, but it was already as far down as it would go, and the old car was shuddering from the unexpected demand of speed.

"He's coming!" his brother said from the back, where he held the girl, his own injuries ignored or even forgotten as he tried in vain to comfort her.

"I know," the driver said.

He risked a glance back, his eyes briefly meeting those of his brother before moving to the pale, bruise-mottled oval of the girl's face. Her clothes were in tatters, her skin streaked with blood. The back of the car was soaked with it. If hopelessness had a scent, he thought as he returned his attention to the road and the onrushing red blinker of the intersection, it would be that high, coppery, thick odor.

"Did you see . . ." his brother's voice choked off into a half-sob. "Did you see what he did to her?"

"Don't think about it. She'll be fine."

He was lying, they both knew it. How could she ever be fine after what had happened to her? Even if they were able to get to help in time, even if she survived and her body mended, her mind would never be the same. Not after what she'd suffered.

The lateness of the hour should have meant that they'd have the night to themselves, but as the car sped toward the intersection, toward that red blinking light flashing its warning into the black, the driver saw the gleam of another set of headlights approaching from the cross street.

Swearing again, he checked the mirror. That white eye was bearing down on them, and if their tired old engine hadn't been banging and rattling, he knew he would have been able to hear the hungry, primal snarl of the motorcycle.

The other vehicle – it was a pickup – stopped at the four-way red and then began to proceed sedately across. Directly into their path.

"Hold on!" the driver shouted. He jigged the wheel to the right.

The headlights splashed across the side of the pickup truck. The driver could see two faces, all wide eyes and mouths like that famous painting of the screaming ghost-figure, in the square of the window. The back of the pickup was piled with rusty tools, old washers and dryers, a mélange of other junk.

The car skated by, tires wailing, and for a moment the driver thought they'd made it. The corner of the pickup was so close that he could have reached out and rapped his knuckles on it. But then the side of their car connected with the pickup's bumper.

Sparks showered. A terrible screech threatened to split his head apart. The car was kicked away, just a little, but enough to make him lose control. The steering wheel tore from his grip, abrading his palms. The back end wanted to slide one way, while the front strove for the other. The driver knew they were milliseconds away from going into a spin that would send them whipping off the road, where they'd roll in a tangle of crumpling metal.

Scarlet flared somewhere to his left and he realized it was the brake lights of the pickup, which they'd already shot past. Tools and ironmongery jolted out of the back, rang like gongs, struck more sparks from the pavement.

Even in the midst of his terror and alarm, the driver found room to silently urge the other driver not to stop, to just keep going, not to give in to the basic human urge of curiosity. The fact of his own mortality was very much upon him. Not only for himself, but for his brother and the girl. Bad enough the three of them were surely done for. He didn't want more deaths on their heads.

He wrested the wheel back into submission, fighting to turn the car away from the gravelly shoulder. But as the tires struck that softer surface, sending a hail of tiny rocks pinging and clanging against the undercarriage, the rear end swung around the other way, skidding on the blacktop, making the car jounce and jolt.

The car plunged nose-first into the shallow ditch. The driver threw his crossed arms in front of his face as he was hurled forward. In the frantic rush to save the girl, he hadn't even thought about buckling his seatbelt. The steering wheel smashed into his chest. His head snapped forward. The windshield imploded, showering in on him, sharp-sticky safety glass cutting his forearms.

The momentum of the crash was almost enough to carry the car up and over in an automotive somersault. The driver felt the sickening sensation of teetering, of facing what seemed to be straight down. But before that mystic balance point could be reached, the back end was reclaimed by gravity and slammed to earth.

He slumped in the seat, blood from his split forehead oozing into his eyes and his ribcage feeling as if the bones had been replaced with hot pokers. Part of his mind clamored that he had to get up, get out, get away. The rest of him just wanted to sink into a comforting fog of unconsciousness.

A hand gripped his shoulder. He laboriously looked around to see his brother's familiar, desperate, battered face only inches from his own.

"We have to get out of here," his brother said.

The driver swallowed, grimacing at the taste, and tried to formulate words.

"Hey! Hey, are you all right in there? Shit! Hey, buddy, you on the bike, how about some help?"

The voice had to belong to one of the people from the pickup. The words, though, struck a chord of panic in the driver's heart that overshadowed his stunned, pained state.

He shook off his brother's hand. The driver's side door had popped open and rested now with its lower edge half buried in the loose fill of the ditch, its frame crumpled and the window a sagging net of fractured, spiderwebbed cracks. He scrambled out and tugged at the back door, but it had buckled and even with him yanking from the outside and his brother kicking from the inside, it wouldn't budge.

"You'll have to climb over," the driver said. "Hurry!"

"I think they're okay," called the voice from the pickup excitedly, and the beam of a flashlight came jogging toward them. "I think I see —"

The beam sliced suddenly up, losing itself in the impassive dark sky. A bleating cry came from the running figure as he was tackled, brought down. Another voice, this one female, shrieked in horror and disbelief.

The pickup had stopped a little ways past the intersection. Between its taillights and the red blinker, the entire scene was painted in uneven washes of crimson. The scant, strange illumination was enough for the driver to see everything in terrible clarity.

A woman, in her twenties and wearing a miniskirt and a patchwork rabbit fur jacket, stood by the pickup's dented rear bumper. Her hands were fisted in her hair as if she meant to pull off her scalp like a wig, and her shriek pealed endlessly, seemingly without the need for her to stop and take a breath.

A motorcycle, a black and chrome machine with gold-edged scarlet flames emblazoned on the gas tank, was tilted at a rakish angle on its kickstand. The rider, tall and muscular, rose up from the unmoving form of the man from the pickup.

The sight was almost enough to freeze the driver into immobility, and surely would have if he hadn't seen it before. If he hadn't known what was chasing them. If he hadn't already witnessed first-hand the terrible strength, and vicious lust, of the creature.

The screaming woman turned to run. The beast was upon her before she'd gotten three steps. A single bound of powerful hind legs propelled the wolfin-draconian-inhuman form with uncanny speed and grace. In the red glow of the pickup's taillights, the beast's claws glistened with blood. The pickup driver was a heap of meat in the road, the life torn out of him.

Luck was with the woman. As the beast leaped upon her, she was driven headfirst into the side of the vehicle. Even from here, the driver could hear the impact, the snapping of her neck. She went mercifully limp.

His brother was trying to move the unconscious girl over the seats. She sprawled with the glitter of windshield-glass making a tiara in her hair.

The driver leaned in through the open door, reaching for her. His hand closed on her slender wrist. He could feel her thready pulse, so weak, barely there. Her eyelids fluttered and opened, dark pools peering up at him in numb incomprehension.

"Take her," his brother said, wriggling halfway over the seat-backs. "Get her out of –"

The rest of his words were driven out of him in a grunt as the roof of the car buckled under the weight that had landed solidly upon it. Metal groaned. His brother was pinned in place, squirming, struggling.

A wild, animalistic scent rich with musk and blood-hunger overwhelmed the driver. He looked up. The beast was there, only inches away. It was crouched atop the car, fangs bared in a feral grin, eyes lambent pools of radiance.

The driver took an involuntary step back, losing his grasp on the girl's wrist. A flush like a fever raced over his skin. His breath slipped like a hot zephyr in and out of his lungs. He raised his hands, ready to fight though he knew he wouldn't stand a chance.

The beast's growl sounded like a laugh. Before the driver could even make a move, one massive pawlike hand swung through the air. Caught off guard, he was sent flying.

A spur of ice ran itself through him. Every nerve stiffened, every muscle convulsed. He felt his spine arch into a curve. Tendons stood out like cables in his neck, jaw, temples.

He coughed, once, and the ice in his chest turned to fire. His head didn't want to move but he forced himself to look down.

A narrow bulge hideously reminiscent of a scene from a space movie tented his shirt. As his spine relaxed its curvature, lowering his body into a slump, the fabric ripped and something dark and wet appeared. He slid down along it until his back came to rest against the slanted metal wall of an up-ended washing machine.

He was in the midst of the debris that had spilled from the pickup, impaled on a bar that poked up at a deadly angle. Other sharp edges gouged and gashed at his legs.

Another cough escaped him, and a warm, thick bubble burst on his lips.

From where he lay, helpless, he could see too well. He could see the beast hop lithely down from its perch and bend to peer into the wrecked car. His brother was still trapped between the bowed roof and the seats.

The girl had gotten to her knees by the mangled driver's side door. Her hands were raised in supplication, shudders shaking her and red-tinted tears glimmering like trails of blood on her cheeks.

The driver grasped the bar that protruded from his chest. The heat and stickiness of it made his throat clench. He tried to lever himself up and off, but even the slightest effort was enough to send motes of blackness spinning through his mind. He fell back weakly, hearing more than feeling a gruesome rending from somewhere within him.

Motes . . . spinning and dancing. In his mind and in his eyes. Through the whirling mothlike specks, he saw the beast reach out, seize the girl. He closed his eyes before he had to witness what it would do to her, but couldn't close his ears to his brother's anguished wail.

That cry followed him down, a resounding echo of failure and loss. When the motes swelled into an engulfing black cloud, he surrendered.

*   *   *

THE HUNTERS

CHAPTER 1
DECEMBER 19, FRIDAY

An hour after the meeting was over – Mr. McGuire liked to call it a meeting rather than a counseling session, but it all boiled down to the same thing in her mind – Aiden Ferguson bundled into her parka with its faux-fur trim and went outside.

The moon, half full and pale as a pearl, hung framed in the boughs of the trees and played peek-a-boo behind the shifting wraiths of the clouds. She gazed up, remembering having read that astronomers expected the lunar sphere to break up one day, cracked into pieces by the Earth's gravity to make a ring, an asteroid belt. As interesting as that might be, she was glad it wouldn't happen until far in the future.

She made her way northward along the beach, finding the best footing by habit and experience. Soon, the terrain turned rockier. She stepped carefully from one slick stone to the next, taking her gloved hands out of her pockets in case she tripped.

The ragged bluff loomed ahead of her. Aiden could hear the distant boom of waves against tumbled rocks. The only hint that she wasn't alone in some remote part of the world, or on some alien planet like the one in her latest painting, was the muted glow of the lights of the town and the buoys, or beacons, or whatever they were, planted far out in the bay itself for the sake of the boats.

Strange to think that only a few hundred yards away, yet out of sight, was an entire town. Hundreds, even thousands of people were over there, going about the chores of daily life and getting ready for the Christmas holidays. While she stood here, alone as she had always been.

Aiden stopped in the shadow of a boulder, startled to realize she was on the verge of tears. For no good reason, either. What could there possibly be to cry about because she lived in a town full of friendly, caring people?

But that was it, that was exactly it. How could she ever fit into their circle? She wasn't one of them, would never be one of them. How could she, when she was too timid to make more than the most basic conversation with the checker at the market, when she buried her nose in a book at the coin-op laundry to avoid having to talk to anyone?

She knew what they must think of her, what they must say to one another. That strange Ferguson girl. Not a local girl but an outsider. The one who'd stayed when the other employees from the Seacliff school had left. Some had gone to prison and others, the innocent ones, had just been happy to get as far away from the scandal as they could.

Calming herself with a series of deep breaths, she eased away from the urge to cry. She'd let the peace of the night work its magic.

An irregular splashing, subtly different from the soothing noise of the surf, made her glance around. She spied dark shapes in the water, out by the furthest of the rocks. Sleek, graceful forms glided cleanly through the waves.

As she watched, one flipped itself onto the slick stone surface. Moonlight silvered its pelt, traced the outline of its form.

A sea lion. Aiden smiled. She'd heard them before, barking their calls, but this was the first time she'd seen one here on her very own beach. And not just one, a pack of them. Would they be called a pack? A pod? Or a pride?

The merry creatures were only a few dozen yards from her, others joining the first on the rock where they groomed and jostled for position and made sounds that could have been taken for chatter. Some slipped back into the water, only to reappear moments later.

Aiden picked her way closer. She counted five of them. The uninhibited joy and playfulness in their movements filled her with delight.

But abruptly, that warm and happy sense turned to a cold prickle of unease. Her breath caught as if her throat had been pinched off.

She wasn't alone in the night anymore. She knew that as surely as she knew her own middle name was Morag, and oh how she wished both facts weren't true.

Someone was near. Someone was watching her just as she watched the leaping, cavorting sea creatures.

Aiden tried to swallow past that pinched blockage in her throat. She slowly looked around. The moonlight was fickle, and the rocks and driftwood offered too many hiding places. The surrounding forest was too close.

Anyone could have been concealed in the shadows.

Someone. Out there in the shadows, just beyond her range of vision. Hiding. Watching her.

She stood indecisive on the spur of rock until the twinge of unease passed. She still felt that there was a presence nearby, still felt watched, but had no immediate sense that she was in danger.

Raving lunatic or curious neighbor, either way, Aiden wasn't going to linger.

Her little house, the diffuse squares of light marking the curtained front windows, looked further away than she knew it truly was. Her hands stayed fisted at her sides, pulse drumming in her ears.

No escapee from a horror movie lunged at her. Neither did an Avon lady or a teenager selling candy bars to benefit the Trinity Bay high school band. She had the night and the shore to herself. Still, she sighed with relief as she set her hand on her own porch rail.

The moment she did so, a sudden sure intuition struck her — *now* was when someone would spring out of the darkness and seize her.

She lunged up the steps and through the door, locking it behind her. She shamed herself more by leaning against it and giving in to a fit of trembling. The fit lasted only a few seconds, because the next thing she imagined was an axe or a claw cleaving through the door beside her head.

Aiden whirled and backed up, narrowly missing the coffee table.

The door stayed as it was, whole and uncleaved. No ominous heavy tread sounded on the porch. The lights didn't wink out and plunge her into blackness.

She did hear eerie music, but that was her own fault for leaving the radio tuned to the classical station, which was currently playing the "O Fortuna" segment from Orff's *Carmina Burana.*

"You," she said, "have been watching too much *Monstorama Theater.*"

Someone *had* been out there. She had no doubt of that. Someone who hadn't wanted to be seen.

Could it be, and this was a thought she found both silly and wryly amusing, that whoever it was had been wary of her? Who could possibly look at skinny little Aiden Ferguson as a threat?

Aiden laughed, stifling it quickly because laughing to oneself was almost as bad as talking to oneself and talking to oneself was only a short step from what the psychiatrists liked to call 'responding to internal stimuli.'

Even so, the silliness of the idea wouldn't go away. Afraid of her? Why would anyone be afraid of *her?*

* * *

CHAPTER 2
DECEMBER 20, SATURDAY

Jerry Forrester slouched in the passenger seat and fiddled with the settings on his video camera. "Can't you at least rough up a suspect?"

"I tried to tell you." Officer Scott James kept his gaze on the twisting coastal road and the shimmering veils of mist that couldn't quite make it as actual rain. "It was your idea to do *COPS* in Trinity Bay, not mine."

"Huah!" grunted Jerry, and sang a little of the classic old reality show's theme song before snorting in disgust. "Yeah, but I expected *something* would happen. Something. Anything. Other than the gripping drama of Mrs. Asherby complaining about her neighbor having his television turned up too loud."

"I suppose you would have liked it better if I kicked in Mr. Havelock's door and wrestled him down, walker and all."

"Hey, yeah. Mrs. Asherby could have been screaming curses to bleep out on the final tape."

"Sorry to disappoint you."

"But, I mean, come on . . . there's got to be more than this. I'm going to get an F in my film class for boring the hell out of everyone."

"Hey, you could have asked the Eureka P. D. Why'd you pick on me?"

"Because I knew you'd go along with it." Jerry grinned.

"Then it's nobody's fault but your own."

"I did learn something, though."

"Yeah?"

"Yeah . . . you guys have a piece of cake job."

Scott spared him a sidelong, sour look. "Piece of cake? You wouldn't have said that two years ago when I busted into Seacliff to save your bacon."

"Oh, yeah, you're so unappreciated . . . who's dating Dani Kensington?"

The radio under the dash crackled into life with Damon Blake's rich deep voice. "Scott, you there?"

"Jeez," Jerry muttered. "No code numbers or jargon or anything."

Scott plucked the handset from its cradle. "Yeah, boss. I'm here. I got Havelock to turn on his closed-captioning. He says he'll get a new battery for his hearing aid tomorrow. The feud is settled for tonight."

"Good deal." Damon Blake, with his habitual wild-west drawl, sounded dry and amused. "But saddle up, son, we just got another call. Out Vista Drive. Ronnie Greene says there's a fight over at the Bakers' place."

Scott's sandy brows lifted. "Domestic? Mike and Stacey?"

"Ronnie says he can hear yelling. Go take a look."

"On our way."

Vista Drive was the only paved road south of town. The rest were dirt roads, mud roads nine months out of the year. They branched off here and there, leading to small lots where the homes were often either ramshackle frame houses or trailers. An ocean view from some of the lots didn't make up for the overall dismal feel of the area.

"If there is a fight going on," Scott said to Jerry, "and you stick your lens in, Mike Baker's liable to feed it to you."

"Think that'd get me an A?"

"Why is it that any idiot with a camera instantly gets a case of Jimmy Olson syndrome and thinks nothing bad can happen to him?"

The Baker house was at the end of a long gravel driveway that grated and crunched beneath the cruiser's tires. As they got closer, Jerry spotted a beat-up no-color Ford, and his pulse picked up in anticipation. He recognized that car even before Scott's headlights picked out the magnetic rectangle pasted to the side. 'Pizza X-Press' was raked across a black and white checkerboard field in slanted red lettering.

"Oh, goddamn it," Scott said. "You better stay here."

"Hell no! This'll be great!"

They got out of the patrol car and heard shouting and profanities from the rear of the house. The December chill soaked into their bones, making Jerry grateful for his Old Navy fleece. He panned across the cars and the small cinderblock box that Mike and Stacey Baker called home. The porch light shed a noontime glow across the yard, eclipsing the red and green Christmas lights that outlined the eaves.

The screen door was standing open on one hinge. On the second step, a cardboard box was tilted on its side with a folded, spindled, and mutilated large pizza spilling out in an ooze of cheese, sauce, olives, green peppers, and sausage. Jerry zoomed in on it, paused, and then hurried to follow Scott around the back of the house.

"All right!" Jerry crowed, as the scene came into view.

Stacey Baker stood on the back deck in panties and a mostly-unbuttoned flannel shirt. Her hair and makeup were mussed, and she shouting and waving a frying pan at a pair of men.

Mike Baker, good-looking in a cigarette commercial kind of way, was bare-assed and bleeding liberally from the nose. This footage, Jerry thought gleefully, would have to be both bleeped and blurred. His glee sank into dismay as it occurred to him that a.) none of them were going to sign releases and b.) Scott would never let him keep the tape.

The other combatant was a pudgy dude with a bad complexion, stringy ponytail and receding hairline. He wore black polyester pants and a red shirt with the Pizza X-Press logo on the back. He was currently engaged in trying to throw Mike to the ground. Where, presumably, he'd use Mike's head for a football.

"Let go of me, you shithead!" Mike roared.

"Cocksucker!" the pizza-man bellowed. "Dirty-ass whorelicking motherfuck!"

"Break it up!" Scott could put out a lot of volume when he was of a mind.

Mike tore away from the pizza-man. "This crazy asshole's trying to –"

He never finished, because the pizza-man, whose nametag read 'Ernie' beside a cartoon smiley-face pizza with sticklike arms and legs, hiked his knee squarely into Mike's exposed genitals.

"Jesus!" Jerry Forrester was pole-axed by sympathy pain, but held onto the camera.

Mike doubled over, emitted a high breathless cry, and crumpled to his knees with both hands clamped to his injured goodies.

"There!" Ernie spat. "There, got you so good your fucking unborn *kids* will feel it." He made to launch a kick at Mike's face, but Scott James got there first.

Scott plowed into Ernie like a charging bull. They landed atop a weathered old picnic table. It gave way with a brittle crack and dumped them onto the soggy lawn. Ernie, cursing even more vilely than before, struggled to get out from under the burly officer.

Jerry moved closer as Stacey Baker flew down the steps to her stricken husband. Her shirt had come the rest of the way open and flapped behind her like wings. She touched Mike's shoulder. Mike jerked away. He fell onto his side with a groan and curled into a ball, retching.

Ernie clipped Scott on the jaw, but Scott shrugged it off, flipped Ernie onto his belly with apparent effortlessness, and braced a knee in the middle of Ernie's back while he cuffed the berserk pizza-man.

"Cool it now or I'll use the spray," Scott said.

"They think this shit is *funny!*" frothed Ernie. "Why not? We tell 'em it'll take twenty, thirty minutes, so they think, what the fuck, we've got time for a quickie. But you get here and you can hear 'em even through the door, going at it like orgy time in the monkey house, and then he fucking comes to the door *naked,* who the hell wants to see that? Like, 'hyuck, hyuck, I got your tip right here.' And it's not just these asswipes, it's fucking *everybody.*"

"Okay, come on." Scott hauled him to his feet and half-led, half-dragged him toward the corner of the house.

"Think it's so fucking funny! You laughing now?" Ernie shrieked over his shoulder at Mike.

Mike didn't answer, but he didn't seem as though he was going to be thinking anything was funny for quite some time. His body was heaving like he was trying not to puke again.

Jerry rushed back around the house to film Scott forcing the rabid Ernie into the back of the car. Yes, fabulous, just like on the genuine show. Ernie threw himself on his back and slammed his heels against the window. Spit flew from his lips as he continued his ranting.

Scott picked up the radio again and, raising his voice to be heard over the din from the back seat, got in touch with Damon to apprise him of the situation.

"Holy crow!" said a high, breathless voice.

Jerry turned around to see Ronnie Greene, the Bakers' nearest neighbor. The rotund little bald man was swaddled in a yellow terry-cloth bathrobe and orange slippers, making him look like the result of a drunken fling between Big Bird and Elmer J. Fudd. Behind rimless specs, his eyes were wide.

Ronnie gawked all the more when Stacey Baker came tearing around the house, shirt still open and upper attributes bouncing like *Baywatch.*

"Let me at that son of a bitch!" she raged. "Did you see what he did to Mike?"

Jerry nodded, a little bit sickly. He'd seen it all right, captured it on tape, and would probably be an old, old man before he forgot it, thank you very much.

Scott urged her away from the car. "Stacey, you might want to . . . uh . . ." He dipped his gaze down, cleared his throat, and gestured. Jerry couldn't be sure, but he thought that one of Trinity Bay's finest might just be blushing to the roots of his blond crewcut.

She buttoned with quick, stabbing motions, not seeming to care that the busybody from down the road and a college kid with a camera were taking it all in. "I'm going to rip his damn face off," she said, and as she possessed acrylic nails of such a length as to make one wonder how she handled her scissors at Red's Salon, it was a believable threat.

"I got him, he's not going anywhere. I just need to find out what happened." Scott looked around. "Mr. Greene, would you mind going inside and calling Marty Arnes over at the hospital? Mike took a pretty bad beating."

When Ronnie Greene had trotted self-importantly past the mangled pizza and into the house, Scott returned his attention to Stacey Baker.

"We ordered a pizza," she said with a shrug that strained her buttons. "I was going to grab a quick shower, but, you know, one thing led to another and we forgot all about it until the doorbell rang."

"Mike didn't put anything on before answering it?"

"He had a towel on." She pointed. A blue flowered heap of cloth was visible just inside the front door. "Last time, see, we called and got that same guy. We didn't open the door right away because we were checking to be sure we had enough cash. So by the time we did open it, he bitched us out for making him stand there all night, and when he left, he hit the mailbox with his truck on purpose. Mike didn't want to keep him waiting and piss him off again, so he just threw on a towel."

"What happened then?" Scott asked.

"He went nuts!" Stacey combed her fingers through her gorgeous fall of chestnut hair, shaking her head at the recollection. "He took one look at Mike, threw down the pizza, ripped the damn screen door off, and hit him in the face. Chased him through the house and out the back door, yelling and swearing the whole time."

"What about you? Were you hurt?"

"I tried to hit him with the frying pan and missed, and he pushed me into the kitchen table." She turned and hiked the shirt, showing a long bruise blossoming on her hip.

Mike Baker was still huddled on the ground, and for the first time Jerry consciously realized how cold it was. California might be known for sand, sun, and surfers, but that was way south of here. Even in high summer, this was no part of the world to be outside naked.

He and Scott helped Mike up, both of them wincing again at the thought of what had happened. Mike couldn't unbend his body more than halfway, and tottered mincingly through the back door. He made it as far as the couch in the living room before falling down again.

The next hour passed busily and colorfully. The ambulance arrived and transported Mike and Stacey to the Trinity Bay Medical Center, and Jerry and Scott rode back to the police station under the constant and inventive barrage of foul language from Ernie in the back seat.

Damon Blake met them there to handle a relative rarity in Trinity Bay, the actual jailing of a prisoner. It was so rare, in fact, that they had to leave Ernie in the car for twenty minutes while they moved a bunch of cardboard boxes out of the cell.

"Jeez," Jerry said when the heavy door was finally closed between the cell block and the outer office, muffling Ernie to a low roar. "The mouth on that guy. Last half of my tape's going to be one long bleep."

"About that tape —" Scott began.

"Aw, hey, come on, don't confiscate it . . . it's the only good footage I've got in five days of tagging along with you. Give me a break, what do you say?"

"Do you have releases from everyone you filmed?" asked Damon.

"I'll get them," Jerry said. "And if they say no, I'll blur their faces like they do on the show."

The police chief didn't look thrilled, but nodded, and tipped back the brim of an imaginary cowboy hat. "So let's have a gander."

Jerry connected up all the wires between the video camera and the small color television Mrs. Dansbourne kept on her desk so she never missed a moment of the afternoon talk shows. He was much more at home on the stage or in front of the camera than behind the scenes or the lens, but the snazzy little device was virtually idiot-proof, so he'd done a better job capturing the drama than he would have expected.

"You are going to have to do a lot of blurring, son," Damon said when Stacey Baker appeared on the screen. "If this wasn't evidence, I'd have to bust us all for watching dirty movies on the city's time."

When that knee landed, all three men turned away with winces and pained groans. "Now, I do wish I'd missed that part," Jerry admitted. "Ouch. Seriously, ouch."

"Marty Arnes gave me a ring after the docs checked Mike over," Damon said. "No permanent damage."

"Luckily," Scott said.

"Hey!" Jerry leaned close to the television, so close that the slightly-too-large nose that was the bane of his existence was almost against the glass. "Did you see that?"

"I went to school with Stacey Baker," Scott said, "so please reconsider whatever observation you were about to make."

"No, not that." He rewound the tape and ran it again, finger poised on 'pause.' When he saw it again, he jabbed the button with video-game reflexes that hadn't decreased much since high school. "*That.*"

Damon leaned close as well. "What the hell?"

The three of them were shoulder to shoulder, staring at the frozen image with narrowed eyes. Jerry couldn't help but think of the first time he and Gary Haverley had logged onto the Countess Madelynne's Dungeon website. If the scene on the screen had been a frozen close-up of Stacey Baker's attributes, that might have made more sense. But the image in question was taken from mid-pan across the back yard, with part of Mike Baker's agonized rolling-around in the foreground.

"Right there. See it?" Jerry pointed.

At the edge of the Bakers' backyard, a tangle of second-growth forest had replaced the redwoods that had been cleared away lots of years before. At the fringe of the back porch light's reach was a shadow between two trees. The shape was suggestive of a man, but there was something about it that didn't seem right at all.

Jerry felt a shudder run through Damon Blake, transmitted to him where their shoulders were touching. The chief's voice was taut as a wire, trying for casual but not coming anywhere close. "Who is it, can you tell?"

At about where head height would be on such a figure were two whitish blurs. "Watch." Jerry advanced the image frame by frame, until the pale ovals vanished from the top down, and reappeared. "Eyes. It blinked."

"Sure did," Damon said.

"*It?*" Scott stressed. "What do you mean, *it?* Even if someone was standing there, and I still think you're imagining things, that'd be a 'him', not an 'it.' Unless you want me to give Chet Underwood a call and have him bring over his Bigfoot kit."

"Come on," Jerry said. "Look at the size. The shape. That's no regular guy."

"Damon, you don't think —" Scott's words trailed off as his boss turned troubled, coffee-dark eyes upon them both.

"I think there was a time not that long ago when some downright peculiar things happened in this town," Damon said slowly. "And ever since then, I've not been a one to dismiss things out of hand."

*   *   *

CHAPTER 3
DECEMBER 21, SUNDAY

Lindie Grantham hated pizza.

She hadn't when she started working at Pizza X-Press. In fact, at the time it had seemed like a great idea, a way to get one of her favorite foods for free. How quickly that plan had palled. Now she could barely stand the stuff. The smell of it, uck, the greasy, oily smell most of all.

By the end of her shift, she could feel it all over her, a fine coating of pizza molecules that had settled onto her skin, into her hair. She had to shower every night when she got home, because she couldn't stand the thought of sleeping and breathing in that cloud . . . having it sink into her skin . . . yuck.

Her usual shift was weekdays six until ten, midnight on Fridays. Thanks to Ernie going ballistic all over Mike Baker, the rest of them had to pull extra hours to cover for him.

Thank God it was Christmas break and she wasn't also trying to fit in six hours of class plus homework every day. She was a junior at Humboldt State University, majoring in computer sciences and business because that's where the big bucks were, but the best she could do in the meanwhile was this sucky minimum-wage job at the pizza parlor. She'd used the job as a reason to avoid going down to Garberville for another fun-filled family holiday, glad for the excuse.

So here she was, at a time she would have normally just been hitting the books in preparation for tomorrow's classes. Instead, she was way out on Vista Drive, squinting in hopes of finding a sign that would tell her which of these dirt roads was Creek Street.

To make matters worse, the news of the previous night's attack had led to a record-breaking number of pizza orders. Every single one of her customers had been convinced that she, Lindie, had the inside story on Ernie's meltdown.

The digital timer on the dashboard ticked over from 24 to 25, warning her that she had five more minutes or she'd have to pay for half the damn double-pepperoni out of her own pocket. But a signpost appeared out of the gloom – ha, ha, a signpost up ahead – and miracle of miracles, it was Creek Street.

She turned right, gritting her teeth as the shocks failed to absorb the jolt of a pothole big enough to drown a cow in. Muddy water geysered over the hood. Lindie flipped on the windshield wipers and succeeded in smearing wide fans of brown muck over her entire field of vision.

"Shit!"

25 became 26. Lindie triggered the wiper-fluid. The rubber blades scraped arcs through which she could, if she scrunched down and held her head at an angle, see well enough to navigate Creek Street.

A dog was lying in the road.

Lindie braked hard, sending the insulated case on the seat beside her sliding to the floorboards. The smell intensified in a gush, that gross pizza smell that now seemed like something that would rise from an open grave, a mass grave, for lepers and plague victims.

Too late. There was no mistaking the feeling of the front wheels thumping over the animal. Already gagging, trying not to cry, Lindie unhooked her seatbelt and got out of the car.

She heard a low whine from beneath the vehicle. The dog was still alive, legs digging feebly at the earth. It was brownish, a shepherd-mix something or other, with fur that was the same color as the muddy road.

Sick at both stomach and heart, Lindie crouched beside the injured dog. She didn't want to be bitten, but she couldn't just leave it there, couldn't roll over it again with the rear wheels as she went on her merry way. Besides, the dashboard timer was at 29 and counting, so there was no way to make the deadline unless she sprouted wings.

She pulled the dog out from under the car. It plaintively licked at her hands, whimpering as if in apology of the mess, the inconvenience.

Its fur was soaked with hot, thick liquid. The splintered ends of bones pushed at its skin, making it feel like a burlap bag filled with thumbtacks. Lindie grimaced helplessly. She tried to slide her arms under its belly to lift it into the back seat and that was when she felt the loose, slippery bundle of intestines that bulged from the dog's torn abdomen.

The car couldn't have done that. Broke the dog's back and ribs, sure, but she'd been going way too slow to rip it open.

The dog shuddered and went limp as she picked it up. She hurled it from her with a wretched scream that turned into a spray of vomit. Blood and worse had soaked into her red smock with the logo on the breast pocket. She stumbled away from the corpse, spitting and sobbing and swiping at her gore-laden hands and arms.

*   *   *

Hunting, hunting, alive in the sweet and wild night. Senses on full alert, every rustle and quiver of prey music to his ears, the forest a tapestry of promise.

Low and stealthy, purposeful and swift. Through the trees, barely disturbing the fronds of the ferns with his passage. His skin tingling, prickling. High overhead, barely seen through the concealing boughs but sensed, oh, yes, sensed in the tides of his blood, the moon a white ship cruising the black.

Light. Sound. Drawing him. New scents teasing his nose. Spiced meat, cheese, dough. Blood. The sick-sweat of revulsion, the tang of tears so similar to the sea. Exhaust.

A shape moving, tall, faltering, hesitant. Female. Finding the dog. Vomiting into the stink of the blood.

The dog. It had come at him in a growling challenge. Gutted and left it for dead. Hadn't bothered with its meat. No liking for the taste of the flesh of other predators. Killing them when he could was a matter of instinct and survival. Eliminate the competition.

A car in the road, lights on, engine idling.

The hunter rising up, nostrils flaring, mouth slightly open.

Movement, there!

*   *   *

Lindie held onto a tree, the coarse and shaggy redwood bark feeling more lifelike than the pelt of the dog, until her gorge settled. She was still making tiny, involuntary, disgusted noises. Stripping off her smock, she used the back of it to wipe her chin, hands, and arms. Her teeth chattered; her coat was in the back seat and her blouse was thin.

Feeling a little better but wanting a shower ten times as much as she ever did after leaving the pizza parlor at the end of her shift, she looked back toward the road.

For a moment, her overwrought brain thought it saw something, a large hunched shape by the rear of the car. She heard a metallic jingling sound, like change rattling in a pocket. When she passed a hand over her face – a very shaky hand – and looked again, she saw just the car, and the dead dog.

Something was different, something was wrong with the picture. She couldn't figure out what.

The dog was where she'd dropped it. The ghastly wound of its belly was clearly visible in the oblong of light that fell out the open door from the dome in the ceiling. Her gaze fixed with unwilling gruesome fascination on the corpse.

What could have done that? Another dog? Fighting over a female in heat, maybe? Lindie didn't know. She wasn't a dog person, wasn't a cat person, had no use for pets of any sort. But not everyone felt the way she did and she knew that it must have been someone's pet. It was too well-groomed to be a stray. Some family, maybe some kid, was going to be wondering where Rover was.

She supposed the thing to do would be what she'd originally intended, put the dog in the car and get to a house to call someone. Find out who it belonged to. Make whatever apologies were necessary, because even if her car hadn't disemboweled poor Fido, the mutt would have been dead anyway from the broken back. In fact, she'd probably spared the dog some suffering coming along when she did. Otherwise, it might have been there for a long time, dying slowly.

That didn't stop her from feeling guilty as hell. But even the guilt wasn't helping her look forward to having to pick up the dog again. She didn't think she could do it, not without heaving up whatever she hadn't heaved up already. Her stomach yawed dizzily just at the thought.

Holding the sodden smock at arm's reach, she went to the car and leaned in to pop the trunk release. The trunk was full of miscellany – tire chains all tangled up and useless, half a dozen soda cans, a towel spotted with oil stains, a bundle of yellowed newspapers tied up with twine, another of the insulated pizza carriers with a broken strap, a can of Flat-B-Gone, a blue plastic box with a white label and red cross, other junk. She dropped the smock in and wiped her hands.

Something growled. Very nearby.

Her heart jumped and the rest of her followed suit. She spun, looking for the other dog. That was what it had to be. The winner of the fight, coming back to make sure. And damn, it had sounded big.

The growl came again. From somewhere in the woods, just beyond the dim light.

"Go on, get out of here, dog!" Lindie commanded, trying to sound unafraid and not let on how that growling had made the fine hairs rise up on the back of her neck.

It growled again, closer, undeterred. Had she thought it sounded big? It sounded *huge*. Huge and hulking, mean, with a mouth like a bear trap. A Rottweiler, a pit bull.

With her butt pressed to the car, Lindie sidled to the corner. She kept her eyes on the woods, the direction from which the growling had come. All thoughts of bringing the dead dog to town or to a house had been pushed to the back of her mind, and the thought of the Villiers' pizza was totally forgotten.

Just a few more steps and she'd be at the door. Hop inside, and get out of here. And if the other dog decided to show itself, maybe she'd hit it on purpose as payback for the scare it had given her.

Bushes rustled. High. Much higher than any dog.

An even crazier possibility presented itself – maybe it wasn't a dog. Maybe it was something bigger, something worse.

Lindie didn't want to even give that idea any air time. She got to the open door and was about to put her leg inside. Paused. What if it had gotten in the car? What if she sat down in the driver's seat only to look in the rearview and have it be full of teeth because it was right there in the back seat?

She took her eyes off the woods and made a quick scan of the car. Empty. Pizza carrier upended on the floor, and by now the pizzas would have folded into weird slumped origami inside their cardboard boxes. The smell didn't bother her at all now. In fact, she welcomed it.

A large, dark shape streaked across the road. Her head was still turned but she saw it from the corner of her eye. The thing moved so silently that it would have been easy to dismiss it as a trick of the moonlight if she hadn't known better.

Lindie was seized by a terror so pure it felt primal. She fell into the bucket seat, banging the back of her head on the edge of the roof. She screamed on the inhale and her throat clenched painfully.

It came at her, a dark, onrushing beast that loped with deadly, deceptive speed. Screaming on the exhale now, loud and ringing, Lindie yanked her legs in and pulled the door shut. It closed with a hearty *tchunk*-sound a split second before something solid slammed into it.

The car rocked sideways. Lindie was thrown onto the gearshift, bruising her hip. She righted herself and slapped at the lock mechanism. Dumb, like a dog was going to be able to try the door handle.

Breathing hard, she hesitantly leaned close to the window. She was braced for the dog to leap up suddenly, barking and spraying saliva on the glass, braced for the surge of adrenaline that would race through her body.

Nothing was there.

Less relieved than she would have liked to be, Lindie locked the other doors too. She kept glancing apprehensively out the windshield, waiting for the moment when the rabid – it had to be rabid, that was the only explanation – animal sprang onto the hood and tried to get at her that way. She didn't see it, but she could still feel it out there, snarling hatefully at the car and the woman within.

The timer on the dashboard had passed 45 minutes. By now, the Villiers would have called in, irate. Dawn would be telling them she was sure their order would be arriving any time, and that of course it would be free. But Lindie had no intention of going the rest of the way to their house. They'd be happy with a free pizza, sure, but not one that was squashed and mangled.

She put her hand on the gearshift and that was when she figured out what she'd almost noticed before. She'd left the car idling, and now it wasn't. The engine was quiet. It had stalled, or . . .

Her fingers found emptiness where they should have found the keys dangling from the ignition. They must have fallen out, she thought, when the dog broadsided the car.

She turned on the dome light again and looked on the floor. Her set was impossible to miss, having more keychains on it than actual keys. A plastic green M&M, the sexy one with the white boots. A stuffed Eeyore. A Hello Kitty figure. Most of them were kid-meal prizes from fast-food places. The last time she'd had a tune-up, the mechanic, Gus Sorenson, had warned her that all the weight would pull on her key at a weird angle, screw up her ignition.

Lindie scuffed her feet along the floor mat and didn't feel anything. She bent down, neck twisted to get her head around her knee and the lower arc of the steering wheel, and saw nothing. She craned the other way, into the foot well on the passenger side, but all she found there was a paper bag of breadsticks that had fallen out of the insulated carrier. The dipping sauce had oozed into a red puddle too much like the one that had been forming under the dead dog.

"Goddammit!" Lindie exclaimed. She sat up.

Now would have been the perfect time for the rabid dog to have sneakily risen up beside the window so that their faces would have been separated by a few inches and a thin pane of glass. She twitched in delayed expectation, but the window was clear.

She knew she hadn't taken the keys with her. The car had been idling.

She remembered hearing it. But it had stopped, about the same time she'd thought she'd seen that shadow, heard that . . .

Heard that funny jingling noise, like a pocket full of change. Like a set of keys.

What was she thinking? That the mad killer dog had, while her back was turned, hurried to the car and swiped her keys so that she couldn't get away? That was beyond insane.

But the keys *were* gone. She patted herself down to be doubly sure, went through the car again. She even opened the ashtray, but it held only an archaic half-roll of Life Savers and a single stick of gum.

Okay, assuming for a minute that the dog . . . or whatever . . . *had* taken the keys . . . what now?

She fumbled for her cell phone, which she kept in the cup holder. What she found was a splintery chunk of casing and electronic guts, smashed beyond repair.

*   *   *

Fear on the prey, worn like a second skin. Confusion edging into panic as the prey examines its device, searches for its keys. Gone, gone, taken. Risky. She'd almost caught sight of him.

The lights going out, casting the dirt road into gloom. The prey possibly thinking that she'd be better able to keep watch if she let her eyes adjust to the dark.

Run at the car again? Batter it with impacts, dent in the doors? Smash through the glass? No, no.

Wrong to take such chances. Wrong to do anything that might give their presence away. But the urges in him, roaring and swelling. The moon in the sky, beckoning, teasing.

The prey's fear. Growing into terror. Sweetening her flesh.

Low. Hugging the ground. Low and silent, keys clasped tight to prevent their clinking.

His mouth watering. Anticipation. Delicious anticipation. Agony, pleasure, rutting. Passenger side door. The key, the lock. Quietly now. Surprise.

*   *   *

Lindie twisted around and groped for her coat, which had fallen to the floor of the back seat. She didn't dare just reach blindly back there, because though she knew she was alone in the car, she could too readily imagine the dog being there, the hot damp breeze of its breath, the gouging pain of its jaws battening on her questing hand.

She fumbled her arms into the sleeves and huddled in the driver's seat. Stay or go? The longer she stayed, the more foolish she felt. After all, it wasn't like she'd actually seen this alleged mad dog. She could have mistaken the groaning of the trees in the wind for growling, could have turned an errant shadow into a lunging shape the way she had turned clouds into elephants, whales, and lions as a child.

Eventually, someone was going to come looking for her. What would happen if they found her like this? All locked into her car and afraid to venture out?

With one hand on the lock and the other on the door handle, she told herself to quit screwing around and go for it. The Villiers' house was half a mile down Creek Street. She could be there in a couple of minutes.

All she could see out her window was darkness and the rising pillars of tree trunks and utility poles. She took several sharp breaths, the way someone preparing to dive underwater might saturate his lungs with oxygen.

A barely-audible, metallic scraping came from off to her right. Panic exploded in Lindie again. She didn't stop to try to identify the sound but threw wide the door and burst out as if shot from a catapult.

She hit the muddy ground running, her sneakers skidding for traction. She had been on the track team in high school and while she hadn't been the best – she'd still been smoking then – she had been decent.

The race was on. Lindie didn't look back, didn't hear anything to make her think she was being pursued, but she *knew*. She tucked her arms close to her sides and ran for her very life. She didn't want to look back and see what was on her heels.

It came in silence, more like some onrushing death-machine or plummeting weight from the inky heavens than a living thing. She couldn't have been more terrified if the chase was set to the accompaniment of earth-shaking hoofbeats or the screeching of a host of demons.

Creek Street was what a housing developer might have called a cul-de-sac, but a dead end by any other name was still a dead end. Two houses and two trailers clustered at the end, where the forest opened up and turbulent Bethany Creek carved a deep cleft on its way to the sea. The view must have been nice by day, nice enough to warrant living where the edge of the land crumbled away into the creek a few more inches every year.

Lindie couldn't have cared less about the creek, the view, or the prospect of the homes sliding away in a mudslide. She saw lights, saw the world's gaudiest life-size plastic nativity scene, saw the big brass numbers bolted to the garage wall at 110 Creek Street.

A stitch dug into her side. She pressed her hand to it and ran on regardless, tapping unknown reserves for the final sprint. A warm draft puffed against her back, the breath of her pursuer, almost close enough to snap its teeth at the nape of her neck.

She screamed and charged across the Villiers' yard. Her shins struck a low fence around a garden. She stumbled over it, waving her arms in a desperate effort to regain her balance, and plowed into the nativity scene.

Wise men, livestock, and Joseph the Carpenter went over like dominoes. Lindie's shoulder hit the rear wall of the manger, tipping it. The angel, all robed in white with a beatific smile, wobbled and took a header into the lawn. A shepherd fell on Lindie. She flung the plastic statue off and rolled onto her back.

The yard behind her was empty.

The front door of the house banged open and Mr. Villiers came out, his astonished expression turning to a scowl as he saw her thrashing around in the nativity scene. He hauled the Virgin Mary out of the way, kicked a sheep, and dragged Lindie to her feet.

"Where the hell is my pizza?"

*   *   *

CHAPTER 4
DECEMBER 25, THURSDAY

Aiden Ferguson woke before dawn on Christmas morning, not because she heard sleighbells or because she had to put a turkey in the oven so it would be done in time for a big meal later in the day.

She woke gasping, from a dream that was mostly memory, a nightmare she'd hoped was long behind her.

The car again, the overturned car. Trapped, in pain, and unable to move except to turn her head.

Even in the dream, she'd known what she would see and tried to stop herself from doing it. Tried to spare herself the sight of the blood, the torn flesh, the dull white gleam of bone. But every time, she couldn't stop her head from turning. Couldn't make herself wake from the cold, and the horror.

Once she did wake, she did not bother rolling over to seek deeper refuge in sleep.

The timer on the heater was set to click on half an hour before her alarm clock's usual buzz, so her bedroom was chilly. She slept in flannel pajamas and thick socks.

She padded into the bathroom. A nightlight in the shape of Mickey Mouse grinned from a socket beside the sink. Clouds of steam from the shower soon filled the room. The heat and the routine of washing her hair drove the last fragments of the nightmare from her mind and she was glad to see them go.

The living room was dark, undecorated. No stocking was hung by the chimney with care, and it had been anything but sugarplums dancing in her head. Her only nods to the holiday were Yuletide Blend coffee and a box of iced cookies decorated with red and green sprinkles, purchased at Tom's Market the day before.

Five Christmas cards were set up on top of the television. One was from the car dealership in Eureka that had sold her the little silver-grey Kia, one was from the real estate agency that had handled the sale of the house, one was from Mr. McGuire, and the last two were from former Seacliff staff members who hadn't been implicated in last year's unpleasantness.

She brewed some of the Yuletide Blend and breakfasted on cookies, and thought of Christmases she remembered from her childhood. When both of her parents had still been alive, and there had been trees and stockings and dinner parties with her father's colleagues, her mother's friends.

After her mother's death, she and her father had made an effort to keep the traditions going, but it was a transparent farce. They gradually tired of going through the motions. One custom after another had fallen by the wayside, unremarked upon by either of them. They'd still exchanged gifts, gone to the occasional party, but their own home had featured less and less of the trappings of the season as the years went by.

And so here she was, alone in her tiny house on a day usually reserved for light and love and family. No wonder people said this was the most depressing time of the year.

She finished her coffee and dried her hair and dressed for a walk on the beach. Her misgivings of the other night had been nothing to worry about, she told herself. Just the dark, just her nerves.

The morning was uncommonly clear, the sky without even a breath of a cloud. In the east, through the trees, gradients of ash-pink, dusty yellow, and pastel periwinkle heralded the sunrise. To the west, cerulean shadows still held sway. Patches of fog curled through the trees and rose in faint tendrils from the sea.

The waves were gentle, as if in respect for the day. Aiden listened, smiled as she heard the vocalizations of her sea lions. She thought of them as 'hers' now, had gone out to check on them frequently, and the unsettling sensation of being watched hadn't been repeated.

She was almost to her usual spot when she realized that she wasn't alone. This wasn't a recurrence of her case of the willies; there was someone sitting on the rocks in plain sight, facing out to sea.

Aiden stopped short. Her initial reaction, surprising her, was one of indignation. What was he doing on her beach?

It wasn't *her* beach, her property didn't extend nearly this far and she wouldn't have a legal leg to stand on by making such a ludicrous claim, but she'd come to think of it as hers because in a year, there'd hardly been anyone else out here.

Now there was.

He sat closer to the water than Aiden usually did, knees drawn up and arms crossed on them, chin resting on his forearms. She couldn't tell how old he was, anywhere from her own age to ten years her senior, because he had one of those faces that was just made to look perpetually youthful, boyish, innocent. His medium-brown hair was cut very short and his skin was a weathered, natural olive-bronze that was unusual in this region where most folks were either the pasty-pale of sun-deprivation or had the deep, fake-looking glow caused by a tanning bed.

She knew that the minute she tried to go quietly back the way she'd come, pebbles would click, hidden twigs of driftwood would snap loudly underfoot. She might slip and send herself crashing down noisily enough to make flocks of gulls take wheeling, scolding flight.

The stranger could hardly fail to notice that. Then, he'd wonder why she was trying to sneak away, and she'd be even more ashamed, even more distressed.

She stood where she was, palms moistening, mouth dry, blinking too often, waiting for the inevitable moment when he'd turn – perhaps glimpsing her out of his peripheral vision, perhaps just feeling her there, sensing her eyes upon him as she'd sensed someone watching her that other night.

Despite her anxiety, it struck her that he was really kind of cute. In profile, anyway. For all she knew, the other half of his face could be some gruesome, twisted, Phantom of the Opera visage.

Unaware of her scrutiny, the man stood up. He wasn't very tall, probably only an inch or two taller than Aiden, who had always been petite. His clothes – brown cords, low-topped hiking boots, and a red-and-brown checked shirt – would have been fine for an autumn day but a little underdressed for winter.

The sea lions were almost directly below him, frolicking in the surf and barking. A thrill of fear pierced Aiden as she thought that maybe he was here to trap them, shoot them. But he didn't have any weapons that she could see, wasn't carrying anything at all. And his expression, grinning down at the sea lions, was anything but cruel. His grin was open, engaging, contagious.

She decided he had to be close to her age. Twenty-three at the most. Young, cute. Cheerful. Seemed pretty harmless. The sort of guy that it might be okay to talk to, at least to say hi, nice day, merry Christmas.

The very idea would have stunned Aiden if she hadn't already been rooted to the spot. Could she really be contemplating talking to someone? A stranger? A *boy?* Well, young man.

Aiden worked her tongue around in her dry mouth, because if she was really going to do this, really *speak*, she didn't want to add to her troubles by having it come out in a rusty croak.

The stranger, standing and grinning down at the sea lions, started unbuttoning his shirt.

The word "hi" froze on Aiden's lips. Her jaw would have dropped if every muscle in her face and body hadn't been rendered absolutely immobile.

He took off his shirt, folding it and setting it on a comparatively dry shelf of stone. A ribbed white tank top clung to his chest, showing a torso that was toned, sculpted. His bare arms, not bunched with gooseflesh despite sea spray and air that couldn't have been warmer than 40 degrees, were as well-defined as anything she'd seen in an anatomy or figure-drawing book.

She could not fathom what he was doing until he took off his hiking boots and reached for his belt. Then the answer, as incredible as it was, came to her . . . he was planning to go swimming! To swim with the sea lions. In water that was barely above freezing.

Naked.

He unfastened his pants and pushed them down over his lean hips, revealing plaid boxer shorts.

"Eep," said Aiden, and followed it up with a wavering little "Ah-ah?" that sounded almost exactly, humiliatingly, like Cindy Lou Who in the cartoon about the Grinch. She'd watched it just last night on Channel 9.

The half-undressed man whipped around, clutching at his pants to keep them from sliding to his ankles. His eyes, a bright and vivid blue, went wide as he saw her there.

They stared at each other while the sea lions barked and yelped. Aiden was braced for his reaction: anger, embarrassment, homicidal mania. What she wasn't expecting was what she got, a flash of pure fear.

He was frightened of *her*, and the realization shocked her all over again.

Quick as a cat, he grabbed up his discarded clothes with the hand that wasn't busy holding up his pants. He leapt down, barefoot but amazingly agile on the slick stones. The rock he'd been on was between them now, so that she could only see him from the collarbones up.

"Oh, I'm so sorry!" she heard herself say, the words coming of their own volition. "I didn't mean to scare you."

Another man might have made some gruff protest. This one blinked. He was blushing, too.

Laugher bubbled up in Aiden like artesian well-water. She knew it was wrong, terribly wrong and rude, but he just looked so mortified and she suspected she did too. What else could anyone do but laugh? She tried to hold it back, bit her lips when they wanted to twitch up at the corners.

But then she saw that he was doing the same thing, undergoing a series of facial contortions as he fought to keep the mirth inside. She looked away, looked at the grey and black shine of wet rocks under her shoes, struggled to get control of herself.

When she thought she had it, she glanced up. He did too, at the same moment, and had to drop his head immediately as a snorting chuckle escaped him. Aiden emitted a shrill giggle and clapped her hands over her mouth.

His shoulders were shaking, and finally he couldn't manage any longer. He threw back his head and barked a laugh that sounded exactly like the sea lions. Aiden had to give in, or else she might have choked. Once she began, she couldn't stop, screaming with laughter until her sides spasmed and she had to hold onto a boulder to keep from falling to the ground and rolling.

When her fit had subsided to hiccups and little spates of snickers, she looked over at him again. He was wiping tears from those direct blue eyes, shaking his head.

"I didn't think there was anyone around," he said. Maybe it was because he'd been laughing so hard, but his voice had an odd, hoarse quality. If it had been lower, she might have called it gravelly, but, like his face, it was youthful, boyish. Except for that rasping undertone. "Didn't expect anyone on the beach at this hour."

"On Christmas, too," Aiden said. "Neither did I."

"You live around here?"

Before she could think better of it, she nodded and pointed at her little house, just barely visible amid the trees. His motions suggested that he was putting his clothes back on, so she averted her gaze even though the rock provided an effective barrier.

"Guess I was trespassing."

"Oh, no," she said. "It's not my property out this far. I just come out here to see the sea lions."

He grinned, the same cheery grin she'd seen before. "Me too. They're cool."

"Are you from town?" She'd never seen him, but that was hardly a news flash, given how she never saw anybody if she could help it.

"Just got here." His grin faded a little. "My family's staying at the campground."

Aiden wasn't sure how to respond to that. It well past tourist season, and something in the way he said it made her think that they weren't vacationing. "Agate River?"

"Yeah."

"Have you seen the otters over there?"

The grin returned, more genuine. "Yeah. Aren't they great?"

"How'd you get out here? I don't see a car or anything."

"I walked. Around the bluff." He gestured off in the direction of Seacliff.

Aiden looked at him with renewed surprise. There used to be a path, a rocky and treacherous one but a path all the same. It had been buried when the bluff collapsed and to her knowledge, no one had found a feasible way to get around.

"Sometimes I just need to get away for a while," he went on, oblivious to her curiosity. "To be by myself."

"I know how you feel. That's why I like living out here. It's so peaceful."

"Until weird guys show up and start stripping." He rolled his eyes in chagrin. "Sorry about that. I deserved to have you creep up and scare the skin off me."

"I wasn't trying to. I didn't even see you until I was right there. Were you . . . were you going to swim?"

A guarded shadow veiled his eyes. "Uh . . ."

"That water's got to be freezing."

"The cold doesn't bother me much." He faltered uncomfortably, then added, "My name's Alex. Alexander Greye, Alex for short. What's yours?"

"Aiden Ferguson."

He stretched up on tiptoe and leaned across the rock to offer his hand. Aiden regarded it for a moment, steeling herself, and reached out. She could tell it didn't slip by him, the way that she approached the handshake as if it were a set of hurdles, or a challenge out of one of those game shows where they made people eat bugs and entrails.

"Nice to meet you," he said.

"You too." It came out little more than a gasp and a squeak.

His hand was very warm, as if he'd had it in a nice deep pocket instead of out in the frigid, damp air. The awareness – not only was she talking to a stranger, she was *touching* him, and had seen more of him than she'd ever seen of a male person in real life – built up like a wave threatening to drown conscious thought.

She was going to have a full-blown panic attack, right here and right now, and if she was lucky it would only end with her fleeing from Alex as if all the devils of hell were on her heels. He'd gape after her, hurt and confused. If she wasn't lucky, she might start wheezing for breath, or even faint, and then what would he think? What would he do?

Letting go of him, Aiden put her hands to her face and closed her eyes. Slow, steady breaths. Calm, calmer.

"Aiden?"

"I'm okay, I'll be okay, honest."

He scrambled over the rock to land beside her. "What's the matter?"

The concern in his voice, the earnest concern, had a soothing effect on her. That had never happened before. Mr. McGuire had a marvelously soothing voice that only served to knot her into even more of a bundle of nerves. But the hitching in her lungs eased off, and she stopped quivering.

"Really," she said, much more steadily than she ever would have believed, "I'm all right."

She'd been right in her estimate. With Alex standing right next to her, she only had to tilt her head a little to look up at him. His shirt was buttoned all the way up, a size too big so that it concealed his build, and he didn't seem imposing at all.

"Are you sure?"

"Yes, I . . . yes." Flustered and overcome with a fit of shyness that was at least real shyness and not a phobic conniption, she scuffed her toe in the pebbles. "I should be getting home."

He hesitated, seemed poised on the brink of a question. Aiden was stricken with the sudden worry that he meant to ask if she wanted him to walk her back to the house. Or, even worse, ask her out.

At this last, she almost laughed again. Ask her out? Why in the world would he do that? He was good-looking, fit, charming. She was a drab little thing who got the vapors just being around anyone else. Plunging ahead before he could do one or the remote-and-unlikely other, she summoned up a smile.

"I'll see you later," she said.

"You mean you don't mind if I come back to the beach?"

She shook her head, a short, rapid gesture that probably looked more like she had a tic. "I don't mind."

"Okay." He made an abashed face. "And I'll bring a swimsuit next time."

*   *   *

CHAPTER 5
DECEMBER 26, FRIDAY

Simone Drachen stretched, catlike, taking a sensual pleasure-pain in the crackling of her spine as she twisted her body this way and that. She yawned deeply, not yet opening her eyes because the memory of her dream was far better than the humble surroundings she knew she'd find.

But wakefulness brought reality home to roost. She couldn't cling to the images of the past with any sort of comfort. All it did was remind her how much she'd lost. How much had been taken from her.

She couldn't bear to think of the ranch, with its fields and mountain wilderness and wide-open spaces. Her heart ached to remember the solid log and flagstone construction of the main house, almost a castle against that majestic backdrop. The fireplaces. The kitchen. The large room that had served as both gathering-place and den, where her father had . . .

No. To remember the ranch was to remember her father, her family, the life that had been torn apart. She turned her thoughts instead to the ones who'd done it, to the people who had come with their taxes and their zoning laws and their development plans, and destroyed everything she'd held dear.

That had been the beginning of her new life. Her secret life. The one she'd tried to keep hidden. But the flame of resentment had become a seething inferno of rage and finally she'd done it. Taken that one step, that one irrevocable step that changed everything.

Once she'd killed, she knew she would never have enough.

It had cost her much. Her home, her children. The love and warmth and companionship that she'd once cared so much about. They didn't understand. They would never understand.

Except . . . one did. Finally. Now that she'd shown him the way.

She opened her eyes at last, and found the sight as bad as she'd expected. The shack was worthy of the name, thin grey light filtering in through gaps where the boards didn't meet. Rain drummed on the aluminum roof. Additional plinks and plonks heralded the four spots where water leaked through holes to be caught by strategically-placed buckets.

The only source of heat came from a layer of ash-coated coals in a small metal barbecue, one of the round three-legged kind. Simone rose from her cot and added wood, stirring new life into the flames.

This was no way to live. Like a beast. On what could be scrounged, or stolen. They would have been drier sleeping in the van, except that with all of their worldly possessions loaded into it, the van barely had room for them to sit while they drove.

This life was nothing like the books she sometimes read. In the books, or the movies, the ones like her were always rolling in wealth. Mansions. Limousines. Chic clothing and expensive antiques. The finest of everything that money could buy, not only in terms of material goods but power, influence.

"Just one more thing," she said, "that they got wrong."

Donovan stirred, responding to her low and throaty voice even in his sleep. His sleeping bag was by the door, where he'd be first to waken should anyone attempt to disturb them. When she did not speak again, he rolled onto his side and pillowed his head on one folded arm.

She loved to look at him, this precious son of hers. Nothing gave her more pride and vindication than to see him there, his features a more masculine version of her own, his hair the same red so dark and scarlet that no one ever believed it could be natural. The rest of him, though, took after his father in the best possible ways. Physically, at least. Mentally, emotionally, he was hers. All hers. As both of her children should have been.

Her son deserved better than this. He'd given up so much to be with her. Given up the safety and comfort that had been his, all to follow her into this uncertain future. She adored him for it, even if she knew his real reasons had been anything but filial.

Tonight, she decided. Tonight, they would go out.

"Donovan."

He came fully awake at once. As his eyes, the pale azure of faded denim, fixed on her, they first widened, and then narrowed. She pretended not to notice the way his gaze followed the long lines of her legs up to the hem of her short silk wrapper. It was belted loosely, the drape of the fabric barely covering the contours of her breasts.

"Yes, Simone?"

"This is no way for you to live, my dearest one," she said. "You have been such a good boy, so dutiful. I know how hard it's been for you, with the restrictions I imposed."

He flushed darkly. "I understand why you made them. I know why it's necessary."

"It is necessary to be cautious, Donovan. But we must survive. No one will give us what we need. They have everything, *everything*, and we have so little. So we must take."

Donovan nodded. "I will do whatever you wish."

Simone knelt beside him and cradled his head to her bosom as if he were a child, stroking his hair. "Oh, my Donovan . . . I am so fortunate to have such a son! I never thought you would leave your father to come with me. I thought you'd reject me, hate me, as your sister did."

She could feel his breath, hot and rapid, through the thin silk. Tension quivered in his muscles. He fought to keep his voice steady, and she did not let on that she heard the huskiness he tried to hide.

"I could never hate you, Simone. Never!"

Murmuring soothing nothings, she rocked him and petted him like she'd once done when he was very small. If any of that lingered in his memory, it had to contrast sharply with everything his senses told him. He could barely remember what it had been like to have a mother caring for him. Was it any wonder that, when she returned to his life, he looked at her and saw her as something else?

"I know what you want," she said, and he stiffened and hissed in a breath.

"You . . . know?" He dared to raise his head and look up at her through sleep-mussed strands of scarlet. The shock was there, the shame, the desire, all brimming in his eyes.

Simone smiled benignly. "Of course I do. What we both want, what we need."

Disbelief was writ large upon his face. Disbelief and a hint of wary hope. "Simone . . ."

"And soon, you'll have it," she said. "We'll go out, find a decent meal. You must be hungry. I know I am."

"Starved," Donovan said shakily.

"And then we'll see what can be done about our accommodations." She swept the shack with a derisive glare. "I'm tired of living like an animal."

*　　*　　*

CHAPTER 6
DECEMBER 27, SATURDAY

Kepler's Wash-Stop was next door to a Chinese restaurant, and Aiden could smell the enticing aromas even with all the windows rolled up. She maneuvered the Kia into a spot behind an old, rusty-black, sinister-looking Chevy and got out into a steady rain.

Her laundry was in the back seat, two plastic baskets full. She stacked one atop the other, balanced the boxes of detergent and dryer sheets atop that, and bumped the door closed with her hip. She splashed through the gutter, thankful for her knee-high waterproof boots, and headed for the entrance.

The detergent started to slide. Aiden thrust her chin forward and stopped it, her hold precarious. She hurried under the overhang that sheltered the sidewalk. The door opened outward. She curled pinkie, ring, and middle around the cold metal handle and scuttled sideways like a crab.

She was able to pull the door open far enough to wedge a foot in, then worked a knee into the gap. A warm, dry, soapy-scented gust of air blew past her. She could hear dryers humming, the uneven clump-thump-ba-bump of someone's shoes going around inside one of the rotating drums. A radio in the back room was tuned to an oldies station.

The Wash-Stop was typical of its breed – a single long room with ranks of machines along the walls and islands of them down the middle. The walls were an unnatural shade of yellow, lemon fading toward mustard, and the floor was burnt orange linoleum. The lights were fluorescent tubes, one of them buzzing and stuttering as if about to go out. A row of long tables was set up along the front wall, under the windows.

Signs around the doorway leading into the back room advised her not to hog the machines, and listed the prices for drop-off service. She'd never made use of that option, finding it only barely preferable to sit here herself for the couple of hours it took rather than leave her laundry in the hands of strangers.

Aiden almost made it to one of the tables without mishap, but hooked her foot on the wheel of one of those carts with the square wire compartment and the poles that rose into a bar. She felt her hold on her belongings slip, knew that disaster was inevitable.

A pair of hands shot out and caught the topmost basket as it gave in to gravity. The detergent thumped to the floor, but it was a new box, unopened, and didn't spray its contents. Aiden looked up into vivid blue eyes.

Alex Greye grinned at her. "We meet again."

A tentative smile tugged her lips, while she marveled that she hadn't noticed before how strong and even his teeth looked, how white against his healthy bronze skin. "Hi."

She set down her basket and he put the other one beside it. He bent to pick up the detergent while Aiden fluttered her hands, not sure what to do with them. She was mortified that he'd had to come to her rescue in such a goofy way, absurdly thrilled that he had. Iron bands tightened around her chest, but at the same time a giddy flush wanted to rise in her cheeks.

The only other guy she'd ever almost gotten to know was Brian Sorenson, who'd done computer work at Seacliff before taking a job with the DMV when the school closed. Brian had been geeky and proud of it, in no way threatening. Even so, Aiden had hardly been able to talk to him.

Alex, athletic and with confidence in his every move, was Brian's complete opposite. He hopped up to sit on the table, running a hand through his short bristly hair. He wore dark grey sweatpants and a college t-shirt, not HSU's dark green and gold but the red and white of the Washington State University Cougars.

"How's the sea lions?" he asked, swinging his feet.

"They're still around," she said, looking at her laundry and wondering if she could sort it while he was sitting right there. He'd see her underthings, the plain white cotton panties and front-hook bras of insignificant cup size. To stall for thinking time, she took off her coat.

At least they weren't alone. Two elderly ladies in jogging suits were discussing bridge and grandkids as they waited for their wash. A thin, harried woman with three children under the age of seven was wearily explaining that the coins were for the washers, not the vending machines. A vaguely dull-witted man in his mid-twenties and a sallow older man – Mr. Kepler – were in the back room, folding and stacking the clothes left to the drop-off service.

"I've been meaning to go back and see them." Alex produced a handful of quarters and arced them from one hand to another like a magician about to perform a trick. "Haven't had the chance."

"Oh," Aiden said, just as if she hadn't been out there every day, sometimes twice, in the pouring-down rain . . . and not solely to check on the sea lions.

She'd told herself that she was making sure he hadn't come back. Making sure she had "her" beach to herself again. But the attempts at self-delusion didn't take, and now, standing here in this bright, mundane place, she gave in and admitted, inwardly, that she'd been hoping he would be there.

One of the dryers let loose with a ratcheting ring that sounded like a chainsaw chewing through wood only to hit a metal spike. Another joined in only seconds later.

"That's mine." Alex tossed the quarters, a flickering silvery cascade worth three or four dollars, and caught them. He went over to the dryers.

Aiden took advantage of the moment and hastily sorted out her laundry, shoving her underwear into a washer and piling her towels on top. She got her wash going, three loads of it, and nested the baskets one within the other. Alex, she saw, was transferring an amazing amount of clothing. Dry items into one of the carts, wet ones from washers into dryers. He funneled in all of his quarters and went to the change machine for more.

He came back to her. Seeing her quizzical expression, he chuckled. "It's not all mine. Got the whole family's to do. Want to sit down?"

The chairs were hard, contoured plastic on tubular chrome frames. They'd once been white, but, like the pattern in the linoleum, had gone dingy. Aiden sat, crossing her ankles and smoothing her powder-blue wool skirt. Alex sat next to her. Right next to her. The next chair over. So close that when he turned toward her to speak, his knee brushed hers.

"Are you in school?"

"No," she said softly. "I . . . I don't do much of anything."

"Work?"

"Huh-unh." Only two exchanges into the conversation, and she was down to semi-articulate grunts. Good going, Aiden, wotta gal!

Her head was down, hair falling along the sides of her face, so all she could see of him was his leg, part of his arm, and the hand laying on his knee. It was a hand that was accustomed to hard work. She saw calluses, and fingernails that were thick, clipped short.

"Am I bugging you?" Alex asked.

"No!" She raised her head, shook it. "No, you're not. I'm just . . . I'm sorry. I'm not used to . . . to being around people."

"Me either. We're on the road a lot, always moving around. Makes it hard to meet anyone, and then I never know what to say."

"You don't have a place to live?" She didn't mean for it to come out sounding scornful, or like an accusation, but there didn't seem to be any other way to say it.

Alex didn't mind. "You mean, are we homeless? I guess you could call it that, except it's not like we're broke. My uncle's got a motor home. He prefers the term 'nomadic.' Like the Gypsies. Thinks it sounds cool. Cooler than 'vagrants,' anyway."

"What do you do?" It was rude to ask, but the question popped out before she could contain it.

"Whatever there is. Handyman stuff. Farm work. I'm good with my hands, not a machine out there that I can't fix with the right tools. We get by."

"I'm sorry. I don't mean to be nosy."

"I don't think you're being nosy at all."

The door opened, letting in the sound of the rain and an eddy of cold air. It also let in a plump young woman with wild black curls that had a dyed lock of burgundy at the front. She was lugging a giant navy-blue drawstring sack, which she heaved into one of the carts. Her hair was sparkling with raindrops, some of them flying free as she tossed her head and looked back over her shoulder at the man who was holding the door.

"Thanks, handsome," she purred brassily.

Something about her was weirdly familiar to Aiden, but she couldn't put her finger on it. All she knew was that she'd certainly never met the brunette before, never even seen anyone who wore leopard-print stretch velvet pants and a low-cut black sweater-dress. Her neon purple purse was the size of a small suitcase.

The man who'd held the door now came in, a grocery bag from the deli across the street cradled in the crook of his elbow. He raised a dubious eyebrow at the woman who'd called him handsome, though from what Aiden could see, it wasn't unwarranted. His face was angular, striking, reminding Aiden of a bird of prey. He had buff-colored hair, a lot of it. Untamed, like pampas grass. Anime hair, she thought it, because of the way it was long and flowing and spiky all at once, like something you'd see in Japanese animation.

Alex stood up. The new arrival saw him, nodded in acknowledgement, and fished a carton of milk out of the bag. He lobbed it across the banks of machines. Alex caught it.

"Thanks, Jeff," he called.

Jeff nodded again. "No problem." As he started across the room, he saw Aiden sitting beside Alex, and came to a sudden stop. His sharp blue eyes filled with suspicion and a touch of anger.

Alex slowly lowered the hand that was holding the carton of milk, and a defensive wariness seeped into his posture. "What?" he demanded.

"What are you doing?" Jeff's voice was deeper, not a lot but some, and had the same raspy undertone that Aiden had noticed in Alex's. It also had a quality of either jealousy or barely-suppressed anger.

"Nothing," Alex said, throwing Aiden a rather guilty look. "Just talking."

The brunette in the leopard-print velvet was keeping a sidelong eye on the three of them as she dumped clothes, unsorted, into a washer. The sardonic tilt of her ebon brow and the matching tilt of her smile told Aiden that the brunette was thinking along the same lines as Aiden was trying not to. Was this a jealous lovers' spat?

"Talking," echoed Jeff, almost in a sneer. He put the bag on the table and it tipped, several packages of beef jerky and another carton of milk sliding partway out.

Alex straightened his shoulders defiantly. "Yeah, talking. Aiden, this is my brother, Jeff."

Wishing she could melt through the floor like a phantom, Aiden murmured a nonsensical sound that was meant to be a greeting. The word 'brother' had brought a rush of relief, but being the evident cause of dissention made her stomach knot. And the relief itself troubled her . . . it wasn't like she was interested in Alex, so what difference should it make if Jeff was his brother or . . . or something else? The eyes, of course, they had the same striking blue eyes. She should have realized.

She'd never been good at lying, not even to herself. Alex *was* cute. She *was* interested. Not that anything would ever come of it.

"Hi," said Jeff grudgingly. "Alex, got a minute?"

"Yeah, sure."

Jeff led Alex over into the nook where the phone was. They leaned close together, Alex on the receiving end of what looked to be a stern lecture.

Aiden blew out a sigh and slumped unhappily in the hard plastic chair. She bent her head into her cupped palm and closed her eyes. Over the rumble of dryers and the high-pitched voices of the harried woman's kids at play, she could barely pick up snatches of speech. Jeff wanted to know what Alex thought he was doing, was worried about what someone called Gideon would think. Alex protested that he knew what Gideon said, and that he hadn't done anything wrong.

"Your boyfriend's in trouble, huh?"

She opened her eyes to see the brunette, leaning her ample backside against the table. Aiden shrank in on herself like a turtle. She was sure that she'd never met this woman before, but that sense of familiarity wouldn't leave. She looked more closely.

Genial face with pouty, wine-red lips. Honey-colored eyes framed by heavily-mascaraed lashes. The brunette was overweight, maybe forty pounds or so, and most of it was in her bust, hips, rear, and thighs. She held herself with the comfortable, cocky poise of someone who didn't care what everyone else thought, and the outlandish way she dressed proved it.

"He's not my boyfriend," Aiden whispered.

The brunette snickered. She held a bottled Starbucks mocha drink from the vending machine, shaking it well before opening, as the label directed. "Not yet, you mean."

"Not at all, I mean!"

"He's a babe. Too short for me, though. He'd only come up to about here –" she held her hand at collarbone level, "– and even the ones who are at eye level hardly ever look at my face. The brother, though . . ." She made a feline *mmrow!* sound, and winked.

"Um," Aiden said, nonplussed.

The brunette threw back her Betty Boop curls and laughed with abandon. Once again, a tantalizing hint of familiarity teased Aiden. Recognition danced close to the surface, and was gone.

A gout of chocolate flavored coffee-milk splashed out of the bottle and onto the front of the brunette's black sweater-dress. She broke off her laughter and made a moue.

"Oh, crudbunnies," she announced in rolling tones that carried to every corner.

With nary a care in the world, she shucked the garment over her head and added it to one of her churning, sudsy loads. Her bra was black satin with a heroic underwire structure. A small tattoo, of a deep red rose on a thorny stem, graced the white swell of her left breast.

Aiden goggled. The thought that maybe this was some hidden-camera stunt came to her, but she had to dismiss it.

Nonchalant, the brunette plopped into the chair that Alex had recently vacated. Alex himself, and his brother, were staring across the room incredulously. So were all the others. The elderly ladies, whom Aiden would have expected to be the most offended, only giggled.

"So," said the brunette. "I'm Birdie."

"Aiden," she said tremulously.

"What do you think you're doing?" squawked the harried woman, trying to cover the eyes of three kids with two hands. The math didn't work out.

"Laundry, for pete's sake," Birdie said in exasperation. "It's no worse than a bathing suit."

"Do you want my coat?" Aiden offered as the sallow-faced man came out from the back room, looking like he was about to have a fit.

"All right." She sighed extravagantly and took the coat, wrapping it around herself because anyone could tell that if she'd put it on regular, it never would have closed in the front. "Thanks."

Alex and his brother had either finished their argument or forgotten all about it. Although Jeff was six inches taller than Alex, they had the same sort of build. Not weight-lifter muscular, but awesomely fit with hardly any body fat to speak of.

Aiden wasn't sure how it had happened, but all at once there she was, in the middle of a group. And the weirdest part was that despite Jeff's banked-coals glare and Birdie's flamboyance, she wasn't about to keel over. Her breathing was normal, and she wasn't clammy with sweat.

Jeff gathered up the items that had fallen out of the bag, opening the second carton of milk. He kept glancing at Alex as if waiting for him to say something. Alex cleared his throat. Birdie and Aiden looked at him expectantly.

After a few seconds, Birdie grinned. "Ooh, an awkward silence, what fun!"

Thrown even further off his stride, Alex stammered out the opening bid in another round of introductions. Jeff and Alex Greye, meet Aiden Ferguson and Birdie Yale, and vice versa.

"I've seen you somewhere before," Jeff said to Birdie.

"Possibly," she allowed with a twinkle in her eye.

"I was thinking that too," Aiden said. "But I can't figure out where."

"Lemme give you a hint." Birdie set down her coffee drink, bowed her head for a moment as if to collect herself, and then raised smoldering eyes to Jeff. In a husky, sultry voice that seemed to push her words forward as if every syllable was a kiss, she cooed, "Hello, boys and ghouls, and welcome to another fright-fest . . ."

Aiden jerked in her chair.

Jeff slapped his thigh and cried, "Son of a bitch! *That's* where. You host

Monstorama Theater!"

"That's right, handsome." She fluffed her hair. "You have to imagine the long black wig. And the corset."

Two sets of blue eyes bugged a little, and Aiden guessed that's exactly what they were imagining. But it all made sense now. She didn't watch Channel 12's low-budget late-night features every Friday and Saturday, but did so often enough to be familiar with the cheesy graveyard set, the vampire-slut getup, and the caressing, smoky tones of Lady Nocturna.

"You were in all those movies," Alex said. "All the Wilfred Ghostman ones from a few years ago. *Revenge of the Wasp-People, Immacula,* those ones."

"My ill-spent youth," chuckled Birdie. "Yep. That's me."

The three of them started talking horror films while Aiden sat and listened, soaking it all up. Alex and Jeff demonstrated encyclopedic knowledge of the topic, mentioning titles she'd never even heard of. Some, though, she had seen, and was surprised to find herself actually contributing to the conversation with less and less reticence. Mr. McGuire wouldn't have believed it. She could barely believe it herself.

Alex held out one of the packages of beef jerky. "Anyone want some?"

"I've got a better idea," Birdie said. "We're still in time for the Saturday lunch buffet next door. What do you say? Six bucks a pop, all you can eat. Mua-ha-ha, the fools . . . they don't know what they're in for when Birdie comes to town."

"The laundry's not done," Aiden pointed out. "I only just put mine in the dryer."

"And I doubt they'd let you in like that," Alex said, indicating the coat that Birdie still had wrapped loosely around her.

She almost dislodged it with her shrug. "So loan me a shirt. Your stuff's dry."

The brothers exchanged a look but couldn't come up with a reason not to, so Jeff gave Birdie a roomy blue chambray workshirt. She eyeballed them meaningfully until they turned their backs so she could change, then snickered as they did so.

"What about our laundry?" Aiden tried again. "Maybe I'll stay here and –"

"No way, Fergs," Birdie said. "Let me go off alone with these two? With no chaperone to protect my virtue? I think not. A girl's got to think of her reputation."

Aiden looked to Alex, to Jeff, but all of them were helpless in the face of Birdie's forceful, yet oddly likeable, pushiness. They both wore uncertain half-smiles that said they'd be more worried about who would protect *their* virtue.

"Well, all right," Aiden said. "But the laun–"

"The laundry, the laundry, sheesh and jeepers, the laundry." Birdie waved to the sallow man, who was peering at the four of them with a pinched, pursed scowl. "Keep an eye on our dryers, would you? Make sure nobody raids our undies. We'll be back in a bit."

She led them out and they had no choice but to follow, like iron filings drawn in the wake of a powerful magnet. Jeff and Alex broke away long enough to stow their baskets in the back of the sinister-looking Chevy, and joined them in the foyer of Hunan Palace. The blended aromas of spices and sauces made Aiden realize how hungry she was.

The interior was dimly lit, with lots of dark wood, red fabric, gold trim, and aquariums filled with exotic, frilly-finned fish. When a dapper Asian man in black slacks and a white shirt led them to a high-backed booth, Birdie slid in beside Jeff and left Aiden to sit with Alex. Like they were on a date. A double date.

That was almost enough to bring on one of Aiden's panic attacks, but she successfully fought it down. Dining in restaurants was a rare experience for her. When she did eat out, she tended to just hit the drive-through. To be sitting here, with a short glass of ice water and a white ceramic teacup, with a parchment placemat that had the various Chinese astrological years around the border – she was born in the Year of the Rat, she read, which apparently meant she was thrifty, easily angered, and brimming with charm and attractiveness to the opposite sex, thereby killing her belief in astrology – was less frightening and more fun than she would have thought.

The buffet was set up along the back wall. A steam table with sunken stainless-steel trays held appetizers, soup, two kinds of rice, and a selection of six courses. She tried a sample of everything, nibbling diffidently at egg rolls, crab-cheese puffs, lemon chicken, beef and broccoli, sweet and sour pork.

During the meal, the talk moved from bad monster movies to movies in general. Birdie told them how she'd gone from acting in the Wilfred Ghostman films to being Channel 12's shlock-jock. Ghostman had discovered her at an after-school job as a waitress when she was sixteen. He'd liked the way she screamed, having been a customer the night a kid with a knife tried to rob the place. Birdie's banshee wail had scared the would-be burglar as well as alerted a passing patrol car. She'd been in ten bad movies over the next three years.

"But then," she said, tweezing a crab-cheese-puff by the crispy ends and pulling it apart to expose the cream cheese filling, "I found out that even ten film credits wasn't much help getting in anywhere else, if they're film credits in B-movie horror trash. I came up here to get away from my family and go to college, take some acting classes. Found out the academic world and I didn't agree. Dated a guy from Trinity Bay, whose aunt knew the owner of the television station. Been here ever since. There you have it, folks, my life story in a nutshell."

She said it lightly, but Aiden had the sudden insight that Ghostman had meant much more to her than she let on. It made her think of Dr. Lundquist, who had been like a grandfather to her, and whose death had left her feeling almost as bereft as when she'd lost her own parents.

"But anyway, enough about me," Birdie went on. "What's your story, handsome?"

She nudged Jeff, who was methodically putting away such enormous amounts of food that Aiden was amazed he stayed so trim. Alex, too, for that matter. The brothers both ate like it was their last meal before facing a firing squad at dawn. There were enough small bones from chicken wings, stripped of every scrap, that she could have constructed a log cabin.

Jeff, wiping his lips, proceeded to say basically the same thing Alex had — they lived with their uncle and grandfather in a motor home, moved around a lot, had only come to Trinity Bay a couple of weeks ago and weren't sure how long they'd stay. Their uncle Gideon had landed a temporary job as a caretaker at the Agate River campground, which got them a free place to park the RV.

Having said his piece, he went back for another helping. Birdie tagged along. "I was going to work my way through all seven deadly sins," she joked as she got out of the booth, "but once I hit Gluttony, I knew I'd found my vice of choice. Though Lust and Sloth have their selling points, too."

When they were gone, Aiden meekly turned to Alex. "I'm sorry if I got you in trouble before."

"Huh? You mean with Jeff? No, don't . . . you didn't do anything wrong. It's . . ." He frowned down at his plate, poking a chunk of broccoli with a chopstick. "We don't usually, well, talk to anyone very much. Gideon thinks it's a bad idea, when we're just going to move on in a few weeks and never see them again."

"That's . . . that's pretty sad," Aiden said in a low voice. "But I guess I can see his point. You don't end up missing people."

"He says, but I don't know." Alex jabbed the broccoli, splitting it apart. "If we never make friends, even for a little while, we're always going to be alone. We'll never feel like we belong anywhere, and there won't be anyone to remember us. Ever."

"I will."

He looked at her, those startlingly blue eyes shimmering like jewels in the amber glow of the parchment-shaded lamp above their table. "I think he's also worried that if we get to know people, if we make friends, we won't want to leave."

Aiden held very still, not sure what she saw in that gaze, not sure what she wanted to see. She didn't know what to say and was afraid to hear what might have come out, if Jeff and Birdie hadn't returned right then and saved her.

*   *   *

CHAPTER 7
DECEMBER 29, MONDAY

The Plaza at the heart of Trinity Bay was an emerald jewel like the centerpiece of a necklace not of gold links but of neatly-kept buildings. The twinkling holiday lights still festooning many of the shops cast shimmering reflections over the wet sidewalks. The air held an unfamiliar tinge of possible snow, which would turn to slush the moment it hit the ground and dash the hopes of countless children who dreamed of snow-days that would close the schools, never mind that school wouldn't even be back in session until the second week in January.

Kel McGuire added a packet of Equal to his orange-flavored double-tall latte and stirred it with a long thin straw. He blew on the steaming drink, relishing the warmth of it through the foamed-cardboard cup and his woolen gloves.

The rain pattered on the slate-shingled overhang of the big stone block that served as the combined police office, town hall, and library. He turned as one half of the brass-framed double doors opened, and Scott James emerged.

"Well?" Kel asked.

Scott rolled his eyes heavenward. "We're releasing him on his own recognizance until the next hearing. The ball's in your court now. Good luck."

"Thanks. I'll need it."

"Town's going down the tubes, Kel." Scott looked out over the peaceful Plaza. "I guess the insanity of the modern world is catching up with us after all."

"Listen to you. You sound like you belong next to the woodstove at the back of the general store, griping about how it was never like this when you were a lad."

"Well, it wasn't," Scott said defensively. "I grew up here, and let me tell you, when I was a kid, no one would have even imagined that Red's Salon would branch out into tattoos and body piercing. It was momentous when they started doing those ceramic nails. They'll be branding people next, wait and see."

"When I was a kid, I never thought that I'd have an administrative assistant who makes more than her salary after hours running a members-only whips-and-chains webcam site," Kel observed. "Times change."

"I guess. But you'd think a town this size couldn't sustain but one full-fledged psycho." He raised his chin meaningfully toward an enormous vehicle that looked like a minivan on steroids.

They watched in silence as the Neeman family poured out of the monster-SUV's many doors. It was like a good optical illusion, or something from a cartoon. The Neeman kids, each born nine months and fifteen minutes apart according to local lore, went in descending size like a series of steps. Rocky, the only boy of the bunch, got imperiously out of the front passenger seat, while his mother was apparently relegated to the back with the youngest.

The patriarch of the clan, John Neeman, very deliberately did not look at Kel and Scott. His shoulders hunched, more out of truculence than in defense against the rain, and he made no move to help his wife unfold the stroller. The girls milled around in identical cheap coats obviously purchased from some outlet store.

"Well, if it isn't the Von Trapp family from Hell," Kel murmured.

Scott snorted as he tried to smother his laugh. "I thought social workers weren't supposed to say stuff like that."

"I thought policemen weren't supposed to refer to citizens as psychos."

"Cynicism is one of the few ways to avoid burnout in this line of work."

"Ditto," Kel said. Just then, something caught his eye and he forgot all about the Neemans, forgot all about the court-ordered anger management counseling for Ernie Warrigan. "But it's not always hopeless and depressing. Look over there."

"What am I looking at?"

"There, by the statue. A miracle."

"If it's someone walking on water, I've seen it. We've all seen it. Done it, even. So long as it's real shallow."

Kel ignored him. To the uninformed, it wouldn't seem like anything out of the ordinary. A young couple standing companionably close, their umbrellas overlapping. But the girl, her face uplifted and alight with a shy smile, was Aiden Ferguson.

"Hey," said Scott, finally catching on. "Isn't that your . . . what's it called? Social phobic?"

"Yep."

"Out in public?"

"Yep."

"Who's the guy?"

"Good question. I've never seen him before."

"Not a local," Scott said. "Not with that tan. Wait, I bet he's with that bunch living out at Agate River."

"What bunch?"

"They moved in a couple weeks ago, talked Harv Leland into letting them rent a campsite even though it's off-season. Damon went out for a look-see, ran a check on their plates."

"Why?" Kel frowned, his pleasure at seeing Aiden actually out and about and conversing not only with a person but with that most daunting of all persons – a young man her own age – giving way to a glimmer of worry and suspicion.

"Seems a little weird, doesn't it? Tourist season's long over, four transient guys show up in an RV, asking about odd jobs. And one of them is huge, according to Damon. I mean, *enormous*. Bigger than Rand Kostas. Bigger than my cousin Paul."

Kel's eyebrows went up. Rand Kostas, boyfriend to Kel's assistant Nancy, was the brawniest man in town, and Scott's cousin Paul made extra money in the summers posing as a yellow-bearded version of the famed lumberjack whose name he shared.

"But they checked out," Scott said. "Harv says they haven't been any trouble. It sounds like they're drifters, but if so, they're clean-cut, respectable drifters. They'll probably stay a while and then move on. I'd keep an eye on your recluse, though, just in case."

"She's not a recluse . . . well, maybe she is, but she's a nice girl. She's come a long way in this past year." Kel looked at Aiden again, remembering how frightfully withdrawn she'd been following the events at Seacliff, and the death of the man who was her legal guardian and surrogate grandfather.

Though he had plenty of reasons to resent anyone or anything having to do with Seacliff's hellish project, Kel had felt sorry for Aiden and wanted to help her. It was a way of doing some good after feeling he'd failed Gwynne, Marge, Eric, and the children. He'd taken charge of her therapy, arranged for the repairs and remodeling on Marge Raney's cottage on Vista Beach, organized the trust funds left to Aiden by her deceased father and Dr. Lundquist, and helped her move in and get settled.

To see her with a friend, especially a male one, should have been a tremendous step in the right direction. But Scott's words about drifters did nothing for Kel's peace of mind. What would it do to poor Aiden when he inevitably moved on?

"There's one of the others," Scott said, cutting into Kel's pensive reverie. He indicated a cancerous blackish car that only heightened Kel's growing unease.

The man standing half-out of the car, rain slicking down his pale hair as he waved and called without benefit of umbrella or hood, gave Kel's nerves a nasty twang. His posture reminded Kel of Eric Raney, or of Joey Mack, the bad-boy member of the pop group that Jenny Forrester was so obsessed with. No leather jacket, no sneer, no dangling cigarette parked in the corner of his mouth, but the rebellious attitude might as well have been glowing around him like a neon aura.

Aiden dipped her head demurely at whatever her friend said, and then waved as he jogged toward the car. When he reached it, he turned and waved back. He got in and off they drove, not revving the engine or peeling out but going at a nice sedate pace in full obedience of the laws of the road.

Standing there in the rain, the hem of her grey coat reaching to the shins of her sensible boots, Aiden might have stepped out of an earlier era. The blue vinyl of her umbrella gave odd highlights to her beige-blond hair and pale skin.

"Tess," Scott James said.

"Beg pardon?"

"Tess Trueheart. Dick Tracy's girl. That's what she looks like. She's got that air of good-girl purity."

"Right." Scott, Kel knew, was as obsessed with the famous gumshoes of the past as he was with the latest high-tech crime solving gadgets. As if he couldn't decide which he wanted to be – Sherlock Holmes, Batman, or Bond. "Maybe I'll go over there and –"

He broke off as the door behind them opened again and Ernie Warrigan emerged.

The day, already dark, darkened even more. Ernie's expression would have made a Doberman think twice about barking. His eyes burned with nuclear-fire hostility, but at the same time, incongruously, his pudgy lower lip poked out in the sullen pout of a kid who'd had his feelings hurt at recess.

Not, Kel thought glumly, that there was anything funny about that. Kids getting their feelings hurt in the playground nowadays were kids who might respond by bringing a gun to school.

Steeling himself, Kel approached. His job was to help people. His mission in life was to help people. But the dedication that had sustained him through years deserted him when that searing gaze flicked out at him like a laser.

"I'll see you on Tuesday, Ernie," he said all the same. "If you need anything before then, or want to talk, you have my card."

A single crinkle of the corner of one of Ernie's eyes conveyed exactly what Kel could do with his card. Silent, apparently having either used up his supply of invective or realizing that his threats and curses weren't doing much to improve his case, Ernie jammed both hands into the pockets of his scuffed brown coat and headed down the stairs. He trudged around the corner, toward the parking lot. Moments later, his battered old Ford came to blatting, snarling life.

"What a mess," Scott said. "Wonder what he'll do now."

"Hopefully, see the error of his ways and turn over a new leaf," Kel said. "None of the previous incidents ever landed him in jail. This might be the wake-up call he needed."

"Some people can't be helped," Scott said with a shrug. "They've got to want to change. Someone like our buddy Ernie there, anger's all he's got, so he's going to hang onto it. As long as he can blame everyone but himself for his problems, he will."

"That's an awfully grim view."

"Maybe so, but am I wrong?"

"I'd really like to think so."

"Trust me. Our troubles with Ernie aren't over. Not by a long chalk. You'll see."

Kel gazed in the direction of the departing car, and a dull but bleak sense of trepidation settled over him like an overcoat. "With my luck, I'm sure I will."

*   *   *

CHAPTER 8
DECEMBER 30, TUESDAY

"Royce? Are you coming up yet? It's almost midnight."

"It is?" Royce sat back on his heels and stripped off his gardening gloves.

He looked around but the room gave no clue to the hour. The light from the full-spectrum bulbs shed the same steady, warm radiance 24/7, and all the year long. The generator that ran them was powered by the stream that ran beneath the house. It was Royce's way of avoiding detection by virtue of a higher electric bill. He knew that many in his line of work met their downfalls just that way.

The concrete walls of the cellar chamber were windowless, bare but for the shelves on which Royce kept his tools and implements. And jugs of fertilizer and insecticide, though hadn't he and Ginger had some go-rounds about that!

She came partway down the stairs, the tiny metal beads threaded onto the fringe of her calf-length skirt jingling like distant bells. Royce's gaze moved slowly up the body of the woman he'd married when they were both barely out of their teens, marveling at how little Ginger had changed.

The same imitation-Birkenstocks. The same thick woolen socks almost as bristly as the unshaven legs they covered. The long broomstick skirt with its earth-tone paisley pattern and fringe of jingling beads. A shapeless cro-cheted sweater reached to her narrow hips, and the loose weave of the yarn gave him occasional glimpses of pink nipples as she moved.

Well, some things had changed . . . twenty years of going braless had made what was once small and pert into small and saggy. The sweater was sleeveless and he could see how the flesh of her upper arms had gotten a little flabby too.

Her hair, though . . . that hair was what had first attracted him to her, and it was still as long, glorious, golden, and kinked as ever. He had seen her on campus, one of a group of four sitting on a grassy slope. One of the guys, dirty-blond dreadlocks hanging around his long billy-goat's face, had been playing the bongo drums. The other was idly tossing a hackey-sack, bapping it around with his elbows. The other girl, in a calico granny dress, was making jewelry. And then there was Ginger.

Royce had grown up in the area, and was in fact a descendant of the original Lelands who had come to Trinity Bay with Jacob Cliffwood back in the later years of the 19th century. Scenes like this were nothing new to him. Some people were just trapped in the 60's, although it had been 1982 when he saw Ginger there with her golden hair frizzing and falling around her like Stevie Nicks.

The more things changed . . .

She still had the hair, still dressed like what the students called a "Humboldt Honey," and still disdained cosmetics of any sort. She made her own soap, scenting it with jasmine or spices, and her own shampoo as well. The house was full of her macramé and pottery, and her garden was all-organic.

Which was why, as she stopped halfway down the stairs, she gave the jugs on the shelf a sour frown. But she couldn't deny that they did the trick. The crop was thriving.

Royce stood up from where he'd been kneeling beside one of the raised trays. There were six of them all told, held up off the floor on cinderblocks. Each tray was four feet by ten, and eight inches deep with dark, moist soil. Rising from the soil at regular intervals were thin stalks with long, slightly-serrated leaves. He'd spent years perfecting this strain of *cannabis sativa*, and often thought what a shame it was that pot growers couldn't register their creations the way the rose growers could.

"Someday, that'll all change," he said.

"What will?" Ginger asked.

"Nothing, babe, just talking to myself." He put his gloves on a stool next to the drying oven, another of his own designs. It had been inspired partly by Ginger's pottery kiln and partly by some show he'd seen about chicken incubators, with several closely-spaced racks and heat baking from three sides.

The only other piece of furniture down here, if it could be called furniture, was the safe. He'd picked it up at an estate sale in Eureka, brought it home under cover of darkness and under cover of a canvas tarp, and nearly given himself a rupture trying to get it down the stairs. It squatted like a dead robot or some strange metal idol in the corner, the black dial of its combination lock masquerading as a blank cyclopean eye.

He knew it was tempting fate, keeping the safe with his earnings down here in the same room as the crop. If he ever got raided, they'd take everything. Money, weed, the works. But where else was he going to keep his cash? Couldn't very well walk in to the bank and deposit it, not without raising uncomfortable questions. Neither his day job as a clerk at Tom's Market – and wouldn't his ancestors be rolling in their graves to know that one of the last of the Lelands, originally partners in the mill and one of the town's leading families, was working bagging groceries – nor Ginger's seasonal business of selling soap, pottery, and jewelry at area craft fairs and swap meets would explain sudden influxes of bucks.

Besides, in some dimly superstitious way, he believed that the moment he gave in to paranoia and moved the money, he would get raided. By leaving it here, he was showing faith in whatever rural deity looked over the small independent farmer.

Someday, though, as he'd mused aloud, it would all change. They'd legalize it. That day was coming closer all the time. First it had been okayed for medical use, and then loss or theft of the medical use marijuana had been covered by insurance . . . it was only a matter of time until it was all legal and above-board.

He wondered if that would be a good thing or not. With it legalized, everyone and his dog would be growing their own instead of buying on the sly. Prices would go down. He might have to look into things like brand names and marketing campaigns.

The very idea gave him an acid stomach. He liked the business fine the way it was. He had his trusted cadre of buyers who paid quite well, and no one had any cause to suspect. He and Ginger were careful with their spending, and it certainly wasn't like they had high-maintenance lifestyles. Royce did make a point of staying clean-cut and respectable-looking.

Take poor Charlie Forrester, for example – didn't even smoke it, let alone grow it, but because he would have fit right in with Ginger's pals from the U. C. all those years ago, everyone in town was convinced that he did and simply hadn't been caught yet. Or that the police knew all about it, but given that Charlie was now one of the richest men in town thanks to a bizarre series of events a few years back, they turned a blind eye.

Leaving his crop, Royce went upstairs with Ginger. He left behind the earthy smell of the soil and the lingering oddly potato-like scent from the dryer, and came into an environment of incense and spices and the yeasty aroma of the home-brewed mead than Ginger had fermenting in the pantry.

The house bore the heavy stamp of Ginger's personality. It was dark and cluttered, with Native American blankets thrown over the couches, a swath of patterned cloth pinned to the ceiling to filter the overhead light, Celtic music softly playing, and cats everywhere. He'd given up trying to keep track of them long ago and only knew that the big grey one with the leonine ruff was Gandalf, the black Manx was Wicca, and the battle-scarred tabby tom was Jimi.

Ginger paused, and as Royce turned to close the concealed door that led to the cellar stairs, he realized that the cats were all on their feet, tails lashing, ears flattened back, and alien eyes in a dozen shades of yellow, green, and blue were fixed furiously on the two of them.

"Royce?" Ginger asked.

"What the hell is up with them?" Damn, but it was creepy . . . he'd never realized before just how creepy the direct, unflinching, slit-pupiled stare of a cat could be.

They were silent, not a hiss to be heard, and that unnerved Royce all the more.

"Gandalf," crooned Ginger, squatting and reaching out to the big grey. "Here, kitty-kitty."

"Don't do that, babe." He scanned the sea of felines, not finding Jimi.

He did see something else. He saw that the front door was standing ajar. A spark of anger bloomed in him. He kept telling Ginger that when he was down in the garden, she had to keep the door shut and locked. Even if it was the middle of the night. If the cats had to go out, they could use the flap he'd installed in the back door.

Ginger ignored him. Her fingers came closer to Gandalf's lowered head.

"Ginger, don't!" Royce bent, grabbed her shoulder, and pulled her backward just as Gandalf lashed out with a pawful of claws. Ginger overbalanced and landed on her butt.

"Gandalf!" she cried reproachfully.

A wavering, wailing moan arose. It came from none of the cats, but from beyond the partly-opened door.

Cougar! Royce thought, which was crazy because there weren't cougars around here, not even in the woods around their remote house way out Mill Road.

The rest of the cats picked it up, higher keening like a chorus of sopranos joining a tenor in an aria from some opera of the damned.

Ginger shot to her feet. "What is —"

She only got those two words out before a grey-and-black shape sailed through the air toward them. Royce instinctively stepped in front of his wife and straight-armed Jimi. But the cat wasn't attacking. The cat hadn't been leaping. The cat had been thrown, and as it hit Royce's arm and flopped limply over it like a stole, he saw the blood dripping from Jimi's gutted underside.

He yelled in revulsion and shook his arm. The dead cat, head swinging freely on a broken neck and gouged black sockets where his eyes had been, hit the floor with a grotesque smack. Jimi had been laid open from the ribs down, laid open and hollowed out as neatly as if his insides had been scooped out with a melon-baller.

Ginger staggered back, fingernails digging at her cheeks and pulling down the skin below her eyes so that they seemed about to pop out, leaving sockets as empty as Jimi's. A gagging, yodeling noise came from her, and Royce realized she thought she was screaming.

The front door swung open the rest of the way. Twin pale glints appeared, and again Royce thought, *cougar!* Except that these glints were higher off the ground than any cougar ever stood, even if they had lived in redwood country. And the shape of the thing that came into the room was unlike any animal he'd ever seen.

It was catlike, in the way the face pushed forward, and the tail curled into a smug wave. The thighs were short while the bones of the feet were amazingly long, giving it the look of backward-jointed legs. But it walked upright, and the shape of its torso was humanoid . . . humanoid and female.

That was what made Royce's mind really feel like snapping tether and drifting off into the wild blue yonder. The thing in the doorway was female. Its waist was slim, its breasts were high and full with no trace of sagging. But the creature was covered in fur, as russet as a fox's pelt, and a darker mass like a mane framed its inhuman face.

Royce was amazed at the equanimity with which he accepted this apparition. A six-foot-tall walking red-furred cat-woman, mouth all needle-sharp teeth, eyes like milky pale green emeralds, stalking through the sea of cats with the hipshot, slinking grace of a lioness crossing the African savannah . . . didn't faze him at all.

The cats parted around her as she advanced. They weren't afraid of her. Cats didn't have strict pack structures like dogs might, but Royce supposed they had their own way of measuring status, and perhaps by killing Jimi, the avowed toughest of them, the cat-woman had supplanted him as their leader.

Beside Royce, Ginger was making a teakettle noise. She would have backed up further, but the counter was in the way.

Only as the cat-woman languidly raised an arm, and extended a claw like a miniature scythe at them, did Royce understand that what he was experiencing wasn't equanimity but raw terror.

"Kill them," said the cat-woman in a voice that hissed without sibilants, snarled without the letter 'r.'

A river of cats moved as one. The sudden rushing tide, from Siamese to orange tabby to the tailless black of Wicca, broke the horrified spell on Royce. Seizing Ginger's arm, he kicked at the nearest cat – Gandalf, springing at them with fangs bared – and whirled to flee.

Ginger's knees were locked, her legs stiff. She collided with a kitchen chair and went sprawling on the hardwood floor, snowplowing a braided rag rug before her in bumps and folds.

Royce turned back for her, but before he could take a single step in her direction, before Ginger could do more than push herself up on her hands, the cats swarmed over her. They had been silent before but now were hissing, yowling, spitting. Ginger shrieked and thrashed, but for each one that she flung off, another was there to take its place. Claws snagged in her crocheted sweater, opened long thin lines on her skin. A tortoiseshell with one maimed ear burrowed under her chin to bite at her throat.

"No!" Royce shouted. He grabbed the nearest thing at hand – a wooden pepper grinder with a black metal crank on the top – and swung at the nearest cat. Its skull gave way in a sick crunch.

A weight dropped onto his back and pricks of stabbing pain pierced his shirt, his flesh. He lost hold of the pepper grinder and flailed for the cat that had gotten purchase on him, but he couldn't see it, couldn't reach it except to brush its fur with his fingertips and be bitten for his troubles. He tried reaching from under and caught a tail, yanked for all he was worth. His shirt ripped and he screamed in pain as all the claws tore free from his body.

Insanely, he remembered his mother's opinion upon first seeing the little house in the woods where Royce intended to live. *Not enough room to swing a dead cat,* she'd said. But swinging a live one worked quite well.

He whipped it around by the tail like a sling and let fly. The cat, a black and white one whose name, he abruptly remembered, was Patches, spun screeching across the kitchen and smashed into Ginger's windowsill herb garden. Patches rebounded in an avalanche of peppermint, basil, and broken crockery, landing in the sink.

Royce went for Ginger again and stopped short. All he could see of her beneath the fury of cats was one hand, one drowning, bloodied hand reaching futilely toward the ceiling. Other cats were coming at him.

Panicked, knowing he'd hate himself later but unable to prevent it, Royce ran for the back door and left his wife of twenty years on the floor beneath that living blanket. A calico under the table slashed his ankle as he went by but he didn't look.

He hit the door with the heels of his hands, arms rigid as steel beams. Although he made a fuss about locking the doors, and bought good strong locks, the wood itself was too flimsy to withstand the impact and gave way with a splintering crack. Royce plunged onto the back stoop and tumbled into the vegetable garden, narrowly missing getting a tomato stake through the eye.

Ginger's cries had tapered off, lost beneath the triumphant howls of the cats. A pang of loss went through Royce, loss salted heavily with guilt. He'd left her to die, to be killed by her own cats, and run like a coward to save his own skin.

Sobbing hysterically, Royce got up. He was covered with mud, his back a mass of stinging scratches. His only thought was to get out of here and find help. Never mind that the secret panel to the cellar was wide open. Never mind that he'd end up in jail for this. Jail would be a small price to pay.

A low, chuckling growl came from his right side. Freezing in place, every hair on his body trying to stand on end, Royce held his breath and listened to a chuffing sound that made him think of a big dog. His head swiveled of its own volition, bringing him face to face with the beast that stood at his shoulder.

He looked up into lambent, frost-white eyes. The thing stood more than a foot taller than him. Like the cat-woman, it was furred and walked erect, but unlike her, its appearance had a wolfish aspect and it was most definitely male.

A gibbering, terrified scream ripped from his throat and got Royce moving again. He ran, no destination in mind, heeding the helpless urge to get *away*, as far away from this waking nightmare as he possibly could. He heard the beast pursuing him, loping easily on all fours in a way no man was meant to move.

It took him down in one powerful leap. They rolled. Royce got a handful of its pelt, felt the terrible heat of its body, inhaled the meaty stink of its breath. He was beyond screaming now, beyond thought.

The beast swept him up in a bear hug, as effortlessly as Royce might have once swept up Ginger. Its massive arms cinched around him, squeezed. Ribs popped like a string of firecrackers. The last dregs of air were forced from Royce's lungs. He beat at the head of the thing, rammed his thumbs at its phosphorescent eyes.

His back broke with a muffled crack. Everything from the sternum down went slack and dead. Royce only knew he'd hit the ground when the side of his head hit a spongy heap of wet pine needles. He could see his legs, splayed and unresponsive.

His attacker circled him, down on all fours. The long muzzle sniffed at him, poked at him.

Royce's arms still worked, sluggishly. He tasted blood when he coughed and knew the jagged ends of ribs had damaged his inner workings. He felt along the ground, found a stout branch, hefted, swung.

The branch hit the beast on the bony bulge of its brow as it sniffed Royce's leg. Its head whipped up sharply. As he struck again, the beast caught the branch in its jaws and wrenched it from Royce so hard that his wrist snapped. That, he felt, in red-hot pain. He cradled it in his other hand, aware of dampness on his face and mistaking it for rain rather than tears at first.

Shock was taking over. He could barely comprehend what he was seeing as the beast hunkered over him, as it brought its fearsome jaws to his belly. He saw its teeth sink in, saw blood pool and then flow, but he could not feel a thing as the creature burrowed into the soft entrails of him, making horrible grunting sounds of pleasure.

It was *eating* him, Royce realized. Eating him alive!

Something inside him came loose with a gristly slurping. The beast raised its head, a slab of maroon-purple-brown held in its mouth. Royce identified it as his own liver, steaming in the cold night. The beast held it almost daintily, and bounded from Royce's side to bring the organ like an offering to the cat-woman, who stood poised in the back door with light streaming around her.

The beast laid the liver gently at her feet and lifted its head, eyes fixed adoringly on her face. She crouched, picked up the gift in one hand, and caressed the wolfish head with the other.

The last sight Royce Leland saw before death took him was the cat-woman bringing the dripping chunk of meat to her mouth.

*   *   *

CHAPTER 9
DECEMBER 31, WEDNESDAY

Aiden arrived ten minutes early and wasn't sure what to do next. She sat in her dark car, listening to the tick of the cooling engine under the rustle of the rain, waiting for the familiar knot of apprehension to tighten in her stomach.

It didn't come. Some nervousness was there, absolutely, but the usual signs and symptoms were absent. She felt a flutter of excitement instead of the knot, and admitted with stunned surprise that she was actually looking forward to this.

She had parked on Brody Way, a whimsically-curving tree-lined path in one of the older parts of town. The houses were a mix of Victorian and Tudor style, but many of them had been chopped and subdivided into apartments or duplexes. The trees, and high hedges, provided privacy.

Birdie's house was one of the Victorian duplexes, painted slate grey with black and maroon trim. Fitting for someone in her line of work, she'd said. Lights were on in her half, none in the other. Her car, a cherry-red VW bug, was in the driveway.

Should she go up? She was still five minutes early. Dr. Lundquist had sometimes teased her about her "pre-emptive punctuality," as he called it.

She got out and was heading up the brick walk when she heard approaching familiar voices. She was about to speak up when Jeff Greye said, "It's not too late, Alex. We can still back out."

Aiden stopped, holding the rustling bag as still as she possibly could. She was shielded by a hedge, unable to see them, hoping that meant they couldn't see her either.

"Come on, Jeff," pleaded Alex. "It's just dinner."

"I don't think this is a good idea. You've been spending way too much time with her."

"I like her," Alex said, and the simple words warmed Aiden's soul in a way she'd never felt before.

"Yeah, I know, but you haven't thought about what you're doing. Gideon –"

"Gideon wants us to live the way he does, never getting to know anyone, never having any friends. We can't hide from the world forever, Jeff."

"It's not that easy and you know it. Gideon is right."

"I don't accept that."

"You have to. Look, I don't like it any more than you do. I wish things were different too. I wish we could settle somewhere instead of always wandering. I wish we could get to know people . . . girls. Alex, if things were different, I'd be all over Birdie Yale like *that*, believe you me." The snap of Jeff's fingers was so loud that Aiden jumped. "But it's a risk we can't take, and you're going to ruin everything if you carry on with this."

"I just want to be around her," Alex said. "She's so sweet, so gentle."

"That's why," Jeff pressed relentlessly, "you'll hurt her if you keep this up. What happens when we have to leave, huh? What happens if things start getting serious between you? And if Gideon ever finds out, he'd nail your hide to the wall. Mine, too, for covering up for you."

"He expects us to be alone forever." The misery in Alex's voice nearly brought Aiden to tears. "Alone forever, and then we die, and no one will care that we ever even lived."

"He's doing what he has to do."

"And so should I, you mean."

"Yeah. Can't fight fate, Alex."

A gusty sigh was Alex's only answer.

"Let's just go," Jeff said. "We'll go to a movie like you told Gideon. It'll be easier that way."

"That's cowardly. It's just dinner," Alex repeated. "One night. And then, I promise, I'll explain to Aiden."

"Explain? Explain what? You can't tell her the truth!"

"I don't want her to think this is because of her. She can't blame herself for something that's our fault. I won't do that to her."

"Okay, okay. One night. We'll go, we'll have dinner, but that's it. And if Birdie tries to put her hand on my knee again, we're out of here."

"When did she do that?" Alex's astonishment mirrored Aiden's own.

"At the Chinese place. She was rubbing my leg like she expected a genie to pop out."

"She should've rubbed higher."

"Ha, ha. I'm serious, Alex. This isn't funny, and it isn't a game. You know that."

"All right, fine. Help me get the food. Do you think we brought enough chicken?"

"Two buckets ought to do it," Jeff said, with a grudging tone that hinted he wasn't satisfied by the change in subject.

Aiden melted into the shadows. Beside the porch, a path of round cement stepping stones led down the side of the house. She moved hastily from one to the other until she was wrapped in cloaking blackness. The knot of anxiety was present now, full-force, but had nothing to do with the impending dinner and everything to do with what she'd just overheard.

Alex and Jeff came up the walkway and pressed the doorbell. Instead of a plain chime, it played a fragment of spooky organ music. Aiden lurked in the dark as Birdie opened the door, greeted them, invited them in.

A mix of emotions whirled and spun like a cyclone through her mind. She couldn't go in there and pretend as if everything was normal. She couldn't eat, not when sick despair would make sure she couldn't swallow a bite. Like a turtle, her impulse was to withdraw and hide from the stimuli. Like a small timid creature, she wanted to scurry to the known safety of her den.

But neither could she stand the thought of not seeing Alex again. Especially if it was to be for one of the last times. Those vivid blue eyes, that boyish smile. Of course he was going to leave. Everyone did. She'd known that almost from the first. It lent a certain bittersweet, doomed charm to the friendship.

She crept to the porch, meaning to leave the bag of desserts. Even if she couldn't go through with it, good manners dictated that it wouldn't do to leave the hostess in the lurch.

"And where do you think you're going?" Birdie asked, popping the door open with the suddenness of a jack-in-the-box.

Aiden gasped and retreated so fast that she bumped into the hedge, feeling the prickle of it through her coat. One heel sank into the soft soil past the edge of the bricks.

Birdie set her hands on her black-clad hips and regarded Aiden skeptically. "You weren't thinking of bailing on me, were you, Fergs? Leave the treats and run, like Halloween in reverse?"

"Um . . . well . . . it had crossed my mind."

"Get in here."

"Birdie, I'm sorry, but I can't. I'm not feeling well."

Calling, "Back in a sec, guys, make yourselves cozy," over her shoulder, Birdie stepped out and closed the door behind her. "Does this have anything to do with why you were skulking about in the bushes? I saw you out the kitchen window."

Her face flaming, Aiden stared at her shoes.

"Spying on the Brothers Greye?" Birdie added. She chuckled richly, the audible equivalent of velour. "What, are they planning something kinky?"

"No!"

"I should hope not. It's only our second date. Even if I'm that kind of a girl, I doubt that you are. So what's the story, Fergs, what's the scoop? You promised you'd come."

"I meant to, I really did."

"Then come on."

"Birdie . . ."

"Lordy, but it'd take a crab-cracker to get you out of that shell." Birdie grasped Aiden's arm above the elbow and steered her toward the door. "Not that I'd object to having both of them all to myself, but a deal's a deal. Now get your heinie in here and have fun."

Unable to object or pull away, Aiden acquiesced. She surrendered her coat in the cramped foyer and followed Birdie into a living area that might have once been two or three rooms but creative remodeling had turned it into one open space of weird angles and jutting corners.

The burgundy wallpaper and drapes, gold braid hangings, and gaudy chandelier made Aiden think of Victorian brothels, but the furniture tended toward futons, burl-wood tables, and nestlike papa-san chairs with matching ottomans. The fireplace was fronted in fake marble, with a mirror in a stained-glass frame above the cluttered mantle.

Bookshelves had been squeezed into every available space, but they held videotapes, stuffed animals, and knickknacks that had to be memorabilia from Birdie's early horror movie career as well as books. Everything was packed in without rhyme or reason. The computer desk was almost lost beneath stacks of papers, shoeboxes of mail, and CD cases.

But as cluttered as it was, Aiden still had the impression that Birdie had done what she considered a fairly thorough cleaning in preparation for the party. She wondered what Mr. McGuire would make of all of this.

A doorway curtained in strands of plastic beads led into the kitchen. Birdie sashayed that way, primping her hair as she went. Aiden looked at her, at the clinging black pants and the wine-red peasant blouse with its neckline scooped so low that it exposed most of the rose tattoo. She was barefoot, flashing ruby-red toenails as well as long crimson fingernails, one of which had been drilled so that a small diamond stud could be inserted, another of which had a gold-painted cursive letter 'B' on it.

Next to Birdie, Aiden felt like a boy. A boy in a modest honey-colored dress, and a copper-gold-brown scarf she'd had doubts about because she'd thought it might be too bright and busy. Now it looked drab.

The kitchen was a visual shock after the living room. All clean white and glossy black, with the only color being cobalt-blue accents in the tile, drawer-pulls, cupboard-knobs, dishcloths and mitts, and the matched set of canisters beside the space-age microwave.

"Aiden, hi!" Alex said as she came in. It sounded forced, but if she hadn't been expecting it based on what she'd heard outside, she probably wouldn't have noticed.

He and Jeff were by the table, next to an amazing array of food. In addition to the two red-and-white buckets of the Colonel's finest, there was a huge bowl of salad, a round loaf of bread holding what looked like spinach dip, a platter of meat and cheese cubes, a veggie tray, a pyramid of sandwiches, an economy-sized bag of chips, a brick of cream cheese, a slab of smoked salmon, and two boxes of crackers. A pot of pasta and another of sauce were on the stove.

Jeff only nodded, but his mouth was full. He was well across the room from Birdie, as if he was anticipating her to leap at him any minute and bite the buttons off his shirt.

Aiden smiled, still troubled and nonplussed and even more taken aback by the amount of edibles. "How many people are we expecting?" she asked.

Birdie laughed. "In case you didn't notice at lunch the other day, these guys are big eaters. As for me, a bod like this doesn't maintain itself." She skinned her hands down the well-padded sides of her ribcage and grinned.

"I guess it's a good thing I brought all this." Deciding to stick it out and make the best of it, Aiden unloaded the bag. "Chocolate cream pie, lemon meringue, fudge-frosted brownies, raspberry jam-filled cookies, and a caramel-swirl pudding cake."

"Dig in, folks." Birdie drained the pasta and dumped the sauce in, stirring. "This is as served as it gets."

"Way ahead of you," Jeff said, reaching for another cube of ham.

"Sodas are in the fridge. Also beer, wine coolers, and I've got mixers if you fancy something stronger. Except for you, Fergs, you're underage. Not that I'd tattle."

"We, uh, don't drink," Jeff said.

"And I'm technically underage too," Alex added.

"You guys are too much," Birdie said. "Either you have some killer metabolisms or you work out all the time. Don't drink? Bet you don't smoke, either."

"Or drink coffee," Jeff put in with a teasing glint in his eye.

"Well, as Adam Ant said, what *do* you do?"

"Who's Adam Ant?" Aiden asked.

"God, I'm old . . . no, blame it on Gary Haverley. Him and his damn 1980's fetish. Never mind. There's milk in there someplace."

They loaded up plates and got beverages – a wine cooler for Birdie, 7-Up for Aiden, milk for Alex and Jeff – and went into the living room because the kitchen table was too overloaded to allow a sit-down meal. Birdie sprawled on a futon like Cleopatra, somehow not spilling everything, and punched buttons on a remote. Music issued from hidden speakers, the CD player on random selections so that they were listening to thunderous classical music one minute, grunge rock the next, movie soundtracks after that.

Aiden nibbled, mouselike, at a little of everything. She couldn't help noticing that Birdie was right – Alex and Jeff really knew how to pack it away. She also noticed that they skimped on potato chips, crackers, and veggies, but went heavy on the meat and cheese. That had to be how they kept so fit, on an all-protein diet.

Later, as Jeff and Birdie were engaged in a heated discussion that was almost an argument about Hollywood's portrayal of werewolves, Aiden went to the kitchen for another soda and Alex joined her.

"You're quiet tonight," he said.

"I'm always like that."

From the living room, Birdie's lusty laugh rang out. Alex glanced that way and grinned wryly. "I'm glad."

"Alex . . . oh, gosh, I've never been good at this . . ."

He came to her, concerned. "Is something wrong?"

"I heard you. Before. Outside. You and Jeff."

"Oh." Wariness turned his eyes opaque, guarded windows through which he could watch her, but she couldn't gauge his reaction.

She busied herself scraping plates and stacking dishes, unable to look at him while she spoke. "I just wanted you to know, Alex, that . . . that . . . I understand, about your family. I won't be upset when you have to go. I mean, I will be upset, I'll be sad, but I won't be mad at you. I won't think I did something to make you not like me anymore. So please don't worry about that. I really do understand."

"Aiden, I don't know what to say." He rolled the top of the bag of chips to close it. "I wish it didn't have to be like that. I don't want to hurt you."

"Can you tell me one thing?"

He rolled the chip bag too hard, and the trapped air exploded out one of the seams. Crumbs and fragments scattered all over the white tile floor with its cobalt-blue accents. With an air of strained casualness, he asked, "Tell you what?"

"Why? Why do you have to keep moving around? Why doesn't your uncle want to stay in one place? Are you . . . fugitives, or something?" She giggled a little to show how silly she thought that was, but the giggle wasn't very strong to begin with and it curled up and died when she saw his expression.

"I can't talk about it." His voice had dropped, turned more raspy than ever.

"Okay. I'm sorry."

She went to the sink and filled one of the stainless steel basins with hot water, adding a squirt of soap. Alex moved up behind her and she knew a moment before he did it that he was going to put his hand on her shoulder.

"I guess you could say that," he said, pitched low so that she could barely hear. "We're on the run. We've always been. Our parents died when Jeff and I were little. They were murdered."

Aiden turned to face him. "Oh, Alex, I'm sorry."

"The ones who did it were never caught. Gideon's afraid that they'll find us someday and want to finish the job. That's why we can't stay in one place very long."

"What about the police? Can't they protect you?"

"I don't think so. None of us want to risk it. And that's also one of the reasons Gideon doesn't want us to get too close to anyone. I'd die if someone I cared about got hurt because of me. If *you* got hurt because of me." His hand slipped up from her shoulder to her cheek. "You're so pretty, Aiden, and so gentle. Your skin is soft as moonlight. I can't let anything happen to you."

Her mind was an utter blank. She knew she should say something, but the touch of his fingertips on her cheek had apparently shorted out every circuit in her brain. All she could do was gaze at him, into those eyes that weren't opaque at all now but clear, as deep and inviting as a cerulean pool.

Plastic beads rattled. "Let me just get another – hello!" Birdie came to a halt, seeing them standing so close. "Whoa, hey, are we interrupting something?"

Jeff pushed past her. "*Are* we?" he asked, his tone of voice the snap of a whip.

Alex pulled his hand away as if Aiden was made of fire. "No."

"No," she echoed. She *felt* made of fire, felt like she might spontaneously ignite at any second. She held up a dishtowel and wouldn't have been surprised to see the marks of her fingers scorched into it in shades of soot. "We were cleaning up."

"Pff, heck, you're guests, leave it for the maid," Birdie said. She looked curiously between Jeff and Alex, at the challenge and tension in their stances.

"You have a maid?" Alex asked, not breaking the stare-down with his brother.

"Well, no, there's only me, but I meant leave it for tomorrow. We were thinking of putting in a movie. Any druthers?"

"Maybe we better not," Jeff said. "Maybe we better get going."

"We told Gideon we were going to see a movie," Alex replied.

"*You* told him that. I didn't."

"If we watched one, it wouldn't really be lying, would it?"

"Can I talk to you outside, little brother?" Jeff spoke without unclenching his teeth, his lips barely moving.

Now Alex dropped his gaze and bent his head contritely, but didn't give in completely. "Later, okay? Let's just watch a movie."

Birdie nudged Aiden, shot her a questioning look. Aiden spread her hands helplessly.

Jeff glowered a moment longer, his eyes almost ablaze like gas jets, his brows knit into a fierce scowl. Then he relented. "One movie."

"We'll save the all-night marathon for another time," Birdie said, relaxing as the palpable energy between the brothers ebbed. She plucked the dishcloth from Aiden's grip and tossed it onto the counter. "And leave the mess. I mean it."

They returned to the living room. Birdie may have scrimped on furniture by buying futons, but she spared no expense with her entertainment center. The television screen was so big they might have been in a private theater, and the hidden speakers that had provided a low-volume mix of music during dinner contributed to a Dolby-esque surround-sound effect. Once the lights were doused, the illusion was complete except for the lack of cinema seating.

Aiden curled into one of the papa-san chairs, not trusting herself to sit by Alex. She still tingled where he'd touched her, and if she'd imagined the marks of her hand burnt into the towel, she could also imagine his fingerprints pleasantly seared into her skin.

He made as if to sit on one of the floor cushions near her, but a warning look from Jeff put a quick stop to that and he settled onto one of the futons instead. Birdie took advantage of Jeff's preoccupation to sidle next to him, and then leaned across him to reach the remote. She must have pressed against him in some provocative way as she did so, because Aiden saw Jeff's eyes widen, saw the flexion of his throat as he swallowed.

The movie was a 1980's classic, *Fright Night* with Chris Sarandon. Aiden had seen it before and enjoyed it, but this time she couldn't keep her mind on the story. She kept stealing glances at Alex, at the way the flickering light and shadow played across his features.

Oh, this was bad. This was very bad. This was not supposed to be happening.

She knew it was wrong, but knowing it didn't make one bit of difference.

When it was almost time for the sexy bite scene, Aiden realized she had to leave the room. She couldn't sit there while that went on and not look at Alex, but if she *did* look at Alex, who knew what he might think? She drained her glass and mumbled some excuse, rising from the round bowl of the chair.

Birdie had gotten her hand on Jeff's knee after all. He was sitting bolt upright, his face a mask of studious concentration, his jaw tight.

Aiden recoiled from the blinding white glare of the kitchen. Blinking like an owl rousted at midday, she found another can of 7-Up and popped the last few ice cubes into her glass. As she went to the sink to refill the tray, she saw her reflection in the window.

Another visage overlaid hers. It was hairy and monstrous and had a mouth filled with dripping ivory teeth. The twin orbs glaring in at her threw back the overhead light in hot white sparks.

She screamed and flung up her arms. The ice tray spun into the air, spraying water. Backing away from the sink, from the window, Aiden's hip slammed into the table hard enough to rock it and cause a bucket of chicken bones to tumble.

As she pivoted to run, Alex was there, bursting through the strands of plastic beads. She collided with him and thought sure they'd both go bum over teakettle, as her father used to say. But he caught her with that easy, deceptive speed and grace, steadied her.

"What? What's wrong?"

"Something . . . something at the window." She pointed.

The rectangle of glass was dark and empty.

Jeff and Birdie rushed in too. Aiden stammered out an explanation of what she'd seen, realized partway through how absolutely insane it sounded, and trailed off. From the other room, as if in mockery, she could hear the dialogue and shrieks of the horror movie.

"I saw . . . at least, I thought I saw something." She made a noise meant to be a sheepish laugh and cut it off quickly when it came out sounding like the titter of a mad woman, like a junior-high girl portraying a witch. "It was nothing."

Alex and Jeff exchanged a look. "Maybe we better check it out," Jeff said.

"We'll all go," Birdie said. "I've got a flashlight."

"Guys, really," Aiden said. "There wasn't anything there."

"You don't need to come," Jeff said.

"You're forgetting who you're talking to, mister. I've seen every scary movie there ever was, acted in almost a dozen of them, and if there's one thing I know, it's that the minute you two big strong men go outside to look around, the nasty baddie will come in some other way and imperil our chaste young bodies. We all go."

Wholly embarrassed, Aiden tagged along as they filed out the back door and Jeff beamed the flashlight. Alex kept protectively close to her, and while she normally might have liked it, now it only made her feel more like a fool.

"What did it look like?" he asked. "Did you get a good look?"

"No. I saw something, or thought I did, and screamed. It's no big deal."

A volley of gruff barks boomed from the other side of the hedge. Something large bounded away through rustling bushes. Aiden bit back another scream and clutched Alex's arm.

"Oh, for crying out loud," Birdie said. "It's Blitzen, the Brinkers' dog."

"Yeah, right, isn't that always how it is in the movies?" Jeff said with a faint jeer. "It's the dog, or it's the cat, and everyone relaxes, and then . . ."

"And then, whammo, here comes the monster," Birdie finished. "I know the drill. But that really is Blitzen. He's always prowling around my yard. I bet that's what you saw, Fergs."

"A dog?"

"Sure. He's part Great Dane and part horse, or at least he looks it. On his hind feet, he could poke his snout up to the window."

"Good." Jeff jerked his head back toward the house.

"Of course," Birdie said in the same jeering tone, "the minute we go inside, it'll be right there, big as life and twice as ugly, some slavering beast from the pits of hell . . ."

"Enough already, huh?" Aiden was shivering, more from the cold than from the scare, and Alex's arm went around her as if it was the most normal, natural thing in the world. She pressed against him. He was warm, incredibly warm, although he wasn't wearing a coat.

They went back in, and no slavering beast appeared to attack them. Jeff gave Alex the evil eye until Alex released Aiden, but when he sat next to her for the rest of the movie, Jeff voiced no objection.

Once good had triumphed over evil – at least mostly, because there had been a sequel – it was almost time to ring in the New Year. Birdie brought out champagne, but Alex and Jeff declined and Aiden insisted that she had to drive home and had no tolerance for alcohol. Grumbling, but good-naturedly, Birdie substituted a bottle of sparkling apple cider instead.

After that, the evening's festivities came to an end. Birdie refused to let anyone clean up, claiming that she would get to it in the morning. Jeff seemed quite eager to escape. He was the first one out the door and down the walk, calling to Alex that they'd better hurry because it was getting late.

Birdie pouted as she handed Alex his sweater. "Is your brother gay or something?"

Alex couldn't have looked more shocked if she'd slapped him. "What?"

"Does he not like girls?" She arched her back and inhaled, and Aiden felt more under-endowed than ever.

"It's not that." Alex floundered, chewed his lip.

"Every time I touch him he acts like he's trying to endure a dentist's appointment on sheer grit and determination. What's the deal?"

"I think you scare him," he said candidly.

"Alex! Come on!" Jeff waved from the car.

"Got to go." He turned to Aiden, started to say something, stopped, and settled for smiling at her. "Bye."

"Bye," she said quietly.

He was gone into the night, a closed door between them. Aiden fetched a sigh and reached for her own coat.

"Scare him," huffed Birdie. "Puh-lease! I saw the way he was looking at me. That was not the look of a scared man."

"Intimidated, maybe" Aiden said. "But they move around so much. I bet that's it. He wouldn't want to start something and then walk out on you."

"Good grief, Fergs, it's not like I'm out to marry the guy."

"Thanks for having me over –"

"You mean thanks for snaring your silly butt when you were about to turn yellow."

"That, too." Aiden bundled into her coat. "It was a lot of fun. Thank you."

"Anytime, Fergs. Happy New Year. Don't be a stranger."

*　　*　　*

CHAPTER 10
JANUARY 1, THURSDAY

Donovan Drachen prowled the house one last time, scanning what remained to see if any of it was worth the trouble of taking. They had little use
for the electronic gadgets that most of the world saw as so essential.

What was it to him if he could choose from dozens of channels, when
it was all drivel and trash? What use would it possibly be to him to have
online access when he preferred real pleasures? Why should he bother with
a microwave, when he liked his food still fresh and body-temperature?

He would regret leaving this place, though. They had been comfortable
here. Two nights without the wind and rain coming through the walls of the
shack. Two nights with electric lights, hot water, heat against the winter's
chill. They'd had plenty to eat as well, not only from the carcasses of the
man, the woman, and the cats, but from the well-stocked refrigerator and
the pantry. They'd slept in real beds instead of on cots and in sleeping bags,
or curled uncomfortably in some car.

This was the way it was supposed to be. Ease and comfort. This was
what they should have. What they deserved. What Simone, most of all, deserved.

But the world was different now, and people didn't live like the beasts of
the forest. There, if Donovan had his eye on a nice dry den that belonged to
a bear, or a wolf, all he'd have to do would be to challenge, to overcome, and
then to claim it as his own. That didn't work in the human world. Having
killed the man, he couldn't move in and take over.

They'd stayed as long as they dared. Sooner or later, others would wonder what had become of the ones who'd lived here, and come looking for them. Not that they'd find much.

Simone appeared in the doorway like a vision. Few of the scrawny woman's clothes had fit her, but she'd done what she could to replenish her wardrobe. As had he, though with slightly better luck. Royce Leland had been fairly broad-shouldered and tall.

The gauzy cream-colored dress trimmed with red and brown braided cords and threaded rows of seashells would have billowed on the dead woman like a sail. On Simone, the fabric was snug over her breasts and hips, and swirled sweetly around her knees. Donovan was entranced by the way the thin cloth molded each curve, by the way he could see – or imagined he could – the triangular russet brush at the juncture of her thighs.

Hot with shame, he forced his gaze higher but didn't dare meet her eyes. He lived in constant fear that she would see into him, that she would know what lurked in his mind. She was his mother! If she knew what he thought and felt, what he dreamed . . . if she knew what had really happened to Erala . . . he couldn't bear to contemplate what she might say or do.

"Donovan, I need you."

How those words sent a tremor to the very core of him! He suppressed a yearning shudder and rose from his crouch. He towered over her, but standing before he never failed to feel small, weak. Hers was the true power, one not born of sheer physical strength but of presence.

"Yes, Simone?"

"Come with me."

She led him down the stairs into the secret cellar, and he followed just as he would have followed her anywhere. Even into the depths of the earth, or into the fiery furnace the humans called Hell.

The green scent of the plants tickled his nose. "Are we going to take any of that?" he asked.

"Why?" Simone swung her head, the thick plait of her hair falling over her shoulder. She wore it the very way that Erala had always worn hers, and Donovan's throat tightened. Did she know? Or had it been Erala, unaware, copying the style from their mother? "It doesn't affect us. Why should we?"

"To sell it," he said. "Some humans pay highly for it."

"True," she said. The plait of scarlet slid off her shoulder and pendulumed in slow arcs across her spine. He watched, transfixed, as it came to rest along the line of her back. "But their laws, and their police, and their traps . . . no, my darling one. It would be too risky. If we were caught, arrested . . . no."

"No, of course not," he said, chagrined for even saying it.

A flush came up in her cheeks, a hard diamond sparkle in her eyes. "Oh, they've got it all set, don't they? We can't do anything in their world without the proper paperwork. How, Donovan, I ask you, how are we supposed to manage? Our kind . . . we are superior to them in every way! We used to rule this world, and they lived in terror and awe of us. Look what they've done to us!"

He bowed his head, familiar with this sermon by now. Simone, however, was only hitting her stride.

"We used to be able to get by," she said. "We used to be able to pass for them, to go among them unnoticed. In your grandsire's day, a man's word was good enough. He could buy property, conduct business. Not like now. It won't be long, you'll see, before they'll be taking blood samples for even the simplest transaction. They've turned this world into a labyrinth of security and numbers, when we don't even have the most basic of birth certificates."

"Couldn't we obtain false ones?" Donovan suggested. "They do it all the time in the movies."

"In the movies!" She withered him with a glare and he would have given anything to take back his impetuous blurting. "I suppose they do, but how are we to know how to go about doing that? Where are we going to come up with those connections, that kind of money? And even if we did know where to go, we couldn't trust them."

"Simone, forgive me."

"Oh, Donovan!" She came to him and reached up, cupping the side of his face in her delicate palm. "I'm not angry with you, my dearest. You have given me reason to hope again. But at the same time, it only makes me more aware of the trap we're in. I can't give you the kind of life I'd hoped to give you, and it burns me."

"You gave me life." He covered her hand with his own and held it there. "You give me reason to live. I just want to be with you, Simone, no matter what."

Her smile was as beatific as that of any angel. "My loyal Donovan. What would I do without you?"

"You'll never have to wonder."

They were close, so close . . . he kept her hand pressed to his face because he didn't want her to draw away. The bitter self-loathing – she was his *mother!* – battled with other, more primal urges. She was female, she was beautiful, she was only inches from him and he could almost taste her wild, natural perfume.

Simone's gaze softened with loving tears. "My son," she breathed.

Donovan closed his eyes, feeling a pain that was very nearly physical. He let go of her, let her hand slide away from him. She couldn't know, *mustn't* know, of the effect she had on him. He had to keep it hidden at all costs. Even if it drove him mad.

"We will get by," she said. "Somehow. They've made it their world, taken it from us, forced us to live by their rules and scavenge on their leavings, but we will survive."

He nodded.

"To that end," Simone went on, "we must have money. I suspect that if you can open that safe, we'll have all that we need. For a while, at least."

The safe, in the corner of the room, was squat and imposing. Donovan studied it with sinking heart. "I'll try, Simone."

"I know you can do it." She perched on the stairs, knees drawn up. "My fine, strong Donovan."

He looked at her and his mouth went dry. The way she was sitting, the sides and back of her skirt dropped away in a bell-shaped swoop. The hem was modestly down over her knees, but he could see the undersides of her thighs, and if he moved just a bit to the left, he thought he might be able to see the dark red shadow of . . .

No.

His fists were clenched so tightly that his nails, which grew fast and pointed and sharp if he didn't keep them clipped very short, gouged at his palms. He turned from Simone, whose innocent, encouraging expression was in such marked contrast with the unaware display of her body.

The safe.

Donovan went to it. He examined it closely and knew that he would have to tear the front panel free. He was no safecracker, no skilled master of locks. In matters such as this, he relied on brute force.

"I'll need to change," he told Simone.

"Go ahead."

She made no indication of leaving. Donovan felt flushes and chills race over him in alternating waves. She meant to stay there and watch him, and it shouldn't have bothered him. Their kind had no nudity taboo. They only wore clothes to better pass among humanity. It certainly wasn't as if they needed clothing for warmth. She'd seen him many times, and he'd seen her. When they hunted together. When they bathed. Why, the first time he'd seen her in his adulthood, she'd been bathing in a stream in the lush forests of Oregon.

Shaking that memory out of his mind before it made matters worse, Donovan pulled his shirt over his head and let it fall to the floor. He unfastened his jeans and pushed them down.

"You are such a magnificent creature, Donovan," Simone said. "Such an example of our species."

Was that just maternal admiration in her tone, or was there something more? Something akin to what he felt whenever he looked at her? No, and why should there be? She loved him as a son, nothing more. How could she know that he would have given anything, done anything, to love her as more than a mother? It was wrong. He had to control these urges, or . . .

Thinking of what Simone might do if she ever found out put a quick end to Donovan's hunger. She'd leave him. He would be alone, because his father would never take him back, not after the betrayal, not after Erala. Alone . . . and worse, he'd be without Simone. It wouldn't matter if he was surrounded by hundreds of others if it meant being without her.

The change rippled through him. Beginning as a bright-burning heat at his bones, it spread outward. He still couldn't believe how much easier it had become since Simone had taught him, shown him, persuaded him to eat the forbidden meat. She'd promised him that he would be faster, that his abilities would increase tenfold, and she hadn't been wrong.

His flesh shifted, bones re-shaping with a deep pleasure/pain. His already muscular frame filled out, swelled, bulged with sleek strength. The fine hair on his limbs turned to downy fur, then thicker, merging with the dense, curled mat on his chest. His jaw creaked as it stretched forth into a muzzle. Teeth elongated into slicing edges and impaling points.

His vision blurred briefly as his eyes changed, their azure fading into silvery-pale. When he blinked to clear them, he saw the room in the heightened clarity that the transformation always brought. Colors lost their definition but outlines and details were sharp and crisp.

He saw the heat falling from the lamps, the residual warmth of the soil, Simone herself blazing like a torch. Not infrared like they showed in movies and on television, not patterns of reds and yellows and oranges . . . he couldn't describe what it *was*, but it wasn't that.

"I never get tired of that," said Simone.

To his improved ears, her voice was intoxicating. Just as her scent curled and eddied, teasing to his even-keener sense of smell. There was a tinge to it that made part of his mind want to shrivel and recoil, that similarity of scent that spoke of their mother-son bond and the age-old taboo. Rutting with close kin – cousins, aunts or uncles – was permitted. Necessary, even. Without some degree of inbreeding, they'd have died out generations back. But to rut with his mother . . .

Or his sister?

Donovan cringed and with a great effort of will shoved all thoughts of rutting, no matter who with, to the bottom of his consciousness. He set his large, clawed hands on the safe. A grunt of exertion escaped him as he pulled with all his might.

"Oh, yes," breathed Simone. "So strong, Donovan, so forceful!"

He growled and gritted his teeth, lacerating his lip. Muscle and tendon and bone strained to the limit. Dazzles of not-light burst in front of his eyes. He had no idea how long it went on, that mostly-silent struggle, but his limbs were quaking, and he wouldn't have been surprised to hear and feel his joints give way before the seal and lock and hinges. His hind claws, sprouting from the agile, splayed toes at the ends of his exaggerated calves, scraped grooves in the concrete cellar floor.

"Yes, go on, you can do it!" Simone encouraged. He had been on the verge of giving up, of exhaling in one giant whoop, but he would rather die than fail her, and threw himself into the task with every last fraction of his concentration.

Metal screamed, sounding uncannily like the way the man, Royce Leland, had screamed as Donovan's muzzle had dug into his soft white belly and brought out the choice liver. The man hadn't seemed to realize he was making any noise. It was dangerous, that . . . letting the prey scream. But the house, out at the end of the long, winding Mill Road, was remote enough that they'd gone ahead and enjoyed themselves. A quick kill was efficient, businesslike. But the chase, the suffering . . . those were so much more delightful!

The front panel of the safe ripped free and clanged resoundingly on the concrete. Donovan nearly fell at the sudden release, catching himself. His breath rasped hotly. He leaned against the wall, waiting for the rush and pound of blood to drop to a tolerable level.

Simone cried out in glee. "I thought as much! Well done, my darling!"

Donovan looked into the safe. Neatly stacked and rubber-banded currency, mostly smaller bills by the look but a lot of them, filled the upper shelf. The lower section was taken up with a metal strongbox. Simone snapped off the clasp and lock with one claw, scoffing as she did so. The larger bills were within, possibly twenty thousand altogether.

They stared at it for a while, Donovan not sure what to say and Simone with eyes glittering. She ran a thumb along a sheaf of bills, riffling the paper and releasing a variety of scents. Ink, human sweat, and general dirtiness were chief among them.

"Very well done indeed, Donovan," said Simone.

He towered over her more than ever in his beast-form, and she seemed so slight and vulnerable. He could have overpowered her easily, borne her to the floor, torn away that flimsy dress to bare her lush body, taken what he so desperately wanted. In her excitement, she was more beautiful than ever.

But if he did, she would hate him forever. The pain of that fate was a thousand times worse than his aching need. The sating of his body would never be worth the irreparable damage to his soul.

So he accepted her congratulatory embrace and tried valiantly not to notice the heat of her skin through thin fabric, the soft press of her breasts. He tried not to think of her lips anywhere else as she kissed his furry cheek. He hoped that his urgent passion wouldn't betray itself, or, since that seemed inevitable, that she would somehow not realize it.

Luck was with him. Exclaiming happily over the money, Simone turned from him and gathered it up, stuffing bills into a large garbage bag. Donovan edged away from her, a different sort of hunger taking him over now as the demands he'd put on himself by undergoing the change began to make themselves felt.

He went up the stairs in three loping leaps, bringing him into the kitchen. They hadn't feasted as well as they might have liked on the contents of the pantry – most of the items were strictly vegetarian. The cans of cat food would have proved more to their liking than the organically-grown produce.

Finding a packet of smoked turkey-jerky they'd missed, he ripped it open with his teeth and hunkered down by the kitchen table to eat. As he did, he willed himself back through the change, bringing himself to human form again. Shed hair fell away in reddish-brown drifts. The outer layers of his claws cracked and broke off in thin ivory flakes and crescents.

Human again, he sat in a chair to finish the jerky. Simone came up behind him.

"Well, Donovan, I think we won't need to worry about money for a while." She sighed. "Not that it'll do us a lot of good, really. We can buy food, clothing –" here he remembered that he'd left his clothes downstairs, "– but even this much still won't buy us a proper home. Or even a new car. We'll still be stuck with dealing with shady people who'll take cash without ID. Still, it's something. Thank you."

She leaned over him from behind. Without his thick pelt, he was even more aware of the touch as her breasts brushed him again. He felt the nubbly little prod of firm nipples through the cloth, and was very grateful for the table that concealed him from the waist down.

"That was very impressive," Simone said, setting down the bag and massaging his shoulders. "I forget sometimes how incredibly strong you are. My, Donovan, you're tense."

"Yes," he said thickly.

Her skilled hands worked, worked. "You'll ache tomorrow."

He ached now, though nowhere near his shoulders. "I'll be fine." Which was a stupid thing to say – suppose she stopped? He didn't want her to stop. Couldn't bear it if she continued. Never wanted this moment to end as she rubbed his back, his neck, his upper arms.

Chuckling faintly, Simone left off the massage and nuzzled her face into his untamed hair. She slipped her arms around his neck and rested her chin atop his head.

"Oh, Donovan. I'm so proud of you. You can't know how happy it makes me to have you with me."

He could barely think, let alone speak. The smoked meat was forgotten. His forearms were crossed and in his lap, pressing down as he tried to will a change over which he had no voluntary control.

"Do you remember," she said, "when we met? I was so nervous. I'd been following you for weeks, trying to gather my nerve enough to approach you. I had no idea what your father had told you about me, about why I left, and what I'd done. I was worried you'd hate me. Run from me. Even attack me, like he once did."

"He attacked you?" Surprise let him find his voice. Rage coursed like poison in his veins. That anyone could try to hurt such a wonderful creature! Let alone his father, who'd been privileged to be her mate, to know every inch of her!

"It was long ago. But I didn't know what he might have told you. Whether you'd even be willing to look at me. I knew I shouldn't have interfered. I should have gone on my way and not bothered you. All I could do, I thought, was bring pain. I'd already made myself an outcast, but I could at least pretend that my children might harbor some fondness for me. I didn't want to ruin it by finding out otherwise. But I couldn't resist. Oh, darling Donovan, you have no idea what it's like to want something so badly, and know you shouldn't do it!"

"Yes I do."

She went on as if she hadn't heard. "I had to see you, just to make sure you were all right, that you'd managed without me. I felt so terrible for letting your father drive me away from my children. I wouldn't have blamed you if you'd hated me for it too, for abandoning you."

"Never that, Simone, never," he said fervently.

"And then, I saw you. I'll never forget it. Seeing you, seeing myself in your features and in the color of your hair, grown up so tall and handsome. I thought nothing would make me more proud. But you did, Donovan, didn't you? By accepting me. By loving me. By turning out to be all that I ever could have wished for."

He was back to being unable to speak again. The feel of her against him was weaving a spell more binding than chains of iron, and the love in her voice turned him helpless as warm butter.

Simone sighed again, contentedly, and Donovan couldn't help thinking that she might sound that way after love, sated on the pleasure he longed to give her.

"Well," she said, with a mild laugh. "No point dwelling on the past when we have our future to chase! We can't stay here anymore. With luck, the authorities will assume the fire was the result of someone trying to cover up the murders — astute of them, don't you agree, darling? — and they'll assume it was some rival in the field, or a robbery that got out of hand. As for us, it's back to the shack for now. I've got an idea or two about what to do with our newfound wealth." She kissed him squarely on the top of the head. "Now run along and get dressed."

"Yes, Simone."

He had to wait until she'd moved off and begun arranging kindling and kerosene for the upcoming bit of arson, had to wait until her back was turned and her attention was elsewhere, because the proof of his passion was very prominent.

In the cellar, as he re-donned his discarded clothes, Donovan told himself that he needed to get these thoughts out of his head before he destroyed his life. He told himself this as he stood in the darkened forest and watched the leaping flames take hold, consuming the Lelands' house as hotly as the fire that burned within his heart.

He told himself this all the way back to the shack. And knew that if he didn't find some other outlet for this pent-up crazed lust, he'd absolutely lose his mind.

* * *

CHAPTER 11
JANUARY 2, FRIDAY
EVENING

On the outside looking in.

She'd spent her whole life doing that, and Aiden was tired of it. All of a sudden. Just over the past week or so . . . no, don't be coy, since Christmas. Since meeting Alex. And, by extension, Jeff and Birdie. Since making friends.

It had given her a confidence she'd never known. She had even joined a reading group when Alex promised to go with her. The group met at Malachi Edwards' bookstore every Friday evening and consisted of Mal himself, local author Theresa Zane, a black-clad teenaged girl named Eva, Officer Avery Scribner, and Mr. Grant the town librarian. Plus Aiden and Alex. They started with coffee – Alex had milk – and chatting, the main topic of conversation being the fire that had consumed the Leland house the night before.

Aiden did more listening than talking, and was more awed into silence than usual by the presence of Theresa Zane. She had both *Mourning Glory* and *The Witchfire Girl*, signed copies, but only because she'd plucked them that way from the shelves of this very bookstore after being too shy to attend any of Theresa's events.

The group decided to start with a classic, *The Three Musketeers* by Alexandre Dumas, and spent a cheerful hour planning out the other books they'd read and discuss. As they walked out into the rainy twilight, Aiden astounded herself by asking Alex if he wanted to come over for dinner.

He agreed readily. Only then did she realize that she had little in the way of groceries suitable for company, having planned on nothing more complicated than a chicken pot pie when she got home that evening. They stopped by the deli for sandwich fixings and were on their way out dark Vista Drive toward the turnoff to her house when Alex suddenly asked if she'd known the people who died in the fire, the Lelands.

"I knew who they were, I guess, sort of, but I didn't know them. Why?"

"I heard they weren't burnt. I mean, that they were dead beforehand." He sounded tense, strained. Now that she noticed it, she realized he'd been edgy all day.

"I heard that too."

"Cut up."

"What is it? What's wrong? Did you know them?"

"No, gosh, no." He looked at her openly, guilelessly. "It's just . . . well . . . I told you about my parents, how they died. The ones who killed them set a fire after."

"Alex, this is completely different. They say Mr. Leland was growing . . . was . . . were your parents into that?"

"No! No way. It wouldn't . . . I mean . . . never mind," he said, gazing out into the wet night with edgy distraction. "I never thought about it much before, but you're pretty alone out here, aren't you? Don't you have neighbors?"

"A few. No one really close."

He was so pale, so drawn, in the faint illumination of the dashboard lights. Heavy shadows lay across his face, giving him a strange, almost sinister look.

Chills on tiny mouse feet scampered up and down Aiden's spine. She had slowed the car without meaning to, and for no good reason found herself thinking of something she'd heard the other day.

"It is kind of spooky," she said. "Brian's girlfriend Dawn told me that one of her drivers got a bad scare out here. She hit a dog, but she swears someone killed it and dumped it in the road, then chased her when she got out to investigate. These woods are weird at night. The beach, too."

Alex was watching her now, that pale, drawn expression more intent than ever. "Why do you say that?"

Aiden tittered a shrill, unconvincing laugh that did nothing to lighten the strange mood that had permeated the car out of nowhere. "No reason. Just . . . well . . . a couple of nights before I met you, the first time I saw the sea lions, I kind of felt it too. Like someone was out there. Watching me. It wasn't very scary, though. I felt . . . I don't know, safe, I guess. Later, I mean, after I got back inside and had time to think about it."

She was babbling and made herself quit. Besides, she'd come to her driveway and needed all of her concentration to navigate the ruts and bumps.

It didn't help that Alex was still looking at her with that eerie, intent expression.

"Does anyone live in that trailer?" he asked.

"The one we just passed? No. I don't know who owns it, but it's been abandoned as long as I've lived out here."

"I thought I saw something moving."

"Alex, don't," she pleaded. "I've got the willies already."

"I don't know if it's a good idea for you to be out here all by yourself."

She wondered if this was some peculiar come-on, some way of hinting that he'd like an invite for more than dinner. The mere notion boggled her, seeming more like something Birdie would think than anything that would dwell in Aiden's own mind. And yet, Alex wasn't acting flirtatious. He was deadly earnest, and some secret shadow in his eyes brought back that shiver of fear more strongly than ever.

"I've been fine out here for over a year now," she said. "Besides, what could be out there? It's not like Bigfoot lives out Vista Drive. We're only half a mile from town."

"Let's go back," he said, gripping her forearm where it extended to the steering wheel. "I want to check it out. Or let me out here and I'll run back, take a quick look."

Eyeing him warily, believing now that he wasn't trying to scare her but was honestly concerned, Aiden put the car in reverse and began backing carefully up the road. She ran the right-hand wheels off once into mud, but the little Kia forgave her and didn't get stuck. At last, the dim bulk of the trailer was in the mirror, cast in red by the taillights.

"Stay in the car," Alex said. "Lock the doors. If anything comes at you, drive. Drive fast. Do you have a weapon?"

"A weapon?"

He got out, holding the door open heedless of the rain. She could have sworn that he was scenting the air like an animal. The alert posture of his body, lithe and full of at-bay energy like a leopard or panther, added to the odd impression.

He's hunting, she thought for no good reason, and shivered. "Alex, let's just go."

"I have to check it out."

"You're frightening me," she said.

As softly as she said it, he heard and it got through to him. He bent and looked in at her, apology in every line of his features. "Aiden, I'm sorry. Maybe you should come with me. That way, neither of us will be alone."

Aiden got out of the car, keys clenched in her fist like a makeshift set of metal claws. She dispensed with the umbrella and rain pasted her hair to her head in a wet cowl.

Alex made no sound as he moved toward the rusting trailer. Aiden felt horribly loud and awkward, brushing against branches and stepping on twigs, as stealthy as a drum salesman. She struggled to keep up.

The trailer had once been white and economically neat, a rounded capsule made to hook to the back end of a tow vehicle. It was up on blocks that had been covered by undergrowth. The sides were cracked and peeling. Fans of rust framed the porthole-style windows and a doorway that was the right shape to belong in a submarine. The door that should have filled that gap was gone, and the metal folding stairs were askew. If either she or Alex stepped on them, she knew, they'd tear free in a pained screech.

She didn't see anything within, only blackness so complete it could have been cut from the cloth of the universe before the Big Bang. There was no way Alex could have glimpsed anyone, or anything, moving around in there. Even if he had seen something, it had probably only been a shadow, cast by her own headlights as they drove by.

As she was about to say so, Alex ignored the metal stairs and sprang through the dark oval of the doorway in a smoothly graceful movement that left her stunned. The only noise he made was the soft thump of his feet landing on the floor.

Aiden had convinced herself the trailer would be empty . . . or thought she had. She was bemused to find that when Alex jumped inside, she was braced for shouts of discovery, even the din and ruckus of a fight. When it didn't happen, she felt absurdly let down.

And watched.

She felt watched.

The sensation was similar to the one she'd felt on the beach that night, and yet different. Angry. Angry eyes upon her. Violent, murderous eyes. Like what Dawn's driver must have felt.

"Alex?" she whispered. The feeble sound died inches from her lips, unheard above the diminishing patter of rain on the roof of the trailer. He didn't reply.

More unnerved by the feeling emanating from the woods than the opaque darkness of the trailer, Aiden moved. She caught the sides of the doorway and boosted herself up, not trusting the tilted metal stairs.

A puff of mildewy air rose around her as her feet hit what felt like damp, moldy carpet. She couldn't see anything, couldn't hear anything. For all she knew, she was standing only bare inches from the gory museum of some serial killer with a head collection, boiled down to leering skulls, a row of white-domed skulls all set up neatly, maybe by some altar to a squelchy, nasty Lovecraftian deity with a multisyllabic, unpronounceable name.

Aware that she was working herself into a fit of terror, Aiden fought to get a grip. She was just reaching an acceptable state of calmness when a pair of hands fell upon her shoulders.

"Aiden, it's me," Alex said.

A breath that would have been a scream came out in a coarse pant, but only because Aiden thought her vocal cords had flown south for the winter.

"There's no one here," he added, with unmistakable relief. "I was wrong."

"Out there," Aiden said, again in a feeble whisper.

"Where?" He went past her to the door, leaned out, a silhouette against the night that was only slightly less dark than the interior of this recreational tomb. Moments later, he hopped down with that same easy grace. "No. It's fine. We can go."

Aiden was only too happy to go. As they returned to the car, she noticed that despite his assurances that all was well, Alex made a point of peering into the back seat and under the car before opening her door for her.

Neither of them spoke as she drove the rest of the way home, but as she parked the car in the welcome glow of the porch light, Aiden had to ask. "Alex, what did you think was there?"

"There wasn't anything."

"You were expecting something. Or someone."

He shrugged it off, and she let it go. They went into the house with their deli bag. She saw that Alex secured both the lock and the deadbolt, and his first circuit through the living room was more for the purpose of examining the windows than the furnishings and décor. When he was satisfied, though, he made another trip, and came to a stop in front of the easel, the canvas.

Aiden, in the kitchen laying out the sandwich makings, paused and anxiously looked at him as he looked at her newest paintings. *Europa Night* had turned out so well that she, emboldened, decided to hang it on the wall rather than tuck it away in the second bedroom closet with all of her other pieces. This new one, almost-finished, showed the pack of sea lions on the beach near the bluff. Some were at play in the water, others sunned themselves on wide rocks. She was especially proud of the way she'd captured the translucent quality of sunlight through the waves.

"This is really good," Alex said after so long a silence that she was about to rush headlong into an apologetic explanation of how she'd never had an art class. He glanced back at her with something like awe before returning his attention to the scene. "*You* did this. You created this. It's amazing, Aiden."

"When it's done," she said, "I want you to have it."

"You do? Really?"

"Really. You're . . . you're my first real friend, Alex. When you go, if you take the painting with you, maybe you can look at it sometimes and remember this place . . . and me." She was blushing, bent her neck to hide her rosy face in fans of hair.

"I wouldn't need a painting for that," he said. "But thanks."

His smile was so bright, so cute, that she let the bizarre business with the trailer drift to the back of her thoughts, and forgot about how the rainwater in her hair had come to be there. All that mattered was that they were here, together, enjoying each other's company and the simple meal they'd bought.

They made sandwiches, Alex piling his high with rare roast beef while Aiden opted for thin-sliced turkey, lettuce, and cheese.

"Hey," said Alex. "It's almost nine. Time for *Monstorama Theater*."

Friday nights on Channel 12 were given over to bad movies on a supernatural theme – ghosties and ghoulies and horrors from beyond the grave. Saturdays were dedicated to bad movies of a slightly more sci-fi theme – aliens, experiments run hideously amok, and the effects of nuclear testing on ordinary insects.

"Birdie told me she offered to give Jeff a tour of the studio," Aiden said. "But he turned her down."

Alex snickered. "Yeah. I think he was afraid she'd corner him in the dressing room or something."

"Doesn't he like her?"

"Oh, he does, sure. She just comes on kind of strong, and, well, you know." He sobered. "Gideon found out where we were on New Year's Eve. Boy, was he pissed. If he knew where I was now . . ."

"Alex, I don't want you to get in trouble because of me," Aiden said.

"I'm old enough to make my own decisions." Setting down the mostly-devoured crust of his second sandwich, he squeezed her hand. "And you're worth it."

"But if your uncle's mad at you –"

"I can't help it. I understand all his reasons, and I know he's right, but I can't help it. I like you, Aiden, a lot. So it's wrong, so what?" His hand, holding hers, was warm. His gaze, also holding hers, was soft and deep.

"Why's it so wrong?" she asked. "That's the part I don't get."

"I wish I could explain, but there's no way. I wish . . . I wish a lot of things." He looked down at their linked hands and she did too. Hers was so small and pale, like a dove held gently in his grasp. "I wish I could tell you everything."

"You can, Alex."

"No, not all of it. You wouldn't believe me, and if you did . . . I don't want you to be scared of me. I don't want you to hate me."

"That'd never happen."

On the screen, the Channel 12 logo was replaced by the movie-poster red lettering, like dripping runes of blood. At the same time, a demonic male voice boomed out, "Mon-sto-rama . . ." and a high-pitched witch's cackle finished with, "Theeeeeeeater!"

Seemingly glad of the diversion, Alex turned his attention to the television. He still held Aiden's hand, now cradled in both of his own. They watched as the scene faded in on the tacky, cobwebby mock graveyard, where Lady Nocturna sat on the edge of a crypt's lid, fishnet-stocking legs crossed. One high-heeled, pointy-toed black shoe swung back and forth in lazy challenge.

"Hello, boys and ghouls," she purred, just as she'd done in the Wash-Stop. Her hair, an ebony wig that fell to her hips, shimmered in the faux moonlight. "Tonight we have a special treat for you, a movie most near and dear to my own heart, Wilfred Ghostman's *Deathwalkers*."

Birdie went on, prattling about the making of the movie and sharing some juicy tidbits about the cast and crew. Aiden snuggled back on the couch to watch. She lost all track of the plot – such as it was – when Alex's arm companionably encircled her, and drew her against his side. Her head fit perfectly against his shoulder. She was very conscious of how warm he was, how right it felt to be so close to him.

"I know I'm crazy to even ask this," Alex said, "but if I tried to kiss you, would you slap me and throw me out?"

Aiden went very still, feeling a pleasant fluttery shiver that seemed to begin just below the tip of her sternum and rise, tingling, into her neck and face. She was sure she must be blushing again, beet-red, but with only the pale light from the television and the bulb over the kitchen sink to reveal her, it didn't matter.

Was this what they meant when they talked about desire? This melting-trembling butterfly sensation humming all through her? Because she wanted him to kiss her, was dying to know what it would be like, her first kiss.

The way he'd phrased it, though, was rather strange . . . it had almost sounded like he'd made a request. *Please stop me before I do something I shouldn't.*

"Why would I do that?" she asked in return.

"Because if I thought you were going to, it'd be easier to behave myself."

"If you want to kiss me, Alex, I'd like that." She said it in a breathless, timid rush before the shyness that welled up within her could take control.

She saw something in him then that she'd seen once before, that first day on the beach. A starkly fearful look, as if he were frightened of her, frightened of this and what they were about to do and what it might mean. But resolve firmed his chin, and he tenderly took her face in his hands and bent to kiss her.

Their noses bumped, and it was clumsy and hesitant, and Aiden had never dreamed that anything could be sweeter. The kiss was gentle and nearly chaste, he kept his hands where they were and didn't attempt to touch her elsewhere, but at the same time she sensed a striving, yearning passion in him that he struggled to keep buried. The only real proof of it came through in a sort of smothered groaning cry in the back of his throat.

The room swirled around Aiden. She thought she might faint. No, not merely faint, but swoon like they did in the novels. That was what it felt like, a swoon, a looping, dizzying spiral as her nerves flooded with the unfamiliar, but so very welcome, rush of sensation.

And then he was gone, leaping off the couch as if shot from a cannon. He stood in the center of the living room, hands fisted at his sides, chest heaving.

"Alex?" Aiden was mortified. "Was I that bad?"

"Oh, no, Aiden, no . . . you're wonderful. Too wonderful. That's the problem. I think you'd better slap me and throw me out after all."

The only thing she could think of to say was hopelessly foolish, but she said it anyway. "It's raining." Just as if he hadn't been walking unconcerned in the rain plenty of times. Just as if they couldn't both hear perfectly well the silence on the roof that meant the rain had stopped. But foolish as it was, it made Alex laugh, and much of the tension ebbed from him.

"The movie's back on," Aiden added, as a commercial for Jordano's by the Bay ended and a younger, though still queen-sized, Birdie Yale in a frilly nightie backed away from a shambling corpse and loosed her trademark scream.

Alex sat down, stiffly and cautiously.

"You didn't do anything wrong," she added. "I liked it."

"I did, too." His smile was a little strained. "Even more than I thought I would. That's the problem. It's . . . it's different for us, Aiden."

"Guys, you mean?"

"Uh, yeah. Guys. I didn't think it would be that strong."

"Me either. But then, I've never kissed anyone before."

"Neither have I." His admission surprised her. She'd thought that every guy, no matter how inexperienced, would lie wildly about it for fear of being seen as less than manly.

"Wow," she said quietly.

"Yeah. Wow." He leaned against the back of the couch, keeping his arm to himself this time.

They watched the movie, which had something to do with a carnival fortune-teller discovering he had the power to raise the dead, but couldn't control them as they rampaged through the county fair. After a while, as if of its own accord, Alex's arm snuck back around Aiden and she leaned into him.

She was never sure exactly how they'd ended up kissing again, but they were. Both of his arms had gotten around her, and hers returned the favor. Those first tentative, almost-chaste kisses evolved into ones of considerably more passion, long searching kisses with no more nose-bumping, no more clumsiness.

A rising, furious roar made them jerk apart. Aiden was disoriented, not remembering that from the movie and initially wondering if they'd somehow lost track of time all the way into the second feature. But the walking dead had cornered the hero in the highest car of the Ferris Wheel, clambering slowly and shedding parts of their decaying selves as they went, and the roar had been loud, so shockingly loud . . .

Alex bolted to his feet, his eyes wide and wild with guilt and fear. The front door shuddered under several hard blows, rattling in its frame. Another blow, this one like a sonic boom, snapped the locks. An enormous shape loomed in the doorway.

Aiden screamed, and at the same time the screen-Birdie did, and Birdie's was much more impressive. But Aiden's was more heartfelt. She lunged sideways and yanked at the chain-pull on the end table lamp. A cone of clean white light poured out.

The man in the doorway – it *was* a man, though her first thought had been more along the lines of *bear*, given that terrible roar – was the biggest man she'd ever seen. He reminded her of Michael Clark Duncan, the actor from *The Green Mile*, seven feet or more of mountainous muscle. His shoulders looked like he could have broken a railroad tie across them.

His skin was a dusky dark tan, looking even darker by contrast with his white chambray shirt. A fall of dark hair, the rich brown of sable and thick as a horse's mane, framed a face that looked like a master artisan had quickly chipped it from granite. It was a hard face, all square jaw and Roman nose and chiseled planes, a face that might have been handsome had it not been contorted with the most intense fury Aiden had ever seen. His eyes almost seemed to blaze with it.

"Alexander!" he bellowed, and it was the voice of doom, bass thunder that shook the floorboards and pressed Aiden into the sofa cushions.

"Gideon, I –" Alex began.

His uncle didn't let him finish. Gideon crossed the room in what looked like a single stride, and seized Alex by the scruff of the neck. "Didn't I tell you?" he raged. "Didn't I warn you what would happen? You disobeyed me, Alexander. You know the rules!" He shook Alex back and forth, even lifted him off the ground like a mother cat with a recalcitrant kitten.

Aiden wanted to leap up and stridently protest, tell this bullying brute a few things about family violence and abuse, but her body was in no mood to obey her mind. She cringed in the corner of the sofa, holding her breath against the moment when Gideon would raise Alex up, bring him down over one lifted knee, and break his back like a pencil.

"Gideon, stop!" yelled Alex with surprising volume.

"You were not to see her again! I made that clear to you! Now I find you here . . . like this! You know this is wrong, Alexander, you know this is forbidden!"

He hurled-shoved Alex from him, so hard that Alex staggered into the easel and knocked Aiden's half-finished painting to the floor. Alex went to his knees. Gideon turned his baleful, fiery gaze on Aiden. She thought her skin might blister from it.

Rather than shout at her, which she was expecting, he just *looked* at her, so hatefully that it was worse than any torrent of verbal wrath could have been. She dissolved into helpless tears, burying her head in her arms to avoid having to see that horrid, hateful look.

"I didn't want to cause any trouble," Alex gasped.

"You *knew*," Gideon said, not roaring now but still with such a deep tone of menace that plants wilted and stars fled for cover. "You knew, and still you disobeyed. Get up. We're going home."

Alex slowly rose, head bowed and shoulders tucked forward. He shuffled forward, and to Aiden, observing through tear-filmed eyes and under the crook of her elbow, he looked like a beaten dog slinking up to offer his neck and underbelly to the leader of the pack. Gideon's hand, as big as a canned ham and hard as a steel clamp, closed on his upper arm. Alex didn't dare so much as glance Aiden's way. If he had, Gideon might well have viewed this as further defiance and crushed his skull on the spot.

Gideon led Alex out, not bothering to close the door behind him. The wind was slicing in but Aiden hardly noticed. She had been so happy, *they* had been so happy, and now everything had come smashing down around them like a house of cards.

She knew that she'd never see Alex again. Gideon would make sure of that.

*   *   *

CHAPTER 12
JANUARY 2, FRIDAY
LATE NIGHT

Stacey Baker dusted herself with powder and slipped into a slinky black negligee. She fluffed her hair around her face and surveyed the final effect in the mirror. Satisfied, she left the bathroom and passed through the darkened house into the living room, where Mike was bathed in the blue glow of the television.

He had a beer propped against one thigh, the remote in his hand as he popped endlessly through the channels in the firm belief that if he stopped long enough to watch one program, he'd miss the televised event of a lifetime on some other station.

She posed in the doorway and waited for him to notice her. When his attention was a while forthcoming, she cleared her throat and posed again, more dramatically, one hip a rounded, aggressive jut.

Mike glanced up, grinned. "Well, look at you!"

"I hope you're going to do more than look," she said.

A shadow of doubt flickered. "I don't know, babe . . ."

Stacey wanted to snarl and pout and make a scene, but knew that wasn't going to help. She had to be comforting, supportive. She slid into the room and onto the arm of his chair, letting her fingernails dance through his hair. "Come to bed, Mike."

He hesitated again, threw a surreptitious glance at his lap. His khakis were undone in the wake of a big hamburger dinner, and the pale expanse of his underwear hid the lingering remnants of the bruising. The swelling, which would have been the source of many a joke if this had been a laughing matter, had gone down.

"I'm not really in the mood," he said.

All of her intentions to be comforting and supportive flew out the window. "There's nothing physically wrong with you. The doctor said so."

"I'm just not in the mood, didn't you hear me?"

She took his wrist and brought his hand to her breast. "I am."

"Stacey . . ."

"You haven't touched me in weeks."

"I don't think I can!" he blurted, wearing a shameful, furtive, truculent expression at the admission. "I don't think I can, okay? Maybe the bruises are gone, but it's going to take longer than that to get over what that rotten bastard did to me."

"He'll get what he deserves," Stacey said with the confidence of a vengeful Amazon warrior. "So they let him out. He still has to show up in court, and he's bound to go to jail. That doesn't have anything to do with us."

"It does, though. Every time I think about it, I . . ." he shook his head and shuddered.

"So don't think about it." She pressed his hand against her breast more firmly, felt him respond with a gentle squeeze. "We can at least try, can't we?"

"Try? What if I can't?"

"Well, as the old saying goes, if you can't stir the batter you can still lick the bowl."

Mike scowled in faint distaste, and Stacey suppressed a sigh.

Six years they'd been married, and despite all the copies of *Cosmopolitan* she left lying around, strategically open to articles like "Ten Moves to Drive Her Wild In Bed," Mike remained strictly a meat-and-potatoes guy in the bedroom. Oh, he didn't mind her going down on him, no sirree, but he never volunteered to do the same for her. When he couldn't pretend not to get the hint anymore, he'd eventually comply, with poor grace and poorer ability, until it just wasn't worth it to even ask. As for anything else, anything even remotely kinky, well, forget it. Which wasn't to say they had a crappy sex life, at least before all this. As far as strictly missionary went, Mike had been enthusiastic and possessed of great endurance.

She eased into his lap, kissing him, aware of the resistance in his body but determined to overcome it. He put his arms around her and gradually warmed to the makeout session. She detected the stirring in his lap and smiled against his mouth.

"In the bedroom," Mike said huskily. He pushed at the remote. The television went dark.

Stacey wouldn't have minded doing it right here in the chair, testing out some new position, but wasn't about to ruin her chances by arguing. She led him, undressing him as they went. Their bedroom was at the end of the hall, illuminated by the red and green bulbs still strung along the eaves outside.

Their bed was a queen-sized with a rattan headboard and sheets with a vaguely Oriental pattern – fans, pheasants, the suggestions of sunsets and pagodas. Stacey sat on the edge and urged Mike to stand between her knees, bending her head forward. He muttered something that might have been meant as a prudish protest, but never finished as her lips closed warmly around him.

Everything seemed to be in fine working order, Stacey noted. Her hand that wasn't encircling Mike burrowed down between her own legs, finding the damp softness there. Mike didn't notice, which was just as well because he could sometimes be weird about that too. Once, only once, he'd expressed an interest in watching her, but had found the experience more intimidating than arousing.

"Oh, yeah, I think I can after all," he said.

"I know you can." She gave one last flick of her tongue and reclined, pulling him down with her.

Mike pushed her nightgown to her waist, pulled the neckline down. He had no problem with her tits, not at all, loved to bury his face between them and lick and suck. Of course, the one time she'd offered to let him slide something else between them, he'd looked at her like she was crazy.

He entered her and fell into his usual rhythm. Stacey clasped his shoulders eagerly, scissoring her legs around his hips and working her ass for maximum stimulation. As hot as she was, as deprived as she'd been, she could tell she was going to go off like a rocket.

Under the familiar groaning and creaking of the bed, she heard a distant click, like the sound the front door made when it was being quietly closed. And a low thump, like a step.

Someone's in the house.

She started to say something, but Mike was oblivious. His face was a mix of desperate intensity and bliss, and if she ruined the moment it might be weeks more . . . and besides, her own climax was building, rushing rapidly toward its peak . . .

Mike voiced a glottal, strangled cry and strained against her. A sudden hot flood soaked Stacey's chest and stomach. Her first thought was that he'd already come, pulled out and shot it all over her for a change. But she could still feel him inside, stiff. He collapsed onto her, that flood pumping and hot pouring over her chest. So much of it, gushing in spurts, and the smell was strange, oddly familiar but strange.

All at once, Mike lunged up and off. Stacey cried out in confused frustration as he slipped out of her, leaving her writhing on the edge.

The world went upside-down. Stacey was flipped off the bed amid a series of crashing noises. Her head hit the nightstand, dizzying stars whirling in her mind. She tried to push herself up and set her hands in a hot sticky puddle. A soft weight was on her, pressing her down. An untucked corner of sheet flapped in her face and she realized it was the mattress, the mattress on her.

It was pulled off, and then strong hands seized her. Reeling, her head pounding, Stacey didn't know what was happening. The only thing that made sense was that Mike had gone a little nuts, decided to play a rougher game than she ever would have expected. Or wanted. She mumbled a half-sensible protest that went unheard.

He threw her down on the mattress, which was leaning at an angle half off the bed. She landed on hands and knees. He braced a hand between her shoulderblades and pushed her down onto her elbows, the side of her head pressed to the sheet and her butt waving in the air. His other hand dove between her thighs, probing urgently and quelling her resistance.

Stacey moaned in mingled pain and pleasure. "Mike, baby, take it easy," she said, and it came out muffled because her cheek was flattened against the mattress.

If he heard, he didn't heed. Stacey felt his hands, large and coarse, clamp on her hips. His nails dug in, sharp, cutting, bringing more little bursts of pain that were swiftly forgotten as a hot, heavy, rigid length pressed against her. He raised her lower body high onto her knees, positioned, and thrust hard. From above and behind, she heard his lustful groan, and echoed it.

God! They'd never done it in this position, despite her increasingly unsubtle hints. She'd read that it would let the woman feel penetration more deeply, and it was more true than she ever would have thought. He felt enormous, stretching her and filling her like never before.

"Oh, yes, yes, Mike, God, that's so good!" she panted as he grasped her hips, those fingernails still digging in, and commenced a swift pumping movement that sent sparks of delight whirling along her nerves.

She had been on the verge already, and her arousal had only dimmed a bit in those confusing, chaotic moments, but now it came raging back fullforce. She rocked back to meet him, and he was grunting now, like a wild animal.

Stacey tried to raise up a little, turned her head the other way and looked into Mike's wide eyes. Something was wrong about it, about the way he was staring back at her. The way he was sprawled on the floor, leaning against the wall on a slant, his head tipped so far over that his cheek was resting on his shoulder. She shouldn't be able to see him. His mouth hung agape. A darkness stained his neck and chest. His breathing was a harsh gurgle.

Horror and orgasm exploded over her in the same instant. She shrieked, a terrible sound, coming like she never had in her entire life, every muscle fluttering and aflame, slick convulsions grasping at him, drawing him deeper, even as her eyes bugged from their sockets and ice ran down her spine because it wasn't Mike, it couldn't be Mike, Mike was way over there in the corner, not on the bed at all, not touching her, not hammering against her. It wasn't Mike who, reacting to her climax, gripped her tight and moved in slow, persuasive, forceful thrusts.

Mike was staring at her, and the gurgle of his breath was the awful sound of air bubbling through a slashed throat. The dark bib he wore, the flood that had drenched her, was his life's blood spilling out. He was dying, dying, but not dead yet, unable to speak or move but conscious, *aware*, and the last thing he was going to see was his wife screaming as she came, screaming as some murderous stranger drove into her and laughed.

"No! Oh, God, no!" Stacey cried, but even as she uttered this denial, she came again in helpless shuddering release, and that final 'no' became a long, drawn-out wail. During it, she saw something indefinable change in Mike's eyes. That bubbling breathing stopped. She knew he was dead.

The man arched against her for one eternal moment of tension, frozen but hot, his fingers gripping so hard that the nails punctured her skin. He spasmed within her, and it was even hotter, the copious jets of his fluid like molten metal.

The aftershocks of her two shattering orgasms were still quaking through her, but Stacey fought her way through the maddening pleasure and tried to wrest herself away from the man. She was sobbing, frantic and sobbing, kicking and struggling but he held her in place easily, the pace of his motions slowing as he exhaled a desert-wind gust of sated breath against her back.

Telling herself that this couldn't be happening, just couldn't be, that she'd banged her head and the rest was hallucination, Stacey looked into the corner again. But Mike was still there, a life-sized doll in the shape of her husband, those glassy eyes still riveted on her in accusation and disbelief.

Above him, at the window, was a shadow pierced by two lambent eyes.

Fresh terror burst through Stacey. It gave her a sudden spate of strength that let her pull away from the stranger. He snared her by the hair that she had so carefully fluffed before going out to see Mike in the living room, a lifetime ago. Now her hair was matted with Mike's blood, and the filmy black nightgown was clammy with it.

He yanked her head back, her neck bending in a vulnerable curve. She knew that he meant to finish her now. The knife that had torn Mike open would find her throat. In the extremity of her emotion, she was ready to welcome it, that brief cold touch and the slicing pain, because it would mean an end. She wouldn't have to live a moment longer with the shame of it all, with the knowledge that the last thing her husband's eyes had seen was his wife fucking like a madwoman with his killer.

The shadow at the window smashed through it in a hail of glass and a shredded cobweb of the curtain sheers. It rose up, a hunched and inhuman form that she was glad she couldn't clearly see. Christmas lights outlined its shaggy head, glimmered red-green on the mouthful of fangs.

Stacey was beyond comprehending. Her assailant shoved her away and she tumbled down the askew slant of the mattress, hitting her head again on the same nightstand. As a flurry of commotion erupted in the room, the sounds of fighting and furniture being destroyed, she curled herself into the tiniest possible ball.

She stayed like that for a long time. For ages. Even after another window broke, and the cold air swept in like a living thing bent on having its turn with her, she stayed where she was. Curled up. Hugging her knees to her chest. Not letting herself think about the blood that was congealing to a sticky glue on her chest.

*   *   *

CHAPTER 13
JANUARY 3, SATURDAY
AFTER MIDNIGHT

Ronnie Greene shuffled to the front door in his slippers, undid the chain and both deadbolts, and drew his bathrobe snug around himself as he let in the winter chill.

The hem of his robe and the cuffs of his pajama pants flapped in the rising wind. It had torn the clouds to tatters, revealing a ghost-white moon almost straight up in the sky.

Aside from the rustle and whisper of the wind in the trees, the night was quiet again. But it sure hadn't been a moment ago. His curiosity getting the better of him, Ronnie stepped out onto the porch and peered in the direction of the Baker house.

An insomniac since college, he'd been watching some old monster movie on Channel 12. He'd dozed off in the chair and woken up just past midnight with a crick in his neck and the taste of stale pizza in his mouth.

He had headed for his bed, hoping that there would still be a good night's rest in the cards for him, and that was when all hell broke loose. Breaking glass, splintering wood. Screaming.

Through the trees, all he could see of the Baker house was a twinkle of Christmas lights. That was just inexcusably lazy, in Ronnie's opinion. He'd taken his down on what the Brits called Boxing Day.

He was sure that he had heard what he'd thought he heard. Fairly sure, anyway. Trouble at the Bakers', again. Ronnie turned to go in and then hesitated. If he called, and the police came, and there wasn't anything, what would they think?

And if there *was* something, Ronnie wanted to see it. He didn't want to be shunted aside by Scott James this time.

His overcoat was on a stand by the door. Ronnie got into it, and pulled galoshes over his slippers, and trudged across his yard and into the woods.

*   *   *

"You *what?*" Lindie Grantham asked, hoping that she had misheard. "You didn't really send Ernie on a delivery."

"Well, somebody had to take it," Billy Ritter replied, peevish and defensive. "*I* can't drive, and Dawn called in because her kid's got the flu."

Lindie pinched the bridge of her nose in an unsuccessful attempt to forestall a headache. "Jesus, Billy. When did he go?"

"He left over an hour ago. Hasn't come back, or called in, or anything."

"Jesus," Lindie said again.

"He's not going to do anything. I mean, he talks big and all . . ." Billy trailed off, his big moon-face twisted in doubt.

"Dawn didn't want him doing any deliveries," she said. "You knew that. He was just supposed to stay in the back, out of trouble, until his two weeks' notice ran out."

"But I couldn't drive it," he whined. "What else could I do? Tell Mr. Greene that he had to wait?"

Lindie shook her head. "The point is, where the hell is Ernie? Did you call him?"

"No answer. Shouldn't you go look for him?"

"Out Vista Drive?" Lindie shuddered. "No thanks."

"I can't close out the cash register until he brings in the money. It's already past midnight, past closing time. What do I do, wait here all night?" The weight of the world, as well as Billy's own three-hundred-plus pounds, seemed to pile down on him heavily.

With a resigned sigh, Lindie came around the counter, pulling off her red baseball cap and dropping her insulated carry-case onto the pile. She picked up the phone and thumbed through the battered book until she found a listing for R. Greene.

It rang. And rang. And rang some more. No answer. No machine picking up.

Unwelcome images kept rising in her mind. Ronnie Greene, the little bald man from the post office, leaning back in an easy chair. The way Mr. Gordon had been found last year after his crazy son Lucas killed him. Except Mr. Greene wasn't smothered in her vision. Mr. Greene had a pencil jammed in his eye. She could even see the embossed No. 2 on the yellow shaft, and a bead of blood hanging from the eraser like a ruby pendant.

One of Ernie's pencils. The ones he kept sharpened to needle-fine points. He gnawed on them sometimes while hunched over one of the endless successions of cheap notebooks in which he scribbled his observations on life, squeezing out rants like pus from an infected sore.

Yes, she could see that pencil, buried so far in Ronnie Greene's eye that only a few inches stuck out and his popped eyeball oozed down his cheek. His gaping mouth had been stuffed with an entire slice of pizza, wadded up in a bulge that dangled strings of mozzarella over his chin.

Her next shudder was so severe that Lindie dropped the phone. It swung at the end of its cord, bumping along a stack of white plastic tubs that held tomato sauce. Billy caught it and replaced it in the cradle.

"You don't think . . ." he did the trailing-off thing again.

"Come on. We'd better go look for him."

"Me?" he squeaked.

"I'm not going out there myself! I mean, if Ernie has lost it, I'm not going to deal with him on my own."

Billy looked at her like she'd taken leave of her senses. She instantly understood his line of reasoning – what possible good could *he* be if Ernie had gone off the deep end again?

She couldn't tell him that it wasn't really Ernie she was worried about. The thought of having to go back out there, along that dark, wooded road, made her tense up and turned her mouth dry as cotton batting.

What good could Billy be? Well, reasoned the vicious little animal of self-preservation in her subconscious, he couldn't run very fast and he'd make a decent shield.

Still fretting and complaining, Billy limped – with deliberate exaggeration, Lindie was sure – to get his coat. Her car leaned steeply to the right as he wedged his bulk into the passenger seat. Lindie got in, and drove toward Vista Beach.

*   *   *

Heartsick and unable to even think about going to bed though it was nearly two o'clock in the morning, Aiden sat in her chair and pretended to read *The Three Musketeers.*

The guilty feeling that had clutched her when Gideon burst in on them was gone, replaced by growing indignation.

Who did he think he was, anyway? It wasn't like she and Alex had been doing anything wrong. They weren't children, and Gideon wasn't Alex's father. Why was it any of his business? Who was he to 'forbid' Alex to do anything?

And what an archaic word, anyway. Forbid. Practically right up there with 'rue the day' and 'beseech' and 'forsooth.' Who talked like that?

Her temper snapped and sizzled. She was grumbling under her breath, turning the pages with excessively brisk flips.

The miserable, hangdog look in Alex's eyes. Just her luck. The first boy, the only boy, she'd ever really liked, and it had to end this way.

Sirens warbled in the night. Aiden sat up straight, thinking for a moment that Gideon had called the police on her. Which was a crazy thought . . . kissing wasn't against the law. She listened as the sirens blasted past the turnoff to Vista Beach Road without slowing.

She went to the window. The clouds had gone and moonlight thin as skim milk shined on the dripping trees. Nothing stirred except for boughs in the wind, and a car creeping slowly along the road on the bluff.

Aiden stopped and looked again, a frown knitting her brow. A car, up there? But the bluff road, which had been the back way up to Seacliff – what Dr. Gwynne McGuire had referred to, with haughty cool snobbery, as the servant's entrance – was closed off. Portions of it had crumbled away on that cataclysmic night a year ago. The road was deemed unsafe.

Yet there was a car up there. Headlights off, it was little more than a dark moving. She couldn't tell what kind or color it was.

The driver's side door opened and the dome light briefly illuminated a figure getting out. The person braced against the frame of the car and pushed. The car rolled, driverless now, picking up speed as it rumbled off what was left of the road.

"Oh gosh!" Aiden exclaimed.

She could see the figure, standing and watching as the car reached the edge. Its undercarriage hung up for a moment on the rocky lip, striking a few sparks, and then it went over.

The car plunged in silent grandeur, fifty feet or more straight down toward the jumble of rocks that had once made up the southern wall of the bluff. It struck with a grinding, crunching squeal. Aiden instinctively squinted against the inevitable fireball. But apparently, she'd watched too many movies. The car didn't explode as metal folded in on the gas tank. It bounced, sailing an impressive distance up and out, before coming down on its roof and tumbling end over end.

It came to rest nose-down, half submerged in the churning surf.

Aiden couldn't believe her eyes. Above on the bluff, the figure leaned out, peering down, and brushed both palms together in a 'that takes care of that' gesture.

She hadn't heard any scream on the way down, but the thought that someone might be trapped, pinned, in that mangled wreck spurred Aiden into immediate action. She grabbed her coat and banged out the door, heart hammering.

The old memory rose up like bile. She was in the car again, her leg caught, the seatbelt cinched so tight that she could barely draw a breath. Already freezing from the snow that slid in the gaps where the windows had been. Scrabbling madly to free herself, crying out for her mother to help her . . . and then turning and seeing her mother's face, her eyes blank blue marbles.

She ran, trying to outrace that terrible image. Bad enough it came to her in her dreams. She couldn't handle it in the waking world.

The waves rushed against the wreck and withdrew. Each time one hit, the car moved a little as if the tide meant to suck it out to sea. Closer now, Aiden could see how the doors had sprung open, how one had been torn off. The interior looked empty, except for a strew of trash that had spilled around, as if a whirlwind had gone through the car.

She picked her way quickly over the slick wet rocks, her breath like fire in her throat, a stitch pulling tight in her side. She'd abraded most of the skin off one elbow in a barely-noticed slip.

Something was draped over a rock ahead, a bright spot against the black. Too small and flat to be a body. She reached it and stared down at it, initially mystified at how an ad for a pizza place had ended up here. Then she understood what it was, the magnetic rectangle strip from the side door.

*   *   *

Donovan tried to sit up as Simone came in. He stifled a whimper, but she knew he had to be hurting. He looked up at her from his cot with large, imploring eyes.

"What a mess we have now," she said, her tone acid and ice.

"Simone, I'm sorry." His voice was rough, still partway between forms like the rest of him. The wounds showed vividly against his mottled skin and pelt.

"I don't understand, Donovan. What possessed you?"

"I couldn't help it. Couldn't resist. When I saw . . . I *had* to, Simone. I didn't mean to, but it came over me. Like falling. I couldn't stop." He hung his head, long red hair falling to obscure those wet and pleading eyes.

"Do you have any idea what you've done?" She could tell that he did, oh, yes, he knew, it was in every abject line of his body. That didn't stop her from lecturing. "You could have been killed. Caught. And now they'll know we're here."

He said nothing, bringing the back of his hand to his mouth to lick at a seeping scratch.

Simone turned her attention to the unconscious man in the corner, tossed there indifferently like a heap of laundry. His shabby black coat was open around him. A pencil had fallen from his pocket and she picked it up, examining the gnaw marks.

"And what, by the moon, are we going to do with him?" she asked.

"He saw me," Donovan said, speaking more clearly as his jaw shifted, receded. "He has to die. Doesn't he?"

"Oh, well, of course," Simone said. "We can't let him go, that's for certain. But we can't let him be found, either. I took care of his car. Let them make of that what they will. Hopefully, they'll think he ditched it himself for some reason, and fled on foot or left town by bus."

"So all we must do is dispose of the body far from here."

"That's not half as easy as it sounds after all the commotion you've caused."

He bowed his head again. "Yes, Simone."

"And there may be a problem. Someone else saw me. She might not have gotten a good look. It was dark, and their poor sight isn't half so keen as ours."

"Who was it?" Eagerness made him lean forward, heedless of his pains. "Was it the one who lives by the sea? The little one?"

Simone raised an eyebrow at him. "You know of this girl?"

His grin was feral. "I've seen her with her boyfriend."

"Oh, have you?" The way he said it made Simone turn it over in her mind, speculatively. "Then we'll certainly have to deal with her, won't we? But not tonight," she added as he moved to get up. "You're hurt. You need to rest, to heal."

Disappointed but accepting, Donovan settled back onto his cot. Already, the rent flesh was drawing back together, the flow of blood stopping, the bruises fading. He'd been lucky.

"But what about him?" he asked, pointing to the man who was showing signs of waking. Donovan's desperate wish to please came through in every word, in the way he lifted his hopeful face to her. "Permit me to finish him for you. I caused this. Let me solve it. Let me set things right."

"Not here," Simone said. "Not now. He'd scream, and might be heard.

This neighborhood's a bit too busy at the moment."

She went to the man, sweeping her gaze over him with mocking scorn. He was paunchy and scrawny at the same time, his arms both flabby and spindly. His tee-shirt, visible beneath the open coat, was black with the thought-provoking message in white: *Life's a bitch and so are you.*

"How true," murmured Simone. "I think I'd like to hunt this one, Donovan, what do you say? We'll take him far out in the middle of nowhere – which, given where we already are, won't be much of a drive – and turn him loose in the woods. We'll hunt him together, you and I. Just like old times. Just like when I was a girl. Except then, of course, the prey was elk, or deer. This will be much more enjoyable."

Donovan beamed at her. Under his look of boyish enthusiasm, she could see what he thought he kept hidden from her. He knew what it meant to hunt as a pair. To run together in the secret forest night, blood racing, every sense alive. To bring down prey as a team, working as one. The bonding of it. The bonding usually reserved only for close siblings . . . or mates. The thrill of the hunt, the excitement of the chase, the violent conclusion as they savaged, and feasted. That it was the forbidden prey only made it that much the sweeter. And after . . .

She saw that yearning for 'after' in his eyes, which burned briefly from azure to frost-hot with suppressed passion and need. Saw it, and pretended not to see it. With calculated gentleness, she raked her fingers through his mussed hair.

"My Donovan," she said softly. "My dear one. My son."

At the last, he was once more cast into the teeming confusion of his feelings. Simone hid her smile and went back to the man on the floor. He was waking, groaning, rubbing at the swollen knot on the side of his head where Donovan's blow had struck him down. He saw her.

His first reaction was typical. There she stood, in her short silky tunic, not minding the cold that came in through every loose board of the shack. Her hair was a ruby torrent around one bared shoulder. He thought he was dreaming, and a good dream indeed, the sort of dream that men of his type would boast about to their friends or write in letters to magazines as if fantasy had become reality.

Then came the realization that he was not dreaming, because of the pain and discomfort he had to be feeling. A perplexed scowl replaced the sly lustful sneer that had been forming on his face.

"What's your name, human?" Simone asked.

"What's it to you?" he flung back, wincing as he found the gouges under his arms, the gouges where Donovan's claws dug in as he lugged and dragged the man through the woods to the security of the shed.

Then it trickled into his awareness, her use of the word 'human' and the way she'd said it, as if it were a vile thing. Which it was, of course. Vile and hated.

"Who the fuck are you?" he added.

She only smiled, and let her teeth show. Her jaw strained in a pleasant ache as they pushed out, longer and longer, white and pointed. She blinked a slow, languid blink, and when she raised her lids again, she saw him through the eyes of the beast. The pattern of his fear was visible around him, yellow-white and expanding. He'd be seeing glowing white orbs with neither iris nor pupil, set in a face that was rearranging itself. Her pale skin blurred under a fine growth of autumn-colored fur. Upstanding triangular ears peeked through her hair.

He lurched back, slamming into the wall of the shed. It rattled. A gibbering slew of nonsense spilled from his lips.

Donovan watched avidly, hungrily. Simone acted as if she did not notice the way his hand fell to his lap, caressing. Possibly, Donovan himself wasn't conscious of it.

"What is your name?" Simone demanded again, this time with a throaty growl.

"Eh-Ernie."

Her nostrils flared at the acrid stink of fresh urine, Ernie voiding into his patched corduroy pants. It mingled nicely with the scent of raw terror coming out of his pores.

"He won't be much sport," she commented idly to Donovan as she lifted a hand and flexed miniature ivory scythes from the ends of her fingers. "But he'll do. He'll do for now."

*   *   *

CHAPTER 14
JANUARY 3, SATURDAY
MORNING

The sun hadn't even come up and Scott James was having the longest day of his life. He'd been roused from a sound sleep by Dani knocking on his head with the phone, and groggily fumbled it around to get the speaking end to his mouth.

What Damon Blake had to say had shaken the sleep right out of Scott in a hurry. Five minutes later, half of the Trinity Bay police department was assembled on the Bakers' lawn, trying to make sense of what had happened and being bombarded with information from Ronnie Greene and a couple of employees from the pizza place.

Mike Baker was dead. Stacey was clinging to life but deep in shock. The front door was ajar, and the bedroom window smashed inward. The bedroom itself was trashed, totally trashed.

That was where things started getting weird. Scott could fit it all together nicely in his mind up until that point. His words to Kel kept coming back to haunt him. One psycho . . . town this size . . .

The suspect – he made himself think in those terms, though everyone already seemed to know who it was – had been lurking around. Looking in the window. Watching Mike and Stacey. He burst in through the window, grabbed Mike unawares, slashed his throat, threw him in the corner to bleed to death.

It had to have been that way, by surprise. Mike didn't have any other marks on him, no defense wounds hacked into his hands, forearms. Then, while Mike was lying there, gurgling out his last, the suspect had turned to

Stacey.

She had a thin line of red on her neck, as if the suspect had held the knife there in preparation of a cut, leaving an imprint of her husband's blood. But then, rather than finish the job and kill her, he'd shoved her to the floor and torn the holy living hell out of the room.

But the wreckage didn't have the deliberate quality Scott might have expected. What his mind kept coming back to was the phrase 'collateral damage.' As if there'd been a fight, a fierce one, and the furnishings and walls had just incidentally gotten in the way.

He turned it over mentally as he went through the motions of doing what he needed to do. Once the scene was secured and the county professionals showed up with their forensic kits, Damon sent him straight over to Ernie Warrigan's apartment.

Grudge against the victims, witness putting him in the vicinity a short while beforehand, all that good stuff.

Scott drove through town toward North Valley, thankful that the early hour and the remoteness of the Baker house had kept the gawkers at bay. Tom's Market and a gas station were open. Everything else was buttoned up for the night.

Ernie's address was in a two-story structure with a view of the concrete rear wall of the market, where stacks of milk crates and flattened cardboard boxes added to the ambiance. The apartment building had wood paneling that looked in late-stage leprosy, and didn't offer covered parking among the amenities. It had a gravel lot where straggling weeds fought for their lives among the tires of the residents' cars. Ernie's Ford was nowhere to be seen.

The curtain was drawn over the window of Unit 8, giving it a sulky, closed-off look. Scott stepped onto the cracked cement walkway and pounded on the door.

"Police, open up!"

The door obeyed of its own accord, the flimsy lock giving way at the second blow of his fist. It stuttered open. No knife-waving maniac leapt out. Scott looked in at cluttered shadows, smelled old greasy smoke. His instincts told him that the apartment was empty.

He flipped on the lights. The studio was small, cramped, with barely a clear spot to stand. Dirty clothes were draped across bins of oil-smeared engine parts. Books and unwashed dishes competed for space on the table. Thrift stores would have turned up their noses at the furniture, the dominant piece of which was an avocado-green vinyl recliner with a split and cracked seat mended with duct tape.

The walls were covered with posters, bumper stickers, pinups, and felt marker drawings. These last made Scott's skin crawl. They could have passed for the work of a disturbed elementary school student, crude doodles of guns and guillotines and people being hanged. A dartboard was mounted on one wall, its concentric rings almost completely hidden beneath pictures that had been tacked to its surface. Some were torn from magazines – politicians, actors, rock stars. Others looked like they'd come from yearbooks.

Scott moved to the bathroom. A quick look was enough to convince him there was nobody in there, unless the thick mat of mildew on the shower curtain counted as a life form. The sliding door to the closet was off the track and hanging open. Nobody was hiding in there, either, but Scott's blood cooled a few more degrees as he saw what was in the open footlocker against the back wall.

Knives. Nunchucks. Throwing stars. A taser. A length of chain with one end affixed to the black rubber grip from a bicycle handlebar. Other stuff.

"Goddamn," Scott said, staring down at Ernie's collection.

The closet also contained stacks of magazines. Most were skin mags, but there were plenty of hardcore military and survivalist periodicals mixed in.

On a warped metal TV tray table, Scott found a cheap notebook, three-quarters full of pencil longhand. He was no graphologist, but didn't need to be to know that the jagged script, and the way that the pencil had been pressed down so hard that it nearly went through the paper were the signs of an angry mind.

There was a folded piece of paper tucked in like a bookmark. Unfolding it, Scott blanched at the words SHIT LIST raked across the top in inch-high slashes. The rest of the paper was taken up on both sides by five and a half columns of names.

Be time for a new SHIT LIST soon, Ernie-old-chum, he thought. *This one's almost out of space.*

Scott's own name was on the list, in a clump with the Bakers, Ronnie Greene, and Jerry Forrester. They were in good company. People that he was sure Ernie had never even met were on there. The President. Julia Roberts – what had she done to earn Ernie's hatred, besides being one of the most gorgeous and highly-paid women in the world?

He re-folded the list and put it in the notebook, and tucked both under his arm.

Apparently a town this size could support more than one psycho after all.

*   *   *

Aiden sat in a booth by the window of the Trinity Bay Bar and Grill, looking out at the misty Plaza and the people crossing it. She had come into town meaning to visit the campground and try to talk to Alex, but driving by, she'd seen Gideon working, and lost her nerve.

She ordered orange juice, and the children's pancake breakfast because she couldn't handle the portion size of anything else on the menu. When she was done, she intended to stop by the Municipal Building and report the car she'd seen go off the bluff. She should have done it before now, should have called or something, but her heartache over Alex had taken precedence over everything else.

The entire restaurant was abuzz with rumors and speculations about what had happened the previous night, out on Vista Drive. Aiden's appetite drained away as she listened to the grisly recounting of Mike Baker's death.

"The cops will get sued for this!" a large blond man proclaimed, his tone one of great satisfaction. "They had the guy right there in jail, and let him go. Probably, McGuire'll be sued too. It was on his advice, after all. Bleeding-heart social workers. He's still out there, too. We should all file suit. They've endangered our public safety."

"I can't believe it was Ernie," an old man said between sloppy bites. "He always struck me as all talk."

"Not me," the waitress said. "He'd come in here sometimes and I swear, you could just smell it on him. Crazy. He's crazy. I bet his high school class voted him most likely to end up on *America's Most Wanted*."

Half of the children's breakfast — two silver dollar pancakes, a single strip of bacon, and a few forkfuls of scrambled egg – sat in Aiden's stomach like a lump of lead. She pushed the rest away, paid her bill, and left as the patrons were speculating on how long it would take the police to catch Ernie.

She entered the police office, tensing up helplessly. How could she not, when she associated all the worst moments in her life with uniformed officers? The events had never been their fault, their doing, but they'd been first to arrive at the overturned, snow-filled car. First to arrive after her tearful 911 call when she found her father dead in his study. And at Seacliff, just when she'd been beginning to feel safe again, it had been a police officer who knocked on the door and informed her that everything going on there was a lie.

In fact, it had been this very police officer, Chief Damon Blake. He started to rise from his chair as she came in, then dropped back into it as if understanding that she'd be nervous enough without him towering over her.

"Miss Ferguson," he said. His voice was warm and deep, touched with a cowboy drawl. "Come on in and set a spell."

A polite smile like quicksilver lightning tugged at her lips and was gone. She lowered herself into the chair opposite him, not yielding herself to it but stiff, ready to spring up and run at a moment's notice. She held her purse in her lap with her hands clamped tightly to it.

"What can I do for you, ma'am?"

She told him what she'd seen. Damon Blake had been affecting a relaxed pose, but he straightened up and his coffee-brown eyes sharpened. He jotted down notes as she spoke.

"What makes you think it was Ernie Warrigan's car?" he asked when she finished.

"I found one of those magnetic things. That they stick on the side. It said Pizza X-Press. Then, just now when I was eating, people were saying —" She gestured vaguely in the direction of the Bar and Grill, and Damon nodded.

He stood. "I think you better take me out there and show me."

Ten minutes later, Aiden led Chief Blake across the beach. By daylight, even wet and pearly daylight such as it was, she could see the fresh crumble of earth at the edge where the car had gone over. Rocks were scraped in long streaks. Broken glass had showered in a corona around the spot it had first smashed nose-down, before bouncing the rest of the way to the surf.

The tide couldn't rise high enough to reclaim the wreck. Waves beat at the twisted hood. The magnetic placard still lay where Aiden had found it.

Damon Blake surveyed it, climbed around on the rocks to look from all angles, and came back down to where Aiden waited with wringing hands on the beach.

He took off his hat, ran a hand through his close-cropped cap of hair, and scowled distractedly at the crunched metal carcass. "About this person you saw —"

"Once the car went over, the person did this." She slapped her palms in that same dusting-off motion. "It was on purpose, not an accident, not like he or she jumped out because the car was out of control. It was on purpose."

* * *

CHAPTER 15
JANUARY 3, SATURDAY
AFTERNOON

Full consciousness returned like a slap. Ernie Warrigan sat bolt upright. His hands were tied in front of him, and his feet bound at the ankles.

He remembered. Delivering that little bald fuckwad's pizza, and sitting in his car at the end of the driveway, clenching his fists on the steering wheel as he contemplated the road.

A left turn to take him back to town. A right turn, and he'd be at the site of his humiliation. The latest and most aggravating in a lifelong series.

He remembered stalking toward the house. And then hearing them. The man grunting, and the bedsprings creaking, and the breathy gasping moans of the woman.

They were at it again. The assholes didn't ever seem to get enough!

After that, it was a blur in which hazy images surfaced. Coarse, hairy hands grabbing him. A burst of pain in his head. A redheaded woman standing over him.

But then . . . she'd . . . she'd . . .

She'd changed. There had been a wild, horrible light in her eyes. As she came toward him, terror cramped his body so hard that he pissed himself.

Now, the grey light around him was steady and dim. Fog light. Forest light. He was in a clearing, the sky above the flat pale overcast of a typical Humboldt County day.

Ernie was cold, damp, and stiff. His wrists and ankles chafed from the cord that bound them. His stomach complained of emptiness, but food was the last thing on his mind.

"What the fuck?" he muttered. It was starting to make a cohesive picture, one that he didn't much like.

He went to work on the knots, freeing his arms and then his legs. The pins and needles of numb-asleep limbs pricked at him as he stood up. His clothes were rumpled and caked with pine needles. His pants reeked of piss. He was passingly thankful that he'd left the Pizza X-Press smock in the car. If he'd seen that damn fucking stick figure grinning inanely from his chest, he would have puked.

So what the hell was the plan? They'd tied him up and dumped him in the woods . . . now what?

Ernie swore at the ferns and redwoods. He picked a direction at random and trudged through the underbrush.

All he had to do was get to the freeway. Couldn't be that far. He'd hear it sooner or later, the drone of the big logging trucks. In fact, he heard one now. That rumbling sound, almost like the snarl of an animal . . .

No, it *was* the sound of an animal.

It was a growl. Coming from off to his right. Low, but wanting to be heard.

I think I'd like to hunt this one, Donovan, what do you say?

That was what she'd said, the redhead, and now her meaning was coming all too clear.

He turned, thinking of the thing she'd turned into, the red-furred *thing* with eyes of white fire and claws like a handful of thin, curved knives. He didn't waste time trying to talk himself into believing that there were no such things as monsters. Or werewolves. Or whatever the blue fuck they were.

All that mattered was getting out of this alive. Payback had ceased to be a concern.

Ovals of pale radiance gleamed at him from the shadows. Eyes. Four of them, two sets. Advancing. He picked up a stick and brandished it at the eyes.

"Come on! Come on, you sick fucks!" he gasped, his voice hoarse and clotted. "Hunt me, is that what you want? Think I'm going to run? Eat shit!"

They moved into view, nudging aside the leafy fronds. The larger of the two was wolflike, on all fours, his chest deep and broad, his tail a russet banner sweeping in slow fans behind his haunches. The smaller, leaner one had a feline shape, pantherlike, fluid and hideously sexy in some perverse way. Her hair, that tumbled mass of red waves, had formed a mane undulating around her head and along her spine. Her eyes glinted, mockingly.

His legs were locked in place. He couldn't move. More warm piss was trickling toward his shoe.

The female opened her jaws and hissed. It broke Ernie's paralysis. He screamed and hurled the stick, missed by a mile. The male took a step, muscles playing beneath his pelt with the promise of sheer killing power.

Ernie bolted. He ran in clumsy, bounding strides, trampling through bushes and arming low-hanging boughs out of his way before they slapped his face.

*   *   *

Agate River met the sea in a setting that took Aiden's breath away. A shore of ocean-smoothed pebbles and driftwood gave way to pale sand and tufts of long grass. The massive outcrop of Agate Head formed the balance opposing Seacliff's bluff. It was surrounded by smaller rocky islands that glistened in the sea spray.

A bridge of natural stone, shaped and reinforced by the hand of man, stretched to one of these rocky islands. The clean white column of a lighthouse stood upon it, ringed by a fence and a garden of hydrangea bushes that would, in the spring and summer, become a riot of pink, blue, and purple.

Beyond the beach was a campground. Lightly-wooded hills backed onto a stand of thicker forest where hiking trails to challenge any level of fitness crisscrossed through the trees.

The campground parking lot was deserted except for a single motor home parked in the furthest space. It wasn't what Aiden had been expecting. When she thought motor home, she thought one of those enormous recreational vehicles, with more square footage than her house.

The one in which Alex's family lived looked more like a refurbished tour bus than an RV. It had dark lines and high, tinted windows, and a motorcycle on a rack on the back end. Jeff's, it had to be. He was just the type. The idea of him in black leather chaps, buff-colored hair streaming from under a helmet, would probably make Birdie drool.

The Chevy wasn't here, which was the only reason Aiden was. She'd seen it head out, with Jeff behind the wheel and a grimly somber Gideon in the shotgun seat.

An old man was asleep in a folding camp chair beside the motor home, in a patch of thin morning sun. Aiden could see a vague family resemblance. In his youth, the man in the chair had probably been as fit as Jeff or Alex, though nowhere near as awesomely muscled as Gideon. Age had softened him somewhat, made him stocky but still strong-looking. His hair was greyish-brown, long for a man his age, and his full beard flowed over his chest. The left side of his face was a gnarled mat of scar tissue. A stub was all that remained of his ear on that side, and it looked as though he'd come close to losing the eye as well.

The door to the motor home opened and there was Alex. He twitched upon seeing her, and that fey look of fright she'd seen a few times before appeared again in a flash. He masked it, but his gaze strayed tensely to the road and she knew he was worried that Gideon was going to catch them.

"Alex?"

"Aiden, what are you doing here?" He glanced at his grandfather to be sure he was still sleeping, and hurried to her. He almost grasped her by the shoulders, but caught himself and, honest-to-gosh, put his hands behind his back to keep from touching her.

"I wanted to apologize," she said. "For last night. And I wanted to see you again. To say goodbye, if that's what we have to do."

His eyes clouded over. Being so blue, so bright, like a June sky, that's just what they did. Clouded over, dulled, dimmed. It broke her heart to see it.

"Yeah. It is goodbye. It has to be. We're leaving."

"Oh, no . . . no. I was so afraid of that."

"Tomorrow. Gideon was . . ." he chuckled weakly. "Really mad. When he got me home, I thought he was going to tear strips out of my hide. He stormed out instead. I guess if he'd stayed, he was afraid he might kill me, he was so upset."

"He didn't hit you, did he?"

"No, no, nothing like that." Alex spoke reassuringly, but his face had gone drawn, and uneasy. "He told us that today we had to pack up, because first thing tomorrow we're heading out."

"But his job . . ."

Alex shook his head. "It wasn't much of a job. He says he'll find a better one in the next place we stop."

"Oh, Alex, I didn't want this to happen!"

"Neither did I. But there's nothing I can do. He and Jeff went to buy supplies, and first thing tomorrow, we'll be on the road."

"It's all my fault." She bowed her head, tears stinging.

"No, Aiden." He overcame that strange reticence and took her gently by the upper arms. "Aiden, look at me."

Reluctantly, she did so.

"If it's anyone's fault, it's mine. I knew better. I shouldn't have disobeyed Gideon. The only thing that's your fault is that you're so pretty, so gentle, so nice. I didn't care what was right. I wanted to be near you. I don't regret that."

The tears welled and overspilled. "I think I'm in love with you, Alex."

He winced like she'd struck him, like she'd put a knife in him and twisted it. Aiden could hardly believe the words had come out of her mouth, but there they were and she couldn't take it back. She started to stammer an apology, but he put his fingertips over her mouth.

"Don't. Don't say it," he said.

"But —"

"It's crazy, it's wrong, I didn't mean for it to happen, I don't know what to do, but it's the truth." He seemed agonized, as if this was some horrible confession she was ripping out of him. "I don't want you to be sorry. I don't want to be sorry. I love you, too, Aiden."

"Do you have to leave?" She hated the way it came out sounding, weak and plaintive. Before he could answer, she went on in a rush. "No. You do. I understand that. It's your family. I just wish I'd thought to bring the painting. I still want you to have it."

Alex turned his head side to side, making sure there was no one around but for the two of them and the elder napping in his chair. He pitched his voice low. "If I can, I'll sneak out tonight. I'll come see you. He'll sleep. He'll never know."

"Only if you're sure it's safe," she said.

"I promise. But now you'd better go. I don't know when they'll be back."

*   *   *

The prey was not fleet. The prey ran with a heavy, lumbering stride. It was not silent, either. The snap and rustle of its passage was laughably noisy, a giveaway.

All the same, Donovan Drachen thrilled at the hunt. He knew that he and Simone could bring the human down whenever they wanted, and they took pleasure in tormenting him. Playing with him. Like cats with a mouse.

Not the trophy, but the race. Not the quarry, but the chase.

The old saying had never seemed more true. The result was inevitable. They would have him, bring him down. When it pleased them.

He caught sight of Simone, sinuous and lovely as she raced on all fours. Her scent reached him, wild and musky, and hot energy ran down his spine.

What would happen when Ernie was gutted, his entrails a loose pile bulging through the fatty curds of his soft belly? When they were wet with his blood, and the meat of his flesh tore satisfyingly between their teeth? Did they truly hunt as a pair now? Would she turn to him, his beloved Simone, with her eyes shining like white suns? Would she look at him as something other than a treasured child?

He was no child! He was full-grown, an adult. He had hunted, he had killed. He had done murder for her, and worse. If he nipped her on the flank, or seized the loose skin of her nape in his jaws, lightly but firmly, what would she do? Would she lash out at him in revulsion? Surely not! She couldn't! She wouldn't! She adored him, loved him.

Ahead, Simone burst from concealment and Ernie shrieked. Simone's claws flashed out, viper-quick, and tagged him with four parallel scratches along the side of his face. Bleating like a sheep, Ernie lunged up and onward. They could have tracked him by smell alone. His fear splattered from his pores in droplets.

Simone, chuffing in the way they showed amusement in this form, trotted to Donovan and bumped her feline muzzle against his longer snout. It was his turn, the gesture said. His turn to harry and mark the prey.

Anxious to make a good showing, to impress her with his speed and strength and cleverness, Donovan bounded in pursuit. He hoped she was watching him, the way his muscles flexed and moved, the glossy good health of his pelt. He had mended completely from the previous night, having luckily escaped with only minor wounds. Not even a scar remained.

Ernie looked back, saw Donovan bearing down on him, and shrieked again. His hand was clapped to his face, blood flowing between his fingers.

Showing off, Donovan leaped not at Ernie but over him, a single agile spring that launched him several feet in the air. He tucked and rolled as he did, wearing a form akin to a wolf but more lithe than any true wolf could ever be, and altered his form mid-air. Not much, just enough so that when he landed on his hind legs, his shape was almost humanoid.

Donovan roared. This, too, was nothing that a true wolf could ever do. It wasn't a howl, but a sound more like a lion, or a bear, or a dragon might make.

Ernie, unable to stop his reckless forward plunge, tried to go around Donovan instead of slam into him. Donovan thrust out a foot and swatted Ernie hard in the back of the head. Ernie's shins hit and he tumbled to land flat on his back in a bed of ferns.

Simone loped up to them, mouth split in a grin and eyes twinkling. She rubbed her side along Donovan's thigh as she oiled past him to look down at the prone Ernie.

Donovan dropped to all fours again, hurriedly, to hide the erection that thrust forth with aggressive suddenness. The touch of her fur against his was sensual wonder. He would have happily forgotten all about Ernie if he thought he could mount her and be accepted.

But the hunt . . . the hunt wasn't done, and that was what Simone was intent on. She hadn't meant to put him into such a state, he knew that.

Ernie scrambled to his feet. His eyes were so wide that the whites showed all around. His chest heaved, his limbs shook, not a body used to so much exertion. He looked from one of them to the other, almost sobbing. He was close to the point where he'd beg, not for his life but for them to get it over with, to make it quick. To kill him and put an end to the fear and misery.

Simone rose up, altering smoothly as she went. She stood before Ernie as a cat-woman, full-breasted and alluringly inhuman. Purring, she ran her palms down the curves of her torso and sank her fingers into the tuft of curled scarlet plush at the joining of her legs. Her tail swished. Ernie stared.

Donovan stared too. His loins were steel and fire and hot throbbing blood.

She reached out. Took Ernie by the wrist. He was unresisting, slack-jawed, as she brought his hand to her breast and arched into it. A glazed, mindless look filled Ernie's eyes, as if all thought and reason had been drained out of them and replaced with insanity. He groped Simone with a greedy crudeness, thin threads of saliva unraveling down his chin.

Violent jealousy spurred Donovan into motion. He went between them, knocking Ernie sprawling. How *dare* he touch Simone like that? How dare this wretched human presume to do what Donovan himself was forbidden to do?

The hand that had been cupping her furred breast flailed up as Ernie fell. Donovan whipped his head around and bit it. Savagely. Bones cracked and splintered. His teeth met through the flesh of Ernie's hand and Donovan shook his head, snapping it side to side. Blood flew in a thick spray. He was growling, a growl that would have been words if his shape had allowed speech, words cursing Ernie and promising him a slow, agonizing death.

Ernie screamed, shocked back into the here and now. His other hand beat uselessly at Donovan.

"Yes!" said Simone gruffly, barely more than a snarl. She went at Ernie, shredding away his clothes with decisive slices from her claws.

He struggled, he thrashed, and Donovan mauled his hand until there was nothing left but a red pulpy mess attached to his wrist, with a few bones sticking out of it at helter-skelter angles, like porcupine quills.

Simone laid his skin bare. She dropped to her knees between his legs, her hair spilling over his pimply white thighs. His organ, a puny and pathetic thing even in its state of arrested arousal, poked through the torn remains of his underpants. Simone exhaled a hot gust, stirring the coarse bush of hair around that sorry excuse for a manhood.

Ernie raised his head, screamed anew at the sight of her leaning over him. Her tongue crept over the pointed row of her teeth. Donovan let go of Ernie's mangled hand and rocked back on his haunches to watch. His gut was in turmoil. In a way, he wanted to see her take this human, lower herself onto his pinned and helpless body, ride him as he fought and wailed in terror. But more than that, much more, he wanted to see her tear open Ernie's throat and let the life out of him.

She went one better. Arching her neck and throwing her head back, Simone stretched her mouth as wide as it would go. Then, with unerring speed and accuracy, she bent down and engulfed Ernie's genitals, and closed on him like the serrated jaws of a trap. His scream was almost beyond hearing. She reared up and spat the severed, bloody mess into his ashen face.

"Now," Simone said.

Donovan rumbled in assent, and they fell upon Ernie together. It was an orgy of blood and warm, fresh meat, claws ripping through to expose tender internal organs, flesh marbled with tasty veins of sedentary human fat. He didn't die right away, as neither of them went for his heart or his throat. His cries, his feeble struggles, only intoxicated Donovan.

This was the way! He'd spent most of his life heeding the laws of the pack, hunting only animals and having as little to do with humans as he could. Resigned to a life on the outside, having nothing while they had everything. And then *she* had come, Simone, appearing to him like a vision in the forest as he'd hunted alone one night.

He would never forget that first sight of her, by a clear pool, the moonlight caressing her like an ardent lover. His nose had caught her scent and told him at once that she was kin, that she was his mother. All of his other senses had cared only that she was female, of his own kind, and so breathtakingly beautiful that he feared his heart might burst.

She had come back. Risking terrible punishment. Come back for the sake of her children. And when he'd made clear to her that he didn't blame her for leaving, that he wasn't appalled by the things she'd done, she told him the great secret that was the real reason behind the pack's law. The power that could be theirs, the versatility of form, the quickness and ease of change, the added strength that could be theirs if they broke the pack's most ancient taboo.

The eating of the forbidden meat.

He did so now, gulping it in raw, quivering chunks that slid down his throat in a sauce of blood. The taste was beyond any beast of the wilderness, powerful and heady, sweet, rich. As he ate, he felt the renewed energy coursing through him, until his fur felt as if every hair stood on end, as if sparks might crackle from him at the pure unadulterated force of it.

Simone nuzzled him, pressed tidbits to his mouth as she must have done when he was a cub, except this was no chewed-soft deer to be brought back to the den. This was the way he'd seen his aunt and uncle share kills, nibbling at the same pieces, nose to nose and eye to eye, joined in the ceremony of the hunt, the feeding.

Donovan replied in kind, digging deep into Ernie's pulsing abdomen for a ragged strip of liver, her favorite. He offered it, clutched gingerly between his teeth, and she took it.

He made a low, needful noise in his throat and moved to her, rubbing all along the length of her side. Simone stood rigid, the morsel of liver still in her mouth. Donovan licked blood from her pelt, prodded his nose beneath her twitching tail and breathed of her vital female scent. The heat in his loins was maddening. He would mount her here, over Ernie's eviscerated but trembling, still-living body, and it would be the best he'd ever known.

Planting his forelegs on her back, he positioned himself. He was whining with desire, but relief and release were only inches away. He would thrust, and it would be done, the deed would be done, he would be hers and she would be his, bonded as a hunting pair.

Simone twisted out from under him before he could gain entrance. She gulped down the bit of liver and coughed, staring at him with shocked eyes that had lost their lambent white and were shading back toward turquoise. He cringed under that look, flattening his belly to the ground.

For an eternity, neither of them moved or made a sound. The change crept over him in slow stages, fur shedding, bones grinding as they re-shaped. Simone shifted to her human form, and the view of her nakedness almost overwhelmed him but she still had that *look*, that absolutely stunned look, and it held him at bay.

"Donovan . . ." she said.

He could hardly stand to meet her eyes. "Simone, I . . ."

"I think," she said in a shaky, but kind voice, "we got carried away. Forgot ourselves."

"Yes!" he seized on it gratefully. "Yes, I think so."

"Goodness," she laughed. "Can you imagine? The two of us? Rutting?"

His laugh was squeezed through clenched teeth. Could he imagine? Hadn't he imagined it every night since she found him? Didn't he go to sleep with hopes that it would follow him into his dreams?

"Sometimes, though," she said, still chuckling as if at her own foolishness, "it's hard to remember you're my son. That's what I get for not seeing you since you were a cub. You've grown up so strong, so handsome, my dearest Donovan. Any female couldn't help but look at you with wanting."

"Simone . . ." It almost poured out of him, almost spurted out, the words like the hot seed pent up in his tormented body. He withheld the words with Herculean effort, knowing they'd do nothing but harm.

She rose from her feral crouch, Ernie's blood and gobbets of flesh clinging to her creamy skin. "Let's clean up and go home. Do you still plan to tend to that little matter of the witness tonight?"

Witness? It made no sense to Donovan and then he remembered the girl. Slim and fair and tiny, a mere wisp of a thing, elfin and meek. Who had seen Simone dispose of Ernie's car. She probably hadn't gotten a good look, even with the moon so full and round, but in the interests of safety she had to go.

"I do," he said, thinking of her. She had to die anyway, for other reasons. But before she died . . .

Ernie hadn't really been very good prey. His love for life had been weak, bitter as the dregs of cold tea. It hadn't spiced the chase or the meat with the urgency of genuine death-fear. This girl, this Aiden, would be young and sweet, fresh, innocent.

And female.

A poor, pale substitute for Simone, but he supposed it would do.

*   *   *

The Change

Chapter 1
January 3, Saturday
Evening

When she heard the engine grumble to a stop, Aiden leaped off the couch. Dumas went flying. A soft cry of joy escaped her and only then did she realize how much she had really been expecting him not to come, not to be able to get away.

Only when she reached the door did she pause, troubled by a nagging sense of something wrong.

The engine, that was what it had been. The sound hadn't been that of a car.

Footsteps creaked on the short flight of stairs leading to her porch. Through a gap in the curtains, she saw a shape move.

A motorcycle! The one that had been secured to the rear of the motor home, it had to be.

Laughing at herself, Aiden opened the door.

Her laughter died on her lips as she looked up. And up.

The man standing silhouetted in moonlight was so tall he seemed twice Alex's height. His faded jeans and matching denim jacket fit tight as an azure second skin. His face, at once sharp and chiseled, was framed by shoulder-length hair of a deep red. His eyes glittered. So did his teeth, lots of teeth, when he smiled at her. It was a hungry, knowing, terrible smile that made fear burn and race along Aiden's nerves like dynamite fuses.

"Aiden, is it?" he asked in a too-wise, mocking tone. "Pretty little Aiden."

She stepped back and swung the door. The red-haired man blocked it with one outthrust arm and waved a finger at her – *tsk, tsk*.

"Who . . . who are you?"

"Donovan."

The name meant nothing to her. But there was something strange, eerily familiar, in his voice. It was low and husky, raspy, like Alex's. Like Jeff's and Gideon's. He had the same athlete's build, the bulge of his muscles truly epic beneath the snug sleeves of his jacket.

Still holding the door open, he let himself in. Aiden backed away from him, one fist curled at the base of her neck. In hopeful anticipation of seeing Alex, she'd dressed nicely. Dressed, she now realized, much too much like a damsel. White silk blouse, knee-length skirt in a soft pastel pattern, a twilight-lavender sweater.

"Pretty little Aiden," Donovan said again. He closed the door behind him. "What a pity she has to die."

Scream! But there was no one to hear, no one near enough to help even if they did.

Okay, then . . . run!

Aiden whirled and fled. Donovan, who had been leisurely moving toward her and sweeping his ravenous gaze over her small slim body, was taken aback. One hand flashed out. She felt it in the wind of its passage, too near a miss for comfort.

She ran, deftly avoiding furniture and keeping her eyes fixed on her goal – the kitchen.

Behind her, Donovan bellowed in rage. She heard the crash-crack of the coffee table as he either kicked it aside or jumped onto it. A shattering tinkle marked the end of a lamp, pitching the room into shadow.

The bulb over the sink was Aiden's beacon, her lighthouse. She went for the knife rack over the stove. The big bread knife looked like a bayonet in her tiny hand. She spun to face Donovan.

"Get out! Go away!" Hysteria raved in her words.

He scoffed at the sharp silver wedge she poked at him. "The mouse has claws, does she?"

"I don't know who you are or what you want but you'd better get out now. I'll call the police."

"They'd never get here in time."

"I'll cut you! I will!" The way she was shaking, she thought that if she actually hit him it would be a miracle. The blade threw off silvery reflections, bright shapes flitting across the ceiling. "What do you want?"

"Your flesh, pretty Aiden."

Donovan flung the kitchen table aside with one swipe. A bowl of fruit went over in a litter of apples. Salt and pepper shakers rolled like dice into the corner. The napkin holder shed its contents in a startled flock of origami birds taking flight.

He moved closer. Confident. Lip curled into a sneer that exposed his teeth. How white they were. How long and sharp.

"Get away from me!" She jabbed the knife at him.

Donovan snatched at it. She screamed and twisted. The edge caught his palm more by accident than design. Then the knife was gone.

Her back was pressed against the counter. She leaned back, far back, over the sink, and groped with both hands for something, anything, that might serve as a weapon.

"The mouse *does* have claws," he said, holding up his hand and looking at the scarlet stream coursing sluggishly down his wrist. He turned it, showed it to her.

Before her eyes, the cut in his palm was healing. The blood stopped, new white-pink skin grew together, and in seconds there wasn't so much as a scar left over.

"Who are you?" *What are you,* that might have been more what she meant, but couldn't bring herself to say it.

"Claws," Donovan said again. "I'll go you one better. Watch this."

His fingernails lengthened, thickened into moon-white curves. At the same time, a ripple of rust-colored hair dusted his skin and grew into a fine pelt. His eyes, glued to hers so as not to miss a nuance of her spiraling, spiking terror, flickered into glowing pale orbs.

"Werewolf." The word came out of its own accord.

"Not exactly." His voice had changed, too. It was lower, more of a growl in the form of speech. The outline of his body was altering, the seams of his clothing straining.

The rest of her might have been held spellbound by the transformation taking place in front of her, but one searching hand had continued its quest, and found the pull-knob of the drawer that held cooking implements. She pulled it open – stab of pain as her arm was made to work at that awkward, unnatural angle – and found a wooden handle.

"Stay back! I'm warning you!"

Donovan burst out in hilarity. Aiden looked at the old-fashioned potato masher as if she had never seen it before. She'd never even used it, didn't know why she had it, the hand-mixer did a much better job at that sort of thing anyway.

Before he quit laughing, she threw it into his face. The sound of his mirth cut off in a startled yip as the wavy metal smacked above his eyebrow. He recoiled.

Aiden shot past Donovan with fright-powered speed. He snatched out and caught hold of her sweater. She was pulled halfway around, felt the scrape of claws on her back. With a frantic tug, she tore away from him and left the pale purple cardigan hanging in his grasp.

She ran back the way she'd come. Jagged ends of wood from what remained at her coffee table raked at her legs.

He roared. In the confines of the small house, it was loud as a jet plane taking off, loud as a Metallica concert. Aiden risked a glance back and wished she hadn't.

The beast hulked in the doorway between kitchen and living room. Dexterous paws neither human nor animal shredded the denim jacket from his body. The tight jeans split down the side seams and fell away. Before his spine contorted, dropping him to all fours, Aiden saw something dark and stiff jutting from a fur-covered sheath, and all-out panic overwhelmed her.

She reached the front door and was across the yard toward the beach by the time her front window smashed out in a glassy, fragmented cascade. The beast shed the ruined curtains and raised its head. In the cold moonlight, she could see it more clearly than she wanted to. The triangular ears. The long muzzle.

Werewolf, she'd said, and he had denied it. But what else *could* he be?

Aiden looked toward the road, but it offered no safety. The beach didn't either. The muted glow of Trinity Bay around the bluff had never seemed so distant.

She went that way anyway. Toward the beach, toward the bluff, toward the distant barking of the sea lions. In some unfocused way, she was thinking that she could swim for it if she had to. The chill of the water would quickly kill her even if the churning and slamming of the surf didn't, but given the alternative . . .

Aiden ran, her breath pluming around her head.

Donovan pursued.

She reached the heaped driftwood and began scrambling over.

A hot hand, furred and feverish, closed over her ankle.

Screaming, beyond all reason, she grabbed up the nearest length of wood and bludgeoned him with it. He turned the blow with a forearm and retaliated with a backhand that knocked her head over heels. She came down on her left wrist and felt it break. Pure white pain drowned out the night.

He dragged her up. Battered and bleeding, her head spinning, Aiden flailed uselessly at him. The feel of his pelt was revolting and coarse. Her slaps were effective as the flick of a moth's wing. Her kicks thumped into his bunched thighs. His steaming breath blew her hair back. She could smell rancid meat, and gagged at it. He lowered his head toward hers, whether to bite or kiss she didn't know.

Her thumb went into his eye purely by accident. Donovan yelped in anger and pain. He spun her, slammed her down onto a slab of rock. Thin ribs cracked. A raw bolt of pain went up and down her spine like lightning.

In everything she'd read, when someone was being beaten to death, they reached a point of detachment. When it didn't hurt anymore. When it could have been happening to someone else. She was ready for that. She was eager for that. It didn't come. She felt everything, from the slightest scrape to the jagged prodding of bone ends into the tender sacs of her lungs. She coughed, and tasted blood.

Movement was a symphony of pain. Aiden rolled onto her side, coughing up more blood. Not a gout but more than a mist. She bumped her broken wrist and moaned helplessly.

"Oh, no you don't."

She thought that was what he said. His beast-voice was all but unintelligible. She got her right arm up to protect her head as he lashed out. Her elbow was driven the wrong way in a flare that swallowed up all her other agonies. Her arm and hand flopped against her face. They didn't seem to belong to her anymore.

Where was that merciful greyness? Why wasn't she losing consciousness? She strove for it, yearned for it, more than anything else wanted to slip away into a dark haze and feel nothing.

Donovan hauled her up. Ends of bone scraped together. Aiden's scream was more of a groan. He threw her flat on her back, on knobs of sea-smoothed pebbles. Her head struck a driftwood log, not hard enough to knock her out. She lay there, sprawled with stones for a bed and water-worn wood for a pillow, taking air in choked gasps and releasing it in weak coughs.

He stood over her on his hind legs. Above and behind him, she could see the towering heights of the trees, and the relentless press of the incoming clouds.

She knew what he was going to do, prayed for the unconsciousness that still eluded her.

I'll listen to the waves, she thought. *And to the sea lions. It'll be over soon. He'll kill me. I'm dying already.*

That realization should have filled her with despair, but it left her empty. As if her emotions had slid into the grey, numbed area while her nerves stayed keen and singing with pain.

"Nooo!"

It was a drawn-out, almost inhuman cry encompassing more rage and grief than Aiden had ever heard before. Even so, she recognized the voice instantly. The gravelly quality of it.

Donovan's head jerked up and around. He had been bending over Aiden, reaching with his claws for the torn mess of her clothing. Now he rose up, black lips curled all the way back.

A dark, sleek, dripping shape hurtled out of the night and slammed into him. They went down a few yards from Aiden, thrashing in combat.

She couldn't move. Couldn't even lift her head, let alone sit up, or even think about getting up and escaping. She watched uncomprehendingly as the thing that was Donovan slashed and bit at something else . . . a manlike form covered in wet, oily-looking dark fur. Its head was streamlined, from the tip of its black nose to the flap-covered holes of its ears. Its wide-splayed fingers and toes were webbed, and tipped with short, blunt, black claws. It looked like a cross between a sea lion and a man.

"Alex?" Her lips silently formed the name. He seemed to hear her anyway, turning his head to look at her, a brief look filled with anguish.

"You!" Donovan spat. "Will you never learn?"

Alex fought like a maniac. But that initial advantage of surprise didn't last as the larger, russet-colored beast retaliated with a series of vicious blows. Their struggling bodies rolled over Aiden, driving her to new levels of agony as she was ground between their weight and the pebbles.

Donovan got his hands around Alex's neck and throttled him. Alex's dark claws raked long furrows through his hide.

A third beast came out of nowhere. Lean and tawny-pale, a long fast shape like a spotless cheetah. It leaped on Donovan and tore him away from Alex.

The grey haze that Aiden had wanted began to seep across her vision. But it didn't dull the pain. Every injury hurt more keenly. Every breath was torture.

She heard a resounding crack, the solid sound of a baseball bat connecting with a good pitch. Donovan plunged headlong, his muzzle plowing a trench in the gravel. The tawny one raised a length of wood, eyeing him, ready to hit him again if he moved.

Something dropped beside Aiden. Her eyes met ghostly white ovals in a streamlined sea lion's head. Alexander Greye blinked, and his eyes were clear blue again, peering desperately down at her. She could see the familiar lines of his features, now that she knew to look.

"Aiden, oh, no, please be all right!" He worked his arms under her, gathering her to him. He was wet, smelling of salt and fresh fish.

Her outcry at being moved came out as a high-pitched whimper. The pain was everything. The pain was all the wide world. Nothing else mattered.

The third one, Jeff, with his anime hair giving the effect of a mane to his cheetahlike form, crouched across from Alex. Their gazes met as humanity began to surface in their faces, fur melting away.

"Donovan?" Alex asked.

"Out cold."

"Good. Thanks. Jeff, we have to get her out of here."

"There's nothing we can do for her. Look at her. Alex, she's dying."

Aiden wanted to protest, but couldn't find the strength or the words.

"No!" cried Alex.

"At least snap her neck," Jeff said in a reasonable, yet heartsick tone. "Don't let her suffer."

"I can't let her die! I love her! I'll . . . I'll save her. There's one way."

Utter shock made Jeff seem even paler. "You can't."

"I don't care. I'm going to!"

"Gideon says —"

"Gideon's the last thing I care about right now!" He stroked Aiden's cheek, looking into her eyes. "Aiden, I'm so sorry . . . I let him hurt you . . . I can help. It's all I can do. I'm sorry."

His head tipped back and his mouth opened to expose the stark pointed white of his teeth. The moonlight vividly illuminated an extra pair that slid out from behind his canines, a set of fangs descending into view.

"Alex, no!" shouted Jeff. "Are you crazy?"

"I love you, Aiden," he said, the words distorted by the new teeth. He held her, letting her head loll back to expose her throat. Strands of damp hair and grains of sand clung to it and he brushed them off tenderly.

Aiden sobbed once as he brought his face to her neck. His lips were a branding iron, his fangs frozen glass spikes. Needles. They pierced the beating artery. Out of the corner of her eye she saw Jeff reach out, perhaps meaning to force them apart, but then his hands fell and he shook his head ruefully.

A coolness began to spread through her. As if Alex's fangs were hypodermics injecting her bloodstream with liquid nitrogen. The effect coursed along the network of vessels, and wherever it went, it eclipsed the pain of her wounds, replacing them with an intense tingling sensation.

Alex cradled her against his chest. He finally lifted his head and she could see the stain of her blood on his lips, his chin. A rash of gooseflesh raced over her, clothing her in shivers. Twin stars of fire burned on the side of her neck. He had changed all the way back to his human appearance, naked and smooth-skinned.

"Do you have *any* idea —" Jeff said, and broke off short as Donovan sat up, rocking groggily and holding his head by the temples.

"Later!" Alex jumped to his feet with Aiden in his arms. "Come on!"

"No, this way! I've got the car!" Jeff, also fully human again, also naked, gestured toward the road. He bent to grab the strap of a small backpack. On the way, leading them at a run, he scooped up a trail of discarded clothes.

Aiden closed her eyes as every jolt of Alex's stride jarred through her aching frame. She felt that haziness again and sought it eagerly. She heard Alex asking Jeff what he was doing here anyway, Jeff's reply that he'd seen Alex sneaking out and followed, and both of them stumbling over each other's sentences exclaiming and cursing about the fact of Donovan's presence. Donovan and someone else. That they were here, here of all places, and wasn't there any way to get away from them? Hadn't they done enough to the pack?

Behind them on the beach, Donovan howled his wrath to the moon. The howl was like a sliver of ice into Aiden, snapping her out of the daze in time to realize Jeff was holding a car door open. Alex slid into the back seat with her draped across his lap.

Jeff dove into the driver's seat. "How can he recover so fast? How can he be that quick, that strong? He never was before!"

"It's *her*," Alex said. "*She* showed him. She remade him. Get us out of here, Jeff!"

The car surged ahead, bouncing over the ruts.

"If we take her to Gideon . . ."

"We can't do that. Just get us away first."

"He's coming after."

"He can't outrun a car."

"He can on a motorcycle."

"Then drive, damn it, drive! I don't care where! Unless you'd rather go back and fight."

Jeff laughed wildly. "We got lucky, little brother. Took him by surprise."

Alex gently settled Aiden onto the back seat. She rolled her eyes toward him, hearing but not really comprehending any of it. He cupped the side of her face, his chin quivering.

"Aiden . . ." he trailed off and blinked away tears. Steeling himself, his face turned grim and purposeful again. He looked out the back window.

Jeff had thrown the backpack onto the floor of the back seat. Alex retrieved it, unzipped it, and brought out clothes. He began to dress as gracefully as was possible in the back of a speeding car. She saw that he had a small round scar on his chest, a puckered dimple like a cigar burn.

In the front seat, Jeff was somehow getting his clothes on while driving. When they reached the turnoff to Vista Drive, the car careened around the corner in a squeal of tires, and took the bump-and-dip hard enough to send them momentarily airborne.

The trunks of trees blurred past. The road was a dark ribbon. They screamed up a hill and topped it with an instant's sense of weightlessness before the vehicle met the earth again in a shuddering impact that made Aiden cry out. A single ruby eye winked rhythmically at the bottom of the hill, where Vista Road intersected with Trinity Bay Boulevard.

Jeff showed no signs of slowing. If another car came along, they'd be canned meat. Aiden tried to care and couldn't. One of her hands crept out like a scared mouse and found Alex's. He gripped it, stared imploringly into her eyes. Pleading with her to understand when she couldn't understand *anything*.

"Hang on!" Jeff said as they rocketed toward the intersection.

* * *

CHAPTER 2
JANUARY 3, SATURDAY
LATE NIGHT

"Look, don't get me wrong, I love both of them," Birdie Yale said. "They've each got their strengths. Where is it written that I have to prefer one over the other?"

"It's the usual way, cupcake," Chas Vandermere said. "You can't have two absolute favorites."

"Can if I like them for different reasons."

"She's got a point," Joseph Perrin spoke up from behind the pages of the *Trinity Bay Gazette*. "Their styles are pretty different."

"Oh, like you know," said Chas. "When was the last time you read any Stephen King?"

"I read the one set in the prison. After the movie came out."

Birdie sighed. "There were two prison movies. Tom Hanks in one, Tim Robbins in the other. And really, Joseph, do you want to be telling us about your fascination with men's prison movies?"

"Wait a second, what's this?" Chas eyed him merrily. "You never told me you had a fascination with men's prison movies."

"There's a lot you still don't know about me, dear," Joseph said.

"If you guys want to play 'warden and inmate,' I can go in the other room," Birdie offered.

"We're coming up to a commercial, boys and girls," Chas said, indicating the screen. A group of teens had barricaded themselves inside the video arcade while people in unconvincing alien costumes rampaged through the streets, shooting plastic guns that fired rays the color of lime Jell-O.

Joseph set down the paper. "Time to act like we work here."

Birdie hefted her corset, causing her attributes to jiggle in a way that the two men utterly failed to appreciate. "On with the show."

The *Monstorama Theater* set in the converted fish cannery of the Channel 12 studios was a faux graveyard where the only thing that wasn't faked was the chill. Even in the summer, the chamber was dank and cool. In the winter, Birdie could see her breath, and Chas just said it added to the ambiance.

Joseph hopped into one of the camera chairs. Chas went to his console and began fiddling with buttons. Birdie took her customary place, perched on the lid of a crypt. Once, right in the middle of one of her sultry monologues, it had caved in and dropped her ass-first into the gap beneath. One of Lady Nocturna's finer moments.

"In three . . . two . . . one," Joseph said, and pointed.

Tossing her hair and pursing her lips at the camera, Birdie went into her spiel. "We'll be right back with the earth-shattering conclusion of *Death From the Stars* – oops, did I just give away the ending? Better stay tuned for these words from our sponsors."

Chas cut to the bank of commercials, which consisted mainly of discount furniture warehouses and every item for $19.95 that a body could ever desire.

When Joseph cued her again, she welcomed the viewers back to the movie. She had a good twenty minutes until the next break, when she'd have to freeze her jahoobies off in that graveyard again. In the meantime, she followed Chas and Joseph back to the lounge.

The can of Pringles chips had Marcie's name written all over them in bold black ink. A strip of tape sealed the top, with "Marcie's – Do Not Eat" on it. Birdie peeled it back, opened the plastic lid, and shared the can around to Joseph and Chas.

"Anyway," she said, "as I was saying before we got sidetracked by Joseph's deepest darkest sexual fantasies, what's wrong with liking both King and Koontz? One's just more . . . visceral, and the other's more artsy."

"Visceral, that's a good word, all right," Chas said. "That one, what was it, about the fungus aliens –"

"The shit-weasel book!" Birdie crowed, and slapped her thigh exuberantly.

"Hate to break up such a fascinating discussion, but someone's at the door," Joseph said.

Birdie glanced at the monitor hooked up to the outside security cameras. It was designed to either switch through the rotation of all seven or stay fixed on one, and most of the time it was fixed on the one that covered the main entrance, on what had once been the cannery's rear concrete loading dock. The fog was starting to come in, but wasn't thick enough to obscure the low-slung car parked illegally, or the guy getting out of it and shrugging into a leather jacket as he came up the steps.

"Must be one of your devoted fans," Chas said. "Since I doubt he's here for either of us."

"More's the pity," Joseph said again.

"It's Jeff," she said. "I'll get it." She adjusted her corset again and went through the nice reception area.

"Birdie?" Chas called from the lounge. "I don't like the looks of . . ."

She opened the door. It was Jeff, but his face was haggard and his eyes wild. His clothing was disheveled and spotted with sand and mud. At the car, Alex was lifting something out of the back seat. No, not something . . . someone.

"Fergs!" Birdie burst past Jeff as he was about to speak. Amazing how fast one could move in high-heeled button-up fetish shoes when properly motivated.

She stopped beside Alex, got one close look at Aiden, and whirled on him. Saw a terrible hangdog guilt in his eyes. Unloaded with a slap that nearly spun his jaw in circles around his head.

All of a sudden Jeff was there, grappling with her. And he was *strong*. "Birdie, quit it!"

"What happened to her?" she demanded, heaving this way and that and almost exploding out of the corset. "You bastard, what did you do to her?"

"Alex didn't do it," Jeff insisted. "We need your help. Aiden needs your help."

"Please, Birdie," Alex said. The mark of her palm had come up furious red on his cheek. "She's . . . she's hurt. I tried to save her. I tried."

Chas and Joseph appeared in the doorway. Chas had one hand in his pocket, where Birdie knew he'd hidden a gun, a dinky little derringer that made a surprisingly big hole in things. She thought of her taser, safely in her purse where she couldn't get near it.

"She needs your help," Jeff said, ignoring Chas and Joseph, focusing on Birdie. His bright blue eyes bored into hers.

"She needs a doctor and the cops, in that order."

"We don't have time for this. Birdie, as a friend, please! She needs a place to stay, someone to look out for her. You're the only one we could trust."

"You've got three seconds to explain."

"I can't. Not in three seconds, minutes, or hours. You wouldn't believe me anyway."

"Is there someplace we can put her?" Alex asked. He was holding Aiden like she weighed next to nothing. The honest wretchedness in his expression went a long way toward convincing Birdie that they were telling the truth.

"Birdie?" Chas asked warily.

"It's okay. I think it's okay. Bring her inside, but then you better start talking."

Jeff nodded. He went to Alex as if to help him, but Alex twisted away and carried Aiden up the steps. As he entered the reception area, the overhead lights showed the bruises and cuts and blood in garish detail. Her clothes were in shreds. She was missing a shoe.

Somehow that, the sight of that small, bare, defenseless foot, dirty and scratched, summed it all up for Birdie.

The shared dressing room was at the end of the hall. The couch along the rear wall was a plaid nightmare, the springs sprung and the cushions saggy. Birdie and Jeff attacked the pile of stuff on it – scripts, articles of clothing, magazines, craft supplies – and threw everything onto the floor. Alex brought Aiden to the couch so carefully, so gingerly, that more of Birdie's anger diminished. She no longer wanted to snatch the taser from her bag and make him jitterbug.

"Poor thing's been beaten half to death," murmured Chas.

"I didn't hit her," Alex said, looking earnestly at Birdie. "I tried to help her. If only I'd gotten there sooner. Just a few minutes would have been enough."

"Who did it?" she asked.

"We can't tell you," Jeff said, pinching Alex above the elbow as Alex was about to reply. "Leave it to us."

"Screw that! Who did this to her?"

On the couch, Aiden mewled like a child in the grips of a bad dream. She half-raised her arms in a feeble warding-off gesture, then crossed them over herself and trembled.

"His name's Donovan," Alex said, yanking away from Jeff and rubbing his elbow. "Last time we ran into him, he killed our hunt-broth – um, our friend, and our cousin."

"I'm calling the police," Chas said.

"No!" Alex stepped toward Birdie, and when she flinched away from him, something warm and hopeful in his eyes died. He stopped and exhaled, looking at her feet without seeming to see the shoes, the fishnet stockings. "She'll be all right. She just needs a place to rest until she gets better."

"Was she raped?" Birdie asked bluntly, making them both wince.

"No," Jeff said. "We were in time to prevent that, anyway."

"But he would have," Alex said, a hollow bleak tone in his voice. "He raped Erala. I was with Bernard when he found her, when he saw what had been done to her. We got her out of there but it was just like tonight. Donovan came after us. The crash . . . he killed those other people too. All they did was stop to see if we were all right. He killed them, and he killed Bernard and Erala, and he almost killed me."

He was massaging a spot on his chest, and his gaze had gone blank and far away.

"We've got to get out of here," Jeff said. "Come on, Alex. Birdie will take care of her."

"I love her." Alex announced like it was some terrible confession, and by the look on Jeff's face, in some weird way it was. "Tell her that. Tell her I'm sorry. Tell her I tried to help, and what I did . . . I only did to save her life."

"Come *on*, Alex!" Jeff seemed millimeters away from forcibly hauling his younger brother out of the room, but Alex went after one tormented last look at Aiden.

Chas and Joseph glanced at Birdie, as if to ask whether she wanted them to stop the pair or not. But Birdie was more worried about Aiden, who was shivering all over and sweating at the same time, and her complexion was ashen grey.

At the door, Jeff paused. "Birdie? There's one more thing."

"Better make it good, handsome."

"When she wakes up . . . she'll need to feed."

Then he and Alex were gone, leaving Joseph looking askance at her. "She'll need to *feed?*" he echoed. "What the hell did that mean?"

Chas came in with a blanket he'd found somewhere, a fleece throw with the Harley Davidson logo and an eagle on it. Birdie covered Aiden more for modesty than for warmth because despite the shivering, Aiden was burning hot to the touch.

She moaned and turned her head. Birdie saw something on her neck. Two red marks, pinprick puncture wounds surrounded by purple bruises. She shifted her body to block Aiden from Chas and Joseph.

"Um . . . food. Yeah. Could one of you maybe make a deli run? My purse is on the back of the door. Get some milk, some . . . uh . . . beef jerky, maybe, or a roast beef sandwich, double meat? Maybe some chicken?"

"This is no time to have the munchies," Joseph said. "That girl needs a doctor, not a midnight snack."

"I don't want to get anybody else involved in this. Come on, I'm begging you, please."

"Birdie, what's going on?" Chas asked. "I don't mind running your errands for you, but I'd like to know why we're doing this instead of getting her proper medical attention."

"Right now, anything I could tell you would only make you think I'm crazy."

"We've thought that for years anyway, darling," Joseph said.

"Just make that deli run, would you please?" She let some of her desperation leak into her voice.

"I'll go," Joseph said. He checked his watch. "But you've only got eight minutes until the next commercial break."

They finally left her alone with Aiden. Once the door was securely closed behind them, Birdie drew down the blanket for a closer inspection.

Torn clothes, but sensible good-girl underthings intact. Her skin was mottled with bruises and she was streaked with dried blood. One wrist was a gnarled knot. The lay of her ribcage was what disturbed Birdie the most. Bones were broken in there.

She knew a little about first aid, picked up here and there throughout her checkered career as starlet and student and late night gore show hostess. But that extended to CPR, the Heimlich maneuver, treatment for shock, and vague recollections of pressure points. Fergs wasn't strangling on a chunk of hamburger, had a pulse – thready though it may be – and wasn't actively gushing blood from anyplace visible from the outside. So that left shock.

A back sofa cushion served to elevate her legs. Birdie tucked the blanket securely around her after daubing away the worst of the mud and blood. She collected a few loose hairs in the washcloth as well, and hesitated. Dark red hairs. Wiry, almost, but also soft.

Aiden had stopped sweating and shivering, but she was still so hot Birdie thought she could fry an egg on her forehead. She'd stopped mumbling and moving in her unconsciousness too, but the deathly stillness no more reassuring. Her breath was shallow and quick. Panting.

"Shit, Fergs, what's happened to you?"

The intercom buzzed and Birdie came too close to loosing one of her famous screams. She sprang up, gave it a dirty look. "What?"

"Show time in one minute."

"Jeez, Chas." She heard every acting instructor she'd ever had, including Ghostman, rise clamoring in her head before he answered. "Never mind. Show must go on and all. Be right out."

Aiden didn't seem like she was going anyplace. Straightening her wig, Birdie rushed to the set for the commercial break.

*   *   *

Memory had merged, two nights becoming one. Two chases becoming one. First the female was slight and fair, then she was tall and dusky. Cowering before him. Resisting him with vicious intensity.

Donovan stumbled through the woods. His flesh had healed from the wounds he'd sustained during the battle, but his wits were still addled from the tremendous blow he'd taken to the head. He wasn't sure where he was, when it was, only knew that he was blundering along on remote control.

Remote control. A human term. There was another human term that fit his situation – *déjà vu*. Hadn't he done this before?

Aiden? Or Erala?

He closed his eyes, holding onto a tree to steady himself, and when he opened them, he saw her. Erala. Lovely Erala with her sweeping plait of dark hair, her lean and exciting body. Why she'd chosen to give it to Bernard was incomprehensible. Even before Donovan's final change, when his attitudes had taken a decidedly darker turn, he'd wondered at it.

Of all the pack, why Bernard? Why corpulent, slovenly, lazy Bernard? He was the only one of them with a taste for sweets, a taste that went beyond fondness into shameless gluttony. He spurned the hunt in favor of books. He composed poems of his own, which he'd read to Erala, and somehow that had made her choose him.

"He's loving and kind," she'd told Donovan. "He cares about other things than hunting and fighting."

"What else *is* there?" he'd asked in honest puzzlement, and Erala had raised her eyes to the heavens with that scornful air that only sisters could truly master.

It had offended him. It should have offended all of them. Didn't they live cheek and jowl with the untamed wilderness? Didn't they make "the fittest shall survive" their creed? She could have done better.

"Think of your offspring," he'd said to her. "You're the last female in the pack. The responsibility is yours to take a mate that will give you strong, healthy cubs. A mate who'll be a provider, a protector. He can't be those things to you and your cubs, no matter how pretty his poems are."

How she'd sniffed. So haughty! She'd told him that he knew nothing about love. That there was more to life than finding a dominant male.

Then Simone had come. She'd shown him the truth, shown him what their kind was meant to be. Erala's wish to have Bernard was just the latest in a long string of symptoms showing their kind's degeneration and decay. They were weak enough already, their numbers diminished, their territories taken over, their very existence in constant peril from the humans, and how did the pack deal with these problems? By making laws that hobbled them all the more. By forbidding that which could make them powerful again.

Even by permitting the last female of the pack to choose an unsuitable mate.

That was why he'd done it.

Or so he told himself, until he almost believed it, and could forget the other urges that had driven him to the deed. He could forget how inflamed he was by Simone's tempting presence, how not being able to have her had pushed him to the point of madness. Until it made sense that daughter should provide what mother would not. Ripe and young and female . . . so alive in her movements!

Erala should have been grateful! She was in her season. He could smell it on her, that alluring, intoxicating musk. For the good of the pack. For the good of their kind. She could let Bernard think the cubs were his if she wished; no one need ever know. Their scent wouldn't quite be right, but it would just be assumed that Erala's genes overrode the contribution of Bernard's tepid seed.

But she had rejected him. Turned her back on what he offered. Just as she'd rejected Simone when all Simone wanted was a chance to win back her daughter's love. In that moment, as Erala lashed out at him with fangs and claws when she realized he meant to have her, everything he'd felt for her turned to hatred.

He'd had her anyway, and the roughness of it, the harsh brutal pounding of it, her screams that went from shock and outrage to pain . . . he had lost himself in the act. Not caring that some of her slashes struck home. He healed in seconds, and the spilling of blood only added to his cruel pleasure.

Donovan staggered again and fell to his knees. Points of light spun and danced before his eyes. Instead of Erala's dark-furred form beneath him, he saw the tiny human. She was fleeing. She was the brightest thing in the night, almost aglow with faerie-fire as the moonlight haloed her pale hair, her white blouse. The pursuit had been as fulfilling as his encounter with Erala, although in an entirely different way. Erala had been strong. It had been a challenge to master her. This Aiden never stood a chance, and the aura of her fear had been so delicious!

Somehow, it had gone wrong. Again. Like before, they'd found him. Interrupted him. Stolen away the female. Again, he'd gone after, speeding down dark roads, not even bothering to turn to fully human form. This time, they'd gotten away.

In the echoes of memory, he heard the crash. Saw the car skid into the ditch, saw the pickup truck slew to a halt. He tasted once more the meat of the man and woman, quick kills but delightful. He remembered leaping on top of the car, pinning Bernard, that fat gut wedging him helpless. He had thrown Alex, not really having any particular grievance against him but having to be rid of him all the same. The youngest of the pack, barely more than a cub, should have died impaled on that metal rod.

He remembered dragging Erala from the wreck as Bernard struggled uselessly to free himself. He'd taken her a second time, hard and fast and without mercy, as Bernard cursed and shrieked. Right there in the ditch, in the gravel and broken glass. And then, when he was done with her, he'd broken her neck.

Bernard had fallen silent then, and the life had gone out of his eyes long before it left his body. Donovan hadn't had the leisure to kill him as slowly as he wanted. Not when other cars could happen along at any moment. But he'd done it slowly enough, giving Bernard ample time to wrestle with the knowledge of Erala's death.

He saw Aiden, crumpled like a wilted flower. Then Alex, who had somehow levered himself off the spear of metal, had come at him out of the darkness, with the smells of the sea and fresh fish clinging to him, transformed, attacking.

No. That had been tonight.

Donovan shook his head, which made more lights dance in it. He gripped the sides of his skull and willed himself to complete the change, so that the energies of his body would be freed up to center on healing.

Aiden's death had been necessary because she'd seen Simone disposing of the car. Her terror and pain, though, those had been for Donovan. Because Alex cared for her, and Alex had been the one to escape instead of dying, the one to tell the others what Donovan had become.

There had been no going back for him then. Only exile. Exile with Simone, which was paradise, but it still hurt to be cast out of the pack, the family.

So Alex had to pay, and having his little girlfriend share Erala's fate would have been a fitting matter of revenge.

Revenge, and lust. After the day's hunt with Simone, coming so very close to joining with her and finally sating the urgent need that boiled in his blood, and being denied at the last moment . . . he couldn't restrain himself. He'd *had* to have a female, any female. Not that he ever would have pretended she was Simone, and sullied Simone's glorious nature by so base a means. He'd only wanted to sink his needful flesh deep, find physical release.

It probably would have killed her, as small and slight as she was. To be taken so roughly, tearing at her softest inner tissues . . . yes, it probably would have killed her even without the other injuries he'd done upon her body.

Aiden . . . Erala . . . Simone . . .

But Alex had been there. Full of fury. He had never been able to best Donovan, should have known better than to even try. His reckless caring had almost proved his doom. If Jeff hadn't turned up . . .

Donovan snarled and raked trenches in the bark of the tree to which he clung. Two against one, that was fine, that was fair enough, given that he hadn't exactly been picking on someone his own size. But to sneak up on him like that, and club him . . . the slinking cowardly thing!

She wasn't even one of their own. He could understand Alex and Bernard trying to defend Erala. She'd been of the pack. One of them. One of their kind. But a human? A fragile and weak lesser thing? Why? Why?

"Donovan?"

Her voice was warm silver wine, a balm to his soul. He unhooked his fingers – fingers now, not claws, the nails embedded deep in the bark – and sat back on his heels.

"Simone . . ." It was a cub's plea, and he loathed himself for it. Not the greeting of a virile male, hunter and provider, but that of a hurt youngling who wanted his mother.

"Are you injured?"

"I'm mending." He touched the side of his head, half of his face squeezing in a grimace as he found the receding knot.

"What happened? Did you find the girl?"

"I found her. But . . . I didn't tell you before, Simone. *They* know her. Alexander knows her. He was there. He and Jeff. They attacked me." A ragged gasp, almost a sob, erupted from his throat. "*Me!* One of their packmates, one of their hunt-brothers. To protect a human."

"My poor, dear Donovan!" She knelt before him and used the hem of her shirt to wipe at his filthy skin. "As far as they're concerned, you're no longer with the pack. You're worse than dead. That's exactly how they saw me. A living shame, to be spurned and despised."

"I could understand it with Erala –" He bit his lip so hard he tasted blood, his own, an unwelcome flavor.

Simone's gaze sharpened. "What about Erala?"

"That . . . if it had been her . . . one of our kind . . ." he stammered. For a moment he feared the entire awful truth would pour out of him and struggled against that most damning of confessions.

"I loved your sister," Simone said, stroking his hair. "I had hoped that in time, she would come to see things differently. To embrace what we are instead of denying it. I like to believe that if not for that terrible, senseless accident, she might have come to me as you did." A soft sound of grief sighed from her lips. "And I'm sure that the rest found some way to blame me for her death. Your father was ever quick to lay fault at my feet."

Donovan trembled and said nothing.

"And now . . . what is to become of us? Erala was the only daughter of the pack. Through her, and the cubs she would have borne, our line would have gone on. Now they are only males left. No hope for the future, unless by some miracle they find another pack and mate into it. Oh, but Donovan, and our kind is so scattered, so afraid! Will we ever meet more? Will you? What will you do for a mate? I had looked to Erala to give me grandchildren, and now that is lost."

"What about you, Simone?" he ventured bravely. "You are young, and strong, and beautiful. Any male would kill to be accepted by you."

Her laughter was a doomed, sorrowful thing. "Until such a male learned the truth about me. Would your father take me back? Never! He'd sooner tear out his own beating heart than give it to me. It would be the same with any other. They'd know it as soon as they caught my scent. Or yours."

"Mine?" He knew what she meant; knew how their scents differed from the Greyes or any others who had never partaken of manflesh. It hadn't occurred to him until now that of course, others could smell it too. Even if they were untutored and didn't know what it meant, they'd detect that fundamental difference. No wonder Erala had shied from him upon his return, before she knew what he'd been doing.

"I've shown you the way to real power, to greater strength, but I didn't think ahead. What good is it to be the fastest and greatest of our kind, to have the abilities others never even dreamt of, if we're to be alone? Mateless? No female of a decent pack would ever take you now. Our only hope would be to find others not only of our kind, but like us. And too often, they are rogues and outcasts."

"As are we."

"As are we, truly said." She found a smile for him, which came to her with visible effort.

"We may be alone," Donovan said, as he reached out and took her hand. "But, Simone, at least we are together! We are not outcasts from the pack. We are . . . a pack of our own."

"Your loyalty is more than I deserve. How can you love me so, after all I've done?"

"How can you even ask?" He clung to her hand when she would have taken it away in shame. "I *thank* you for what you've done! You've shown me the way to change more quickly, with less pain. I heal in minutes what would have taken hours, what would take a lowly human days or weeks. And the other gifts, the ones you've learned and will someday teach me . . . all that is worth everything I've lost. Simone, but know this. Even if I had gained no new powers, I wouldn't undo any of it, because I'd still be with you."

*   *   *

"You broke one of our most ancient laws, Alex. Do you have any idea what that means? Didn't you ever listen to the elders?"

"I did what I had to do."

The stony resoluteness in his tone made Jeff blink, but didn't make him let up. "When Gideon finds out, I can't even begin to imagine what he'll do to you. You're worse than Simone and Donovan now."

"Worse? Because I saved a girl's life?"

"She might not thank you for that. She might rather be dead." Jeff took a deep breath and ran his free hand, the one that wasn't on the wheel, through his hair. "Alex, listen. We were born to it, and sometimes even we can't handle it. The transformation, the temptation . . . not being like anyone else, always having what we are hanging over us . . . it's a miracle more of us don't go crazy. I've had days when I've wished it would just all be over. Haven't you?"

"Sometimes," Alex admitted, unable to stay angry in the face of his brother's low, earnest words. "Nights, mostly. When the moon's so full, and compelling."

"Exactly. When we *have* to hunt. When we come so close and know how easy it would be to slip. We were raised with this, Alex. With others who understood. We had elders and parents to guide us. How's it going to be for her when she's got no one?"

"What are you saying? That I should have stayed with her?"

"You shouldn't have done it in the first place, that's what I'm saying."

"And just watched her die."

"If that's how it had to be."

Alex scrubbed shaking hands up the sides of his face. The roof of his mouth ached, long after the fangs had retracted and beating he'd taken from Donovan had healed. "But don't you see that I had to? I didn't even know I could do it until it was happening."

"What was it like?" Jeff asked like he didn't really want to know, but couldn't help it.

"Dying." Alex shuddered. "I could feel my life flowing out of me, into her. It was cold. Like I was turning her to ice in my arms. I could taste her blood, just a little, and . . . and . . . Jeff, I wanted to drink of it. It's what I think it must be like when they talk about drugs. Poison, but you can't help it, you want it anyway even if it kills you, because while it's killing you, all the hurting goes away."

Jeff was looking at him like he was some sort of monster, and it made Alex's heart ache to see that wary, horrified expression in his brother's blue eyes. A silence spun out as they pulled into the campground parking lot. One light shone in the rearmost window of the motor home, and everything was packed and loaded for their early departure in the morning. Jeff returned to his former argument.

"What about Gideon? Do we tell him?"

"He'll skin me."

"He has to know about Simone and Donovan." Jeff's fist pounded the dashboard. "Why can't they leave us alone? Haven't they done enough to our pack? If only we'd killed him! Why didn't we kill him?"

"How many of the ancient laws do you want to break in one night?" Alex asked, trying to make it come out light and jesting, and failing.

"That's what Simone wants, you know," Jeff said darkly. "She corrupted Donovan, tried to corrupt Erala, won't stop until she's gotten the rest of us either around to her side, or dead. We should quit running and trying to get away from her, and stand and fight instead."

"You saw how Donovan was," Alex said. "Stronger and faster than both of us put together. Even Gideon might not be able to take him now. Our whole pack, what's left of it, couldn't take on him and Simone."

"Not by tooth and claw, maybe," Jeff said. "But how come none of us ever think to get a gun and blow their heads off?"

"We're never in one place long enough to make it through the seven-day waiting period," Alex said wryly.

"Just a plain ordinary shotgun. Oh, never mind, you don't have to say it. I know why. That old-fashioned streak of Gideon's. It's amazing enough he lets himself carry a knife."

"Sometimes I think he'd be happiest if we were still living in caves and traveling on all fours. Remember how long it took to talk him into the motor home?"

"It would probably take more than a gun to stop Simone anyway," Jeff said, not listening to Alex. "A rocket launcher, maybe." He opened his door, letting in a damp gale of winter wind. "Come on."

"What are you going to do? Are you going to tell him?"

"No. We're leaving at dawn anyway. Let's just forget it and go."

Jeff stalked toward the motor home and Alex turned his face into the sea spray. His throat closed with grief and despair.

Forget it and go?

How could he?

*   *   *

CHAPTER 3
JANUARY 4, SUNDAY
MORNING

Aiden knew where she was by nothing but scent even before she opened her eyes.

Underneath the enticing food smells that had wakened her, she picked up the odors of hair spray, make-up, paper and ink and newsprint, old coffee, dust and mildew, and as a glossy finish over all, the long-ago olfactory echo of fish.

But it was the food, the fresh and nearby food, that commanded her attention. She sat up, letting the blanket that had been covering her fall to the floor. As she'd surmised, she was in the Channel 12 dressing room. She'd seen it once before, when Birdie had given her and Alex and Jeff a tour. That seemed like it had been a long time ago, but it had been less than a week.

A brown deli bag sat on the cluttered table. Aiden's stomach groaned. She got up and went to it, tearing the paper in her haste. A carton of milk, a bag of jerky, and a wrapped sandwich tumbled out.

The gnawing hunger inside her was scary in its intensity. She could hear a voice from somewhere, identified it as Birdie's and the one-sided pauses as clues to it being a phone conversation, but that didn't matter. What mattered was opening the milk carton, nearly being overwhelmed by the creamy goodness of its scent. She tipped it to her lips without bothering to search for a cup, guzzling it straight from the triangular opening.

Nothing had ever tasted so good. Or so she thought until she got the package of beef jerky open and bit into one of the stiff leathery strips.

Smoky, meaty, salty, delicious! Something savage and satisfying in the way it ripped under her teeth. She heard herself making little animal sounds of pleasure and didn't care.

Her eyes roamed the room. Movie posters, most of them old, covered the walls. The mirror was something straight out of the 1940's, surrounded by bright but somehow dingy bulbs. Pictures were taped around its rim, making an uneven frame for the central silvery glass. Most were from women's magazines, cosmetics pointers and so on, but she recognized Cassandra "Elvira" Peterson and Devila Fontaine among them.

Then she caught sight of herself, and froze.

Could that be her? Aiden Ferguson, polite and timid? Hunched . . . yes, *hunched* over the table, alone in the room but guarding her meal as if someone was going to come along and snatch it away? Aiden, wearing a sloppy white mustache nowhere near as tidy as the ones in the "got milk?" ads? Holding a chunk of meat in the corner of her mouth and her jaw working, knotting and bulging, as she chewed?

She swallowed, the hard jerky scraping down the inside of her throat, and for the first time looked at her arms. The right was fine. But the left . . . the left was fine too. And it shouldn't have been. It was broken, after all. Donovan had broken it.

The night's events came back to her like a slap. She jerked, dropping the carton of milk. Before it could hit the table, her hand had flashed out and caught it, spilling none. She took another drink, just to prove that she could, and set it down.

As she was only in bra and panties, she could see a mottling of darker blotches on her skin. Bruises. But they were faded, faint, old. She ran her fingers up and down the dual xylophone of her ribcage and did not find what she should have found. No jutting ends, no uneven bumps. When she inhaled deeply, the jagged internal stabbings were gone. The places she'd scraped herself raw on the rocks were smooth, unmarked by even the smallest scar.

Moving to the mirror, the demands of her stomach temporarily quelled by her consternation at what she was seeing, she leaned close to peer into the glass. Tilting and lifting her head, she saw the twin scars right where she expected to see them. On the visible beat of her pulse. Not quite an inch apart. Two tiny white marks, not circular but slightly crescent-shaped.

Her pain was entirely gone. She had been so wrapped in agony that she would have given anything, even her life, for it to stop. Now she was whole, hale, and alive. She felt, in fact, uncommonly good and full of energy. And hungry. Hungrier than she'd ever been in her life.

She went back for the sandwich, which she could tell by the smell was rare roast beef. It normally would have been too big for her, the sort of thing she would have cut in two and taken the rest home for later. The meat was piled thick and tall, fine-cut folds of pink and brown. Throwing table manners to the wind, she wolfed straight into it. In minutes, she had nothing left but a bit of crust and five slices of pickle that she had to spit out because they burned her tongue like acid.

As she ate, she finally tipped an ear to Birdie's phone conversation, which came from another room in what sounded like an otherwise deserted building.

". . . that *I* believe it," Birdie was saying. "And you know what a hard-headed cynic I've always been. It used to drive you bonkers. Now I'm apologizing for my smartass remarks — well, not all of them, but the ones pertaining to stuff like this. No, just me and Chas and Joseph. Uh-huh."

Birdie laughed, but it was strained, and tired. Aiden suspected Birdie had been up all night. God knew what she must be thinking. That she might wake up to Countess Aiden, looming over her with the ratty old blanket spread around her like a cape? Or Aiden Talbot, sprouting hair and checking palms for the mystic mark of the pentacle?

"You will? Thank you. I know it's asking a lot, but . . . no, you don't owe me anything! On the contrary! Well, if you insist. Great. I'll see you then. Haven't the foggiest. I'm going to wing it. Love and kisses to you too. TTFN."

Aiden heard the rattle of the receiver being replaced and made a scramble for her clothes. Birdie had probably been the one to undress her and get her cleaned up, but modesty was still and had always been one of her main driving forces.

Her clothes, however, weren't fit for anything but the rag bag. Holding them up and looking at the other side of the room through the long claw-marks, Aiden chilled to the memory of Donovan's attack.

The door opened. She spun, clutching the scraps to her chest although they were stiff with blood and sand and generally nasty-feeling.

"Hey, Fergs," Birdie said, and did a good job of sounding fairly casual. "You're up."

"Hi, Birdie."

"Lemme get you something to wear." She eyed the crumbs on the table. "Still hungry?"

"No, thanks." The pleasantries struck Aiden as wholly absurd, but she wasn't sure how to ask the many questions in her head. Like how she'd gotten here, where Alex and Jeff had gone, or who that had been on the phone. Or why she wasn't in the hospital.

Birdie rummaged, and found a pair of leggings that would have been snug on her but were blousy on Aiden, and a recalled sweatshirt for the HSU women's crew team, which had been unfortunately printed with the words "women's" and "crew" too close together.

"So what's the deal, Fergs? What are you going to turn into?"

"I don't understand," Aiden said, though of course she did.

"By that nifty hickey, I'd be tempted to say that your boyfriend is a vampire. But you reflect, and I've seen him by what passes for daylight around here. Touch this."

She thrust out a cross, and Aiden flinched, but only because the movement was so abrupt. "I'm not feeling any urge to hiss and cover my eyes," she said.

"Touch it."

"Isn't that the prop from *Immacula?*" Aiden tentatively extended a finger toward the crucifix. She found herself surprisingly reluctant to do this, not because she thought anything was really going to happen but because she didn't know what she'd do if something *did.*

Nothing happened.

"No smoke, no blisters. So far so good," Birdie said. "Unless the thing about the faith of the wielder is true, in which case this wouldn't apply 'cause I'm antagonistic."

"Don't you mean agnostic?"

"Nah. Antagonistic. I like to tweak the Bible-thumpers. You got religion, Fergs?"

"My father did, but we only went to church on Christmas and Easter."

"Not thinking about bounding over here and biting me on the neck?"

"No. Birdie, what happened last night? I remember Donovan . . ." She shook and glanced around as if he might suddenly spring out of hiding. "And Alex . . . he's not human, is he? He's a . . . not a werewolf, exactly, though Donovan sure did look like one. Alex was different. A . . . a selkie."

"Like in those old stories about seals who could take human form, and if you hid their sealskin, they'd have to stay that way?"

"Kind of, but not the same. And then Jeff . . . he was more, well, like a big cat."

"Doesn't it just figure? The first interesting guy I meet since breaking up with Gary, and he's not even human. Ah, well, at least I can still hope he's not gay. Who's this Donovan?"

"I don't know. A monster. He came to my house. I saw him change, Birdie. Right in front of me. Like special effects that they could never do, even with computer morphing."

"Hey, don't discount the guys in the creature shop so fast. They've gotten damn good these past few years."

"He wanted to kill me," Aiden went on. "I don't know why. All he'd say was that I had to die. And calling me 'pretty little Aiden' in a voice that would give Hannibal Lecter the creeps."

Haltingly, she told Birdie about the knife in the kitchen, the chase down the beach, the way he'd caught her and struck her and was about to do worse when Alex arrived.

"I knew there was something not quite normal about those two," Birdie said. She nodded toward the table. "The way they ate. That's why, when Jeff told me you'd need to feed, I had Joseph get stuff heavy on the protein."

"Jeff said that? They brought me here?"

"Yeah, and did I have a hell of a time getting Chas and Joseph to go along with it. No offense, Fergs, but you looked like total hell when they carried you in. I was ready to beat the snot out of Alex, too. Would have done it, but he looked so miserable already that I didn't have the heart, and I believed him when he said he tried to help."

"He did. He saved me. Donovan was going to kill me, Birdie. Not 'kill me' kill me, the way people say when they're afraid they're in hot water with their parents or their boss, but really and truly kill me." She hugged herself and trembled. "It hurt, too. I kept waiting for it to be like in the books, when the person who's dying gets detached from it. But I felt everything, down to the tiniest scrape. And then Alex was there."

Birdie looked at her neck. Aiden moved her hand there.

"Yes," she said. "He bit me. He *bit* me, Alex did, right here. But he didn't suck my blood. It was more like . . . I don't know what it was like. But it was cold."

"He grew fangs and bit you on the neck."

"Things got confusing after that."

"Only then, huh?"

"I'm not saying that it all made sense, just that I was able to keep track of things up until that point. The next thing I remember was they were running with me, carrying me to the car. And driving. I was fading in and out by then but I think he was following us. Donovan. To finish the job. And then . . . nothing, until I woke up here, starving and . . ." She touched her wrist, her ribs. "And I'm healed."

"You were messed up all right, broken bones, oozing blood. On fire with fever, too, and delirious. But then, like you said, you healed. In a few hours. It's almost four o'clock, by the way."

"What about Alex? And Jeff?"

"They split. I think Jeff was even more freaked than I was, to tell you the truth. He acted like Alex had committed a major, and I mean *major* no-no."

"I remember that too," Aiden whispered. "Jeff didn't want him to bite me. He said it would be better if they killed me quick, rather than let me suffer."

"Nice guy. And I was really starting to like him."

"Alex didn't mean to hurt me." She met Birdie's eyes. "I believe that."

"He said he saved your bacon. It makes sense if you think about it. This Donovan guy damn near killed you, right? As in, you would have died long before the paramedics could have shown up. But they've got this incredible healing ability, right? So Alex figures the only way to keep you from dying is to take a chomp, and make you be like them."

Aiden nodded.

"What I can't believe is that you're taking it all so well," Birdie said. "A-plus for keeping your cool. Me, I'd be hysterical right about now."

"Well, I . . ." Aiden said, and the next thing she knew, she burst into tears. A huge startling flood of them. She screamed through her sobs, covering her face and knotting her fists into the distressed tangles of her hair.

"Whoa, hey!" Birdie touched her and Aiden jerked away. "Fergs, hey, I'm sorry, I didn't mean it, don't have a hissy on me here!"

"What's going to happen to me?" Aiden hiccupped in a high, shrieking voice. "What *am* I?"

"Easy, Aiden, easy. It's going to be okay." She tried again, getting Aiden into a hold that was part hug and part grapple.

Aiden sagged against Birdie's ample, soft comfort and cried. The storm of tears became a hurricane, her body shaking like a sapling in high wind.

When it passed, she felt weak and wrung out. Irregular sobs turned her breath into watery gasps. She snuffled loudly and raised her head from the large damp spot she'd made on Birdie's shirt.

"This is all so crazy," she said. "I don't . . . I don't know what to do."

"First off, let me get you a tissue. You're kind of leaking."

"Thanks." She glanced in the mirror again and wished she hadn't. Her face was wet and red and runny, and her hair was a witch-wig made out of straw. "What then?"

"We have to get you out of here," Birdie said. "The morning news crew is due in soon. But you'd better come to my place instead of going home."

"He knows where I live. Donovan."

"Knew your name, too, you said. Why was this guy after you? What have you done to piss off the local lycanthropes, Fergs?"

"I never saw him before. The only one that has reason to be mad at me might be Alex's uncle . . ." she trailed off, eyes widening. "He must be one too. They all are."

"Betcha it was him peeping in my window on New Year's Eve. Spying on Jeff and Alex."

Aiden sat on the couch, elbows on her knees and head in her hands. "He didn't want Alex spending time with me. Now I know why. But how does Donovan fit into it?"

"From what Alex said, they've got a history that's none too friendly. At least we can be sure he didn't follow you here."

"We can?"

"Sure. If he had, he would have come in as soon as we were alone. If you're lucky, he'll think you're dead."

"Why didn't you call anyone?" Aiden asked. "The police, or an ambulance? You knew, didn't you? You knew something like this was going to happen."

"I had a notion, yeah."

"How?"

Birdie combed her fingers through her hair, tousling it even more. The dyed-burgundy lock over her forehead bobbed and bounced. "I told you, I had the feeling there was something strange about them. Alex and Jeff, I mean, and not just because Jeff was able to resist my abundant charms. When they brought you in, and especially when I saw the bite, well, I suspected."

"What if you'd been wrong?"

"Roberta Louise Yale is rarely wrong, my precious. If I had been, you would have died on me and I'd have blamed myself forever. Started drinking. Ended up a roaming bag lady who thought the CIA were sending clones to spy on me. Come to a pathetic end in the gutter."

"Birdie, I'm serious. How can you joke?"

"It's a defense mechanism," she said. "A shabby, unfunny one, maybe, but it's all I've got. Besides, Fergs, I *wasn't* wrong, was I?"

"No, but that still doesn't help me know what to do next."

"We're going for a little trip."

Aiden brightened hopefully. "To find Alex?"

Birdie shook her head somberly. "Not what I had in mind."

"But he could explain, help me understand, help me deal with this!"

"Then he should have stuck around. Sorry to break it to you, but he ran like a rabbit."

"He does care about me."

"I'm not saying he doesn't. But this —" she waved at Aiden's neck, "— is a pretty severe commitment. And that's one thing that most guys, human or otherwise, have a problem with."

"You make it sound like . . . like he got me pregnant or something," Aiden said with a feeble chuckle that she didn't really feel.

"Isn't it similar? It's one whopper of a life-change, and he ran out to let you deal with it on your own. You do need someone to help you understand. Lucky for you, I know someone who can help."

Aiden drew back, gazing suspiciously at her. "You . . . you're not one too, are you?"

Birdie snorted. "No way. You've seen my bad habits in action. Did you ever see Alex or Jeff drink coffee, or alcohol? Even a glass of wine?"

"I don't get what that has to do with the price of Beanie Babies on eBay," Aiden said.

"Never mind. He'll explain when we get there. You got credit cards?"

"I didn't exactly have time to grab my purse on the way out the door. Who are you talking about? Where are we going?"

Birdie tossed a fire-engine red rain slicker at her. "Ashland."

"Oregon?" She said it like it was on the far side of the moon. "What's in Ashland? Besides the Shakespearean festival?"

"About a gazillion tourist shops, bakeries, candy-makers, and ice cream parlors," Birdie said. "And Wilfred Ghostman."

Aiden's jaw came slightly unhinged. "I thought he was dead."

"Yup. That's the way he likes it." Birdie snickered as she looked at Aiden. "Oh, that's just perfect."

"What?"

"That damn coat, under the circumstances." She placed her hands on Aiden's shoulders, turned her toward the mirror, and drew up the hood.

"Oh, no."

"Oh, yes."

They said it together. "Grandma, what big eyes you have!"

*　　*　　*

CHAPTER 4
JANUARY 4, SUNDAY
MIDDAY

Noon of a rainy Sunday found Scott James arriving at Trinity Bay's Municipal Building in a mood as foul as the weather.

Damon Blake's office door was ajar. The chief himself was bent over the desk, scowling at the morning paper. The words "Murderous Rapist on the Loose in Trinity Bay" screamed up in bold black type. A scatter of fax papers littered his desk, preliminary reports from the county forensics people from Friday night's mess at the Baker place.

They both knew what those papers contained, and the results weren't encouraging. A knife had been found on the scene and could have easily come from Ernie Warrigan's collection, but the prints on it were nothing like the ones Scott had lifted from the studio apartment. Nor had Warrigan's prints been found anywhere in the Baker bedroom. But two different hair samples had, both coarse, one red and one dark brown. They'd been sent to another lab for a complete analysis.

The car that had gone off the old bluff road was indeed Warrigan's, but the wind and the waves had done a thorough job of cleaning it out. Damon planned to pay a visit to Aiden Ferguson later that day with a picture despite the fact that she'd already insisted she hadn't gotten a good look at whoever pushed the car over the edge.

"Anything?" Damon asked in a tone that said he was already expecting a negative answer.

"I wish." Scott sat down heavily in the chair opposite the chief. "None of the local bus route drivers remember a passenger matching his description, we know what taxi service is like out here, and everyone I've talked to said the guy didn't have any friends he could have called for a ride. He's gone, like he fell off the face of the earth."

"If it was only that, I'd be resting easier with it," Damon said. "It's all this other stuff too. The condition of the room. That looked more like a fight than a trashing to me."

"Me too."

"And I don't know why, but I keep coming back to this report about the dog." When he was under stress, Damon Blake's habitual drawl thickened, and 'dog' came out 'dawg.'

"The one that Don Villiers and Lindie Grantham reported? Why?" Except Scott was getting an idea why, could see where Damon was headed, and didn't like it.

"Then I get to thinking about the tape that Jerry Forrester shot that night he was out riding with you. It seems to me there's been a lot of strangeness going on in that neck of the woods."

Scott went cold, as if someone had pressed an ice cube to the back of his neck. "I hate it when you get that look, boss. Warrigan was probably the one who killed Mike and put Stacey in the hospital. We've got Ronnie Green placing him in the area just a little while before the attack, and the kids from the pizza place back it up. We've got his car taking a nosedive onto the beach a little while after. The only question is where he went, and how. The dog doesn't factor in. Neither does Jerry's tape."

"Why don't we take a drive out that way just the same?" Damon stood, reaching for his hat. "Have a look for anything we might have missed in the dark."

"The rain will have washed anything out by now," Scott protested.

"Can't hurt to try. We've got to do something, and until the lab gets back to us with something useful, Stacey Baker can give us a better recounting of what happened, or someone tracks Warrigan down, we've got a whole lot of not much to work with. On the way, we'll stop and see the Ferguson girl."

"Have you talked to Kel about that?"

"I'm not planning on interrogating and traumatizing his client," Damon said. "Seems to me anyway that she's been doing right better these past couple of weeks. She brought herself in here yesterday all on her own."

They headed out, Damon telling Avery Scribner to hold down the fort. Ave looked nakedly terrified, but Mrs. Dansbourne gave them an encouraging nod and a smile and they were able to leave knowing that even if Avery couldn't cope, the station was in capable hands.

The rain beat steadily as they got into one of the brown police cruisers and drove out of town. Scott sat in the shotgun seat, tense and grumpy. Damon was right. He knew that deep down. His instinct told him so. As cut-and-dried as things outwardly appeared, those extra pieces made it all seem wrong.

The Baker house was deserted when they arrived. Stacey was still in the hospital. Mike Baker was at the funeral home in Arcata and would only be returning to Trinity Bay in an urn. Reverend Carmody was planning to hold a brief service once Stacey was released.

A sheet of heavy-duty plastic was stapled over the broken window. Barrier tape had been strung around the house and across the yard. The place looked forlorn and unwanted. Scott didn't doubt that Stacey would be putting it up for sale, probably hiring someone to go in and pack her things rather than set foot inside ever again. He didn't blame her.

"I can't help thinking about Royce and Ginger Leland," Damon said, and Scott, who had been apprehensively studying the house, jumped a little.

"I thought that was a drug deal gone wrong."

"That kind of criminal usually opts for a clean shot to the head. Coroner said it was hard to tell with the fire, but Royce and Ginger weren't shot. They were slashed up. Like Mike."

"That's clear on the other side of town from here," Scott said uneasily.

"I know. Still, it preys on me."

Damon got out of the car, a black raincoat wrapped around him and water running in rivulets from the brim of his hat. His eyes scanned the gloomy yard alertly, seeing what there was to see in the fan-shaped gleam of the headlights and what little daylight permeated seven thick miles of storm cloud.

Maybe it was the way he was standing, but Scott couldn't help thinking that the chief looked more like the old-time gunslingers he emulated than ever. His stance said he wasn't seeing a rain-swept lawn bordered by underbrush, but a dusty street between wooden buildings, high noon as a tumbleweed bounced by in a bristly ball. But there was no foe there to meet him, stare him down, slap leather and draw and shoot. There was only the billowing snap and flutter of that sheet of plastic over the window, and the secret sound of the rain.

Scott got out. He thought again of the shadow-shape with the pale eyes that they'd seen on Jerry's tape. Or imagined they'd seen. He tried to cling to the idea they'd imagined it. Trick of the light. Yeah. That was it.

Except his nerves didn't buy it. His nerves said it was quite plausible to think that there was something out there. Why not? Gut reaction of man to the untamed wilderness.

The part of the lawn nearest the broken window was a churned and muddy mess. It looked as if the destructive force that had wrecked the interior of the house had spilled over into the yard. The knife had been found nearby, partly concealed under a wild blackberry bush.

"We're not going to get anything more here, Damon," Scott said. "We've already found all there is to find."

Damon ducked under the sagging wet strips of yellow tape and paced around the perimeter. On the other side, he ducked under again and kept going toward the wall of the woods that marked the edge of the yard. He paused to finger some broken twigs, his eyes narrow, teeth chewing thoughtfully at the fullness of his lower lip.

"One of them went this way," he said, and proceeded to do the same.

Scott hurried to catch up, asking himself why they were doing this. It wasn't like they would find a trail that would lead them to the killer's hideout. "The only thing this way is the old fire road."

"Then let's have a look," Damon said implacably.

A few minutes later, they reached it. 'Road' was a stretch – it was two wheel ruts, now turned to muddy canals, with a humped mound of old gravel down the center. The dull shine of dirty metal one way marked the location of a water tower like a huge corrugated barrel. It had once been used to hold several thousand gallons, and the fire trucks had filled up there during the infrequent dry summers in case of forest fires. The tower became obsolete once the water mains came out this far, which had happened about the time Scott was in grade school. Now the tower was just kept as it was, drained dry and locked tight.

"This way," Damon said. He went toward the tower in a brisk, purposeful, I've-spotted-something stride.

Moments after, Scott spotted it too. A brightness in the grey-brown-green that didn't belong there. Something small, rectangular. As he got closer, he saw that it was a notebook with a cover the same blinding-orange shade of a biohazard warning. It was in the shelter of a tree, so while moisture had swelled and warped the pages, it hadn't disintegrated into pulp and a wire spiral binding.

Damon squatted beside the notebook and studied its closed cover, then glanced up at Scott. "Seen one of these before?"

"Ernie Warrigan had a bunch at his apartment. Same cheap brand. They sell them at Tom's Market, packs of three for a buck."

Using the tip of a ballpoint pen, Damon picked up the notebook by the top loop of its spiral binding. The notebook rose out of the mud and then slid free to fall with a sodden thump. It flopped open like the mouth of a dead man, a tongue of smeary paper poking out. The writing on it was in dark pencil scrawls, smudged to the point of illegibility, but Scott had no trouble recognizing it as the same script as on the SHIT LIST.

With this new bit of evidence safely bagged up and put in the big pocket of his raincoat, Damon Blake stood up. "Anything else out here?"

"There's an old equipment shed around on the other side of the tower," Scott said. "That's about it."

"Let's see if we can find it."

The equipment shed had been built in the 1950's when the linemen and pipe layers finally got around to civilizing this part of town, putting in the telephone poles and bringing electricity to those who'd done without. Scott remembered his mother talking about going to a birthday party at Tanya Amberly's house, back when the Amberlys still relied on a gas generator and had their water trucked in. From that same water tower, as it happened. The shed was barely visible from the fire road and not visible at all from any of the houses in the area.

"It's not that overgrown," Damon said in a low voice. "Someone's been here lately."

The foliage around the shed was trampled down, and a rainbow oilslick shimmer on one patch of mud made him believe that a vehicle of some sort had been parked there in the not-too-distant past.

They approached the shed cautiously, in cop-mode. The noise of rain beating on the aluminum roof, an atonal concert, covered any slight sounds they might have made. The shed had no windows and one door, but gaps in the planks were wide enough to peek through. This, Damon did, pressing his eye up to one of them.

Scott was struck by a horrid thought – Damon would scream and reel back, and when he did, Scott would see the haft of a knife quivering in the socket. He was so apprehensively anticipating this that it was a shock when Damon drew back unharmed.

"No need for a warrant," Damon said. "This is town property."

He went around to the door and opened it.

"Someone was here, all right," Scott said. "Smell the smoke?"

The shed had no fireplace, or stove, but a drift of ash on the floor suggested a hibachi or barbecue had been standing there. The single room was empty of everything except a bulging Hefty bag, an ancient broom leaning in one corner, a folding camp chair with a decided lean, and a No. 2 pencil caught in a crack in the floorboards. The room was far cleaner than it should have been. The junk that Scott expected to see – rusty tools, rotting wooden cable spools – was nowhere to be found.

With his face set in a mask of grim expectation, Damon examined the Hefty bag. He prodded it with the toe of his black uniform shoe. Scott winced, braced as Damon no doubt also was for the dark plastic to split open and spill out a noxious pile of dismembered remains or some similar grisly souvenir. Instead, the bag clinked, and when Damon opened it, all it contained was tin cans, milk cartons, and ordinary trash.

They both exhaled in relief, but it was mingled with the peculiar sort of morbid frustration that homicide detectives know all too well. A body meant clues, and clues lead to the killer.

Scott pried the pencil from between the floorboards. It was liberally gnawed and worn blunt. "Bet you anything this is Warrigan's. Dawn Jessec and Lindie Grantham both mentioned how he chews on pencils."

"And have a look at this." Damon held a tuft of loose hairs. Dark red, thick, coarse. "Think these would match those samples that are giving the lab boys fits? I reckon I'd better give them a call and get them down here to go through this bag piece by piece. Damn, but I hate the delay. They're none too happy with it being Sunday and all anyhow."

"Whoops." Scott kicked the garbage bag over and spilled its contents onto the floor.

Damon gave him a dirty look that wasn't entirely serious. Wasn't even mostly serious. "That was clumsy of you, pardner."

"Clumsy me," Scott agreed. "I'd better put it back."

"I'll help."

Bit by bit, they began picking up the trash. The cans were slimy with the residue of tuna, deviled ham, chunk white chicken, beef stew. White polystyrene butcher's-counter packaging was brown with dried blood. The sour smell of old milk drifted from open, empty cartons. Half a bar of jasmine-scented soap . . .

"Hang on a second," Scott said, looking at the soap. "This isn't store-bought. This is home-made. Ginger Leland's making. You may have been onto something after all."

"Here we go." Damon brought out a crumpled receipt, smoothed it. "Tom's Market, Friday afternoon. They bought . . . whew . . . eighty bucks of meat at a whack, plus other groceries. Paid cash. The checkers might remember a ring-up like that."

They piled the trash back in the bag and put it on a spread-out newspaper in the trunk of the patrol car. Scott put the tooth-marked pencil in a zippered plastic bag. Damon held onto the receipt.

"Can we go now?" Scott asked. "I don't know about you, boss, but I'm ready. This part of the woods has always given me the creeps. That damn water tower squatting there like it escaped from an H.G. Wells story . . . and the old-timers say that a woman was murdered out here once. Chopped with an axe. Back in the golden days of the logging boom and old Jacob Cliffwood himself."

"Don't you be telling me the woods are haunted. I think we've got troubles enough without that, don't you?"

"Yeah." Scott managed a shaky grin. "Sorry. Having a *Blair Witch* moment, I guess. Spooky stand of woods, strange shit . . . let's just go."

*   *   *

"Why, yes, I remember," May Sorenson said, squinting at the receipt. "It was on Friday. I rang it up myself. A striking couple. Red-heads, the both of them. Good-looking, but not very friendly. Actually, they came in a few minutes ago if you want to talk to them. I think they're down Aisle 3."

Tom's Market was crowded with the usual variety of weekend grocery-shoppers. Scott saw plenty of familiar faces, but maybe because they all perceived the alertness and purpose in Damon's stride, nobody called out a greeting. Aisle 1 held cereal products. Aisle 2, flour and sugar and other ingredients for baking. Aisle 3, soups and stews and canned meats.

The strangers were midway down, the woman pushing a cart while the man added cans to it. As May had said, they were both red-heads, but their hair wasn't auburn, like Kel McGuire's. Wasn't carroty-orange or strawberry-blond. It was *red*, red as arterial blood.

Red as the hair sample found at the Baker's house, as the tuft Damon had picked out of the garbage bag.

The man was tall and well-built, with wide shoulders that tapered into a narrow waist. The working of his muscles beneath his jeans and denim jacket as he crouched to reach cans of tinned beef on the bottom shelf advertised both grace and strength.

Then Scott's eyes settled on the woman, and he was riveted.

She held herself with the arrogant, lazy sensuality of a lioness, and when she tossed her head in laughing response to something the man had said, her waist-length curtain of hair rippled like a crimson waterfall. She had a better body than Nancy Ellsworth, Trinity Bay's resident sexpot. Her clothing was strictly ordinary, brown slacks and a sheepskin vest, but she wore the outfit like it was a slinky evening gown.

"Ever seen them before?" murmured Damon in an undertone.

"Nope."

Although he would have sworn their voices couldn't have carried more than a few inches, the two strangers turned, instantly sharp and alert. Their faces, even more than their hair, suggested a blood kinship. Brother and sister. Could have been twins if he hadn't been obviously several years younger.

The woman's eyes were sea-green, her companion's sky-blue, but in that first instant as they faced the police officers, their eyes seemed to glow with inner white light, like something out of *Village of the Damned.*

And there was just something about them . . . something that set Scott's nerves to tingling. Something subconscious that his primal instincts recognized and responded to that his waking mind could not.

"Howdy, folks," Damon said, sounding calm and pleasant. Only Scott and Damon's wife Theresa would have been able to hear the tension thrumming under that welcoming deep voice. "Like to talk to you, if you've got a minute."

The red-haired man took a step forward. The woman stayed him with a touch to the elbow. He subsided, but there was a flat, unfriendly glare turning his blue eyes to ice.

"Is something the matter, Officer?" the woman said. She moved partially in front of the younger man, meeting their gazes directly. Almost challengingly.

Scott couldn't get enough of looking at her. It wasn't just the flawless beauty of her features, or the way her vest fell open to show how her blouse clung to clearly braless breasts, or the perfect and supple lines of her body. He hadn't felt so overwhelmingly aware of a woman since he was a teenager, when it seemed that his entire life was ruled by hormones and ever-randy urges. If Dani had been here, right beside him and highly annoyed, he still wouldn't have been able to stop staring at this woman.

"Uhm," Damon Blake said. He shook himself, visible effort of will, and blew out a breath that was almost a whistle. "A few questions, ma'am. You're new around here, I take it."

"Passing through. We're leaving today, as a matter of fact." A hint of fire heated her words. "And why is our business yours? Have we done something wrong? Or are you simply seizing on any excuse to harass and persecute us, as does your ilk?"

"I'd just like to start with your names," Damon said, and now he was stern.

Scott tried to get hold of himself. Her haughty ferocity might have freed Damon from the stunning spell of her beauty, but Scott was drawn in deeper, thinking of unconquerable mountains that men sought to climb anyway, even knowing it would be their death.

"Simone Drachen," she said. "And my son, Donovan. Does that mean anything to you? No. Why should it?"

"Ms. Drachen, have you and your son been staying at the old equipment shed out by the water tower?"

Her eyes flashed. Scott knew he wasn't hallucinating it. They *flashed* with their own inner light. If Damon had done that looking for a reaction, he wasn't let down. The man – Donovan – snarled in rage. He seized the handle of the cart and whipped it around. It came speeding down the aisle at Damon and Scott with tremendous force.

Damon leapt one way and Scott the other. Scott's shoulder hit a shelf of canned fruit and brought it down in an avalanche all around him, peaches-pears-pineapples. A jar of maraschino cherries exploded by his foot and the air was suddenly thick with their gagging-sweet amaretto smell.

The cart clipped Damon, teetered, and went over. Cans rolled all over the floor. They hadn't even come to a complete stop when Donovan was running at Damon and Scott.

Startled but interested cries erupted from the mouth of the aisle, shoppers who'd meandered over to see what their local law enforcement was up to on such a dull Sunday afternoon. The cries turned suddenly to screams of shock and horror as Donovan's eyes burned white, as his lips darkened and peeled back from long, vicious teeth.

Scott grabbed for his gun. What he saw was beyond all sense and his rational mind surrendered to his survival impulse.

Donovan was bulging out of his clothes, bristling with hair through the stretching seams. He leaped the overturned cart and landed in a crouch beside Damon, who had been knocked down in the middle of the spilled groceries. Clawed hands closed on Damon's upper arms and lifted. Damon was not a small man, but Donovan handled him as if he were a child. He slammed Damon's back into the opposite shelf, sending down an avalanche of canned vegetables.

"Let him go!" Scott's gun was in his hand and he leveled it at Donovan. "Right now."

People were screaming, stampeding. It was the setting that made this all seem so crazed and unreal. Muzak oozed from the speakers, so ordinary, so mundane. Overhead fluorescent lights painted everything with clinical, artificial brightness.

Donovan grunted and snorted. His face was pushing forward into a muzzle, and the sound of his bones realigning was a grotesque gristle-popping. He had not split his clothes apart but the shape of his body was becoming hunched, and his low-topped hiking books were struggling to confine feet that were arching up high on their toes.

Damon, staring directly into that misshapen face, seemed to have mentally checked out. His dangling hand hung near his gun but he didn't reach for it. Didn't move at all. He could have been paralyzed from his collision with the shelves for all Scott knew.

"I said let him go!" Scott said.

Simone tackled him, hitting him broadside. The gun went off with a colossal roar. The kick jolted through his arms. He crashed down onto a bumpy, rolling bed of cans with Simone on top of him, her face poised kissing-distance above his own.

She had changed too, or was in the process. Bands of red fur streaked down the sides of her face like weird muttonchop sideburns. Her upper lip was splitting like a cat's. The terrible heat of her body threatened to burn him through the layers of cloth between them.

"Filthy human!" she spat.

Her hand, tipped with ivory points, rose and slashed. Pain sizzled in parallel lines from Scott's forehead to his chin. Blood ran in sheets, into his eyes, or maybe she'd blinded him, he couldn't tell.

He heard shrieking, agonized shrieking, and realized it was his own voice.

*   *   *

CHAPTER 5
JANUARY 4, SUNDAY
EARLY AFTERNOON

"So you've met them," Wilfred Ghostman said.

Aiden had wanted to believe this was all a dream. A nightmare. Delirium. Or even the onset of mental illness that she'd so long dreaded. Anything would be better than having to accept it as reality.

She'd clung desperately to the dream idea during their whirlwind trip out of Trinity Bay. Birdie, veteran watcher of hundreds of horror movies, knew better than to go back to Aiden's house, the scene of the incident. Never mind that Aiden's purse and all of her things were there. For that matter, Birdie hadn't even felt safe going to *her* house.

"We have to leave now, just go," she'd said as she hustled Aiden into the parking lot behind the Channel 12 building. The fog of the early morning hours had turned it every bit as cloaked and ominous as any Victorian gothic, and not even the sight of Birdie's cherry-red Volkswagen bug had been able to shake Aiden from that notion.

It had taken Birdie five minutes to clean out her passenger seat of pop cans and other junk, while Aiden stood edgily staring around at the streetlights with their misty, rain-haloed globes. She wouldn't have been surprised to see Donovan come loping out of the fog, or hear his eerie howl.

That was when she'd first, and eagerly, seized on the dream idea. It had been hard to maintain while having to share the footwell with a box full of CDs.

"*Holst: The Planets . . . Classical Thunder* volumes one through three . . . *Night on Bald Mountain and Other Russian Favorites*," Aiden read doubtfully. "I thought you were into the oldies, 80's stuff."

Birdie had laughed. "I only got into that because of the guy I was dating at the time. Gary was weird that way. Had a real thing for the 80's. The age of the synthesizer. Dawn of the music video mini-movie. But me, well, I guess it is kind of strange, but that right there is what I like. I do occasionally listen to the Flirty Boys, Johnny Harlowe, Blade Ballet, but mostly, it's classical."

She had proved it by popping in Wagner. The ride north on 101, through the winding and hilly region between Trinity Bay and Crescent City, with *Ride of the Valkyries* blasting from the speakers, did nothing for Aiden's sense of unreality.

A dream. A nightmare. A raving psychotic break.

That was harder and harder to hold onto as the mundanities of the long drive set in. Breakfast snatched on the fly from McD's led to Aiden's discovery that she was hungry even after pigging out on the sandwich, and also that the acidic tang of orange juice made her feel like her head was going to dissolve. Just the smell of Birdie's coffee made her heart race.

If it was a dream, it was lasting forever and more vivid than anything she'd ever known. She had never had a dream before in which she had to make potty stops. Birdie, high on fatigue poisons, caffeine, and adrenaline, kept up rapid-fire chatter as they got onto 199 headed for Grant's Pass, Oregon. Aiden had never been there, couldn't have conjured signs advertising the Oregon Caves and Crater Lake from her own imagination.

The dream idea took another serious blow when they stopped at a Wal-Mart after lunch. If anything could be more ordinary and day-to-day than Wal-Mart, Aiden didn't know what it was. Birdie bought clothes, toiletries, and a duffel bag for each of them, as well as car munchies.

By the time they were nearing Ashland, Aiden's last hope for the dream excuse centered on Wilfred Ghostman. Surely they couldn't really be going to see him. He'd supposedly died years ago, leaving a legacy of dozens of low-budget fright-fests. The possibility that he was secretly alive was unlikely enough. That he'd know, really know, anything about what was happening to her stretched into the absurd.

"Ashland, home of the Oregon Shakespearean Festival," Birdie had said, in a chirpy tour-guide voice as she slowed to the speed limit for one of the few times since leaving Trinity Bay. "Also home of Lithia park, a natural-history museum, and too many goodie shops. We're in the off season so I hope you weren't counting on taking in many plays."

"He doesn't really live here, does he?"

Birdie's answer had been to pull up to a gated driveway, with an intercom and speaker mounted on a pole. She rolled down her window and leaned out as the speaker emitted tinny, quavering words.

"Is that you, Roberta? Come in, my dear, do come in."

Now here they were, sitting in Wilfred Ghostman's living room. The sight of the house, and then the sight of the man himself, had finally convinced her that she couldn't be dreaming. Her mind would never have come up with this.

"Well, what on earth did you expect?" Birdie had chuckled when Aiden tentatively brought up her surprise having to do with the house. "A moldy old Hungarian castle brought over stone by stone, crawling with ivy and cobwebs and gargoyles?"

Ghostman's home was a long, low building of white glossy enamel and glass. It looked like a futuristic luxury liner come to rest on a slant on the hill. The interior was sleek and shiny, with hardly any straight lines. The walls curved, flowed, swooped. A runner of carpet, white with flecks of gold and black, undulated in a sinuous S-pattern along the white tile floor. Here and there along the walls were paintings of abstract shapes in pastel, small white tables holding fragile china vases, chrome and glass shelf units with alabaster sculptures and collections of small pewter figurines. The scents of pine air freshener, fresh-baked bread, and faint smoke teased Aiden's nose.

The man himself had met them in the foyer. The legendary monster-mogul. In loose cotton pants and a bright floral shirt, and knitted slippers.

It was the final blow to Aiden's comfortable dream-delusion. If she'd imagined Wilfred Ghostman, he would have looked like Dr. Lundquist, or like Vincent Price. Imposing, commanding. She never would have thought of a roly-poly pink-cheeked cherub who smelled of powder, vodka, and snickerdoodle cookies.

But Birdie had gone right to him and hugged him and greeted him warmly. He'd returned the hug with evident relish, then set her back from him, eyed her approvingly, and said, "Scream for me."

Birdie obliged, tilting her head and pealing a classic scream. It rebounded and resonated through the house. Aiden thought she saw the window glass shiver.

"I never get bored with that," Ghostman had said, turning a beaming chubby little smile on Aiden. "It's how we met, you know. And you must be Aiden."

He had come toward her unflinchingly, with his hand outstretched, and surprised her into shaking it.

That had been an hour ago. In the interim, Ghostman had fussed and fluttered about like a mother hen, getting them settled into guest rooms and giving them time to freshen up before joining them in the living room with all the fixings for high tea . . . high tea heavy on the cold cuts.

"You've met them," Ghostman said again, nodding and folding his tidy little hands over his round belly. "More than met, really. My word."

"I guess I have," Aiden said slowly. "They're like werewolves. Except not quite. And like vampires. A little bit."

"They call themselves changelings," he said. "Not werewolves, not vampires, but the closest thing there is to such creatures in the real world. They've lived among us for thousands of years. They, and their abilities, gave rise to all those old legends."

Aiden's teacup chattered against the saucer and she swiftly put it down. "Selkies?"

"Selkies, Japanese fox-women, any sort of shape-shifter. Every country has its own set of mythos, going back centuries. Someone must have seen a changeling in action and had to come up with a way to explain it. The stories sometimes strayed far from the mark." He chuckled, a smug pleased-with-himself sound. "In fact, most of the legends, particularly the erroneous ones, were purposefully begun by the changelings themselves."

"Like the ones about how vampires don't cast shadows or reflections?" Birdie suggested. "Garlic, stakes, silver bullets?"

"An age-old campaign of misinformation," Ghostman agreed. "No sleeping in coffins of native earth or being unable to cross running water. Preposterous. Though some of the folktales do have a basis in truth. The garlic aversion, for instance. Not because it has any particular power over them, but because they have such heightened senses that the scent is too strong. They avoid anything that's too pungent, or too spicy."

"Pickles," Aiden said. "And orange juice, and coffee."

"First-hand experience. How I envy you, young lady!"

"Envy me?" Aiden gaped at him. "I almost *died.* And now I'm . . . I'm . . . different."

"But you didn't die. And you came through the other side changed. One of them. More than human. How did it happen? Tell me precisely, from the beginning. Roberta here didn't have time to give me the entire story."

Hesitantly, but with more confidence as he hung on every word and didn't scoff or roll his eyes, Aiden told him. She held onto her composure fairly well, though as she was getting to the point in her story where Alex had come to her as she lay dying and extended those fangs, her hands clamped down on the arms of the chair hard enough to hurt.

Ghostman hopped up – he moved with nimble speed for such a rotund fellow – and grasped her jaw. He lifted her head, brushing his fingers over the fading crescent-shaped scars.

"Fascinating," he said.

"But what'd he do to her?" Birdie asked. "He didn't drain her blood, so what did he do?"

"They have glands in the roof of their mouths," he said absently, fingering Aiden's neck as she tried not to squirm away from the tickling touch. "Akin to the venom sacs you might find in a snake. The substance those glands produce would have been injected into the bloodstream, where it would be quickly carried throughout the body and spread out into every cell."

"To change me," Aiden said in a low tone.

"There are, essentially and that I know of, two camps among them," he said, letting go of her and returning to his seat. He gazed thoughtfully at the high ceiling and the rain streaming in rills down the curve of the glass bubble skylight. "Most just want to keep their secret. They know what would happen if the world at large ever found out the truth. They have no real enmity toward us, and would just as soon leave us alone if we'd return the favor. But then there's the other bunch. The ones who've broken the ancient laws of their kind."

"If they have laws, that implies a society," Birdie said. "Organization. How many of these things are there?"

"Far fewer now than once there were," Ghostman said. "It's ironic, really. During the Middle Ages, humanity accepted their existence without question. Then, along came the Renaissance, the rise of science, the Industrial age. The death of superstition. No one believed in them anymore. They should have been safer then than at any previous time in their history, as they were no longer being hunted and killed but instead, their plight got worse. And has gotten worse ever since."

"Why?" Aiden asked.

"Pollution. Deforestation. Increases in communication, transportation. Advances in weaponry. Humanity became stronger, jobs became more specialized. It got harder and harder for them to successfully pass among us. Now we're in the Information Age, and they don't have the plethora of documentation and certification that our world requires. How could they?"

Aiden remembered the hassle she'd had to go through to buy her house, even with Mr. McGuire's help and her considerable trust fund. It had been the same with her driver's license.

A swell of pity rose in her as she thought of Alex. His wistfulness. Always having to stay on the move so that no one would notice that they didn't have the proper paperwork. No wonder they felt so set apart.

She wiped her hands down her cheeks, not liking the way her skin felt.

She wasn't cool, still felt feverish, and was beginning to think that might be normal for her now. Hadn't Alex seemed very warm whenever she touched him?

"They have a higher body temperature," she blurted into Ghostman's rambling about how the changelings couldn't get birth certificates because they were never born in hospitals.

"Yes, that's right," he said. "They look human enough, when they choose to, but certain physical factors will always give them away. Their temperature averages five degrees higher than ours. Their dietary requirements and metabolism and reaction to drugs or alcohol are all different."

"What about mentally?" Birdie asked. "Psychologically? I mean, they read, they watch TV, they do ordinary things like anybody else."

"In that way, yes, they are much like us. They're sentient, after all. They have the same basic needs for affection and companionship and intellectual pursuits. I have noticed that they are much more tactile than we are." Seeing Aiden's blank look, he explained. "They touch much more frequently than we do. Especially in America, we place a high degree of importance on personal space, and discourage physical contact except among partners or close kin."

"Sure!" Birdie said. "Jeff and Alex were always bumping each other, doing that guy-hug thing with one arm around the shoulder. And they stood close to us, remember, Aiden? Not that I minded."

Ghostman poured himself another cup of tea. "You have to understand their culture. You especially, young lady. This Alex must care quite a bit for you, to do what he did."

"It's against their laws, isn't it?" Aiden asked. "Those ancient laws you mentioned."

"Oh, yes. The laws were set down long ago, when there were enough of them to have a society of their own. It was made up of pack-groups, sometimes as large as fifty at a time, gathered under one leader. Most would be related, but mates would be taken from outside of the pack or two smaller packs might join or a larger one might split off. Every so often, the leaders would get together to address matters that affected the race as a whole. That's how these laws came about."

"So what are these laws?" Birdie asked, helping herself to another bit of cake.

"The first and most vital is that no changeling must eat of the forbidden meat," Ghostman said. His brown eyes twinkled, but all of a sudden he didn't look so benevolent any more. Less like a cherub and more like a cruel imp in disguise. "Manflesh, they call it. But before you go thinking that they did it out of benevolent concern for our species, let me assure you it was because they were frightened of what eating the forbidden meat did to them. It changed them. Set them apart. Made them stronger. Gave them powers that most changelings didn't have."

Aiden shivered.

"Of course you're familiar enough with vampire lore to know how some of them were said to have control over the beasts of the night. Those changelings who'd partaken learned to bend lesser creatures to their will."

"Wolves, bats, rats," Birdie said.

"So they ate people, and it made them more powerful," Aiden said, feeling sick. She set down her plate.

"But it was also very bad for them, psychologically speaking. They'd conceive of obsessive hatreds or compulsions. They'd believe, probably validly, that others were out to get them. They'd become convinced of their own superiority or invulnerability and behave in ways that endangered the entire pack."

"Total paranoids and psychotics?" asked Birdie.

Ghostman nodded. "So the leaders, or the elders, decreed that the eating of manflesh was forbidden. Anyone who did it would be driven out of the pack, if not killed outright."

"What were the other laws?" Aiden asked, rubbing at her neck. "As if I couldn't guess. Biting people, right? Changing them. Though I don't see why they'd even do it in the first place."

"Sometimes a pack would lose so many members that there wouldn't be enough hunters to sustain them," Ghostman said. "Or there might be an imbalance between the genders. On such occasions, outsiders might be transformed and brought into the pack."

"Always got to keep things boy-girl, boy-girl," Birdie said around a mouthful of cake.

"But the humans they bit did not die and wake enslaved to their masters, as in the movies. They retained their self-awareness, their memories. Most were horrified by what they'd become, resented it, hated the ones who'd done it to them. The new members might have friends or family who could cause problems too. So the elders made that their second law, deeming it better to let the pack die out than risk attracting so much attention."

Aiden thought of Alex, the anguish on his face and in his voice. He'd known it was wrong, even without Jeff reminding him. Known, but hadn't let that stop him. He hadn't hesitated. Did he regret it now? Did he think that she must hate him for what he'd done?

Did she hate him for it?

"Is there a cure?" she asked. Her heart sank at Ghostman's pursed little frown.

"Folklore cures, as many and as effective as the folklore causes. You didn't get this way by drinking from the pawprint of a wolf, or dancing naked under the moonlight, did you? As for whether modern medicine can do anything, I honestly have no idea."

"Even if they could do anything, they'd keep you to study," Birdie said.

"Although . . ." Ghostman trailed off.

"What?" Aiden asked, clinging to fading hopes.

"If anyone knows of a cure, they might. The changelings themselves. I recall hearing about a renegade changeling who, wanting to lead a pack of his own, went on a biting spree. The other changelings hunted him down and restored his victims to their normal lives."

"How?" Aiden was, in every sense, on the edge of her seat.

Ghostman's pink face folded mournfully. "That, my dear, I'm afraid I do not know."

Disappointment sagged through her.

"What about other stuff? Silver? Fire?" Birdie asked. "Immortality?"

"Ah, more of the misinformation campaign."

"Alex said his parents had been killed," Aiden said.

"Changelings heal phenomenally fast and are incredibly resistant to disease, but, yes, they can die," Ghostman said.

"What about – forgive me, Fergs, but I have to ask – killing the vampire who bit you? That's another one you always see in the movies. Or the coffin thing?"

"All nonsense," Ghostman assured her as Aiden gasped in horror at the thought of killing Alex. "They are not the undead. They are living beings, albeit different from us."

"But they change," Birdie said. "They actually physically change."

"Yes," he said somberly. "And that is one thing . . . Every living being is ruled by some cycle, some instinct. The changelings can change at will, day or night. However, the moon does have a strong effect on them. It exerts a powerful pull, a call. A compulsion, if you will. To change. And to hunt. To feed."

*　　*　　*

CHAPTER 6
JANUARY 4, SUNDAY
AFTERNOON

When Simone and Donovan sprang out of the aisle, caught partway in their change, a fresh sirening whoop of screams burst from the crowd. They lunged back and forth, jostling in their panic.

Simone was tempted to go through them like a living scythe to their standing wheat. She grappled for control, knowing that if she gave in to her urge they would not be certain of escaping before others came. Others with weapons.

She conveyed as much to Donovan, who broke off stalking the humans and leapt to the top of a check-out counter. From there, with a single thrust of his legs, he dove through a pane of the plate-glass window that made up the front of the store.

Simone jumped after him. There were more humans in the parking lot and coming out of the surrounding shops to see what was going on. She saw that one of the shops was a pet store, but any animals there would be too small, and caged, and of no use to her power.

Instead, she ran for the van, seeking human form as she went. Donovan was ahead of her, but veered to intercept a running man who was waving a tire iron and yelling incoherent threats. A single swing of Donovan's arm sent him crashing to the pavement.

She revved the van before their doors were shut, and almost sideswiped a car just entering the lot. Then they were into the street and away, tires squealing on the wet pavement. The boxes containing all their worldly goods and the items they'd claimed as their own from the Leland place shifted and rattled.

"We let them live, the policemen," Donovan panted. "We should have finished them."

"We shouldn't have started with them!"

He flinched from the rebuke, his expression puzzled and wounded. "They knew about us. Suspected, at the very least."

"I'm not angry with you, my dearest Donovan." She ignored the speed-limit signs, blasting through the North Valley shopping center toward the highway. "It's the moon, and the thrill of the blood. It gets my temper high."

"They'll be coming after us. What do we do?"

"What we were going to do anyway. We leave this place. The others already have. They left with the dawn. I felt them go."

"Maybe they were found out, too."

"Maybe." Simone frowned through the sweeping blades of the wind-shield wipers. The van shuddered and groaned at the unaccustomed high speeds. She usually drove carefully to avoid being pulled over, but if another police officer tried to stop them now, she didn't think their identification would prove the main problem.

"So what now?" Donovan asked.

"Stop hounding me!" He flinched from her wrath, and she softened. "Oh, Donovan . . . I am sorry . . . I don't know what's wrong with me. You're depending on me. I will take care of you, I promise!"

"I'm not a cub anymore," he said. "I look to you because you're the leader, and because I love you."

She took her eyes from the road long enough to smile at him. "Still?"

"Always. Now and forever."

"Because of me, you're on the run. A fugitive."

"Because of you, I'm whole. Happy. I'm finally what I was meant to be. Yours."

"We'll have to get rid of the van," she said, pretending she didn't notice the way he looked at her when he said he was hers. Pretending she didn't know what he meant. "Too many people will have seen it and be able to describe it. We'll need another car. We'll get out of town, and then we'll find one."

*   *   *

Damon Blake sat up feeling like every bone in him had been taken out, hammered on, and put back in the wrong places. The most alarming flare of pain was across his back, where the creature had driven him into the shelves, but other parts of him hurt from subsequently being flung down. He'd landed first on the overturned shopping cart and slid from there onto a heap of cans, and felt bruised all over.

Scott was in worse shape. Damon hitched-crawled to him and hissed as he got a closer look at the extent of the damage. Four gashes that ran down his face like some bizarre Halloween make-up job. He couldn't tell if either of Scott's eyes had been spared or not.

"Hang in there, pardner," Damon said. "They're gone."

People came hurrying around, babbling in chopped fragments of sentences. Damon let them help him up, directed them to call for an ambulance. Someone brought a towel for Scott, and as he pressed it to his face Damon spotted both eyes present and accounted for, intact but awash in shock.

The hectic confusion went on, gradually resolving itself into something that made sense. Avery Scribner showed up, positively green with horror. The paramedics arrived to take Scott in. Crowds congregated, and Damon could hear the tale circulating.

An hour or so later, when things were settling down, Damon was on the phone. He told Theresa he was fine, he didn't need to go to the hospital, she should just stay home with Lora and the twins and her father. He'd be there as soon as he could.

"Chief Blake?" one of the men asked, after looking to his friend for encouragement. "If you've got a minute, we need to talk to you."

Damon turned to see Joseph Perrin and Chas Vandermere standing by nervously. He knew them by reputation and because he'd done occasional public service announcements on Channel 12. "Help you, gentlemen?"

"Someone said that the one who attacked you was named Donovan. Is that right?" Joseph asked.

"Yes, the woman introduced them as Simone and Donovan Drachen. Said he was her son. Do you know something about this?"

"We know that someone called Donovan damn near killed Birdie Yale's little friend Aiden last night," Chas said.

They spun their tale. Damon listened with increasingly wide eyes.

"Birdie made us promise we would keep quiet about it," Joseph said, and sought an encouraging look of support from his partner. "But when we heard about this, we knew we had to speak up."

"I'll need to talk to them," Damon said. "I'd planned to see Miss Ferguson today anyway."

"That might be a problem," Chas said. "Nobody answers at either of their numbers. We drove by Birdie's place this morning and it's empty. Her car's gone too."

Things were starting to come together in Damon's head, making a shape that was cohesive even if not readily identifiable, and certainly bizarre. He knew the young men that Chas and Joseph had mentioned. Jeff and Alex Greye, whose family had gotten permission from Harv Leland to stay at the campground in exchange for doing some odd jobs. He'd been out there once to say hello and get a look at them.

What in God's name had come to Trinity Bay? And why?

"No," he said aloud, drawing quizzical looks. "The important question is, where are they, and what am I going to do about it?"

*   *   *

The bus barn was near the small airport between Arcata and McKinleyville. Bill Hartford got there fifteen minutes overdue, given the sloppy weather conditions. He was looking forward to turning in his bus, clocking out, and heading home to Anne's chili and cornbread.

He turned off the ignition and unhooked his seat belt, getting out of his seat to make his final sweep of the shift. Amazing how much stuff got left on buses. Most of it was trash like newspapers, disposable coffee cups, and fast-food wrappers, but every now and then, he stumbled across treasure. Books, wallets, cell phones, parcels . . . once, a shopping bag full of wrapped Christmas presents. A shame he had to turn it all in to Lost and Found.

As he moved to the rear of the bus, stooping to collect some foil packets from trading cards – two *Pokemon*, three *Magic: The Gathering* and a *Star Trek* – he realized he'd found something else on his bus today. A guy was sound asleep near the back, slumped down so that he hadn't been visible in the mirror.

Bill paused. These days, you never could tell. Guy might be faking. Meaning to rob him. Waiting for Bill to walk up and give him a shake, and then he'd pounce.

"Hey. Buddy."

The guy jerked awake with lightning speed. His head whipped around toward Bill, eyes flashing, and for a second there Bill really did think that he was dealing with a maniac, or a druggie. The guy's face was weird. Shadowed with hair. His mouth didn't seem to fit right with itself, the glint of teeth protruding. And those eyes, throwing back the overhead lights in reflective flashes . . .

Instinctively, Bill stepped back. His hip hit the edge of another seat and damn near tumbled him into it. He brought up his hands to shield himself when it looked like the guy was going to leap at him and work him over.

Then the moment passed, and the guy bent over his knees, taking deep, gulping breaths. When he straightened up again, Bill saw that he was no more than a kid, not even old enough to buy booze.

"Guess I woke you out of a bad dream," Bill said. "Sorry about that."

"Where are we?"

He may have looked like a kid, but that coarse voice sure didn't make him sound like one. Even so, Bill no longer felt skittish, and relaxed. "Bus barn. End of the line. You must've been pretty tired."

"Yeah."

The kid peered out the window at the parking lot, which was shoulder-to-shoulder buses in front of the great grey bulk of the barn. Thin pillars of blinking lights on a nearby hill and the droning presence of a small plane indicated the proximity of the airport. Not the most picturesque view. Nothing that would be turning up on one of the tourism board's postcards anytime soon.

"Look, I didn't see you back here," Bill said, trying to come off apologetic as well as defensive. "If I had, I would have woken you up sooner. When'd you get on?"

"College of the Redwoods. Can I catch another northbound bus from here?"

"Nope. There's a phone inside you can use."

"Who would I call?" The kid picked up his backpack and put his arms through the straps, then shrugged into a rain slicker. The combination made him look like a hunchbacked lighthouse keeper.

"Must be someone who can come and get you." Bill thought about suggesting a cab, then thought better of it; by the kid's haggard look, he must not have much cash to spare.

"No such luck." He sighed. "How far to Trinity Bay?"

"About eight, ten miles."

The kid's shoulders slumped but he set his jaw resignedly. "Thanks. I better get going. Got to make it before dark."

"I'm heading into Trinidad after I clock out. I can run you up to the Bay." Anne always told him that kind-hearted was just a nicer way of saying doormat, and that it was going to get him in trouble someday.

"You don't have to do that," said the kid, looking alarmed as if he was the one suddenly having notions of being beaten up and robbed. "I can walk."

"I can have you there in fifteen minutes. You walk it, you'll be out here for hours and probably catch your death. I've got a son myself about your age and I'd like to think that if he were in a bind, someone would give him a help."

The kid looked at his feet, frowning, and finally nodded. "All right."

Bill finished his sweep of the bus, dumped the trash, and raised his umbrella. The kid, his face mostly hidden in the shadows of his hood, followed.

He left the kid in the staff lounge while he went into the locker room to change from his uniform into his street clothes. When he came back out, the kid was watching the grainy black and white television intensely, although there was nothing more interesting on than the local news channel. All the high-school sports scores and city council crap anyone could ever want.

"Ready to hit the road?"

The kid punched the off button and the screen shrank to a bright dot. "Yeah. Thanks."

"My good deed for the day."

The employee lot was almost deserted and the rain-lashed tarmac had an eerie glimmering quality under the orange bulbs.

"Over there, the minivan," Bill said. "I wanted an SUV myself, but the wife said that with the dogs and the kids, we'd do better with this. What I want to know is how come it always ends up me that has to drive it?"

The inside was cluttered with school papers, toys, and other junk. Especially in the damp, the interior smelled strongly of dog. The rear compartment was cordoned off with a heavy wire screen and that section was coated with hair.

Bill's passenger sneezed six times in quick succession as he got into the front seat.

"Allergies, huh? For me, it's cats. My daughters, they're eleven, twins, want a cat for their birthday coming up next month." Bill dropped his lunch pail behind his seat, heard something crack, and groaned as he picked up the pie-shaped silver wedges of what had been a Flirty Boys CD. "Aww, damn, they'll never believe that was an accident. What's your name, son? I'm Bill."

"Alex. Thanks for the ride. I appreciate it."

"Happy to help. You live in Trinity Bay, do you?"

"Not anymore."

The hollowness, the deadness of that reply, made Bill glance over in concern. His passenger was staring out the side window, hands folded on the backpack in his lap, and he looked like someone had pulled his soul out by the roots. Muttering sympathetic but meaningless syllables, Bill stuck to his driving.

It was as if everyone else had been seized by some gypsy urge and run off to sunnier climes for the weekend. The lonely back roads usually didn't bother him, but for some reason as he steered the minivan down those narrow lanes where the dripping redwoods leaned over and knitted their boughs to form a dark green tunnel, he felt his skin go all creepy-crawly.

He shot a glance at the kid, and wouldn't have been surprised to see a homicidal maniac's grin and the gleam of a switchblade. But Alex hadn't moved, wasn't making the least hostile gesture.

Chiding himself for nerves, Bill looked back at the road. He knew this route like the back of his hand. A mile further on would be the turnoff that led to Wally's, a struggling bar that only came alive on Friday and Saturday nights. On a day like this, the only customers would be the die-hard regulars like Tinker Andrews and Bobby Channing, who made it their second home.

He saw an old-fashioned panel van pulled off the side of the road up ahead, amber hazard lights winking. The hood was up and two people were standing over the engine compartment with the blank posture of those who had no idea what they were looking for.

"Must just be my day for good deeds," he said, slowing as he passed them.

Alex looked up from his silent contemplation. "What?"

"Couple of folks stuck back there. You wait here, stay warm and dry. There should be a box of granola bars in the glove box, if you're hungry."

Raising the umbrella again, Bill made sure there was no oncoming traffic and trotted across the street, headed for the disabled van. Through the small windows, he saw that it was stuffed with bundles and boxes and camping gear, all thrown in helter-skelter.

"Hey there –"

He forgot anything else he might have been going to say when he filled his eyes with the red-haired woman. The rain molded her clothes to her skin so closely she might have been wearing body paint.

"Hah . . . ur . . . trouble, miss?" Bill stammered out. "Bad luck."

"Bad for you, good for us," the woman said, pinning him with her gaze. He barely noticed that her male companion was moving around him, flanking him.

Before Bill Hartford could ask what she meant by that, the young man was in motion. Bill's umbrella dropped from his hand, spinning on the glistening roadway like a crippled bat.

*   *   *

The rain was a steady, relentless downpour beating on the roof and windshield of the minivan. Alex slumped in the seat, chewing on a granola bar without tasting it, only needing the nutrients and absently wishing it was meat instead of grain. He supposed he should have gotten out to help Bill and the stranded motorists, but Jeff was the car expert.

Besides, his mind was too brooding and full to be of any help. He couldn't stop thinking about what he'd done.

What he'd *done*. One betrayal and evil deed after another. All he could think in his defense was that it had seemed like the right thing at the time.

He couldn't let her die. Not Aiden. Not innocent, pretty, sweet Aiden. No matter the cost.

Was she all right? He had no idea what the bite might be doing to her. How long would it take for her to finish crossing over? Would she feel the insistent pull of the moon? Would she know what to do? No one in the pack had ever done anything like this before and Alex didn't know enough of the old stories to be able to predict what would happen to her.

He'd never forget it. His fangs sliding out of the roof of his mouth, and piercing her tender throat . . . it had been a feeling greater than sexual, not that he had a whole lot of experience in that either. Aiden trembling in his arms, the rich wine of her blood . . .

Was it enough to damn him? He hadn't drunk of it, but some had welled up around his impaling fangs to flood his mouth with its delicious taste, so filled with life and sweetness. In that instant, he understood the awful temptation that had doomed the fallen ones of the packs throughout the centuries. He could almost grasp the craving that led them to drink, to eat, to feed on the forbidden.

He hadn't drunk of her! Only that one scant mouthful. All right, yes, he'd swallowed it, but it had been pure reflex. Unintentional. Unconscious. Something that had happened of its own accord while he was lost in the release of fangs and flesh. He hadn't meant it, and later he'd tried to sick it up. By then, it had been too late.

Did they know he was gone? Had they discovered his absence yet?

"Coward," he muttered now, inaudible under the rain hammering on the roof.

Afraid to face Gideon. Afraid to admit what he'd done. Pack law was still pack law, and the penalty for breaking it was death.

Running away from his pack. Direct disobedience of his leader. Throwing away his entire world, the only world he knew, and for what? To find a girl who probably would want nothing to do with him? Who would hate him for what he'd done to her?

Alex leaned his head against the cool, condensation-damp glass. He heard footsteps approaching the minivan.

The driver's side door swung open.

Bill's scent? Something was wrong with it. With him.

Alex turned, nose wrinkling and nostrils flaring. The stench of blood and urine and excrement surrounded him in a reeking cloud.

There stood Bill, his posture stiff and odd, his head tipped and his glassy eyes rolled up so it seemed he was observing the dome light in the ceiling. The death-stink was everywhere. And something else, something horribly familiar . . .

A face appeared over Bill's shoulder, framed in sodden red hair.

"Boo," said Simone Drachen, and cast Bill's body aside.

Adrenaline shot through Alex, flooding him with terror and strength. He reached for the handle just as his door was yanked open and he fell sideways out of his seat.

He was caught in strong arms already dense with fur, and engulfed in Donovan's hated musky odor. Above a protruding muzzle of sharp fangs, Donovan's eyes glared with murderous delight.

The change was on Alex, rushing and burning in him. He twisted, writhed, lashed out. Simone's laughter, terrible in its moon-silver beauty, rolled merrily through the minivan as she climbed lithely over the seats.

Donovan's hands, huge and strong, closed around Alex's throat. He didn't react to the slicing blows of Alex's claws, although they parted skin and drew blood. He slammed Alex against the side of the minivan, denting it, trapping him there at the end of his longer arms.

The drumbeats of his pulse pounded in Alex's ears, fast and steady, then stuttering as he slid into the black vortex of unconsciousness.

*   *   *

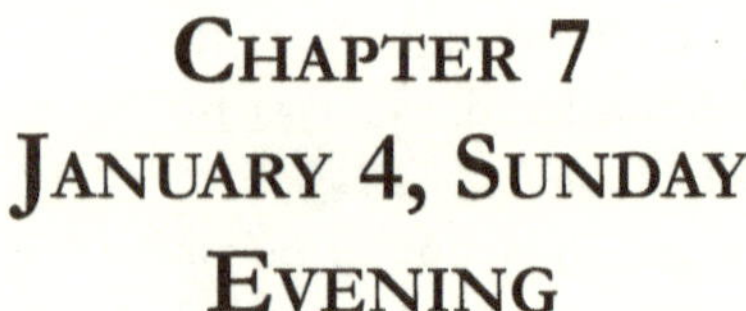

CHAPTER 7
JANUARY 4, SUNDAY
EVENING

Aiden's head throbbed from trying to understand everything that she'd been forced to accept in the past twenty-four hours. She looked at Wilfred Ghostman wanly.

"How do you know so much about them, anyway?" she asked.

He set aside the last bite of his cake and dabbed his lips. "I've met them. Spoken with them. Seen them change with my own eyes."

"I thought so," Birdie said. "The stuff you used to say, like you were testing me to see if I'd believe . . . you've been dying to tell someone."

"It hasn't been an easy secret to keep," he said. "I wanted to tell you, Roberta, but you're right in saying you've always been too hard-headed."

"I think I'm getting over it," she said with a grin at Aiden.

"You knew changelings?" Aiden asked.

"Many years ago. I started off with an interest in parapsychology, even made it my chosen field of study in college. Researching psychics, trying to tape-record spirits, all of that. I spent many a night in haunted houses and graveyards, interviewed countless families complaining of poltergeists. The results? Nada. Not a single verifiable case."

"I was in on an experiment run by one of the HSU psych professors," Birdie volunteered. "Twenty bucks for a couple of hours in a closet, trying to move a steel marble with the power of my mind."

"They should have tried it at Seacliff," Aiden murmured, most of her attention fixed squarely on Ghostman.

"I may never have turned up any concrete proof, but it did feed my lifelong interest in a good spooky yarn and exposed me to a good deal of folklore. Scary stories have always been one of the most popular forms of entertainment. There's considerable psychological reasoning behind that but we hardly need to go into it now. I decided to turn what I'd learned toward making movies."

"Bad ones," Birdie said, and snickered.

"I'll admit it freely. I never had the budget or the connections. The sets, the effects . . . laughable. And yet something in them, something in the stories or the mood, struck a chord. That's why my films endured. Schlock classics, maybe, but I was able to live comfortably doing a job I enjoyed. Not many can say that."

"I can," Birdie said complacently.

"But how did you find out about the changelings?" pressed Aiden, not wanting to see the two of them go off down nostalgia lane.

"It was a tiny town in the Trinity Mountains, northern California. Drachenheim, it was called. Not much more than a wide spot in the road, off Highway 3. Not much of anything there. The sort of place that attracts survivalists, fishermen, and back-to-nature types wanting to get away from it all. There'd been a rash of sightings and wild reports in the area. Hikers mauled. Strange things seen by the light of the moon. It made the papers. Drachenheim's fifteen minutes of fame."

"I bet," Birdie said.

"I was between projects at the time. This would have been twenty years ago now. I thought Drachenheim might make for good inspiration so I took a tape recorder, a camera, and a notebook and pretended I was a journalist. That was when I met Malcolm Drachen."

The name made Aiden shiver despite the fire that felt like it was roaring under her skin.

Ghostman chuckled to himself. "He said he recognized me. I was used to people being familiar with my movies, even if they spoke of them in those tones of guilty pleasure, but I wasn't used to having anyone know me on sight. Malcolm called himself a horror buff and claimed to have an extensive collection of films and film magazines."

"Yeah," Birdie said. "Jeff and Alex are like that, too. With good reason, I guess. It must crack them up to see how we portray them."

"Not all of them are cracked up. Some find it offensive. Luckily for me, Malcolm was one of the former. His only concern was that I'd been asking around town about the Drachen family. They lived on a ranch out in a remote part of the woods and hardly anyone ever saw them. I'd been toying with an idea that would feature just such a family, all of them members of a sinister cult. Malcolm must have thought it hit too close to home."

"Because they *did* have something to hide," Aiden said.

"Did he try to kill you to shut you up?" Birdie asked.

"No. He saved my life." Ghostman got up, so affected by the power of memory even twenty years later that he couldn't sit still. He went to the white-marble fireplace and kindled a cheery blaze. "I'd gone hiking in the woods one night, scouting for locations that would have the right malevolent atmosphere. I was never anybody's woodsman and was confidently sure that I could not possibly get lost in one of the most populated states in the nation. Sure enough, within hours I was lost and thought I'd never see civilization again. I was on the verge of panic when I happened to look up and see a beast looming over me."

Birdie and Aiden leaned forward intently. Aiden had heard the phrase 'hanging on his every word' before, and finally felt it was an apt description. Her own encounter with Donovan burned brightly in her mind.

"She was, I later found out, Malcolm's mate. She'd eaten of the forbidden meat and gone insane. Pack custom demanded that she be killed, but Malcolm couldn't bear to do it. He locked her away instead and told the others she'd died. He still loved her, you see, even as her psychosis deepened."

"I've had relationships like that."

"Birdie, this is serious!" Aiden said, her nerves strained almost to the breaking point.

"Then, that one fateful night, he took pity on her and let her out of her prison so she could see the sky again. He thought that he could control her. She fled from him, escaped into the woods, and was the one who'd been preying on the hikers. Malcolm caught up with her the night she found me. She was like a cougar, all power and muscle and radiant eyes. She would have killed me if he hadn't gotten there in time. Their fight was the most terrible thing I've ever seen. He was larger and stronger, but she had the fervor of her psychosis. In the end, only a lucky blow from his claws opened her throat, and saved us both."

Aiden felt sick, the cakes and tea sloshing in her stomach and bitter bile seeping into the back of her mouth with a taste like sour lemon.

"As she died, she changed," Ghostman said, pale from the recollection. "Right before my eyes. Malcolm did, too. He was badly hurt, half his face torn away, his ear gone, nearly blinded. He should have been dead himself. I wanted to run all the way back to town, get into my rental car, and be a hundred miles from there before I stopped for a breath, but I couldn't."

"You stayed?" Birdie whistled admiringly. "Got to credit you with plenty of guts, my friend."

"You stayed, too," Aiden reminded her.

"That's different. You weren't attacking me."

"But I could have." Her voice went high and wavery. "I could have, you didn't know, and you helped me anyway."

"Easy, Fergs. Let him finish."

"I stayed," Ghostman said. "Not so much through kindness or loyalty as prudence and curiosity. I was still lost, you remember, and had no way of knowing if there were more of those creatures about. More, I couldn't bear to walk away without knowing what they were. I did what I could for Malcolm, but he was healing so fast he didn't need much. He led me back to my car and told me everything that I've just told you."

"How could you trust him?" Aiden asked. "How could you know he wouldn't decide that his mate had been right and kill you himself?"

"If he'd wanted me dead he could have stood back and let Olivia finish the job."

"So that's where you learned all this," said Birdie. "Straight from the werewolf's mouth."

"In exchange for my vow that I'd keep the secret. That's a deal I've kept, until now."

*　　*　　*

The wire cage had been designed to hold the biggest and strongest breeds of dogs. The world's most determined pit bull or St. Bernard would have thought twice about attempting to bust through the screen.

It was more than a match for Alexander Greye.

He'd revived to find himself locked into the back of the minivan. The smell of dog was overpowering. A dirty tennis ball and a knotted length of rope were the only items sharing his confinement.

This time, upon waking, he suffered no befuddled confusion. He woke with the sharp and clear knowledge of where he was and who'd put him there. Rising slowly above the top of the back seat, fingers hooked through the gaps in the screen, he looked over a heap of camping gear and boxes to the two heads up front.

Donovan was driving. Windshield wipers slashed at rain and sleet.

Simone half-turned in the passenger seat to smile mockingly. "Hello, sleepyhead. Finally with us again?"

Alex didn't answer. He squinted at his watch and saw that he'd been out cold for hours. Night had fallen and by the looks of the scenery, they'd driven high into the mountains. Redwoods loomed close, while snowdrifts caked the slopes and frosted the rocks to either side. The road was narrow and winding, with the impression of gorges plunging away and cliffs rearing above. Highway 299, he guessed, the winding road that led from the coast inland to Redding.

Bill Hartford would be stone cold now, probably buried in sodden leaves at the bottom of a ditch. A pang of guilt pierced Alex when he thought of the man who'd just tried to do a favor, and the wife and children now left on their own.

Fear and distress threatened to bring on the change, as intense emotions always did. Alex struggled to hold onto his human form. He didn't want to give Simone the satisfaction of seeing his fright, even though she could probably smell it on him.

"Whatever were you doing out there?" she asked. "So far from your pack, all alone?"

"He's grief-mad," said Donovan smugly. "I killed his girlfriend, and it drove him insane."

"She's not –" Alex broke off, breathing between clenched teeth.

"Not what?" Simone's eyes narrowed.

Alex didn't answer. She'd smell a lie on him as easily as she smelled fear. His rage at Donovan boiled up. If only he and Jeff had finished it on the beach!

"I'm glad you got there in time to say goodbye and have her die in your arms," Donovan said, grinning fiercely into the rear view mirror. "A shame you weren't a few minutes later. Think what you might have seen then!"

Willing himself *not* to think of what he might have seen then, some visions too hideous and obscene to bear contemplation, Alex glared hatefully into that reflected gaze. He said, "I saw enough of that with Erala."

Donovan hissed and snapped his attention to the road.

Simone scowled quizzically. "Erala? What about Erala?"

"Nothing," Donovan bit out.

"You don't know?" Alex was giddy at this sudden turning of the tables. "He killed her. And Bernard."

"That's a lie!" Simone spat. "That fat fool of a male killed my angel. Ran the car off the road and killed her. He was probably trying to find a doughnut he'd dropped and wasn't watching where he was going."

"Is that what you think? Is that what you believe?" Alex stared at her, and at the back of Donovan's head, hunched low as he bent over the steering wheel. The minivan shimmied as it accelerated, as if Donovan were trying to outrace the truth.

"That's what happened," Donovan snarled. "I was there. I saw it."

"I was there too," said Alex, noting with savage pleasure the way Simone was eyeing her son with the first flickers of suspicion. Donovan was ripe with sour sweat, liar's sweat. Alex could smell it all the way back here. "You almost killed me that night too. But you left me to die so you could rape Erala again, and break her neck when you were done with her."

"No!" Donovan roared.

He jerked the wheel to the side and the minivan slewed, inches away from going into a sickening spin on the wet road. Redwood trunks flashed past in the headlight beams. Stacks of boxes went over in a crash. Alex was thrown into the side wall, bruising his elbow and cheekbone. He clung to the wire to steady himself.

"Yes!" he yelled above the din. "That's what you would have done to Aiden, too."

"Donovan?" Simone asked. "Donovan, this isn't true?"

By way of reply, he braked hard, throwing Alex face-first into the metal grid. He sprang from the seat before the minivan had stopped rocking on its suspension and stalked around to the back.

Alex readied himself. He saw Donovan's outline shift as he passed the windows, knew that Donovan was changing and his only chance was in changing himself. Quickly, he sought a shape more attuned to battle, more wolfen than his habitual sea-lion form. Chestnut-colored hair burst from his skin, his clothes falling in tatters around his altering limbs.

Simone rushed around and met Donovan at the door, putting her hand over his just as he was about to throw it open. Her expression was shocked, but her voice was steady. Alex could hear her through the glass. "Donovan, tell me what happened."

Caught halfway between man and wolf, Donovan was all anguish as he bowed his head. It was admission enough. Simone's hurt gasp made Donovan flinch. He knelt on the wet asphalt and offered her his neck, and Alex had to press his ear to the seam in the door to hear him.

"I did it. Simone, I had to. I was trying to talk sense into her, to make her see that she needed a strong mate for the good of the pack. Not that weak, puling sack of blubber. I tried to convince her to give you another chance, to at least do you the courtesy of hearing you out instead of taking Gideon's word for everything. I saw how much she hurt you by her scorn and wanted to make it better. But she wouldn't listen. She condemned me. Called me vile, told me that I was no longer any brother of hers. And I just . . . I struck her, Simone. I beat her. The more she tried to fight back and escape, the more I . . . I fell into the blood haze."

"Did you . . . ?"

"Yes, I took her, too. I was maddened. If she was to have cubs, I thought better they be mine than fat Bernard's. But then he turned up, and Alexander too, and they stole her away from me. I chased them. Their car crashed, that much was true, but it was because of me. I knew then that Erala would never forgive me, never understand, and so I killed her. Her and Bernard. When I went to find Alex to deal with him too, he was gone. Fled, like a coward."

"Oh, Donovan!"

He groveled at her feet. "I did it for you, Simone. I know how it looks, but I did it for you, for us, our pack. Erala never would have joined us. She hated us. She hated *you*. For that, she deserved to die."

Alex hardly dared breathe. He was hoping this confession would cause Simone to strike out at Donovan, that they'd tear each other to shreds. He'd gladly find some way out of the minivan or wait until help arrived, gladly, just to see them go for each other's throats.

"She never would have loved you as I do," Donovan went on. "All that I am is for you, Simone. All I've ever wanted is to be with you. Don't send me away. Kill me if you must, but don't send me away."

Simone knelt beside Donovan and embraced him. She stroked his shaggy head and murmured to him, too low to hear. She soothed him, consoled him, and slowly he reverted to human form.

"I won't say I'm not angry with you," she said, "but I understand why you did what you felt you had to do. You're a good and devoted son, my Donovan."

He practically wept with gratitude. Alex could have thrown up if there'd been anything in his stomach.

They got back in the front seats. Simone shot Alex a reproachful look, as if this was all *his* fault for making her precious Donovan feel bad. He glowered at her, lips wrinkling back from his teeth.

"Were you coming after us?" she asked. "For revenge on behalf of your little human?"

Above all else, Alex knew he mustn't let on that Aiden was alive. He felt like one walking on thin ice, hearing it groan and crackle beneath him. "I owe you for my parents, too."

It was Simone's turn to skin her lips back, revealing very pointed teeth. "Self-defense. They hunted me, they meant to kill me. I had to protect my pack."

"You have no pack! You're a rogue, nothing but a rogue, a renegade."

"Oh, I have a pack."

She set her hand on Donovan's forearm. He'd started up the minivan and steered it back onto the winding mountain stretch.

"Two rogues still doesn't make a pack."

"We are joined by stronger bonds than your almighty Gideon could ever understand," said Simone. "When you're one of us, you'll agree."

"I will never be one of you."

"You will. You'll see." Her secretive smile was as terrible as the face of the Gorgon, and as effective. Alex intuited her plan and froze on the spot.

"No," he whispered.

"I was too subtle with Erala. I see that now. I tried to appeal to her daughterly love and duty. With you, Alexander, I'll take the direct approach."

"We're keeping him?" Donovan asked, appalled. "Why? We don't need him. Why on earth would we need a runty thing like him?"

"We're too few, my dear one," Simone said. "We'll need a larger pack to defend our home. Think of it. No more running. We'll have a place that is ours and we'll hold it. But we need more than just you and I. There must be others. Someday, cubs."

Donovan's entire body stiffened. "You can't mean to have cubs by *him!*"

For once, Alex was absolutely and unquestioningly in agreement with Donovan. The very prospect turned his blood to water.

"We both need mates, Donovan."

"I'll be your mate!" he blurted. "I'll give you all the cubs you could ever want."

Alex recoiled, but Simone merely raised her eyebrows.

"But Donovan, dear one, you're my own son."

"I don't care! Remember when we hunted together, and you said it was the excitement of the hunt? It was more than that for me. I wanted you right then, to take you, to rut with you over his spilled entrails, to roll through his blood with our limbs entangled and our breath mingling."

Simone's brows rose further at this impassioned speech, while Alex huddled in the farthest rear corner from Donovan that he could find, revolted beyond measure.

"You can't want him," Donovan went on feverishly. "I'm taller, stronger, fitter, a better hunter, a better fighter. Think of the beautiful cubs we could create. I couldn't stand it if you mated with anyone else, Simone, I'd die. Let me be yours, as I'm meant to be."

"This will bear some thinking on," she finally said. "But in the meantime, we still need Alexander."

"Why?" Donovan nearly screamed.

"I won't!" Alex did scream.

"For numbers," Simone said as if she hadn't heard the outburst from the back of the minivan. "You and I alone can't keep constant watch, and if I do take you up on your offer, we'll need more hunters to provide for all of those beautiful cubs. Once we've come home again, he will see the wisdom of our ways."

"Home?" Alex echoed. "Not . . . you can't mean . . ."

This, she did acknowledge. "Drachenheim. The humans stole it from my father and I mean to have it back. They will never drive us from our land again. Not with their taxes and their zoning laws and their county assessors. Let them try. Let them claim we haven't the deeds or the money. I'll answer them with tooth and claw."

Alex sank down on his haunches, finally seeing the full extent of her madness. He remembered, although he'd been little more than a cub at the time, when Simone had been given a choice between death at the teeth of the pack, or exile. He also remembered how she'd come back years later, won Donovan over to her side, and killed two hunters – his and Jeff's parents – when she was discovered.

That had been the end of the pack's settled life at Drachenheim. The humans foreclosed on the property and they were forced to leave, splitting the pack. Some joined Bernard's parents and went north and east, while the rest followed Gideon west to the sea. They'd roved up and down the coast ever since, and the only other contact they'd had with their kind was when Simone and Donovan found them last year. Erala, and Bernard who had stayed with her, paid the ultimate price for that meeting.

As the months had gone by, they'd begun, foolishly, to hope they were safe again. Until Trinity Bay.

Now Simone was taking him back to Drachenheim. He knew what she'd want him to do, and rebelled against it with every ounce of his being. He wouldn't. Couldn't. It was against one of the most ancient laws . . .

Then again, so was what he'd done to Aiden.

*   *   *

CHAPTER 8
JANUARY 4, SUNDAY
NIGHT

Sleep was eons coming once Aiden was tucked beneath the covers, and she didn't know if she'd welcome it when it did. She dreaded the nightmares that would surely fill her mind. Her waking thoughts and memories were bad enough.

Everything she'd seen and experienced, combined with everything Ghostman had told her, was jumbled together into a big confusing muddle.

Tired as she was, her eyes wouldn't stay closed. Her body felt jumpy and restless. Skittery. She got up and paced, made herself sit down, tried to read. But her concentration was in shambles.

She couldn't believe they were just going to leave her to her own recognizance. She wasn't the *same* now. She was changed. Inhumanly, horribly changed. It was in her blood. In her bones. Way down deep in every cell of her body.

Alex popped into her thoughts and she tried unsuccessfully to push him out. Her emotions, drawn tight as a garrote, were mixed when it came to him. She missed him, but he'd done this. He'd saved her, he'd abandoned her. She loved him and was terrified of what he was, what he'd made her become.

Her emotions hurt, her mind hurt. Her body was fine except for the restlessness and a feeling like she had a fever. The higher temperature. She wasn't used to it.

Whether she blamed Alex or not, Aiden knew that she could not go on like this. She was grateful for her life but how could she live it as a changeling? Wasn't she outcast enough already? Didn't she already feel so disconnected from everyone that all of humanity might as well have been foreigners to her?

It might be different, the part of her that missed Alex with fierce intensity suggested, if she was with him. And why not? Changelings were pack creatures. They drew their security and strength from being together.

But even if she could find Alex, or others of his kind, she could all-too-clearly imagine the reception she'd get. She could just see herself arriving wherever the Greyes had stopped, approaching the motor home timidly but hopefully. Alex would be there. He'd come to her, and . . .

And what? Take her before Gideon, stand with her, announce that she was one of them? More, that she was *his?* His . . . mate, that was the word Ghostman had used.

Only a few days ago, the thought of being with Alex forever would have delighted her. Now she wasn't sure how it made her feel.

It was too easy to see Gideon, his face twisted with rage, telling Alex that he'd broken the law, and that he had one simple choice. Kill Aiden himself, or he, Gideon, would do it.

"He wouldn't," Aiden said softly to the empty room. "He wouldn't hurt me."

No, Alex wouldn't. He'd defend her. Which meant they'd probably die together.

I don't want to die! she thought. *But how can I live like this? More alone than I've ever been, and . . . what would I do? I have ID and a bank account, the things Mr. Ghostman was saying it's hard for changelings to have, but what will happen the first time I have to go to the doctor? Even if I don't ever get sick again — he didn't say that, but at least implied that they . . . that we . . . are healthy as horses — I might get hurt.*

Even assuming that she was somehow able to duck out on every regular check-up or emergency visit from here on . . . even assuming that Birdie was able to get Chas and Joseph to keep their silence about what had happened that night at the Channel 12 studio . . . even assuming she was able to pick up the shreds of her life and go on . . . what then?

She barked a bitter laugh at the mental image of herself trying to go back to the book discussion group at Malachi Edwards' shop. Maybe she could do it a few times, but sooner or later people would start to wonder about her. Mr. McGuire would be first in line. He'd know the first time they met for a counseling appointment that there was something wrong, something different.

"I can't go back," she said to the phantom of her reflection in the window. Beyond that faint Aiden-outline was a view of the sloping front yard, dark and sheltered and private with high hedges ringing green lawn and garden.

A chill surfaced through her new hot blood as she thought of Donovan. No matter where she went, no matter where she tried to make a home for herself, however fleeting the stay might be, she'd never open a door without expecting to see him looming there. All red fur and sharp teeth and rapacious erection, looking to finish what he'd started.

She looked out the window again and caught her breath. "The moon . . ."

It had risen above the hills now, half-filmed by a cloud but round, white, full. Aiden stood and watched it climb, transfixed by its beauty. She'd always known that the moon was pretty, sure, it was one of those things that everyone knew. Especially when it was full. But she suddenly felt like she'd never really noticed it before.

The moon . . . the full moon . . . so beautiful . . .

Headlights speared in shafts through the hedge. A car. It pulled into the neighboring driveway.

Drawn out of her reverie with a gasp, Aiden realized that the moon had climbed higher, as if she'd been standing and staring at it for an hour or more. At some point, too, she'd shed her garments and had her body right up against the glass.

Face flaming, she backed away from the window and crossed her arms over her nudity. Her nightgown, socks, and panties were in a heap on the carpet and she got back into them quickly.

The clothes felt itchy and confining. Heavy. Without them, she'd felt wonderfully unencumbered and alive, caressed by moonlight like a cool night wind that eased the burning in her veins.

Aiden yanked the curtains closed, cutting off the sight of the moon except where it beamed, like a veiled spotlight, against the fabric. She curled on her side in bed, facing away from the window, and pulled the comforter over her head.

Tears seeped from the corners of her eyes as she squeezed them tightly shut. The comforter was too hot, stifling. She kicked it and the blanket off and kept only the sheet. Even that made her feel like she was roasting alive. She tossed and turned until all the linens were tangled beyond hope, and got up.

A diffuse white circle through the curtains, the moon called to her. The moon, and the night.

"I just need some fresh air," Aiden said in a voice she barely knew as her own. "Just to cool down, and then I'll be able to sleep."

She opened the window, which was thirty feet above Ghostman's front lawn. A wonderful cool draft swirled around her, billowing the hem of her nightgown.

Moments later, her clothes were discarded again. Her bare toes were deep in the dewy green grass. Moving quicker and quieter and more grace-fully than she ever would have believed herself capable of, she passed through a gap in Ghostman's hedge and out into the soft shadows of the night.

Letting her senses guide her, she came to a park that was long and nar-row, following the course of a creek that ran through it in pretty tumbles of whitewater over rocks. The air smelled clean and refreshing, healthy and alive. The special crisp flavor of impending snow was in it.

Aiden knew without needing to be told what each night sound was. Life was all around her. Birds and squirrels, a fat possum contemplating a chained trash can, the fleet whisper of a running cat.

She felt poised on a threshold, teetering, balanced between two worlds while belonging fully to neither. It was a sensation of unbearable excitement and suspense, like how it had been to be kissed and held by Alex, wanting more but afraid to go on.

Playing tag with the moonlight as she moved silently down the path, Aiden came to a pool. It was ringed by stones and benches where people could sit and feed crusts of bread to the ducks and the swans.

Swans!

Three of them, so white they looked divine, had paddled to the edge of the pool and rested there, long necks curved and folded to tuck their heads in sleep, wings backswept. A sort of wooden coop had been set up to pro-vide shelter for the waterfowl, and the dull orange of a heat bulb glowed within. The shapes of sleeping ducks surrounded it.

Entranced, Aiden crept closer. She'd never seen a swan before except in pictures. They were bigger than she'd thought. Not dainty, delicate things. Beautiful, yes, but large. Strong. Well-muscled.

There'd be a lot of meat on a swan.

Appalled to find herself salivating at that alien, intrusive thought, Aiden backed off. But seconds later, she was back by the pool, looking longingly at the birds, wondering how hard they'd be to kill, and what they'd taste like. She'd had duck before, and it was rich but greasy. Would a swan be more like that? Or more like chicken?

She itched as though she'd stepped in an anthill or brushed against poi-son oak. As she moved to scratch her arm, she froze at what her fingers encountered.

Slowly, not wanting to see but having to look, Aiden lowered her gaze.

The backs of her hands and her forearms were covered in a fine downy hair. Her nails were thicker and longer. Not claws, not yet, but headed that way. Curved and hard, extending well beyond the tips of her fingers.

Changing. She was changing.

"No, please, no, I don't want to," Aiden whispered.

Oh, but that was a lie. Part of her did. Part of her wanted to give in, to surrender.

The moon was above her, framed in clouds but not touched by any, as if purposefully showcasing itself.

Aiden shuddered. Fine knots of pain formed like thin wire being drawn taut in her joints. Her fingers were altering even as she watched, shortening and widening while sturdy pads of flesh formed on the undersides and on her palms.

Her skin was covered in a soft white-blond pelt lighter than the hair of her head, mottled with darker markings. The shape of her legs and feet had begun to change, too. Her toes grew longer, her calves shorter, her hips wrenching not unpleasantly as they shifted to an angle.

"No, please," moaned Aiden. The words came out oddly muddled, and she bit her tongue with unfamiliar, sharp teeth.

Her eyes had changed, too. The night was exceptionally detailed. Every leaf had its own rare texture. Each blade of grass, each swan's feather, each rock forming the orderly boundary of the pool, was a work of art. Her ears, her nose . . . all of her senses were keen and alert and sharper than they'd ever been.

Aiden reeled at the influx of stimuli. She knew that she wasn't understanding half of what she was sensing, untutored as she was, but she would learn. And learn fast. That's what predators did. They hunted and they learned. They were quick and clever.

A sudden, strange joy welled in her. The timid Aiden was pushed far to the back, and this new Aiden, this sleek and confident hunter, took over.

She slunk to the pond, body held low, the pointed ears that thrust up through her mane of beige-blond hair pricked and alert. One of the swans, a male with elegant black lines like kohl around his eyes, reared up and beat his wings in challenge or warning.

Aiden crouched on her haunches, suppressing the eager twitch of her tail. She could smell wariness on the prey, and fear. But these swans were over-fed and arrogant in their belief that they were safe, protected.

The male honked, a startlingly harsh and ugly sound coming from such an elegant bird. Ducks yammered and quacked, stumbling over each other as they fled their enclosure for the pond. From high in the bole of a tree, a squirrel chattered warningly.

She sprang.

The single leap carried her across the narrowest part of the pool. She had a momentary impression of her reflection pacing her across the murky green surface, a pale blur that was not the shape of a wolf and not the shape of a jaguar but somewhere in between.

Her hand swept in a scything arc. The swan's honking ended in a gurgle.

Its head had been severed into her grasp. The proud body didn't yet accept it was dead, thrashing and flapping. Warm blood oozed down Aiden's wrist from the ragged flesh. She lapped at it and the taste ignited a frenzy in her.

Tossing the head into the water, she turned to the body of the swan. She dragged it onto the grass and hunkered down over it to defend her kill. The white feathers of its breast tore away under her claws to expose the plump layer of meat.

Some time later, she became aware that she was walking, staggering, down the middle of a street. Tears coursed down her face. Her skin was caked with drying blood and feathers. The taste of blood and rich, rich meat overwhelmed her mouth.

The bright dazzle of headlights found and pinned her too abruptly for her to hide. She froze there, terror-struck.

"Fergs!"

The cherry-red VW screeched to a stop a few yards from Aiden. Birdie jumped out, wearing sweatpants and an electric-blue sleepshirt with bright yellow jagged letters reading *just give me the coffee and nobody gets hurt.*

All those colors . . . all those eye-searing vivid colors . . . Aiden couldn't take it. She crumpled, chest jerking from the force of her sobs, wanting to vomit but unable to make herself do it. The weight in her stomach, that warm, full, Thanksgiving-dinner feeling, was simultaneously wonderful and horrible.

"Fergs, oh, Jesus, Fergs, where are you hurt? Where are you bleeding?"

She couldn't answer, couldn't warn Birdie away like she knew she should. She was too dangerous to be near. After what she'd done to the swan . . .

The story spilled out of her in tangled sentences and tears. Birdie, instead of heading for the hills at roughly the speed of light, put her arms around Aiden and herded her gently toward the car.

"Let's get you out of here. No sense giving the world a free show, huh?"

"Birdie, no, you shouldn't. You can't trust me."

"I trust you, Fergs."

"I could hurt you!"

"Well, that'd make me a shitty judge of character, wouldn't it? Here, I'll see if I can find something to clean you up." She rummaged, found a packet of pre-moistened towelettes, looked askance from the packet to the mess all over Aiden, and tried again. A ratty towel surfaced through the junk in her trunk.

While Aiden stood and trembled, helpless as a baby, Birdie wiped off the worst of it. It occurred to Aiden that Birdie's teeth were chattering and her lips were going blue. It was freezing out, but to Aiden the night felt mild and pleasant.

Birdie wrapped her in an old blanket the color and texture of cotton candy, and coaxed her into the car. Neither of them said much until they were back in the security of Ghostman's garage. Only then did Aiden rouse.

"I can't be like this," she said, turning wide, shocked eyes to Birdie's concerned ones. "I can't."

"It's okay, Fergs. All is cool. No need to get in a tizzy."

"You didn't see it. The swan. What was left of it. I . . . I *ate* it, Birdie. Raw and still warm." Rather than lurch in revulsion, her stomach gurgled contentedly. Aiden burst into tears again. "Ate it, tore its heart and liver out and ate them too, good meat, protein and iron, and then I left the carcass there with its guts hanging out —"

"I get the picture."

"I'm a monster."

"You are not."

"I killed it. An innocent swan. I've never killed anything before."

"It's okay."

"How is it okay?" She slammed the heels of her hands against the dashboard. "How in the world is it okay? I *changed*. I really did. Physically, but mentally, too. I wasn't thinking, Birdie. Not in the way that people are supposed to think."

"Come on inside."

"I'm dangerous!"

"Bullshit."

"I *am!*"

But Birdie wouldn't listen. She led Aiden through the garage, up the elevator, and along the hall. Aiden saw herself in a mirror as they went by. Was this her? This tottering, bony, hollow-eyed creature? Blood was grimed into the corners of her mouth. She looked like a painting by some deranged artist. A hysterical laugh stuttered from her lips and she bit it off sharply, sounding way too much like a chronic schizophrenic for comfort.

"Shh," Birdie said. "No need to wake up Ghostman. We can take care of this. We'll get you showered and back to bed, and nobody will need to know."

"Won't he, though, the minute he opens the paper and sees the article? *Swans Slaughtered in Lithia Park.*"

"Thought it was just the one."

"I don't remember! It was such a blur. It could have been all of them. It could have been a person!"

"Easy does it, Fergs. Here. Into the bathroom."

The bathroom was as white and pristine as the rest of Ghostman's house. It seemed terribly wrong to bring any mess into it, let alone the mess of a killing.

Aiden stood motionless while Birdie got hot water streaming from the showerhead. She felt numbness surround her and clutched at it gladly. Numbness was preferable to mind-shattering lunacy. Steam roiled around the edges of the shower curtain and fogged the mirror, mercifully masking her sunken grey eyes.

She was so detached that she didn't utter the tiniest squeak of protest when Birdie unwound her from the blanket, directed her into the tub with hot water beating down, and shucked her own blood-stained clothes to climb in too.

Birdie's manner was matter-of-fact as she soaped and scrubbed and shampooed both of them. She might have been a nurse, or a mother. Aiden dutifully did as she was directed, bowing her head to let Birdie rinse suds from her hair, holding still while Birdie dried her with a big fluffy towel as white as the pelt of a polar bear. She sat on the closed lid of the toilet, swaddled in white, while Birdie worked the tangles from her hair with a comb.

"There," Birdie finally said. "Better?"

"Mmm," Aiden said.

A strange lassitude had replaced the numbness. Maybe it was the heat and the stream, or her night's exercise catching up with her. Maybe her analogy of Thanksgiving hadn't been so far off. Maybe swans were loaded with the same chemical found in turkey that was responsible for people dozing off during the football games.

"Ready to talk yet?"

"I told you what happened," she mumbled. "All I want now is sleep."

They had gone into her room, and the bed beckoned her as seductively as the moon had done. Birdie was in her way, holding her by the shoulders, fixing her with a concerned, stern gaze.

"We've got to figure out what to do next, Fergs."

Aiden blinked a slow, drowsy owl's blink. "I don't know what to do, Birdie. I can't handle this. What do I need? An exorcism? What? There has to be some way. And if there isn't, I've got to die."

"Whoa, wait, hold your horses. No suicidal stuff. That's not an option."

"Why isn't it?" Aiden sank onto the edge of the bed. "At least I don't have to figure out how to get silver bullets."

"Stop it, Fergs."

"You can't understand. I'm not human anymore. I'm a monster."

"Is Alex a monster?"

"That's not fair." She roused a little at that, and her chin quivered.

"Hell it isn't."

"It's different. He was born to it, grew up with it."

"So? He still changes. He still hunts, I bet you. Does that make him a monster?"

Aiden covered her face. "It's not the same."

"Maybe not," Birdie said, "but I'm not going to let you give up and jump off a bridge or something. You think you're a monster, but look at it this way – you didn't have to go out. You could have gone right through that door to where I was, or down the hall to Ghostman's room. You could have broken into any house between here and the park. You didn't. A monster would have. If anything, you're . . . an animal, and an animal can't help its instincts."

"Is that supposed to make me feel better?"

"I'd hoped. At least you're alive."

"I'm sorry." Aiden wiped ineffectually at her leaking eyes. "You're right, I know you're right. I just want to be rid of it."

"That might not be possible. You know what would happen if you went to a doctor with this."

"I wasn't planning to go to a doctor. I've got one other idea."

"Let's hear it," Birdie said.

"I want to go to the place he told us about. I want to go to Drachenheim."

*   *   *

The Kill

Chapter 1
January 5, Monday
Morning

Grant Kendall found that he needed less and less sleep as he grew older. He had worried that he'd find the days too long once he'd turned his Redding dental office over to his daughter. He'd worried that retirement would bore him. Instead, he had the horses and the chores around the ranch to keep him busy, and probably worked harder now than he had during his forty years of professional life.

Joyce didn't move when he got out of their big peeled-log bed. He slid carefully from under the patchwork quilt, the chill in the air bracing as he got into his robe and slippers.

The kitchen was the only room in the house that always seemed to remain warm. The enormous brick hearth boasted both a fireplace and a woodstove. Copper pots and pans dangled from a cast-iron rack, and more copper gleamed from the pulls of the drawers and cabinets. The room smelled pleasantly of spices, and as the coffee pot began to perk and bubble, its savory aroma added to the cozy atmosphere.

The world seemed much more peaceful before dawn. Grant looked forward to his daily ritual of coffee, a muffin, and a leisurely perusal of the previous day's paper, which he picked up each afternoon on his trip to town.

But something this morning wasn't quite right. A spark glinted, seen from the corner of his eye. Grant laid down the paper and went to the window, leaning over the sill and Joyce's little herb garden.

A vehicle was moving slowly up the driveway. He kept it plowed with the blade attachment that affixed to the front of his all-purpose Jeep, but a fresh layer of snow, wet and slushy, had fallen during the night.

Grant pursed his lips thoughtfully, running through a mental list of any-one who'd be likely to come and visit, let alone at this hour.

The headlights rolled closer. He could see the shape of the vehicle, a minivan. Jeanie and Pete drove one like that, but they weren't given to sur-prise visits.

Belting his robe tightly around his middle, Grant went to the side door and stepped out on the porch. Icicles dripped from the eaves, the soft splat of their substance melting onto the planks the only sound in the early hush.

The minivan stopped in the wide turn-around beside the house. It idled there for a moment, and his misgivings subtly deepened into a case of the nerves that bordered on premonition.

Grant pictured in his mind, clear as could be, the gun cabinet beside the entertainment center in the living room. Decoratively carved, solid oak, a real piece of work. The key was on a string in his desk drawer, upstairs in the study.

This apprehension was out of line, overblown. He wasn't about to make himself look like an idiot by slamming the door and pelting up the stairs in a panic. He'd wake Joyce, and as embarrassing as it would be to have total strangers, or people from town, think he'd lost his last marbles, he couldn't bear to have Joyce think that.

The minivan's doors opened and a man and woman got out. The wind lifted identical banners of red hair from their shoulders. They weren't wear-ing coats or winter gear, and while their breath puffed in clouds around them, they didn't seem to notice the cold.

"Hello there," he called, the words coming out of him in almost a ques-tion.

The woman looked up at him, and in the thin spill of light from the open kitchen door, her eyes began to glow.

*   *   *

The female floundered through deep snow, whining as the wind threw hard granules of it into her eyes.

The blizzard had come up unexpectedly. They'd been ready for snow, but thought it would come later, and never in such a howling fury. Never blow up so suddenly that the pack would be separated in their hunt, unable to catch one another's scents. Tracks were eradicated, familiar landmarks lost in the white opacity.

Alexander Greye was frightened and feeling foolish.

She – yes, he dimly realized, for some reason he was female in this dream, this vision – shouldn't have been out so close to birthing. But she'd wanted to do her part, one last hunt before winter closed in and she was unable to stir from the den.

Now she was lost, cut off from her mate and her pack. The voice of the wind masked any calls they might have made, and swallowed up hers the moment they left her lips.

The snow clung to her fur in wet clumps instead of fluffy flakes that could have been easily shaken off. Her body heat melted it enough to soak her thoroughly and weigh her down all the more. She had to get inside. Had to get warm and dry.

Prey was forgotten despite her aching hunger and the demands of her unborn cub. She turned in a full circle, senses alert, seeking any sign of her pack or the way home. Each direction looked as promising and as hopeless as any other.

She chose one at random, knowing that it was better to be moving than standing still. If she could find her way back, good. If not, she could at least search out some hollow or sheltered spot and curl up, trusting to her pelt to keep her warm enough until she was found. The shame she'd feel at having to be brought in like a youngling who'd strayed too far on a first hunt shrank the longer she was out here and the colder she got. Soon she would even be glad of the teasing she'd take from the others. Anything to be warm again, and dry, and fed.

The storm gained in strength, as if it had a personal vengeance against Alex. She – *he*, his mind insisted, trying to make sense of this – had to go to all fours just to keep her footing in the vicious wind. But on all fours, the heaping snow was up to her bulging belly. The skin there was stretched, the fur thinned, and exposure to such a chill couldn't be good for the little one inside her.

She fought her way onward, shouldering through drifts that went higher than her head. The ground had been frozen even before the storm and the iced rocks cut into the pads of her paws. They were normally tough and callused enough for running over harsh terrain, but they weren't made for this sort of punishment.

In the lee of a fallen log, she stopped to lick at her wounded paws. The scrape of her tongue made the scratches sting and burn, and the taste of her own blood only reminded her how long it had been since she'd fed. But there was no prey to be seen –

Aha! There!

Movement contrary to that of the wind caught her eye. With a predator's keen vision, she saw a fat rabbit, winter-white, hopping toward the safety of a bramble-bush. It was a foolish creature to be out in weather like this, not that she was one to talk.

She stalked the rabbit, salivating at the prospect of hot entrails, fresh blood, and meat. It would barely make a mouthful, but was far better than nothing.

Closer, closer . . . her tail switched, her haunches tensed . . .

The rabbit spotted her. For a moment they stared at each other, its tiny black eyes inkspots in the whiteness of its face. She pounced. The rabbit bounded sideways and her gnashing jaws caught nothing but snow.

Her prey arrowed and zig-zagged. Flagging from weariness and the ungainly weight of her body, she fought to catch up. She leapt over a rock, ducked under a bush, snapped and got a tuft of fur, and then in the wild, driving snow, didn't see the precipice ahead until it was too late to stop.

The land fell away at a steep angle, not quite a sheer cliff. The rabbit darted along its edge but she tumbled toward the frozen river. She scrabbled for a foothold, missed her grip, and did her best to shelter her cub as she slammed and rolled over rocks and hard, frozen ground.

She hit the ice and slid into a dizzying spin. Just as she slowed, just as she began to think it would hold her after all, the surface beneath her cracked and she plunged into the freezing water. Her forepaws clawed at the edges of the hole, but only broke off more chunks.

Howling now, yelping and wailing at the top of her lungs, she tried to change to a more appropriate form. Something otterlike, seal-like, with an oily waterproof coat . . . except that it was too late, she was already drenched, and didn't have the strength to seek another shape. Her head went under and she forced herself up again, snorting water from her mouth and nose.

The sluggish current bore her downstream, trying to pull her under. A hindpaw wedged between two submerged rocks. Kicking desperately to get it out, she snapped the bones in her lower leg. The pain was immediate and awful, outshining everything else. She went under again.

Somehow, she freed her paw and fought her way to the shore. The slope was shallower here, enabling her to drag herself out of the river. She lay on ice-coated rocks, shivering and mewling helplessly.

Soaked through, only three good legs, half-drowned, and on the wrong side of the river. They wouldn't think to look for her over here. The pack didn't cross the river that marked the border of their territory, not while they were hunting. The snow and water would have erased her scent.

She might have lain there until she died, if not for the cub. It struggled within her, fighting for its life with a fire that got her to her feet again. The hindleg wouldn't support her so she hobbled along on the other three. She went into the forest, thinking only of finding a temporary den.

Through a gap in the whirling snow, she saw a gleam of orange. The wind teased her with a whiff of smoke before snatching it away, the way a mean boy might taunt a starving dog with a piece of meat only to leave the beast straining at the end of its leash.

An orange gleam and smoke. That meant fire. It also probably meant humans, but she didn't care. She *had* to get shelter, or she and her cub would die. It was as simple as that.

She hobbled through the woods with her eyes fixed on the spot where she'd seen the glow. Soon she reached the source of the firelight, a gap in a shutter, a window, a cabin. A hunter, or at least a human who presumed to give himself that title.

It wasn't much, a single room with a tarpaper roof and the bent iron cylinder of a chimney poking up, but a palace couldn't have been more inviting. She limped to it, her breath like knives sawing in and out of her lungs.

The door was too much for her in her weakened condition. She scratched at it and made pleading noises, and heard the stir of movement within. Footsteps, heavy booted ones, clomped closer. She waited, waited, and the door opened in a wonderful rush of light and heat.

A man stood there, stocky and bearded, with a rifle held at his side. He saw her, and in the one precious stunned moment before he could react, she leaped. Her teeth closed on his arm and she snapped his wrist with one practiced jerk of her head. The man screamed, the gun falling. He stumbled back. She lunged against his legs to trip him. The cabin shook when he struck the floor.

She tore out his throat with a sweep of her claws. Even with such a wound, he was a long time dying. He gurgled, his legs rattled fitfully, his hands clutched at empty air. She nudged the gun away from him and maneuvered the door shut with her head.

At last, the man's final breath sighed out and he went limp. She looked around the interior. A cot with a sleeping bag, a wood stove and box of split lengths of firewood, a single table and stool, various tools and utensils. The heat baking from the woodstove was more welcome than even her mate's smile would have been.

Her hindleg wanted to heal. She hitched over to the cot and pulled herself up on it, and shifted just enough toward a human form to pull the leg straight. The pain nearly overwhelmed her but she persisted, biting her lip, until the worst of it passed. Then, fearfully weak, she fell back on the sleeping bag and panted.

Being inside, being warm and dry, wasn't enough. She had to change but lacked the strength to complete her transformation. The last of her reserves had been drained.

A massive, monstrous cramp seized her. The cub! It was too soon, a full face of the moon too soon. She clamped her paw-hands over her stomach as if she could somehow stop the inevitable, but the process was begun.

She'd never make it. She was too hungry, having lost pounds already from the effort of getting here. If she didn't eat, she'd never be able to survive the birth.

Shelves over the woodstove held cans of soup and stew. Above her reach. She had no time to search for a can opener and knew even her jaws couldn't do that job.

And the smell . . . the blood-smell . . . was everywhere. It pooled around the dead man, good nourishing blood dribbling through the floorboards to be wasted.

Whimpering, wracked with contractions, she rolled from the cot and crawled to the corpse. She had lost sight of everything except survival, survival for herself and her cub. The laws of the pack paled in comparison to that single driving need.

The first bite made her forget any reservation. It was delicious! Better than rabbit, better than venison.

She gorged shamelessly, blood coursing down her chin. When she couldn't take another mouthful, and the contractions were coming so hard and so fast that she knew it was time, she returned to the cot.

Now she had the strength to take the best form for this, curling around to lick at the cub as it emerged in its birth-sack. She ripped the sack with her teeth and nuzzled the tiny body.

The cub was covered in a downy red pelt. A female. Her eyes were sealed shut, her soft claws scrabbling for purchase as she tried to find her way to her mother's body. The exhausted mother nudged her into position and urged her to nurse, which the newborn did with a fierce hunger of her own.

She dozed then, replete. She had fed, she was warm and safe, she had her cub, they would live.

*   *   *

The trip across Highway 299 in the snow was hair-raising. Literally. Jeff Greye was constantly at war with himself, trying to hold back the change that tension and exhaustion wanted to bring on.

When they'd realized Alex was gone, Jeff expected Gideon to blow up like a nuclear bomb. He couldn't believe, and at the same time wasn't the least bit surprised, that his brother had done such a crazy-stupid thing.

It was noble, in its way. Decent. Romantic, even. But to run from the pack? Worse, to leave *him*, Jeff, in the unenviable position of having to explain everything to Gideon and the elder they called Grandfather? He only hoped they'd find Alex alive and well so that he, Jeff, could have the pleasure of kicking his butt.

He had stood firm, held his ground, and laid it all out for them. The more Gideon's face darkened, the more his eyes glowed, the steadier Jeff made his voice. He tried to emit subtle submissive signals, not cowering or groveling but holding his head low, avoiding eye contact.

When he told them of Donovan, and Simone, he was shocked to see that Gideon only nodded as if he'd expected something like this. As if he'd known all along.

"How long did you know?" Jeff had asked, against his better judgment. "Why didn't you tell us?"

"That is not important now."

"The hell it isn't! We could have been killed."

At this, Gideon had bristled. "Not if you and Alexander had obeyed your pack leader and stayed away from that girl. Now look what's come of it! He's deserted his pack and gone back to her, this female, this freakish neither-kind. When I find them, I will do what must be done."

"You mean kill her," Jeff said flatly.

"That task should be Alexander's. He has done this, and he should set it right. If he is unable, or unwilling, I will do it myself."

They had discovered Alex's absence two hours after they'd left Eureka, the day before. Up until then, they had all believed he'd merely been napping in the back bedroom of the motor home while Gideon drove and Jeff went ahead in the rust-black Chevy. When they'd stopped around midday Grandfather had gone back there to ask him if he wanted lunch, that was when they'd found him gone.

Jeff had known instantly what Alex had done. His young brother had been doing nothing but moping all night and day, not eating, not sleeping, not speaking. Chewing his heart out over what had happened with Aiden.

Nothing would do but to turn around and go back. They didn't know just when Alex had jumped ship, but they knew where he was going. A terse silence had reigned once Jeff had finished telling them everything that had happened in town, and that fateful night on the beach.

Grandfather had broken the silence as they passed Arcata, asking Gideon when he had learned that Simone and Donovan were nearby.

Gideon might have been able to shunt Jeff's questions aside, but he could not deter the elder so readily. He was not really grandfather to any of them, not by blood, but he had been leader before Gideon and had always been a figure of wisdom and respect. The battle-scars only added to his air of quiet power. It was rare for them to be injured so badly that the body could not completely heal, and the fact that he had survived so catastrophic an encounter spoke of his courage and will.

"I saw Donovan Friday night," Gideon had said. He cut his gaze to the side and down. Not lying in his words, not so far, but neither entirely honest. "In the woods."

"You came back late that night," Grandfather remarked. "And wounded."

"We fought. He escaped me and I . . . I lost his trail." This last was evidently a difficult admission for Gideon, who hated to be outdone in anything, and he couldn't look at either of them.

"You led him right to Alex and Aiden," Jeff had said.

"No. It was after. I saw Donovan after I dragged Alexander from that female's den by the scruff of his neck. My blood was high." He said this as if he didn't have the worst temper in ten generations, a temper usually held in check by his iron control but always there, impossible to miss. "If I hadn't gone back out after bringing him home, I don't know what I might have done. That was when I encountered Donovan."

"And the next day," Grandfather said, "you told us to make ready to leave Trinity Bay with all haste."

"To run," Jeff said with more belligerence than was wise. "Like we always run. What happened when you fought with him?"

"I do not have to explain my actions to you," Gideon growled.

"Alex and I fought him too. We almost had him. Why don't we stay, and fight, instead of running? If the four of us were together as a pack should be, we could take down that misbegotten waste of fur."

"The moment we do as they do," Grandfather said, "we become no better than they are."

"That is true," Gideon said.

"What's the difference between that and murdering Alex and Aiden? Is it because they're small, and not too strong, while Simone and Donovan are too powerful? You're afraid of them."

Jeff had known at once that he'd gone too far, but his blood had been roaring and only the firmest lock of will kept him from changing form right then and there. But all of a sudden it was Gideon whose eyes blazed with phosphorescent heat, Gideon's chiseled features that were darkened beneath a spreading pelt of sable.

"I do not fear them," Gideon said, biting out each word sharply.

"Every time they get close, we move on, fast as we can," Jeff said.

"We move on to keep this pack safe. We are too few. I will not risk another life against those . . . those . . . abominations."

"We're dying anyway," Grandfather had taken them both by surprise. "Our kind have been scattered to the winds. We might never encounter another pack. We have no females. There will be no more cubs. This life of ours is hollow and meaningless when we have no future."

Gideon blustered but no coherent words emerged.

"And so," Grandfather went on, "if we are to die anyway, it would be better to do so while attempting to set things right. The root of all this misery, Gideon, began with me. I must end it."

"The humans will be searching for us, and thanks to Alexander they may know everything by now," Gideon had said, a snarl underlying his words. "Are we to hand ourselves over to them? Our kind may be dying, but I will die free, not locked away in a lab!"

"We can avoid the humans," Jeff said. "It's not like any of us have done anything wrong –"

Gideon's posture took on that defensive stance again. He quickly masked the guilty shine that came into his eyes, but quick as he was, Jeff didn't miss it.

"What was that for? What have you done?"

"I do not know what you mean." His lie was apparent in the bitter scent issuing from every pore. In that moment, Gideon had turned weak, and Jeff seized the advantage.

"I'm going back," he declared. "If you are too afraid, I'll go alone. I'll find Alex. If Simone and Donovan come for us, let them try. I'm done running."

"You won't go alone," Grandfather said. "I'm with you."

"I will not allow this!" Gideon had hidden away that look of furtive guilt but it was too late; Jeff had seen it and would never forget, even if he never understood the cause. "I am this pack's leader."

"If you'll *lead*, I'll follow," Jeff said. "If not, I'll challenge you."

He'd heard it come out of his mouth with utter disbelief. He had never even moon-dreamed of challenging Gideon. But Alex . . . Alex had thrown everything to the winds in order to do what he felt was right. Like it or not, Jeff was compelled to follow that example. Even if it killed him, which it probably would . . . and within the next few minutes, if the way Gideon was baring his teeth was any indication.

Rather than cuff him down for an insolent pup and strip the hide from his back, Gideon made a low noise deep in his throat and nodded curtly. "Very well, then. We go back. But we avoid the humans. This is a matter for our kind, not theirs. And when the time comes to face . . ." he brought out her name with an effort, as if it were a bone caught in his gullet, ". . . Simone, and her whelp, I will do so alone."

"That's suicide!" Jeff barked. "Donovan fought you to a draw the other night. You've seen how much faster and stronger he is. Alex and I couldn't take him. There's no way you could beat them both."

"First and foremost, we must find Alexander," Grandfather said. "We can see to the rest as it comes."

"Yeah? What about Alex?" Jeff asked. "I won't help you find him if you're going to kill him."

Gideon's lip curled. "He has turned his back on us, broken our laws. If you are insisting that I punish Simone for her crimes, how could I do less with Alexander?"

"It's not the same. Alex hasn't killed anyone. I remember the histories the elders used to tell. It used to be all right to do what he did."

"The cub is correct," said Grandfather before Gideon could reply. Jeff was grateful for this unexpected support despite being called 'cub'. "The prohibition against manflesh *must* be kept for reasons we know all too well, but I say that Alexander deserves a chance to defend his deed. If he's brought this female into the pack and she's willing to have him, it may be our last hope."

Once the decision was arrived upon, Gideon had lapsed into a smoldering silence. He had barely looked at Jeff, barely grunted in response to anything Grandfather had to say. His only command before heading north was to leave the motor home. All three of them would ride in the car, Jeff and Gideon taking turns driving.

They'd arrived near Trinity Bay at dusk and hadn't entered the town openly. They'd parked out by the sawmill, deserted except for a night watchman, and left Grandfather with the car while Jeff and Gideon changed and loped stealthily across town.

Jeff hadn't missed the fact that Gideon was nervous and keyed-up, and the closer they got to the wooded and muddy shorefront near Aiden's house, the more noticeable it became.

"Was this where you ran into Donovan?" Jeff asked, his speech slightly mushy thanks to the shape of his mouth but otherwise clear.

"Near here," Gideon said.

"Where? Maybe it's not too late to pick up his trail."

"I think not."

"If we can get them now, tonight, catch them unawares . . . or at least find out if they're still here . . ."

Grudgingly, Gideon had led him away from the beach and deeper into the woods. To Jeff's amazement, Gideon's own scent was everywhere here, overlapping in faded hints. And his scent markers . . . they were strange. Jeff paused to sniff at one, but Gideon shouldered him roughly and made him go on.

They'd passed a section of road where the lingering death-smell of a dog haunted the air, Gideon's scent there too, weeks old. In a low place on the other side of the road, Gideon's scent was thick and Jeff stepped on something rounded and hard under a carpet of leaves. He stopped to paw at it and uncovered a keychain ornament in the likeness of the sexy green M&M.

"Come on," Gideon growled.

Jeff had gone, but uneasily. His ears twitched as he caught Donovan's unwholesome scent near a boarded and police-taped house with unlit Christmas lights hanging along the eaves.

"Here," Gideon said. "We fought here."

"How'd you find him?" Jeff asked.

His nose wrinkled from the maneater and kill-smell of Donovan, and the musky odor of Gideon's old presence. Rut-scent. Gideon's marks had a rut-scent to them. That couldn't be right. Who would there be to rut with but Simone? And he would never . . . not with Simone . . . would he? Besides, there was no trace of *her* scent, and Jeff would not have overlooked that. Not the scent of a mature female of his own kind.

Gideon hadn't answered him, but followed Donovan's trail far into the woods, near a water tower. At one point, Gideon had stopped and closely examined a patch of ground where there were signs of a scuffle, tire tracks, and a human reek of sweat and fear and urine.

They'd ended up at a shack, and there Jeff had been swamped by the scent of Simone, ripe and musky, enticing in a way that left him tingling with lust despite his revulsion. Donovan had been there, too, but the trail was lost. Their quarry had gotten into a vehicle.

"They've gone," Gideon had said.

"Following us?"

"If so, we may have lost them by doubling back." This seemed to please and relieve him quite a bit.

Having used up most of the day with travel and much of the night with this search, they'd been too tired to do much more. But Jeff insisted on going to Aiden's little house far out on Vista Beach.

Aiden's house had been deserted, plywood nailed over the shattered remains of the front window. Her little car was parked and somehow forlorn by the corner of the porch. The scent patterns here were a confusing stew – Aiden, Alex, Jeff himself, Donovan, several humans, even Gideon from when he'd found out that Alex had sneaked away from their camp to meet with her. But all of those traces were faint and old.

"What now?" Jeff had wondered aloud. "Can't go to the hospital, can't very well show up at Channel 12 and ask them, can't go to the police."

When they'd gotten back to the car, wet and defeated, worn out and hungry, they'd been greeted by Grandfather with a suggestion of his own.

"Simone has been following us," he had said. "We've known that. Why don't we lead her where she wants to go? Why don't we lead her home?"

*   *   *

Alex woke from the strange and horrible dream of being a hurt, breeding female to find himself in a darkness so complete he was sure he'd been blinded.

Tentatively, afraid to but needing to know, he raised his fingers gently to his eyes. He expected to find them gored out, with gnarled masses of scar tissue that proved his body had tried to regenerate the loss, healing the sockets but unable to regenerate the delicate eyes themselves. His only reason to be thankful would be that he'd been unconscious when the maiming had taken place . . .

He blinked as his fingertips brushed his eyelashes. Closing his lids, he pressed them and sagged in relief to feel the unhurt, rounded orbs beneath. The fact that he saw the dull colors of that pressure made him feel better. Undamaged eyes. Which meant only that he was locked away someplace pitch-black.

With sight useless, he turned to his other senses. A single breath of the room's dank atmosphere told him volumes.

Underground. He was underground, with the smell of damp concrete and slimy molds all around him, overpowering the scents of horses, hay, manure. Whatever he was laying upon emitted puffs of its own sour stink as he moved, and Alex winced in distaste.

Madness. The mattress – for so his questing hands identified it, the mildewed cover pocked with plastic buttons and split in places to let stuffing ooze through – reeked of madness and despair. An old scent, decades old but permeating.

It brought back the confused dream, and he felt himself all over to make sure that he was *Alex*, not that nameless female. He was as male as he'd ever been, which he discovered quite easily because he was also as na-ked as he'd ever been.

The scent. That was it. He had inhaled that scent and read the memory in it, such a strong and terrible one that it lingered even years later.

His head slowly clearing, he remembered. His desertion of the pack. His hitchhiking and bus riding. And then, out of nowhere, Simone and Donovan. Confinement. The long drive. Finally believing that she meant it, that she was taking them back to Drachenheim. The man coming out to see who they were. Simone and Donovan transforming, chasing the man into the house. The screams, the violent shadows moving across the windows. And then silence, for a long time.

They'd come back for Alex. He didn't know how they'd gotten him out of the van, because everything was a blank after he'd seen Donovan ap-proaching the rear door. By the pounding in his head, he surmised that he'd been clouted unconscious again, and that he still hadn't fully healed from the rough treatment.

Alex's stomach grumbled. After that dream, he felt more sick than hun-gry, but he was still empty in the middle and exhausted. Much as the female in his dream . . .

He sucked in a breath as he realized who she must have been. And where, pack help him, he must be.

It had all happened long before Alex himself had been born, but the elders sometimes talked about it in low tones if they didn't think any of the cubs could hear. How the pregnant female had insisted on joining a hunt when she shouldn't have, and gotten lost in the storm. How her mate had gone searching and been away for a week, only to return with a newborn cub and the news that the mother had died.

Except that she *hadn't* died. Her mate had brought her back, secretly, and locked her here. In this very room.

He was home.

A shudder twisted his body.

The scent, and the memory, belonged to Olivia Drachen. Mate of Malcolm, once leader of the pack. And mother of Simone.

Malcolm, perhaps as misguided by his love as Alex himself had been, had spared Olivia even after learning what she'd been forced to do for the sake of her life and her cub's. He'd imprisoned her in a cellarhold beneath an outbuilding, keeping her existence a secret from the pack, bringing her food and hoping for a miracle.

But the miracle had never come. Malcolm's love and kindness had almost led to their destruction. Olivia had escaped and killed several humans, nearly causing the pack to be discovered.

This room. She had been kept here, sleeping on this mattress until it absorbed so much of her scent and her mad-sweat that Alex could relive her worst moments as if they were memories of his own.

He scrambled off of it and brushed at himself, feeling unclean.

Drachenheim. He'd loved it as a cub, had cried when the pack had been forced to leave, and now that he was back he had never wanted to get away from a place so badly.

The darkness was total. Not even his eyes could penetrate it. He moved cautiously, trying to get a sense of the size of his cell. The outbuilding was a stable now by the horses he detected above him. The ceiling would have been oppressively low to Gideon, but the heavy beams were high enough above Alex's head that he didn't have to worry about concussing himself.

"Again," he muttered, rubbing at the still-tender spots where Donovan had probably taken great delight in hitting him.

The space was square, six paces to a side. Roomier, then, than a true cell. He barked his shins on a short flight of wooden steps, and held utterly still, listening for any reaction to the sound of the thump and his muffled curse. The horses upstairs were shifting and nickering, nervous but not yet in a panic. They could probably smell him as well as he could smell them. His predator-scent would have them on edge. He hoped that their response would give him a warning when Simone or Donovan returned.

The steps led up to a trap door in the ceiling. It was four feet square, resting heavy and flush. An experimental push proved to him that it was not about to budge. Heavy, but he could have lifted it. Locked, then. Barred, for all he knew.

Aside from the mattress, the remains of a ladder that had probably predated the stairs, and a stack of cartons and old furniture in one corner, this subterranean cell was empty. The humans who'd bought the ranch must have run out of space in the main house's attic and stored cast-off items here.

Alex made a second circuit, weaving back and forth with his hands raised, hoping against hope to find a pull-chain connected to a light bulb. No luck. He was doomed to darkness for as long as his captors chose to subject him to it.

One thing was for sure. He was not about to spend another moment on that vile, stinking mattress. He lifted it, grappling with the unwieldy thing in the blind dark, trying to get it up on end. It promptly flumped over, raising a murky stench. A horse whinnied shrilly. Alex covered his nose and mouth and retreated, thinking incoherently about spores and disease.

When the stink settled, he went back and wrestled the mattress until it leaned against the wall. He paused for another listen. Did Simone plan to let him sit in the dark until he was willing to cooperate?

"No way," Alex said in a low voice.

He went back to the pile of furniture and cartons, feeling his way and glad that his other senses were so sharp. His investigation found him nothing he could use as a weapon or a lever, unless he pried apart some of the chairs. Even then, they were so old and rickety that he knew they'd be no good against the door, and Donovan would probably just laugh if Alex rushed at him with a splinter in his grasp.

The pile did include a coarse, threadbare-feeling couch under all the boxes. Alex shifted them, deciding that if he had to sleep down here, this would be better than bare floor. He found what felt like clothes in the boxes, most musty but some still with the lingering scent of humans on them.

The cell was cold enough to be uncomfortable but not life-threatening, unlike the snowy extreme of that storm in his nightmare, or vision, or memory-dream. Alex dressed more for the mental value, not wanting to be naked and cowering before Simone and Donovan. He donned paint-smelling pants that fit fine around the waist and only needed a few turns of the cuff to be the right length, and a sweater that had holes in the elbows.

The last box, from which he'd been hoping for socks, turned out to contain blankets. He made himself a crude bed on the sofa. He did not so much sit on it as perch, his feet drawn up under him and his forearms resting on his knees, ready to spring down at a moment's notice.

That left him with little else to do but try not to think about his hunger. He didn't want to count up the hours since his last meal. It would be a futile effort anyway since he had no idea how much time had passed while he was unconscious. He didn't want to torment himself with thoughts of food. But of course, the more he tried not to, the more he couldn't help it.

This was worse than any hunger he'd previously known. He'd never missed so many meals before, never experienced anything this severe. It wasn't even the usual monthly upswing in appetite that matched the waxing moon. This was a raw and empty hole in him, and he imagined he could feel his body already cannibalizing his tissues in order to keep him going.

He doubted he could effect much of a change without draining himself dangerously. Even if he could, without food, he'd never be able to turn back. More, if he was left down here long enough, thirst would do him in long before hunger . . .

Only then did Alex realize that he'd been hearing the quiet but steady sound of dripping, and not paid any attention thanks to his bigger concerns. He held his breath and listened, trying to track the noise to its source. It led him to the stairs – no, *under* the stairs. When he wormed beneath the treads and supports, his hand splashed into a puddle. Groping, he found a cold metal spigot protruding from the concrete wall. He turned it. The dripping became a stream.

Alex thrust his face beneath it and slurped at the water, drinking until he thought he might slosh when he walked. It would give him the illusion of fullness, in body if not in mind. Returning to the boxes, he rummaged until he found a crate of old dishware, mostly plastic and hence nothing that could be shattered to produce an edge, but good enough to put under the spigot and collect more water.

His thirst assuaged, he resumed his spot on the couch. His time sense had gotten distorted, with no clues of daylight to guide him. His grandfather had always maintained that they'd know moonrise even if they were underground, but all Alex could assume was that the moon hadn't risen yet. That wasn't much help.

It might have been only minutes, or as long as an hour later, when the horses went into a spate of neighing and stamping. Some of them rattled the doors of their stalls as if hoping to break free and gallop away before the two-legged menaces dropped to four and tore their guts open.

He heard steps, instantly recognizing the sure and habitually stealthy tread of one of his kind. Then he caught the scent. His nose wrinkled. It was woods-wild and musky, a rutting-scent. Overpowering it, though, and bringing back his nightmare vividly, was the smell of fresh carrion.

Wood scraped as a bar was thrown back. Alex had the presence of mind to throw a hand over his eyes just as the door to his cell was flung up and open. It banged like a thunderclap on the stable floor, sending the horses into a new frenzy.

Light leapt down like a savage white animal. Alex squinted. Silhouettes blocked it, rays streaming around them like something out of a science-fiction movie, except these were no aliens in the accepted sense of the word.

Simone stood on the lip with a battery-powered lantern. Her hair was a scarlet tumble, and she had the flushed and smoky-eyed look of a female who'd just been thoroughly taken, thoroughly sated with rutting-pleasure. Donovan, close behind her, wore what he probably thought was a proud and proprietary grin, but to Alex it looked like a silent scream of horror at what he'd done, what he'd become.

Even if he sprang up, fleet as could be, they'd be ready. A kick from

Donovan would be all it would take to send him crashing back down.

"All comfy?" asked Simone. "I see you've redecorated."

Alex bared his teeth. He was adjusting more to the light now, able to see what Donovan held slung over his shoulder. Not that he needed to see it when he could smell it, and hear the thick patter of blood. He knew what they were going to do, wanted to plead, locked his jaws against giving Simone that satisfaction.

"You must be hungry," she said with a smile that made him want to rend her face from her skull. "Here."

At that, Donovan unlimbered his load and the two bodies sailed lifelessly through they air. They hit the concrete floor with a hideous sound of cracking bone and smacking flesh.

The man and woman, both older though in decent shape for their years, had been brutally mauled. Partly eviscerated, too, and with great chunks missing from their limbs. Alex knew all too well where those missing portions had gone. Blood seeped from the savaged wounds.

"No," he said. "I won't."

"You will," Simone said. "When you're hungry enough, you will. Starvation makes a very good spice. And then you'll be one of us. You'll have to be. Where else would you go? Who else would take you in?"

"I will never be one of you."

"We don't need him," Donovan snarled. "We'll raise up a pack of our own." He leaned close to Simone and nipped lovingly at her ear. Alex's gorge, already churning from the presence of the corpses, took a revolting lurch.

"I've explained that to you, my darling." She raked her fingers through his shaggy red mane and melted him with a look.

Alex turned away. He clenched a fist, not to strike but to bring the veins in his wrist into stark relief. He could chew through that thin skin easily . . .

Simone's voice cut through his thoughts. "You wouldn't do that, Alexander. Your will to live is too strong. And once you've eaten, once you've tasted the power that comes from the forbidden meat, you'll see. You'll change faster, heal faster, have senses keener than ever before. In time, you might learn to control the actions of lesser animals, as I have." She sent a glare over her shoulder, and in the stable, the horses went crazy with kicking and rearing. "You'll wonder why you ever even tried to resist."

She retreated with Donovan, and slammed the door, leaving Alex alone in the company of the dead.

* * *

Chapter 2
January 6, Tuesday
Early Morning

A fresh and silent fall of snow had come during the night, blanketing the landscape. Simone threw the kitchen door wide and stood on the porch, the arctic breeze caressing her nude body, errant snowflakes alighting in the russet of her hair.

By day, she could not see the lights from the town. All around her was white and still. They could have been the last sentient beings on the face of the earth. That would have suited her just fine. Her own small pack, and a world full of lesser creatures to hunt and kill.

Then again, wasn't that already how it was? The humans were clever animals, but animals still. They were meat that could speak, flesh that could invent. With minds cunning enough to make their society so demanding and tricky that Simone's kind couldn't pass unnoticed among them anymore.

Oh, they were cunning enough to weave sly laws and steal away what should have rightfully been hers. This land was her home. Generations of her ancestors had lived here, belonged here. It was wrong that the ranch should have been taken from them. Wrong that her father should have been driven out, a broken shell of a male with his years and his memories weighing on him heavy as boulders. Wrong that humans should come and try to claim it as theirs.

At last, a few of them had learned the error of their ways. It hadn't been that challenging of a hunt, given that they were old and one was still abed when she and Donovan burst upon them with flashing claws and gnashing teeth. But despite the ease of the kill, oh, it had been sweet.

What came later had been even sweeter, a long-denied and long-antici-pated pleasure.

She'd been waiting for just the right moment. So aware of him. His needs, his lusts, his urgent yet conflicting desires. The longer she toyed with him, the more unsettled his mind became. The more malleable. Bending to her will. Desperate to please. To do anything for her, in hopes of a fond look or a touch.

Once the humans had been dealt with, killed but only partially con-sumed because she had other plans for their carcasses, she and Donovan had explored their house. Simone kept one ear constantly toward the exte-rior and the van, listening for the sounds of Alexander trying to escape. A good thing about the new breed of vehicles. Their windows were nigh im-possible to break, even for one with the strength of a changeling.

Much work would be needed to make this place acceptable again. She wouldn't feel fully into her own until every remnant of the humans had been cleared away. Their furnishings and clothing burnt. Their scent driven out by windows thrown wide to the winter wind.

She had won back what was hers. It didn't matter that these humans might have had kin or friends who'd wonder what had become of them. Let them wonder! Let them come and investigate. More food for her pack. She would fight them all, to the last one. She would not be driven from her home again.

In time, perhaps even other changelings would come. There had to be more of her kind out there who were dissatisfied with the foolish old laws and sick of living on the edges of comfort. She would make this place a haven for them. The outcasts. The exiles. And they'd find one of the most wonderful truths of all – when enough outcasts gathered together, they stopped being outcasts.

Alexander would be the beginning. He'd resent it at first, as his entry into their pack was not an amiable one. Not with being kidnapped, stuffed into the back of a van, carted cross-country, and then gassed senseless.

A bug bomb, found beneath the sink and meant for wasps and spiders, had done that trick nicely. All she'd had to do was open the door, toss the hissing and spouting smoke canister into the van, slam it shut, and wait.

The foggy mist had been absurdly floral-scented to disguise the poison fumes. Not nearly powerful enough to kill one of them, but more than enough to temporarily incapacitate. That had enabled her and Donovan to move Alex's unconscious body down to the cellar beneath the stable. He'd be se-cure there, and it wasn't as if he would starve. No, he might think he would. He might even think he'd prefer it. But the instinct of the beast was too strong in them. Survival came before all else. He'd eat. He would eat, and then he'd be hers. Just as Donovan was.

No . . . no one would ever be hers as fully and completely as Donovan was. Cub of her womb, devoted follower, impassioned lover, he was son and mate and more to her now.

A delicious thrill went through her as she thought of it. He'd been angry about Alexander, but she knew that his anger only masked an unacknowledged fear. He was afraid Alex might supplant him in her affections. That she'd want Alex for her mate instead, leaving him bereft. That had never been her intention, but she'd seen right away that she had to make it very clear to Donovan. Before, in a fit of jealous rage, he decided to eliminate the competition.

Better to assure him in no uncertain terms where her affections truly lie. After delivering Alex to his confinement, they'd gone for a run and a hunt to explore the region around the ranch. She remembered it well, but Donovan had still been so young when they left that it was almost new to him.

They could have released a horse to hunt, but Simone decided to save those in case game grew scarce. Provided, of course, that they lived and didn't panic and batter themselves to death against the walls of their stalls. The fresh horsemeat would be their reserve, along with the well-stocked pantry. That one reminder of the humans, she was willing to keep.

But in the meantime, she and Donovan had hungered for the hunt. He'd never seen such snow before, deep and soft, muffling scents and hiding contours of the ground. It made him a cub again. The sight of him rolling in a drift, paws waving in the air, or burrowing his head and coming up with a *whuff* and a shake to fling snow in all directions, made her laugh as she hadn't laughed in years.

The woods surrounding the ranch were much as they'd always been. The snow cover was thinner beneath the trees, some of it held above by interlocking branches in a waiting trap that could suddenly give and shower them with the powder. Icicles gleamed like fangs.

She led, with Donovan loping effortlessly alongside. He seemed more eager than ever to show off for her, to make sure she saw the flex of lean muscle, the sheen of his pelt, the speed of his running and the agility of his leaps. In every way, he was a perfect specimen of a male in his youthful prime.

Pointless now to pretend he had no effect on her. She brushed against him, rubbed her flank along his, nipped teasingly at his ear. He brought her a bird, a small but tasty token and she wolfed it down bones, feathers and all. He crowded close to lap blood from her muzzle and continued, his tongue roughly smoothing her fur, long after any trace of the blood had been cleaned away. She groomed him in return, noting and relishing the tremble of his body.

Oh, how he wanted her. She could smell it, see it in his eyes, feel it in the suppressed tension of him. Simultaneously, he was in agony that she'd deny him. He could have overpowered her, had her by force. It might have cost him some skin, but a male his size could handle any female no matter how lithe and ferocious if he was willing to endure her claws. He held back out of his damned, doomed love for her. Or perhaps he thought she'd hate him because of Erala, whom he *had* overpowered.

Could she blame him for that when she'd all but driven him to it? And did it matter so much? Erala had been her daughter, yes, precious girl-cub coddled by the entire pack. Spoiled, really. Unwilling to listen to her mother even before Simone had been exiled. Father's little darling. Always taking his side, blindly and stubbornly. No, Erala never would have joined her. Whereas Donovan had.

He'd whined with pent-up passion, this magnificent male of hers, but instead of seizing her scruff in his teeth, he'd been cowering, submissive. His words about wanting to sire cubs on her must have spilled out of him unbidden, his true feelings as vivid as a bloodsplash on the snow, and he didn't know her reaction. Wanting her so much, yet paralyzed into inaction . . .

Simone had nuzzled him and crooned low in her throat. Her absolute power over him was such a warm and tantalizing joy that she was almost sorry to see the game come to an end. But she knew that if she kept him in this state of contradiction, he'd go mad and she'd lose him as surely as she'd lost the rest of her pack.

Donovan had been stunned when, therefore, she moved a few paces from him and presented herself, tail held to the side, neck craned that she might peer invitingly along the length of her body to meet his wide and startled eyes. He made a chuff so interrogative that she wouldn't have been surprised to see the steam of his breath form a question mark mid-air.

Speech was difficult when fully in beast-form, but she growled her assent. He rose slowly from his crouch and approached her, circling her as if thinking she might suddenly change her mind, whirl on him, lay him open to the bone. When she didn't, he came closer, breathing deep of the musky rut-scent that surrounded them. He could barely stand straight, and his breath puffed in quicker and quicker plumes.

He moved against her, side to side and nose to tail, probing with his muzzle at the swollen heat of her genitals. Simone, chuckling inwardly, dipped her head to view with great appreciation his glistening and rigid length protruding from its furry sheath. She licked. He froze, but she could feel the tremors transmitted to her where their bodies were pressed together.

She licked again, craning her neck to enable her to roll her tongue in a slow and coaxing circle. A shudder wracked Donovan and his soft howl of need brought an answering cry from her. Then, like one in the grips of a dream from which he feared he'd be rudely ejected, Donovan swung around and reared up on his hind legs. She had a clear glimpse of that jutting shaft as he braced his forelegs on her back, and then he drove forth with a sure and strong thrust.

The shock of that complete and intimate contact was like a thunderbolt to them both. Simone, the moment she felt him plunge hotly into her, was suddenly horrified. This was her son, and while she'd pushed him to it, she couldn't believe he'd actually done it. Donovan was like a thing possessed, his movements frantic to the point of brutality. He was rough and quick, forelegs clamped tight on her sides to yank her back against him as he lunged.

Her instant of horror was blown apart by the onslaught, and her own eager response to it. Nothing else mattered except for the glorious feel of him, and if it was over too soon, that was all right because there would be a next time. And a next. And a next.

It *was* over too soon, Donovan's climax a shattering explosion that crashed over him and made him bay to the sky. Simone, striving, bucked and writhed and sought every last bit of sliding friction as he spilled his seed and began to soften.

She keened with frustration at the thought she wouldn't reach her own release, but Donovan, aware of and inspired to new lusts by this evidence of her desire, stiffened before he could slip free of her and went at her again. She loosed a howl of her own as a bonfire roared through her, lava in her veins.

Her legs went weak and she would have fallen, but he looped an arm – yes, an arm, for he was halfway between man and beast forms now – under her waist and lifted her hips. Having spent once already, he was in better control for this encore and serviced her so diligently and relentlessly that Simone thought she'd never stop climaxing.

But young and energetic though he was, and as determined as he seemed to go until moonset and beyond, it was all too much for Donovan too and he strained against her, the both of them poised in stark, immobile relief for a timeless moment before they collapsed together, chests heaving, limbs entangled.

Even now, on the porch of the house with the breeze gusting snow-flakes against her rosy skin, Simone had to fan herself from the mere memory.

They had hunted no more that night, with good reason. It was a wonder they'd made it back to the ranch at all. An hour later, with the resiliency of such a fine young stud as he was, Donovan wanted more. She was glad to oblige.

They'd passed much of the night in rutting, trying out combinations of forms and positions and locations. The humans' bed, their bathtub, the rag rug before the huge fireplace. At one point, Simone had regained enough of her wits to remember they needed to provide Alexander his meal, and they'd gone out to the stable with the sweat of their rut-play still drying on their skin. He wouldn't have been able to miss that, and she no longer cared. Let him think what he would. He'd soon be in no place to judge.

At last, neither of them able to bestir themselves for anything more than murmuring kisses and gentle caresses, which seemed a strange end to a night of such frenzied lust, they'd fallen into an exhausted slumber.

The morning had revived Donovan. Filled with renewed strength and purpose, he'd set off at once to hunt. Simone smiled at this adherence to old custom. He'd be wanting to bring back some large piece of prey, a token by the male to his mate, proving his willingness to provide in case the rutting was fruitful.

She placed her palm on her bare belly. It was far too soon to tell, for even the first subtle changes in a female's scent wouldn't come after only a few hours. But if his stamina and enthusiasm were even half of what he'd demonstrated last night, she supposed it wouldn't be long before she was with cub.

The idea warmed her with a happy glow quite different from the one brought on by passion. More cubs, who would be raised her way. Weaned from the teat onto manflesh, so that from the beginning they would wholly belong to her and never have reason to wonder why their scent differed from others of their kind. Because, if she had her way, they'd never meet others who weren't just like them.

The land was white and the sky was a leaden grey, so the bright red car caught her eye at once. It was at the end of the driveway, which had been plowed when they arrived but was buried now under the fresh fall of snow. A woman got out and went to the post that held the mailbox, and began brushing snow from it to read the name.

Simone retreated into the kitchen, and from there to the bedroom where she put on her clothes. They'd get ruined if she had to change and kill, but she was hoping to send this inquisitive human on her way with some story. The man and his wife had . . . what had they done? Gone to visit kin? That would work unless this unwelcome guest was their kin. They'd been called away? Left her to look after the place? Yes, that might do.

She kept an eye on the red car through the various windows as she came back downstairs. It was creeping up the driveway unsurely, like a timid little animal, like the driver was unaccustomed to snow and thought that at any moment, a glacial crevasse might open up and swallow the car whole.

The red car stopped behind the van. Simone cursed herself for leaving it out and visible, and for leaving the kitchen lights on. If she'd had the presence of mind to have Donovan take the van out behind the stable, she could have lain low and stayed quiet and the human would have concluded no one was home. Unless she was some meddling relative or neighbor who had a spare key. There hadn't been any indication that others besides the man and his wife dwelt here.

Waiting by the door, she held the curtain at the side window open just enough to see, without letting it look like she was watching. The human got out of the car again, a small female in an open coat, a sweater, and dove-colored pants. Her hair, beige-blond, fell around her pale face. There was something familiar about her . . .

As the girl leaned back into the car to sling a purse on her shoulder, it came to Simone. She was astonished, incredulous.

Her? But Donovan had killed her!

All right, it was remotely possible that she'd somehow survived, but even so she would be in a hospital somewhere, breathing through a machine. She could not, simply could *not*, be walking toward the porch of Drachenheim without any signs of injury. And how had she found them? What was she doing?

All of the questions buzzed like bees in the disturbed hive of Simone's mind. She would have answers for each of them, and perhaps a few words for Donovan later. Maybe he'd killed the wrong girl? But no, he swore he knew who she was, the one who was Alexander's . . .

A tentative knock sounded on the door and interrupted the fevered flow of Simone's thoughts. Smoothing her blouse and her hair, she opened it with a polite but puzzled smile that cost her much to maintain.

"Can I help you?"

The girl spent a long moment gawking, thoroughly nonplussed. It gave Simone ample time to study her in return.

Yes, she was the same one. If this was Donovan's idea of a sure kill . . .

"Mrs. Kendall? I'm sorry to bother you, and I'm probably in the wrong place, but I was hoping you could help me."

"Kendall?"

Ah, she realized, the name on the mailbox. The man and his wife who were probably having their entrails chewed this very minute. She hoped so. The longer Alex tried to resist the inevitable, the less appetizing the corpses would be by the time he gave up and got down to it.

"Isn't this the Kendall house?"

"Not anymore," Simone said, more harshly than she meant. "Who are you?"

"My name's Aiden Ferguson," said the girl. She looked up at Simone with awed but shy grey eyes. "I asked in town and they said that Dr. and Mrs. Kendall lived here now. But I'm looking for the people that used to live here. I'm looking for the Drachen family."

Just then, the wind shifted and Simone fully caught the girl's scent. The truth struck her between the eyes with all the dazzling force of a sledgehammer blow.

"You're . . ." She couldn't finish.

It was impossible. She was one of them? How could that be? How had he not known? Donovan might not be the cleverest thing on two feet or four, but neither was he stupid. How could he have overlooked something as obvious as this?

Mentally backtracking, she said, "I'm Simone Drachen."

The girl sniffed delicately, but not delicately enough. An unknowing observer might have thought she had a mild cold. Not Simone. The cubling was seeking the scent, in a very unpracticed way.

"I think you'd better come in, child," said Simone. She stepped back and let Aiden precede her into the house, closing the door firmly behind her.

*   *   *

"Damn it, Fergs," said Birdie Yale. "This was not the plan."

She'd slept in and hey, who could blame her? The past few days had been pretty hectic. Finding out that your new, nice, sweet, innocent best friend had been turned into something that wasn't a vampire and wasn't a werewolf but had qualities of both would shake anybody up.

Add to that a whirlwind trip to visit a man the rest of the world believed was dead, get the skinny on a race of shapeshifters who'd lived among humanity since the dawn of time – mostly benign and uninvolved but for the few psychos who decided that them's good eating – and then deal with the selfsame friend chowing down on one of the tourist attractions . . . so her nerves had been strung a little tight lately.

Was it any wonder, then, that once her head had hit the pillow, she'd gone out like the proverbial light? They'd left Ashland around noon over

Ghostman's objections and the going had been fine as long as they were on I-5. But the moment they'd taken the turnoff onto Highway 3 and headed up into the mountains, all bets were off. Even with the chains, and Birdie'd had to do some pretty heavy flirting with the gas station attendant to get him to do her the favor of putting them on.

The town of Drachenheim was dinky by anyone's standards. It was the sort of place that eked out a living providing goods and services to seasonal hikers and fishers, but the locale wasn't prime for skiing and so in the depths of winter, they might as well have folded up the houses and rolled up the sidewalks and flown south.

One motel was open, and it lent new meaning to the word 'dive.' Hot and cold running roaches, double beds that looked like someone picked them up cheap at a whorehouse yard sale, water-spotted walls, burnt-orange carpet with paths worn between door-bed-bathroom, and a black and white television older than Birdie herself. But by then, it was heaven. Just to be indoors, out of the snow.

Neither of them was in the mood to go out, but neither of them was hungry for pizza either and that severely limited their options. They'd walked two blocks through the snow to a diner that was nothing to write home about but at least served plentiful portions.

By the time they got back to the room, Birdie was already regretting the extra-spicy chili that had sounded like a good idea when she'd seen it on the menu. She'd been worried that she might be up half the night doing the outhouse fandango, but her body wanted sleep more than anything.

Sleep. Eleven solid hours of it. And it had felt awfully damn good until she woke up a few minutes ago, checked the clock, scraped her tongue around the inside of a mouth that still tasted of chili despite a liberal application of Crest, and peered over at the other bed to find it empty.

That was enough to get her up in a hurry. She didn't even have the momentary luxury of dismissing it as "oh, she's just in the bathroom," because the bathroom door was open and she had a better view than she wanted of the cracked tile and the cat-puke yellow shower curtain.

Only when she pulled back the nasty-textured drapes and saw that the parking slot in front of the unit was empty, instead of containing a sporty red VW like it ought, did Birdie really realize what her meek and mild little chum had gone and done. She had known all along but hadn't admitted it to herself, clinging to the delusion that if she didn't say it, it wouldn't turn out to be so.

"Damn it," she said again, and hurried to get dressed.

She'd hoped for a shower this morning even if she had to arm-wrestle the roaches for possession of the tub, but that was no longer an issue. Fergs had taken it on herself to pay an early-morning visit on the Drachens without her.

Okay, so maybe she had her reasons and maybe they were valid – there was no way of knowing how the Drachens would react to Aiden turning up on their doorstep, but having a full human in tow would probably just make things worse. And Birdie doubted she'd be much help if the changelings did decide that Aiden had to die; the only assist she could offer her friend was to die right along with her because if Donovan was any example, a whole pack would make short work of the two of them.

Still, for pete's sake, she had come all this way. Driven Aiden around. Footed the bills because Aiden had run out the door without her purse. Didn't she deserve to be in on the end game?

She got out the door into the brisk winter light, pawing in her purse for her keys, when she stopped and smacked herself in the head. No keys, of course. Aiden was no more likely to know how to hotwire a car than she was to bellydance. And no car. What was she thinking? That once the keys were in her fist the car would automatically appear?

"Dummy."

Drachenheim, like most wide spots in the road, had been more palatable by night when merciful darkness concealed the dismal truth. Maybe once, it had been a pretty place. Some of the buildings looked like there'd once been a push to do a theme, like Solvang or Leavenworth or those other Scandanavian/Bavarian/German villages specializing in bratwurst, beer, guys in lederhosen, and Oktoberfest. It hadn't worked in Drachenheim, and the scallops and decorative woodwork here and there only made the rest of it look sadder.

Not a taxi in sight and she wished she could say she was surprised. Didn't appear to be much of a bus system, either. And by the sidelong frowning glances she got from people on the street, she somehow had the feeling that a busty gal with faux-snakeskin pants, multiple earrings in each ear, and a burgundy lock bobbing at the front of her unkempt curls wasn't going to have much luck begging a ride.

What was she going to do? Hoof it? Yeah, right, as if! The Drachen farm, if it was still the Drachen farm, was miles out of town. They'd tried cruising by on their way to the motel, but the dearth of streetlights had made them give up. Ghostman's hand-drawn map and directions had been on the dashboard, too, so Birdie didn't think she could even find it on her own.

"Okay, I'll give you an hour," she said as if Aiden could hear. "One hour, and then I'm doing something about this."

The only one near enough was an elderly dude with a newspaper and the world's ugliest dog on a leash, and he gave her a narrow, suspicious, disapproving look. She blew him a kiss off the tips of her fingers and went back to the diner, atoning for the chili by having cold cereal for breakfast. Not even three cups of coffee perking through her bloodstream could give her any bright ideas.

"An hour," she repeated, under her breath. What she'd do when time was up, she hadn't a clue.

*   *   *

When the red-haired woman opened the door, Aiden could barely summon the wit to speak. Beside Birdie, she felt like a boy. Beside this woman, *Birdie* would have felt like a boy.

Faltering, she stammered out her introduction, sure that she'd come to the wrong place and would find no answers here. But then she caught the woman's scent, complex and wild and strange, and knew she was right. They were of the same sort. Had to be.

She entered the kitchen, and reeled from the dizzying barrage of smells. She didn't understand half of them but picked up, very clearly, a presence of violence, danger, and sex. Blood had been spilled here. Recently.

The woman, Simone, was regarding her with curiosity and a greedy hunger that made Aiden all the more nervous. She held tight to her new Wal-Mart purse and made no move to take off her coat although she was stifling. Cold was barely anything to her now but old habits died hard and she'd bundled up well before leaving the motel.

"Let me get you something to drink," Simone said. Without asking, or needing to, she poured Aiden a tall glass of whole, creamy milk.

"Thank you." Aiden sat at the table when Simone motioned to a chair. "I shouldn't have just shown up like this, but I didn't know what else to do. I was hoping you could help me."

"Of course." Simone patted her hand, and lingered, until the heat of her skin made Aiden yearn to pull away. That look, that hungry look . . . "Why don't you tell me about it?"

"First, you are one, aren't you?"

"A changeling?"

Aiden closed her eyes briefly in relief. "So you do know."

"Yes. And you're one of us too, but . . ."

"I wasn't always." Aiden pushed back the hair at the side of her neck.

They'd faded some, the crescent scars, she'd seen in the mirror earlier that morning while Birdie was sound asleep. But they were still visible, whiter against her pale skin.

Simone did not move except to drop her jaw slightly, but something flashed in her eyes. Aiden hurried on.

"I know that someone like me, someone who wasn't . . . who wasn't born this way . . . is against your pack laws. I was hoping you could tell me a way to fix it. Cure it."

Simone rocked back in her chair and pealed amazed laughter at the ceiling. "Of course! That explains everything!"

"Sorry?"

"I should have thought of it myself!" She tipped forward, the legs of her chair thumping on the floor, and seized Aiden hard by the chin. Her fingertips skated over the scars. "Bitten. You were bitten. To save your life?"

"Yes." Aiden tried to pull away, disliking the feel of Simone's touch, but the woman's grip was too strong.

"What a brilliant idea! I can't believe I didn't even . . . oh, what I fool I've been. All this time, I could have been bringing others into the pack, recruiting likely souls. Humans, yes, low and wretched, but I could raise them up. Elevate them. Bestow upon them this incredible gift and earn their undying gratitude."

Aiden succeeded in freeing herself and scooted her chair away from the table. "The law, though . . ."

"Pff. The law. And to think I'd been so desperate to win over the others, yet it simply never occurred to me that I could have made my own pack . . . how could I have been such a fool?"

She laughed again, a bright and beautiful and thoroughly insane laugh. Her teeth glittered, longer and sharper than were right for her mouth. Her blue-green eyes danced brightly.

"Please," Aiden said. "If you know anything about a cure, please help me."

Simone broke off and looked at Aiden as if *she* were the crazy one. "A cure? Are you serious?"

"Yes, please." She spread her small hands and stared at them, in her mind still seeing them tacky with blood and feathers. "I can't be like this. Not me."

"Well, you wouldn't have been my first choice for the bite," Simone said with a snort, "but what's done is done. How could you possibly want to give up what you've gained? The speed, the strength, the healing, the power? You're other than human now, girl, *above* human. Better. You should be thankful!"

"You don't understand." Tears stung Aiden's eyes. "I'm no hunter. I don't want to hurt anything, let alone kill. I'm so afraid that I won't be able to control it, too, and I'll hurt my friends."

"Control can be learned." Simone patted her again, but with an ersatz sympathy that didn't fool Aiden for a minute. "All you need is guidance. Didn't he tell you anything?"

"No. There wasn't time. He . . . how'd you know it was a he?"

"When you're such a pretty young female? Now, tell me how it happened."

"That's not important. I need to know if you can help me."

"If that's what you really want."

"It is." Aiden stifled a sob. "More than anything. I just want to be normal again."

"Then I'll help you. Poor child." She toyed with a few strands of Aiden's hair. "You can rely on me."

Despite her severe misgivings, knowing that she had nowhere else to turn, Aiden told a very abbreviated version of her tale The milk sat untouched on the table as she talked about Alex, about falling in love with him.

Her voice fell to a hushed whisper as she got to the night of Donovan's attack and what had come after. Her eyes were fixed unseeingly on her hands, in her lap. She sensed Simone leaning closer, the better to hear you with, my dear, and when Aiden finished a long silence unspooled between them.

"That's quite a story," Simone said at last. "So this Ghostman knew about our pack, you say. And told you how to find us."

"I'm sorry if that's against the rules. He was only trying to help. I was so lost and confused and didn't know what was going on."

"He told you about our laws."

"Yes, that's how I knew it was wrong for Alex to have done what he did. I also think that Donovan, the one who attacked me, must have broken another."

"The eating of the forbidden meat," Simone said.

"How'd you know?"

Just then, the kitchen door opened in a swirl of snow and a shaggy form stepped in. The carcass of a deer was slung over his shoulder, its hooves and antlers dragging. The smell of blood and meat was everywhere, filling the room like smoke from a blaze. The creature, whose lamplike eyes went wide at the sight of Aiden, was seven feet tall and covered in red hair, with a long toothy muzzle better suited to a crocodile or a dragon than a wolf.

The claws . . . those were claws that she recognized all too well.

A scream snagged in her throat. She bolted up, but Simone, fast as a shot, kicked the chair into her legs. Tangled, Aiden went down. Her arm hit the table as she fell and the milk glass spilled, rolled, shattered on the brick floor.

"Because," said Simone with a smile in her voice, "Donovan is my son."

"*Her?*" It was an inhuman, astounded bark. The deer slapped wetly as he dropped it. "What's she doing here? What's she doing alive?"

Aiden scrambled, kicking loose of the chair and springing upright. Pure panic took over her brain, all rational thought ceasing and escape being her only driving impulse. A change was burning through her, bringing blondish downy fuzz in a tickling pelt as she leapt up. She didn't know whether to fight it or give in, but the choice wasn't hers.

Simone slammed the heels of her hands against the table. A heavy, solid-wood construction though it was, the table slid like a hockey puck and crashed into Aiden. Her breath burst out. Her back hit the kitchen wall. She was pinned there, a belt of pain across her middle, the short but sharp claws that tipped her fingers digging shallow trenches in the wood.

Donovan, reverting partway to human, drew in a deep breath through his nose and snorted it out disbelievingly. He shook his head and turned to Simone in bewilderment. "She . . . I don't . . . she wasn't . . ."

"Our troublesome little Alexander," Simone said, "our audacious cubling, our stubborn guest with all his lofty ideals and holier-than-thou attitude, was willing to do anything to save this little sweetmeat. Anything at all, whatever it took, laws or no laws."

"He didn't!"

"Oh yes he did."

Seams ripped and cloth parted. Aiden's bones creaked and cracked. Her downy pelt was fur now, beige and faintly dotted with darker rosettes. Donovan watched her with a horrid, evil fascination. She'd heard them talking and was dimly aware that something important had been said, but the change had her fully in its grasp. She braced her spine against the wall and pushed with all her might.

Simone had been leaning casually on the table, her weight sufficient to keep Aiden trapped. As the table legs skidded on bricks, the red-haired woman was knocked off balance. Aiden had breathing room again and sucked in as much air as she could hold. She sprang straight up like a cat just as Donovan recovered and shoved the table back the other way. It collided with nothing but wall and Aiden landed crouched atop it, teeth bared and eyes blazing.

"Catch her," Simone said. "But don't harm her, not a hair of her pelt."

The male – Aiden no longer cared what his name was; he was male and an enemy – reached for her with two massive hand-paws. She tore at his arms, gouging hair and flesh. He yipped and recoiled enough for her to shoot past him.

She hit the floor on all fours, running, and would have been out the open door and into the snow before either of them could get to her, if not for the deer. She slipped trying to jump over it, and in that moment of clumsiness, Simone hurled a copper-bottomed saucepan with deadly accuracy.

A gong went off in Aiden's head. She veered off course, ears ringing, and rebounded from the doorjamb to sprawl on the floor. Her limbs skittered around spasmodically. She shook her head, blinking madly, stars wheeling behind her eyes, bleeding from a split scalp.

Donovan was there before she could regain her scrambled senses. He lifted her like she was a paper doll, immobilizing her by clamping her arms to her sides and holding her firmly around the waist, her back tight against the solid muscles of his chest. She raked the air with her hindclaws but wasn't jointed the right way to scratch at his legs. His hot snort of amusement and triumph blew her hair into her eyes.

"Not so fast, little one," Simone said. "You wanted my help."

"You . . . you . . ." A million questions, and she couldn't put any of them in coherent words.

A new and different terror dumped adrenaline into her system as she realized just what that stiff bar was that prodded at the small of her back, and how defenseless she was, with her clothes in ruins so that she wore little else but fur.

She could smell his excitement, first from the hunt and then from having a different sort of prey, female and vulnerable, struggling in his arms. The more she fought him, the more he liked it, rubbing against her backside with increasingly lewd urgency.

Simone set her hands on her hips and cocked her head, looking Aiden over. "Tsk, tsk. Is this how you repay our hospitality and my kind welcome? To answer all those questions you're unable to ask, yes, I am Simone Drachen, daughter of Malcolm. I was driven out of the pack long ago for the same crime that saw my mother imprisoned and killed, although mine was committed by choice and hers out of desperation. I wanted greater power, and I wanted revenge on the humans who stole our home. I also wanted revenge on the pack that cast me out, but I also hoped to win some of them to my side. I succeeded with Donovan here, and now I've regained my son, and my ancestral home."

"Let me go," Aiden said. It wasn't a beg, and she was inordinately proud of herself for it. Because what she wanted to do was scream and plead and cry. Except she knew that those reactions would arouse Donovan even more that her continued struggles.

"But you're one of us now," Simone said in an attempt at a soothing tone. "Or, very nearly. You need a pack, Aiden, and we need more members in ours. There's a place for you here. You belong here."

She shuddered. "Please, no."

"What other pack would take you? Your Alexander abandoned you because he knew the truth. Gideon, the ever-righteous and sanctimonious Gideon, would snap your neck in a heartbeat."

"The hypocrite," snarled Donovan, and pressed his hips firmly against Aiden.

"Even if you could find others of our kind, scattered as they are," Simone continued, "what makes you think they'd welcome you? Only we, who've dispensed with all those ridiculous old laws, are willing to accept you among us. You'll have a home here, Aiden. A family."

"I don't want to."

"Idiot girl, what choice do you think you have?" Simone glanced down, and chuckled. "Stop that, Donovan, the poor thing is terrified that you're going to throw her face-down over the table and deflower her before she knows what hit her."

A tiny, plaintive wail of fear came from Aiden's throat.

Donovan quit rubbing, and actually sounded abashed. "It's the thrill of the hunt, the heat of the chase, that's all. She's nothing to me, Simone, I swear."

"Good." Simone stepped closer, and Aiden was sandwiched between them. Simone raised a hand and caressed, lovingly, the side of Donovan's face.

Disgust would have brought Aiden's breakfast up, if she'd had any. Naïve, she might have been, but totally ignorant, she was not. The way they were looking at each other was more than enough. More than she could stand.

"What do we do with her, then?" Donovan asked.

"She needs some time to think," said Simone. "And perhaps some additional persuasion is in order. She must be hungry, too."

Aiden was hungry, ravenous, the demands of the change on her metabolism asserting themselves in a gnawing emptiness, although she couldn't imagine eating a bite without throwing it back up.

"That should give them both something to think about," Donovan said with a cruel laugh.

She didn't know what he meant, what they had in mind, but was so glad in that instant to understand that Donovan wasn't going to rape her that she didn't really care. Nothing could be worse than his touch, nothing.

He carried her, with Simone in the lead, out of the house and across a snow-covered yard. Aiden could see Birdie's car, and a wild flare of hope lit up in her. Birdie! She had mentioned Birdie's part in all this during the course of her explanation to Simone, but she had purposefully made it sound like she'd come the rest of the way alone. She wasn't sure why she'd done it, obeying some instinct or maybe just ashamed that she'd deceived her friend, but now she was thankful. Birdie knew where she'd gone, and when Aiden didn't get back in contact, hopefully Birdie would figure out that something had gone wrong.

Just what good that would do, Aiden had no guesses. Birdie was many things, but a one-woman commando team wasn't among them. And even an actress like her would have a hell of a time convincing anyone that there were werewolves. She might be able to get the local sheriff out on the grounds that a girl had gone missing, but there would be no way to prepare them for this. Aiden didn't think a full SWAT team would be prepared for this.

The long, low building ahead was a stable. One side was ringed by a split-rail fence, and a door high in the wall promised a hayloft. Simone opened the lower doors and they went in, into a warm and fragrant space filled with the frightened sounds of horses. Aiden had quick glimpses of rolling, white-rimmed eyes and the tossing of maned heads.

Braced for being tied up and thrown in a stall, or maybe the hayloft so she couldn't get down without falling and risking broken bones, Aiden was surprised when they took her to a small trap door.

They were going to entomb her in the dark. In the dark and in the cold.

A new fear that had nothing to do with Donovan came bellowing up from the depths of Aiden's heart. She shrieked high and piercingly. Her mind was years ago, in the car, the snowbound car with drifts pouring in through the broken windows, cold and dark, trapped and helpless, freezing and sobbing and unable to move, while her mother sprawled lifeless in the seat beside her with her flesh turning to ice.

Her shriek was cut off when Simone slapped her and brought blood to her lip. She heard, in the silence after her scream ended, something rustle down there. Every monster from every movie she'd ever seen jostled for center stage in her frantic imagination, but the one that pushed all the others aside was the most horrible of all — her mother's frozen, mangled corpse brought hideously back to life and ready to embrace her with dead, icy arms.

Simone lifted the latch and moved the bar, and heaved the door open to reveal a black hole in the ground. Before she could begin a new scream, Donovan pitched her head over heels into the pit.

* * *

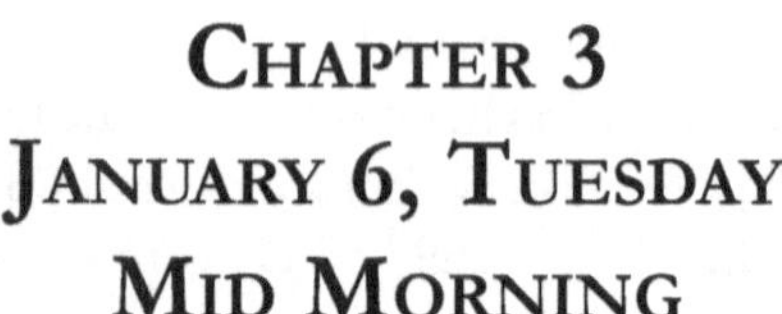

CHAPTER 3
JANUARY 6, TUESDAY
MID MORNING

Jeff was grainy-eyed and in no mood to be overwhelmed with the nostalgia of homecoming. He'd only been a gangling adolescent the last time he'd seen Drachenheim, and it hadn't been much to look at then. Now, especially at the end of a drive that had been grueling in the extreme, between the conditions of the road and the way Gideon maintained his silent glower, the sight of the town depressed him.

Grandfather's reaction was the exact opposite. He'd spent most of the trip sleeping in the back seat, but as they cruised slowly through the streets, their big wheels churning up muddy slush, the elder sat up straight, looking wistfully and with fond remembrance at the shabby buildings.

"We were happy here," he said to Gideon.

Gideon uttered a noncommittal grunt.

"What now?" Jeff asked. "The ranch was sold, remember? What are we supposed to do, go up and knock and say hi?"

"Simone will come," Gideon said. "We'll be waiting."

"Great plan. Got anything a tad more specific?"

"I'm tiring of your insolence, Jeffrey."

"Well, fine. I'm tiring of your whole attitude. I'm tiring of all of this. Shit." He banged a fist on the dashboard. "We spend our lives slinking from town to town like raccoons going from one garbage can to the next, we can't make friends, we can't trust anyone, we've got no home . . . what's the use? Shit."

A hand fell on his shoulder, another on Gideon's. Grandfather warned them both with a look. "It's been a long night. Before we do anything, we need food, and sleep."

By way of response, Gideon eyed Jeff scathingly and drove into the core of Drachenheim, through the bustling downtown with its diner, general store, bank-slash-post-office, and motel. A brown sign with a picnic area symbol on it came up, and Gideon turned off the road.

The entrance to the picnic area was supposed to be closed off by a chain, but others had been here before them and cut the lock so that humps of link poked above the snow like the spine of an immense snake. The open space was crisscrossed with ATV and snowmobile tracks, sled marks, and footsteps punched deep through the crust.

The Chevy slipped a little in the snow. Gideon parked it beneath some trees, with branches hanging so low they scraped the roof. It was a spot that would be out of sight on a casual drive-by inspection.

Grandfather bent to the floor of the back seat and rummaged through their hastily-packed provisions. Jeff peered down and groaned. "Are we stuck with cold canned stew, or can we get something in town?"

"The impression I had was that you didn't see much of value in Drachenheim," Gideon said.

"There's *food*, though. Look, I'll walk. It's not that far. I'll bring back something."

Gideon started to object, but Grandfather stepped in. "Let the cub go. The exercise and fresh air will do him good and improve his mood."

Jeff bit back an objection or two of his own. He was getting a little sick of being called cub all the time, and if anybody needed his mood improved, it was Gideon. But he wasn't up for another argument, and all he wanted right now was to get out and away. Food was a secondary concern.

He trudged through the snow, not minding the cold but thinking how much easier it would be to change and go on all fours. But he couldn't take the chance, not in broad daylight, not in a populated – barely – place such as this. He was stuck with human form for now.

The general store had a sandwich counter, but that didn't open until eleven. He kept going. The diner up ahead was probably his best bet. Could grab a few burgers, at least.

People were watching him with the suspicious small-town looks usually reserved for his ilk: long hair, leather jacket, boots. The bike would have completed the ensemble, but it was still strapped to the rear of the motor home and he would probably never see it again.

The scent of frying bacon was a lot more appetizing outside of the diner. Inside, it was a greasy cloud overhanging the other scents of eggs, pancakes, and coffee. He paused in the entryway to knock snow off his boots, stamping the ribbed rubber mat. A blackboard on the wall announced the specials in smudgy pink and blue pastel chalk.

A waitress who looked worn out finally got around to him and disinterestedly took his order for six ham-and-egg breakfasts to go. He waited, keenly conscious of the eyes upon him and the comments, pitched so that he was definitely supposed to hear them despite their seeming confidentiality. A group of young men, the kind who looked like they'd be lucky to make it out of high school by age twenty, were particularly obnoxious.

Jeff willed them to let it go. His blood was still simmering from his conflict with Gideon, worry for Alex and the future preyed on his mind, and if someone started it up with him now, he was too grimly sure what the consequences would be.

Ignoring their remarks to the best of his ability, he paid for his order and accepted the six plastic containers in a brown paper bag. It made for a tall stack, and he had to crane his neck to see over the top as he made his way back to the door.

The instincts of his beast's nature served him well. He didn't see it, but was aware of the foot stuck deliberately into his path. He deftly avoided it and, without turning to confront whoever had tried to trip him, continued toward the door. He reached it, groping for the handle around his load of food.

It opened and he heard a gasp. Then a voice.

"Handsome, I'm telling you, we gotta stop meeting like this."

Only a quick juggling act prevented six orders of ham and eggs dumping all over the floor. He got them safely set down on top of a coin-operated newspaper vending machine and goggled into Birdie Yale's hazel eyes.

"Huh-wha?" he said with all the wit and intelligence that would have made any sensible female run in the opposite direction.

This female wasn't sensible, and threw her arms around him. Lots of curvy girl was pressed against him as the entire occupancy of the diner quit even pretending to mind their own business.

"I am *so* glad to see you, you've got no idea," she said. "Your timing and sense of location is perfect, just perfect. We need to talk."

*　　*　　*

Alex Greye was on the couch, eyes tightly shut, his body rocking in short back-and-forth motions. He was trying, with no real success, to take himself *away*. To distract his mind so that he didn't keep thinking about his stomach, and the ravening pangs in it. But every time he started to make it, all his other worries would jostle up and get in the way.

Hours had passed since Simone and Donovan had dumped the corpses. Maybe days. Time had become elastic, stretching and snapping in patterns that made no sense. He hoped that his hunger would reach a peak and stop there, but so far it only kept waxing, like a runaway moon getting bigger and bigger on a lethal collision course.

He heard them approaching, first by the warning cries of the horses. And then by a shriek and the sounds of struggling, coming closer. Incoherently, he thought that maybe they'd decided carrion, cooling and stiff in the cold cellar, wouldn't be so appealing to him as fresh, live human prey.

They'd have to open the trap door. It would be his only chance to get out. But they'd be expecting just such a move. How to do it?

And then, like a lightning bolt, like a slap, he recognized the shrieking voice just as it was cut off by a hard slap.

He couldn't believe it. Wouldn't. It had to be a trick, some cruel, crazy trick.

The door was yanked open. Thin daylight streamed in, enough to blind Alex. He had a blurred perception of a dark shape hurtling at him, trailing a scream.

His other senses moved him even as his eyes failed. He caught her, and her scent was all around him. Poignantly familiar but subtly different, the *my-kind* scent now instead of the human scent. His hands met a silky-soft pelt and warm flesh beneath.

Aiden screamed anew and lashed out at him, in a complete panic. The door slammed shut again. Darkness engulfed them, darkness in which the laughter of Simone and Donovan could clearly be heard.

Claws scored Alex's cheek. He wrestled her arms to her sides.

"It's me! Aiden, it's me, it's Alex."

The fight went out of her in a rush. He could feel her chest rising and falling rapidly against his, the gentle push of her downy-furred bosom through shreds of a sweater.

"A . . . Alex?"

"Yeah."

He let go of her, having no business holding her even though she'd probably strike at him again, lacerate his face, slice out his eyes. He'd done this to her, all of it, first been careless enough to let this attraction develop, then drawing Donovan to her and nearly getting her killed, and finally, the worst act of all, the bite that made her into something inhuman. He closed his eyes and stood motionless in the dark, trying to ready himself for the sharp pain of her claws. Pain that he'd earned, that he deserved.

"Alex, it's really you?" He heard her sniff, but through her tears she couldn't be picking up much in the way of scents. "What are you doing here? How . . . ?"

"I was going back to Trinity Bay," he said. "To find you. To apologize. I don't blame you if you hate me for it. I just wanted a chance to explain, and say that I'm sorry."

She was crying. He could smell the salt tang of her tears.

"I never meant things to turn out like this, Aiden, I swear. It was all my fault. If not for me, Donovan never would have found you. He would have killed you. I . . . I couldn't stand there and watch you die."

Her hand, the fingers shortened and furry, the palm and undersides of the fingers thickened into pads, touched his face. The scratches on his cheek were already healing but her fingertips came away wet with his blood. She made an anguished sound.

"I hurt you."

"It's nothing. I'm the one who hurt you."

"I don't hate you, Alex."

"What? You . . . you don't? But . . ."

"I know what you did, and why. I know about the law you broke. But you did it to save my life. You did it because . . . because you cared about me."

He could barely breathe with the hope that she understood after all.

Now both of her hands were on his face, and he felt a tickling against his skin as the shape of them altered, her fur melting away as they resumed human form.

"You were going to come back?" she asked in a whisper. "You weren't going to leave me?"

"I didn't know what to do," he said, choking up. "Jeff was sure that Gideon would flay me alive if he found out. I thought you'd hate me forever. There wasn't any time to think. Gideon was in a hurry to leave but the further we got from Trinity Bay, the more wrong it was. I had to go back."

"I wasn't even there. Birdie whisked me away before it was even light out. But how'd you end up here?"

Head down, he told her of his bus ride, the fate of Bill Hartford, and what had happened when they'd reached the ranch. At that point, Aiden hissed in shock.

"The bodies. Yes, I can smell them . . ."

"They're over by the stairs," he said. "Simone . . . she wants me to . . ."

"No!"

"That's her plan. To starve me until I have to eat. Once I've done that, I'm damned forever. She thinks I'll join her. But I won't, Aiden, not ever."

"It's what she wants for both of us," Aiden said. "I didn't understand her before, but it makes sense now. She's going to leave us down here until we do what she says."

"I'm not going to let it be that way. I'll open my own wrists first."

"It can't come to that."

"She's gone mad," he said. "It's the meat that does it."

"That's what Mr. Ghostman said. It makes them psychotic even while it makes them stronger." It was her turn to tell, and Alex listened in amazement as she related everything that had happened to her, everything she had learned from Birdie's old mentor.

"I should have told you about Simone," he said, furious at himself. "You would have been warned —"

"I don't think it would have mattered," Aiden said. "I couldn't have gotten away from her."

"So Birdie's here, in town?"

"Yes, and I'm so afraid she'll come looking for me. She wouldn't be expecting this much trouble, and Simone will catch her. Bite her, even. She was kicking herself for not coming up with that idea sooner. She'll make Birdie into one like me, unless she kills her outright."

Alex went numb. Of course he should have thought of that. By the sounds, Simone would do anything to increase the numbers of her pack. Even something as unspeakable as the bite. And here he'd gone and given her the idea.

Aiden was shaking. Alex put an arm around her and led her away from the corpses, toward the couch. Halfway there, he once again realized what he'd known all along but had pushed to the back of his mind — Aiden was nearly naked, and now that she'd returned to human form, no pelt gave her the illusion of covering. He couldn't see anything, but he felt her bare skin and jumped away as if scorched.

"There's clothes here," he said. "Not great, but something, at least."

She said nothing but he could practically feel the blush radiating off her. Fumbling in the dark, he found some things in one of the boxes and stood prudently aside while she dressed. They were too big, baggy, and smelled of paint like his shirt, but she thanked him as if he'd just given her an expensive evening gown.

They sat side by side, worrying about Birdie and trying to convince each other that she was savvy and wouldn't walk right in if she suspected trouble.

Not that there was much else she could do.

"And . . . Donovan . . ." Aiden said with difficulty and loathing.

"He didn't . . . do . . . anything, did he?" Anxiety spiked Alex's voice louder than he intended, loud enough to echo off the concrete walls. The idea of Donovan touching Aiden made him want to go foaming-at-the-mouth mad.

"Not really," she said, though a tremor of revulsion went through her. "I think he's more interested in . . . in Simone. But isn't she his . . . ?"

"Yeah, it's sick, all right," Alex said. "Sick but true. She'd have done anything to win him to her side, and I mean anything. He raped and killed his sister, and he would have . . . if I hadn't gotten there . . ."

"I know." She leaned against him, resting her head on his shoulder. It was so tender and trusting that Alex could hardly believe it. All the proof of her forgiveness and understanding he'd ever needed was in that simple and sweet gesture.

He didn't want to say it, but sometimes it was better to have everything out in the open. "He might still try."

"Simone told him to stop," she quavered.

"But, see, I know her, the despicable bitch. She didn't have to put you in here with me. There's other places they could have locked you up. She wanted us in here together so that she could get what she wanted from us by threatening one or the other."

"You mean, she might try to hurt me in order to make you do what she wants?"

"She's got to know that I love you, because she'd know that I never would have broken the law if I didn't. She'd think, and she'd be right, that if it would keep you safe from Donovan, I would eat."

"Alex, no!"

"I'd have to. I couldn't stand to let that happen to you."

"I couldn't stand it either. Or to see them torture you. I'd have to go along with them."

"No, Aiden, no. I'm not worth it. I'd rather die."

"I would too." Her laugh was a hollow and desolate dirge. "What now? Do we make a suicide pact? Despite all Mr. McGuire's concerns, I've never been suicidal. Even if I was, I'd . . . I guess I'd take pills or something. Anything else would be too scary, or too painful, or too gross. I couldn't . . . what did you say you'd do? Open your own wrists? With your claws, or teeth? I could never do that. I'd chicken out. You'll have to do it for me, Alex."

His breath hitched and he instinctively tightened his arms around her. "I don't want to hurt you any more."

"But if it was that or . . . or Donovan . . . would you?"

"Aiden, don't."

She was clinging to him, her head burrowed into the juncture of his neck and shoulder. Her tears scalded him where they soaked through his shirt. "Promise me, Alex. Please. Promise you won't let him, even if it means killing me."

"I . . . I promise. If it comes to that, *only* if it comes to that. We can't give up hope."

"We can't eat, either. Whatever else, we can't do that. I didn't want to be like this, I came here hoping to find a cure, but I can learn to live with it. If you're with me, I mean. But I can't, I won't, let myself get any crazier."

Alex could hardly believe his ears. "Aiden, do you mean it? You want me with you? After everything I –"

He was cut off by her sudden, fierce kiss. It was clumsy, given that he didn't expect it and she couldn't see very well yet, but her lips were on his and she was holding him by the sides of the head. Alex, stunned, spent a few seconds immobile, but then reacted by embracing her and returning the kiss with desperate fervor.

"Of course I want you with me, you silly," she said when they parted. "If you want *me*."

"You know I do. Even before. I would even if you were just –"

"Just human?"

"That's not why I bit you, though. I never would have done that."

"I know," she said with some exasperation, and kissed him again.

"If we get out of this, will you be my mate?"

"Oh, Alex!"

He went on hastily, stumbling over his words, mixing up the traditional speech with his own rambling. "I left my clan and don't have much to offer, but I'm a good hunter, and I'll do whatever it takes, get a job somehow, I'll protect you and care for our cubs, and . . . damn it, I can't remember the rest of the words. There's words. A pledging rite."

It made her giggle, though, and that lightened his spirits more than anything since surfacing off Vista Beach to see her running from Donovan.

"It's okay," she said. "I get the idea."

"This is hardly the place for a proposal anyway," he said. "I'm supposed to offer you a fresh kill to prove I can provide."

"No diamonds?" She giggled again.

He chuffed. "Two months of *my* salary wouldn't buy you much of a rock."

"I don't need diamonds. I bet jewelry makes it harder to change shape, anyway."

"You're really all right with this?" he asked. "The change and all?"

"It was scariest being alone," she said. "Which is funny, really . . . ever since my parents died, I thought that all I wanted was to be alone. Nobody could hurt me if I didn't let them get close. I hardly went out, I didn't talk to anyone, I had no friends. Once I met you, and Birdie, and Jeff even if he doesn't really like me, I finally started to see what Mr. McGuire and Doctor Lundquist had been telling me all along. It's riskier to love, to trust, yeah. Riskier, but better. Worth it."

"Jeff does like you. It wasn't because he objected to you personally that he acted that way. It's the principle of the thing."

She shrugged, unconvinced, but since they'd probably never see Jeff again, Alex let it drop.

"When I realized what the bite had done," Aiden said, "I suddenly saw that I was more alone than ever, because as good a friend as Birdie is, as nice as Mr. Ghostman is, I'd always be different from them. They could intellectually get what I was going through but they'd never really, deep down, be able to understand. If there's someone around who does, who knows what it's like when the moon comes up all white and round like that, to have the need to hunt setting fire to your blood, if there's someone to share it with me and help me get used to it, I'll do just fine."

"That'll always be me, then." He sealed it with a kiss, and for a while, with her in his arms, was able to forget his fears and his hungers, to forget everything except for Aiden. His mate.

*   *   *

The phone kept ringing, until Simone unplugged it with a hard yank and threw it, trailing its cord like a tail, into the fireplace. The casing shattered against the back wall of the hearth, and the pieces fell into the embers, sending up a puff of ash.

"Won't they come looking?" Donovan asked. "When no one answers?"

"Let them come," Simone said, glaring at the door and the world beyond. "We have retaken our own and nothing will force us from our home ever again!"

He looked doubtful, but she drew him down and caressed him until he forgot all about such petty concerns. This was their place now. He was hers now, more than ever. Soon they'd have a proper pack, and cubs, and everything would be as it was before her father had grown weak and let the humans take away what was rightfully theirs. The only thing that would have made it perfect was if her father and the rest of the pack were here to share this victory with her . . . or to wallow in their shame for having let it all go in the first place.

Later, languid in the afterglow of passion, Simone rolled over and got up, leaving Donovan snoring by the fire. Young as he was, she'd depleted his energies at last. He slept, a manlike wolfen form with his head cradled in the pillow of his crossed arms, the orange-gold light glinting on the rusty strands of his pelt.

All the rutting wore him out, but it filled Simone with vigor. She paced the room, aware that the sky had darkened with the shortening of the day and that a heavy snow was falling, whipped by the howling wind. It would be a fine and stormy winter night, just as she remembered from her cubhood. On such nights, the pack would gather and share meat, and tell stories of the olden days, the old country, times when their kind had been powerful and feared.

It had been on a night such as this that she'd left her warm den, the younger cubs – Alexander's parents among them – curled in a fuzzy heap. She had only wanted to prove that she was adult enough to hunt instead of shaking and worrying at pieces of raw prey carried home by the elders.

Gideon was only a little bit older, so she felt she should be allowed to do as he did. True, he was bigger, with paws the size of saucers that made the elders say he'd be a giant when he reached full growth, but she was quicker. Couldn't she outrace him every time?

So she'd sneaked out, meaning to find and kill something all by herself. How surprised they'd be when she returned, dragging her prey! They'd see that she was a cub no longer.

The first cold blast of the wind as she slid out a window nearly made her reconsider, but before she could fully decide to save the hunting for a warmer night, she'd seen a shadow slinking toward the outbuilding where slaughtered prey was kept until it was needed.

Incensed by the thought that some scavenger meant to make off with meat that belonged to her pack, she headed that way. Her dreams of glory as a hunter were supplanted by ones in which she was lauded as a fine and strong warrior, having defended their lair and their food.

When she got closer, though, she recognized the dark shape as it rose to man-height and opened the door. She would know that silhouette anywhere, the last one she saw when she was bid good-night. Her father, Malcolm, brave leader.

Whatever could he be doing, out here in the middle of the night?

Simone crept closer, heard his movements. Heard his voice. She could barely make out the words, the wind snatching them like a cub wresting a toy from another, but she thought he said a name. Her mother's name.

She'd gone in, hiding in the shadows, and seen him near a small door that was usually latched and barred, and that everyone else in the pack stayed away from because sometimes strange sounds came from behind it. Strange, terrible, tormented sounds. The cubs whispered to each other in delighted shivers of terror, speculating on what misshapen beast might be imprisoned there.

Malcolm Drachen had opened the door. Simone flattened herself to the floor, trembling but determined not to flee. The looks of awe and envy on the faces of her den-mates would make any scare worthwhile when she told them what she had seen.

So she thought, but she wasn't prepared for what emerged from that black cellar. It was no misshapen beast at all, but one of their own kind. A female. With a scent that was uncannily like her own, though different in a sour, peppery way that made her hackles rise.

But her mother had died years ago! She'd been caught away from the den and died birthing Simone, her father finding them too late to save his mate but in time to bring his cubling daughter home.

They left the outbuilding, slinking as if they knew they could not let themselves be seen. Simone, heart in her throat, followed. Or tried to. She lost them in the snowy forest night when they loped ahead on longer legs, leaving her behind. She wanted to yip and call, wanted to have a closer look and a better sniff of this female, because if it *was* her mother . . .

She couldn't keep up. She nearly got lost herself. When she admitted to herself that it was no use, she found her way back to the building. The small door was still standing open. She peered down, her nose wrinkling at the foul air. That disturbing scent was here, too. She sneezed.

And yet, as not-right as it was, she was more sure than ever that she was smelling her mother. Olivia Drachen was alive!

Simone would not go to bed until she had answers. She settled herself down to wait for their return, hidden behind a stack of tanned hides. But as she warmed up and relaxed, she fell asleep. When she awoke, the storm had blown out and dawn was almost rising, and the door was shut again, barred. A fresh trail of her father's scent hung in the air.

Only his. Not hers, not Olivia's.

She went to the door and listened, hearing nothing even after she tapped and whispered. The dark little room beyond was empty. She sniffed at the traces of her father's scent, the sweat of his hands as he'd replaced the bar. Weariness and misery were predominant in that odor.

242

A few nights later, the killings had begun. The elders spoke in horror of a rogue of their kind, one who'd eaten the forbidden meat and gone mad from the poisons humans carried in their flesh. The other cubs, even Gideon, took joy in frightening each other with stories about what such a crazed changeling could do. Simone took no part in that, troubled by what she suspected.

Her father forbade the rest of the pack to go hunting as long as this danger was out there. His decree didn't stop him from going alone, sometimes staying out until morning, coming back shaking his head in defeat. He never told any of them what he was doing, or who he was seeking.

And then he had vanished for more than a day. The elders were in despair, unwilling to disobey his last order by going out in search of him, while others like Gideon urged action. Before it could come to a violent dispute, Malcolm had come home. Simone had barely recognized him, with his face and body torn into a scrawl of healing scars. All he would tell them was that he'd found the rogue, and killed it.

They never discussed it. Even when Simone was grown. She kept that secret knowledge like a festering sore on her soul. She believed that he had done what he said he'd done. Killed the rogue. Killed his mate, her mother.

It was the end of him. He lost all fortitude after that. He ceased caring about the pack, no longer had the desire to hunt, became glum and weak. Simone's adoring love for him waned, shadowed by what she knew. When they learned that the humans meant to take their land for these made-up laws of taxes and foreclosures, Malcolm hadn't been able to fight them.

Well, what he had lost, she had regained. When she'd matured, and had a mate and cubs of her own, she decided to avenge her mother by following in her pawprints, finishing what Olivia had begun.

The land was hers now. She'd proved that it was possible, even desirable, to prey upon humans. That old law was foolish, put into place by soft and cowardly ancestors who were afraid of the greater gifts it could bring. Not poison, but power!

She paused by a window, Donovan's gusty snores behind her. Something had moved out there in the snowy dusk.

Her senses came to full alert. Was it beginning so soon? The humans wondered about their inability to contact the dead usurpers, and just had to stick their noses in. They would live to regret that, at least for the few seconds it took for their eviscerated hearts to stop beating in her fist of claws.

*　　*　　*

Chapter 4
January 6, Tuesday
Late Afternoon

Birdie Yale sat in the stolen car, wondering which would happen first —
getting arrested for grand theft auto, or having the window crash in on her
as some horrible werewolf punched through the glass to get at her like the
Tootsie Roll center of a Tootsie Pop.

Or she could freeze. She was used to Trinity Bay, that coastal cold that
was always damp and somehow comfortable. This was a frigid, bone-biting
chill that threatened to suck the moisture right out of her body. Her breath
had fogged everything up so that all she could see was a blurry expanse of
dark grey and white, and kamikaze snowflakes plunging to their doom on
the windshield. An occasional gust of wind rocked the car.

"As long as the heater's on, you're not going to freeze, you goose," she
told herself, and blew into her cupped hands while wishing for gloves. Couldn't
remember everything, especially when one was shopping or packing in a
hurry.

How long was he going to take? It wasn't that far to the house.

She rubbed the side of her forearm on the glass until she'd cleared a
space, and squinted out. But Jeff had been prudent and parked in the lee of
a high drift, so she wouldn't have been able to see the house even if the snow
hadn't been blowing around.

"This sucks," she announced. "Here I sit, doing nothing."

And yet, she knew it was really the only thing to do, until Jeff got back.
If Jeff got back.

He'd told her how the ranch had been sold, and the lettering on the mailbox read Kendall, not Drachen. All this way for nothing. Drachen had been one of the names of their pack, Drachen and Greye, two packs merged into one. But both had left this area years ago.

Fergs hadn't come back. With each minute that ticked by, Birdie was more and more sure that her shy friend had walked smack into big-time trouble. Maybe the Drachens had moved on, but some other pack could have come in and taken over. Sure. All of them savage man-eaters. The numbers of this alleged pack and the grisliness of their eating habits climbed the longer she sat.

By now, they'd probably dissected Fergs and noshed on the best bits. Or, for all she knew, they were right this very second chanting around her in a circle, about to gruesomely sacrifice her to some nasty unpronounceable Lovecraftian god.

Lambent eyes peered in at her through the fogged window.

Birdie's heart lurched. She was about to unleash her trademark scream, the one that could make dogs drop dead bleeding from the ears, and then she recognized the inhuman face, with its long buff-colored mane.

She opened the door and slid over, admitting a lynx-like creature the size of a man, and a spitting torrent of snow. A quick scan showed her that Jeff was unhurt, but he was also alone. No Aiden.

"Well?"

He held up a paw, asking her patience as he groaned and contorted. She'd watched him change from man-form to animal. Prior to that, he'd unashamedly stripped to his birthday suit, while Birdie ogled openly and for one of the few times in her life could not come up with a witty remark. Lordy, lordy, but he was as fine out of his clothes as her imagination had suggested.

Burgeoning horniness, however, had taken a sudden drop when Jeff transformed. The popping of cartilage and other assorted gross biological noises were enough to sweep thoughts of romance from anybody's mind.

When he was done, he was spotted and furry, feline, with wide paws covered in thick tufts. She dimly remembered something from high school or a nature show, about how certain critters had spreading paws like that to help distribute their weight. Nature's snowshoes. They worked well enough for Jeff, who'd gone bounding away like a rabbit on springs.

Now the reverse of the process was occurring, fur giving way to bare skin, muscles sliding around to rearrange themselves. Moments later, he was fully human – and fully male, hubba-hubba – again. He brushed snow from his long hair and turned toward her, either comfortable with his nudity or oblivious of her appreciative checking-out.

Or, as she found out as soon as he started to speak, too concerned with more important things.

"We've got a problem, all right," he said. "Simone's there. Donovan, too."

"What?" Birdie whapped herself on the side of the head as if to shake stuffing from her ears. "I didn't hear you right. How can they be *here?* They're in Trinity Bay."

"Not anymore."

"Oh, shit. Shit, shit, shit. You mean to tell me that Fergs walked right up and knocked, and it was *them?*" Now Jeff's admirable bod was the last thing on her mind. Despair welled huge and overpowering. "That's the worst thing that could have happened."

"Your car's there, behind a minivan with a plate-holder from a Eureka dealership. And a purse. I saw it in the kitchen as I was making a circuit of the house." He shivered. "Boy, the memories. The place has hardly changed at all."

"Forget that, what about Aiden? You didn't see her?"

"No. But I couldn't see into the upstairs, and not all of the downstairs rooms have windows. They could be holding her somewhere."

"If she's alive."

"Yeah."

"Wrong answer, handsome, you were supposed to tell me not to worry, that of course she's alive, they wouldn't just kill her."

"Except that they might."

"I know!"

"What do you want to do?"

"I suppose busting in Governator-style is out of the question."

Jeff looked grim. "I can't fight them both. And you, no offense – "

"Weak and puny human, yeah, tell me about it." She socked one fist into the other palm. "But we have to do something!"

"Birdie, it's probably too late."

"Ask me if I care."

"Look, I like her too, she's a sweet kid. But what good would it do to get ourselves dead too?"

"What would Alex do if he was here?"

"Bust in Governator-style," Jeff admitted. "He isn't, though."

"Because he took off to try and help Aiden."

"I see where your logic is going." See it, he might . . . look happy about it, he didn't. "You want me to save her for Alex's sake."

"Bingo."

"I can't beat them. Simone is probably on her guard. They'll be waiting. They'll shred me."

"Can we get to my car first?"

"What are you talking about? If I'm not going, you're not going. And even if I'm going, you're staying here."

"Look, maybe I am a weak and puny human, but I'm not useless. Especially if I can get to my car."

"Whatcha got in there, a bazooka?"

"No such luck."

Sputtering yellow-white headlights appeared behind them. Jeff slid down in the bucket seat, grabbing for his clothes. Birdie could just imagine the expression on some hick local cop's face when he beamed a flashlight in and saw them. One busty brunette in sweats and a parka, one blond hunk totally stark-buck-naked. In a stolen car boosted from behind the local supermarket, no less.

The approaching vehicle slowed. Either a cop, or maybe just a passer-by. They were far enough off to the shoulder that the other driver would have plenty of room to get by, and Birdie wished he or she would do just that. But people in the sticks were more neighborly and nosy than in the disaffected urban jungle.

It was choppy, rumbling-lumbering, and stopped behind them. As the engine died, Jeff sat up again with blank white dread in his eyes.

"What?"

"Gideon."

Birdie's spirits sank too. All the while as they'd been discussing what to do in her motel room, and as Jeff had hotwired the car, and all the way out here on their way to do a little reconnaissance, he'd continually muttered how Gideon was going to kill him.

"He delivers, huh?"

Jeff didn't answer. He had wriggled back into his jeans – she'd watched with an inward grin that a dozen pissed-off Gideons couldn't quash – and thrust his arms into the sleeves of his tee-shirt. He opened the door and stepped out.

"In for a penny," Birdie said, and got out on her side.

She hunched into her coat, would have given a lesser-used body part for a scarf or a ski mask, and watched as the driver's side door of the old Chevy opened, and Gideon Greye slowly emerged.

"Aye *caramba*," she breathed.

It was like watching the opening scene of *Star Wars*, when Vader's ship like the Energizer Bunny keeps going and going. Gideon was massive, and so buff that he made Jeff look like a 98-pound weakling. Her first coherent thought was to wonder if he was proportionate, and it resulted in an immediate mental crossing of the legs. Bigger wasn't always better.

He was all male, the kind that spoke to millions of years of biological conditioning. So brimming with masculine magnetism that Birdie felt a physical pull. It was as if every piece of metal on her, ferrous and non — the underwire of her bra, the fillings in her teeth, the silver studs and bangles in her earlobes — reacted to that unseen force. She warred with herself, torn between taking a step forward and a step back.

Then she registered the flatly hostile glare in his eyes and that settled it. She stepped back.

Like Jeff, Gideon wasn't dressed for the cold and didn't seem to feel it. The snow turned his sable hair prematurely grey and did nothing to soften the granite lines of his face. He came toward them with his body hunched forward, not against the wind but out of pure anger. His fists were each as big as Birdie's head and considerably harder.

All that, and a werewolf too. Changeling. Whatever.

Another man, this one stocky and needing no snow to grey his hair, got out on the passenger side. He looked upset by the whole mess, stroking fitfully at his beard and massaging a nest of scars that covered the side of his face like a lumpy mask.

Jeff stood his ground, so naturally Birdie had to step back up beside him. She wasn't about to cower and whine.

"Explain yourself," Gideon said to Jeff, glowering so fiercely that nobody would have been surprised to see sparks shoot from his eyes.

"They're already here," Jeff said with what Birdie felt was impressive calm. "Simone and Donovan. They're at the ranch. They've probably killed the humans who lived there."

The old-timer sighed and bowed his head. "We did not anticipate her quite soon enough."

Gideon's brow was low and ominous as a tornado warning. He shifted his attention to Birdie and she could have listed five thousand places she'd rather have been. Vegas. An ivory tropical beach being brought rum drinks by a shirtless guy named Ramon. Shopping. Even a duty visit to Aunt Margot would have been an improvement over standing here in the frigid wind, being studied like something loathsome under a microscope by a guy who could have taken on the entire WWF with one hand tied behind his back.

Fergs, I love you dearly but I could belt you one for getting me into this, she thought, conveniently forgetting how she'd bulled and bullied her way into it in the first place.

"And who's she?"

Not directed to Birdie herself but to Jeff, in the exact tone Birdie had once gotten when she took a grunge rocker to a family get-together. Aunt Margot's, again, that had been, and it just went to prove how bad this situation was. Most of the time, she was able to block Aunt Margot from her memory. It was a defense mechanism. Knock someone through a glass-topped coffee table just once, even on accident, and they never let you forget it.

Jeff went with honesty, probably the only choice under the circumstances. "Aiden's friend. She knows."

Gideon stepped closer and to the side. Downwind, Birdie realized. He sniffed. He scowled. Birdie was indignant. She was used to being scorned for the way she looked – forty pounds overweight in a world where thin was in and fat meant lazy. She was used to similar treatment for the way she dressed, which was as outrageously as she could get away with, and even the brassy and irreverent way she talked. But this was the first time anyone had given her that look because of the way she *smelled*.

The older changeling, who walked gingerly and chafed his hands together as proof that he, at least, wasn't immune to the cold, came closer. "We have no time to lose, Gideon. They'll kill the girl, if they haven't already."

With a grunt that clearly expressed his hope that they already had, and spared him the exertion, Gideon took another step toward Jeff. "You left us."

"You followed me."

"Your trail was easy enough to find." His scowl carved deeper lines in his face as he flicked a contemptuous glance Birdie's way.

He had to be talking about the motel room, where she and Jeff had hidden out for a while to discuss their plan. What a shame they hadn't had the time or the inclination to give him something incriminating to smell. He'd probably been so busy, in fact, sniffing for just that evidence that he'd entirely missed Aiden's scent. She was beginning to comprehend just how much input these people . . . creatures . . . beings . . . pick your term . . . took from their noses and their instincts. Reason was very much a secondary factor. And instinct was a lot harder to argue with.

"We can discuss it later," said Jeff. It was a gutsy move on his part; Birdie sensed that he'd backtalked Gideon once too often and another infraction might well turn this roadside confab into a brawl. "If we're going to face them, we've got to do it now. If we're going to run like rabbits, we'd better do that now, too."

"I've got a plan," Birdie offered.

As far as Gideon cared, her voice might have been nothing but the hooting of the wind in a tailpipe. But Jeff and the old-timer glanced at her in curiosity, if not exactly hope.

"But we've got to get up to the house to do it," she said. "So Jeff's right. We'd better get moving."

*   *   *

Simone decided the dark shape she'd seen had been nothing more than a phantom of her imagination. She didn't bother going out to check for tracks, because as strong as the wind had gotten, it would have scoured them away already.

This decision did little to calm her nerves. Donovan was still sleeping, still snoring, still with that blissful smile of absolute contentment. She thought of snuggling against him and dozing herself, but the fire was dying and she was hungry.

She added some wood, stirred the flames into renewed life, and went into the kitchen after a quick pause to relish the sight of Donovan bathed in orange-amber flickering light. What a lovely beast he was!

The pantry was well-stocked, if not quite so exceptionally as it had been in her father's day. The contents now tended toward more grains, and canned vegetables, and not nearly enough meat. Maybe in the morning, they'd butcher one of the horses and rig a smokehouse.

Thinking of the horses made her think of her captives, and wonder how they were doing. Had they reconciled, those two young lovers? Or had they turned on each other in spite? It would be a shame if they killed each other, a waste, but now that she knew how she could increase her pack, she didn't mind all that much the prospect of losing one or both of them.

As she chose cans and carried them to the counter, she marveled once more at her own forgetfulness. All this time, she could have been judiciously choosing prime examples of humanity. The ones whose bestial natures were already well-advanced. The strong. The sly. Not the puny and whiny ones, like the myopic pencil-pushers who'd cheated them out of Drachenheim in the first place. Not the ones who needed rules and rights and laws because they were too feeble to defend themselves.

It would be carefully done. She couldn't just start biting people wherever she pleased. They'd have to have the right desirable qualities.

Soup heated on the stove, sending tendrils of warming aroma into the air. Chicken stock, golden-greasy but good. Simone fetched a package of sliced ham from the refrigerator and forewent the bread. She peeled one slice after another from the stack, rolling them into balls and tucking them into her mouth as she made a list of the qualities she'd look for in future packmates.

The narrow pad of paper, with a magnet on the back and "Joyce's Kitchen" printed across the top of each sheet, had been halfway filled in when someone knocked at the back door.

Simone's pen skidded, leaving a startled swoop of a line. She dropped it and rose, turning off the burner beneath the simmering soup and swallowing the last morsel of ham. In the living room, the pattern of Donovan's snoring altered, then resumed.

She opened the door to find yet another young female standing on the stoop. This one was as unlike little Aiden as the night was unlike the dawn. Her body was lush and ripe, her hair an ebony tumble with one wine-red lock at the front. And her scent was fully, undeniably human.

This one would make a fine feast. Plenty of well-fed flesh on her. The ham was suddenly far less than fulfilling.

"Yes?" she asked, presuming this was a daughter of the dead couple, or perhaps of friends of theirs.

"Simone Drachen?"

Hearing her name took her aback. The dark-haired girl stepped into the kitchen as if she owned the place.

"Who are you?" Simone demanded, bristling with incipient change.

"Avon lady. Want to try a perfume sample?"

With that, the girl brought up a hand that had been partly hidden by her ample thigh. She held a small vial with a silvery top, and when she depressed it, a cloud of stinging mist puffed right into Simone's face.

She screeched, leaping back and shaking her head, but the droplets clung. They burned into her eyes, filled her nostrils with their gagging, apocalyptic stink. She couldn't see, couldn't scent, felt as if acid was eating into her skin and leaving pitted craters.

Blindly, she clawed out and got nothing but air. She heard, as if from very far away, Donovan shouting her name, and then the crash-tinkle-smash of shattering glass and a roar.

The roar pierced Simone like a lance. She'd know her one-time mate's voice anywhere.

Water was gushing copiously from her eyes, cleansing them but leaving her viewing the world through a streamy blur. Another figure was in the kitchen now, light-colored so that she first thought it was Aiden, but too tall, too wide. Jeffrey.

Snarling in hatred and challenge, she leaped. Not at the young male, but at the she-dog human bitch who'd sprayed her. The brunette's other arm shot out, and with her leaking eyes Simone saw something black, something the wrong shape to be a gun, something that looked vaguely like a . . .

The tiny metal prongs on the end of it touched her, and everything went electric-white. A jolting numbness slammed through Simone's body.

The next thing she knew, she was flat on her back staring up, still through a veil of tears, at the copper-bottomed pots hanging from the rack. Jeff's shadow fell over her, claws scything, but if he thought she was going to lay there and let him carve her into slices, he was as gullible as his fool of a mother had been.

She flipped herself to her feet in one fluid motion, drawing an amazed exclamation from the black-haired she-dog. A swipe of her hand, claws only partly formed, was sufficient to send Jeff staggering back with scratches on his neck. A little harder, a little more length, and she would have had his larynx in her palm like a dripping corrugated tube.

But Jeff wasn't her concern. Her concern was the terrible sounds of battle she heard coming from the living room, as two bodies – one large, one larger – demolished furniture and slammed around. She raced that way, shriek-ing for Donovan.

The two in the kitchen gave chase, the human brandishing her taser and loosing a war-cry that would have been better suited to an Amazon. Simone outdistanced them and didn't falter even as she took in the scene.

Gideon, even more powerful and imposing than she remembered, was wrestling with Donovan in the center of the room. They were almost of a height, but Donovan still lacked a few years before he would have reached his full growth, his full genetic potential. He was slowly bending. Slowly giving way under the force of his father's strength.

Simone sprang at Gideon with a feral hiss. Any fondness she'd once felt for him had long since curdled, and now here he was trying to take her new mate away from her. With a brutal ferocity that surprised him, she landed on his back. All four sets of claws dug in, and she bit hard at the nape of his neck.

Blood and fur filled her mouth. He roared again, this time in pain, and tried to fling her off. Donovan came in low, going for the belly. Gideon kicked him, a rib-cracking kick that sent Donovan tumbling.

Jeff, moving so fast he was a light-colored streak, snatched up a poker from the overturned rack of fireplace tools. His shadow danced crazily in the light thrown by the leaping flames. He swung it at Donovan, but Donovan twisted and the blow meant for his skull took him in the shoulder.

"No!" Gideon cried. "He's mine!"

His huge hand, sable-dark with long blunted claws like those of a bear, reached around and tangled in Simone's long red hair. He meant to rip her off of him but she clung like a burr, drawing up her hind legs and pistoning them down to open deep gashes all the way from his shoulderblades to his buttocks.

Donovan kicked Jeff's legs out from under him. They fell in a snarling, spitting tangle. Simone's senses were returning and she could smell the blood, hot blood and fury and the smoky scent of males in deadly competition.

Gideon whirled and went to slam his back against the wall, which would have crushed Simone if she'd been stupid enough to stay where she was. Instead, she scaled him like a tree, swung around, and they were face to face. She ripped at him with her teeth, hoping to take off his nose but mauling a cheek instead. He backhanded her and she went flying into the wreckage of the couch.

Dazed, she shook her head and looked up, but it wasn't Gideon standing over her now. It was an older male with a careworn, bearded face full of scars. He regarded her sadly.

"Simone, it is over. Surrender and it will be quick."

A column of clear fire rocketed up inside of her, and brought her to her feet with the power of that righteous rage. "No, Father. This is my den now. What you lost, I've won back. *You* surrender, and there will be a place for you in my pack, an honored place."

"We'll never follow you," growled Jeff, as he and Donovan strained to get leverage. Despite the blond-furred male's smaller size, he was fighting with incredible vigor. "You were cast out."

"Gideon leads our pack," her father, said in a soft, yet carrying voice.

"Hah!" Donovan was slowly but surely bending Jeff backward, just as he himself had given way beneath Gideon's greater strength. "Your precious, mighty Gideon. So honorable. So noble. You don't even know what he is. He's a man-killer."

Gideon's bellow shook the house. He knocked Jeff aside, but Donovan ducked away before those monstrous mitts could close on his neck.

"You scorn *us*," Donovan went on, in a vicious hiss. "You follow him, but I've seen what he does. He hunts, he rapes, he kills. He's as much a murderer as we are. Worse, because he hunts for pleasure, and does not eat his prey."

"Be silent!" Gideon's punch landed dead-center on Donovan's chest, the sort of blow that caved in bones and could stun the heart into stillness.

Simone threw herself from the ruins of the couch. Her father caught her, and despite her teeming, turbulent emotions she could not bring herself to lash out at him.

Donovan hit the wall and slid down it, rasping for breath. He looked squarely at Jeff. "Ask him . . . about the man in . . . Trinity Bay. The . . . dead man. And his . . . his wife. The . . . ravished one. I got there . . . before he could . . . cut her throat and finish her."

"The Bakers?" came the voice of the brunette human, who'd been standing in the kitchen doorway with her hateful perfume in one hand and her taser in the other as if unsure whether she should join the fray. "Mike and Stacy Baker?"

Gideon swelled and changed, leaving his humanoid form behind. He filled the room, towering more than eight feet high on his hind legs, the fur at the crown of his head brushing the roof beams. His roar was deafening, his tread an earthquake. Jeff dove aside as Gideon bore down on Donovan, too shocked by what had just been said to do much of anything else.

*   *   *

Alex had fallen into a thin sleep, tossing and mumbling every time his stomach grumbled. Aiden sat with his head cradled in her lap, stroking his hair and his brow and trying not to think about how hungry she was, too. Her complaint wouldn't be anything compared to his. She'd had a big, if bland, dinner last night and several strips of jerky on her way out to the ranch. He'd been without food a lot longer than that.

Telling herself that didn't help the fact that she was still hungry. The kitchen of the big house had been full of tantalizing scents. The pantry door had been ajar, giving her a view of the well-stocked shelves. All of that food, so close, and they couldn't get to it.

Scratch that . . . there were horses right over them. Tons of meat on the hoof, and only a few yards away.

You can't eat a horse! her mind squealed in horror and alarm. It was the inner voice that had protested the death of the swan, the voice that sought to convince her she couldn't live like this. Better to starve than to feed on innocent creatures.

"Oh, phooey, tell it to the animal-rights activists," she whispered into the total darkness. It wasn't like she'd been a vegetarian before all this, and was it really so different to contemplate a nice body-heat slab of horsemeat than a sizzling hamburger?

Her stomach made such a loud noise that Alex, whose ear was pressed against it, woke with a start. He flailed a bit, gasping, and then settled down as he remembered where he was, and who he was with.

"Sorry," she said ruefully. "I shouldn't have been thinking about food."

"The horses?" he asked, with a rueful tinge of his own.

"It's awful, isn't it? I used to love horses. Looking at them, I mean. Pictures, toys. I was always a little scared of them in real life, and never rode one except for pony rides when I was a kid. But right now, I could literally eat a horse."

"Nothing wrong with that. It's the natural order."

"That doesn't make it seem any less mean."

He chuckled wryly and sat up, stretching. "Well, killing them in their stalls wouldn't exactly be hunting. Sometimes, though, ideas about what's sporting and what's fair just aren't all that important."

Above them, the horses nickered and stamped as if they were aware of, and didn't like, this conversation. They didn't calm down but continued, distressed.

"What's wrong with them?" Aiden nervously looked up, not that she could see anything but more blackness. She could just imagine their hooves breaking through the floor, which was her and Alex's ceiling. Wouldn't that be poetic justice if they were squashed to death under the very animals they'd been talking about eating?

"Something's got them upset." He eased from the couch like an eddy of wind and was gone.

Aiden could barely hear his stealthy movements but judged he was headed for the stairs. It was probably Donovan and Simone, come to see if they had given in yet, or if the bodies were still where they'd fallen. Cold. Stiffening. The blood sinking, settling like sediment. Eyes gone cloudy. Skin waxy and cool.

She hugged herself, but at the same time it was *good* to be thinking that way. As long as she focused on the corpses being just that, cold and unappetizing cadavers, she wouldn't think the unthinkable.

A stair tread creaked under Alex. He evidently froze, for there were no further sounds except those made by the horses and the wind keening outside. Aiden listened for footsteps above, or the grind and grate of the bar being moved.

Nothing.

Just horses and wind. And something that might have been a distant roar.

"Was that Donovan?" she gasped out, feeling faint.

The trap door banged as Alex threw himself against it. "Come on, Aiden, I need your help here."

She scrambled off the couch and shuffled, arms out in front of her like a sleepwalker, in the direction of his voice. "But how – *oof!*" She tripped on something solid and yielding, waved her arms, and fell across the body of the dead woman. She thrust her hands out for balance and they plunged into a clammy, slippery mass. Her forehead whacked what felt like a chin.

These are the witch's guts, she thought out of nowhere, some childhood Halloween game turned grotesquely real. In the game, kids stuck their hands into gelatin, or cold pasta. Now she knew how inaccurate that game had been. The texture was all wrong, not slick enough, or lumpy enough.

She rolled off and squatted, making helpless cawing cries as she shook and wiped the sludge from her hands. Alex called to her again, urgently.

"Okay," she said unevenly, and crawled up the steps to find him.

"If we both try, we might be able to break it."

"Alex, I don't know . . ."

"It's our only chance. The longer we wait, the weaker and hungrier we'll get. We have to get out of here now."

"Tell me what to do."

"We'll need to change. We're stronger that way."

Cloth rustled. A zipper went *zeeep!* in that metallic way. Alex was undressing, and Aiden's mind darted to the first time she'd seen him, standing on the rock watching the sea lion colony at play, with no idea that he was observed. She understood so much better now.

Understanding, and darkness, didn't prevent a blush from rising in her cheeks like the tide. He was only inches away, increasingly naked with every move and every moment, and in the confined space she couldn't keep from bumping into him. His skin, so smooth yet so tough . . . so warm.

"What are you waiting for?" he asked.

"Huh?" She was blank, and then it came to her. She'd rendered one outfit useless already today. Although the clothes she wore were someone's cast-offs, ill-fitting and smelling of paint, she'd have an easier time with the change if she got out of them.

Her face hot, she undressed with as much grace as she could. Which, of course, wasn't much. She managed to get her foot snared in the cuff, and Alex had to feel his way down her leg to free it. His hands were none too steady. Aiden found it kind of flattering, embarrassing as it was.

"Ready?" he asked huskily, and had to clear his throat. "Ready?"

"Yes, let's try."

It was the first time she'd consciously willed the change. Mr. Ghostman had asked her for a demonstration at his home in Ashland, but she'd been too afraid to try even before the swan-slaughter. After, it had been out of the question. Suppose she had changed, and fallen upon him and Birdie in a murderous frenzy? There hadn't been time for any real experimentation later, even if she'd been so inclined. Her transformation in Simone's kitchen had been brought on by sheer terror, uncontrollable.

"You can do it," Alex said as if smelling her doubts on her scent. For all she knew, he was. There were patterns and meanings to scent that she had only begun to discover.

He was already well along in the process. Brushing him, she felt the silky-bristly fur covering his arm. Very much like an otter's. Mildly oily. Moisture-repellent. He'd swim like a shot, she knew.

"How come we all look different?" she asked as she dug deep into herself and tried to effect the change.

"The elders said it was all in our minds," Alex replied through his reshaped mouth. "That any of us could look however we wanted, mammals at least. Wolf, bear, tiger, seal . . . it's a personal thing."

Aiden closed her eyes, entering an inner darkness no less black than the real one surrounding her. She envisioned herself as the furred, catlike thing she'd been on those two brief occasions, striving to overcome her helpless fear of what she had become.

Alex is with me, she thought. *Alex loves me, I love him, and if this is how we are, it can't be wrong.*

An ember of heat grew within her, and spread. Her skin tingled. Her jaw ached as sudden sharp teeth forced themselves longer, reconfigured her mouth, pushed the lower half of her face forward. Her eyes throbbed, stung, and she felt her pupils stretch and narrow into cat-slits. Hands turned to paws, fingernails burst out as claws. Her slight form thickened, mass coming from somewhere — at the same time, her hunger pangs spiked into extreme discomfort. She knew she was burning fuel she couldn't spare. An unbelievable surge of energy filled those newly-developed muscles. Alex was right. Stronger this way. Faster. But still herself. Still Aiden.

"On three," he said in a guttural growl. "One . . . two . . ."

When he said 'three,' they rammed their shoulders against the underside of the trap door, lifting with their legs like the exercise instructors always said, bending and straightening, and the stairs groaned and wobbled and Aiden just knew the stairs would give way long before the trap door did, spilling her and Alex to the floor in a deadly welter of jagged stakes that would kill them as surely as any length of sharpened ash ever hammered through the chest of a vampire in the countless movies they showed on *Monstorama Theater* . . .

Wood cracked and splintered. The trap door jumped in its frame, letting in thin streams of horse-scented and horse-warmed air. Something heavy and metallic clanked around, a padlock jittering in its hasp. Pain pounded into Aiden's shoulders and back.

A long sliver fell out of one of the planks. There wasn't much light, but it was moderately less pitch-dark. Alex attacked the gap, clawing it, tearing away chunks and splinters that showered down on their upturned faces. He widened the opening enough to snake an arm through, groped around, found the bar, shoved – Aiden heard something in his shoulder pop – shoved harder. The bar squalled against the planks and slid free, and now only the padlock held them in.

They resumed their battering assault on the trap door. The sound of the twisting, bending, rending metal was unbearable. Nails on a blackboard. The cat-gut scream of a violin in untrained hands. Aiden was on the verge of screaming herself when the lock gave.

The trap door jumped up a few inches, dropped back down, took them by surprise, and smacked them both smartly on the head.

"Owww," Alex said, crouching on the staircase and rubbing his head, but he sounded more delighted than hurt. He stood up and pushed, and the trap door levered slowly open. "Out you go."

Aiden scurried into the stable, grabbed the edge of the trap door, and flung it all the way open. It was dusk-dark in here, storm-dark, all in shades of purple and deep grey rather than inky black. Her vision adjusted far better than it ever had before, letting her see shapes and outlines.

Alex emerged. Even bruised and holding himself as if it hurt to move – she was standing with the same careful, bent posture herself – he was even more of a striking and handsome figure than he was when human.

"We did it," she said, laughing in amazement.

"Look at you, Aiden . . ." His large eyes, glimmering and reflective, moved slowly from her head down over her body, lingering where he couldn't help but linger, and then returning to her face. "You're beautiful!"

Already, her accelerated healing was leaching the pain from her aching bones. She went to him, and they embraced, fur rubbing against fur. Desire threatened to sweep her away and she would have been ready to give herself to him right here, right now, consummate their agreement in this stable . . . except that another hunger had to come first.

The horses knew it, too. From the moment they'd appeared, the whinnying and restless stomping had intensified. Alex let go of Aiden and turned toward the stalls. A stallion reared up, hooves striking the air, but Alex ignored him and sprang over one of the gates, onto the back of a mare. The horse screamed and tried to bolt, colliding with the gate full-force and snapping the latch.

But by then it was over. Momentum carried the large body out into the barn proper, where the mare's legs folded like broken stilts and she landed nearly at Aiden's feet with blood spewing from the carnage of her throat. Alex, hunkered atop the animal, tore into the hide and burrowed around. He came up with a lump of something, marinated in thick red sauce. He brought it to Aiden and, with a graceful movement, bent and laid it at her feet.

She picked it up, warm and sliding in her grasp, hot with the fading life of the mare. Somewhere deep in the core of her mind were revulsion and abhorrence, the civilized Aiden's last despairing cry. The rest of her, thrilled by the symbolism and sparked by ravening hunger, did not hesitate. She brought the organ – the liver, packed with the nutrients her body craved – to her mouth and bit into it. Blood and juices spilled down her chin.

Alex made a joyful baying sound as she accepted his offer of food, then fell upon the carcass and began pulling off ragged strips of meat for himself. When Aiden had devoured the liver, she joined him.

The rest of the horses had gone deathly quiet. Without their noise, Aiden heard another roar rise and fall. She lifted her head, looking at Alex. He, gulping down a chunk of meat, tilted his head to listen.

Roars. Howls. Inhuman cries of pain.

Then, faintly piercing the crevices between boards in the walls of the stable, a dim orange light.

"Something's happening," he said.

Aiden swiped the back of her hand across her bloody lips. She went with him to the door, helped him drag it open.

They could see the back and side of the lodge from here. The downstairs windows were alive with flame, some coming out through an opening of shattered glass and scaled the outer walls like a troop of fiery monkeys. The wind snatched at them, the snow pelted them, but the fiery troop climbed on regardless.

From within the burning house arose such a wail of agony and torment that it almost froze Aiden's marrow. She'd never heard anything so terrible and never wanted to again. A blazing comet burst through another window, glass flying in a sparkling spray. The thing had a long and lean shape, and was wrapped in and trailing fire like the gown and train of some hellish bride. It plowed into a snowdrift.

Alex went to all fours and raced toward the house. Aiden followed close behind.

The thing that had gone into the snow rose up again, smoldering. Even at this distance and in this poor light, Aiden recognized Simone Drachen.

She was in catwoman form, struggling upright with what was left of her hair hanging around her in blackened, charred clumps. She looked back through the window, and whatever she saw made her shriek even more terribly than the wail of only moments before.

Simone stood as if spellbound, rending her face with her claws and pealing that awful cry. Fire roared through the house, finding fuel aplenty in its wooden construction. More windows exploded outward from the heat, and above the crackle of the flames, other voices could be heard. Coughing. Shouting. Indistinguishable.

Alex, like a thing possessed, went for Simone. Some instinct prompted her to turn at the last second and let her see him leap. Despite the hideous pain that must have enveloped her, scorched over most of her body as she was, she dodged him and struck, clubbing him on the side of the head. He pitched sideways into a snowbank.

"Alex!" Aiden threw caution aside and charged.

Hearing her, seeing her, Simone's lip lifted away from her fangs in a cruel snarl. She met Aiden halfway. Her skin was flaking, peeling away in great scorched patches, bubbling and red and raw, yet she came at Aiden with claws extended.

Those claws sped toward her face. Aiden automatically raised an arm in defense, and screamed as Simone's claws shredded her flesh and grated off bone. She ducked barely in time to save her eyes from the other handful of death, taking slashes across her forehead and scalp.

Shedding snow, Alex tackled Simone and knocked her away from Aiden. They rolled, thrashing, Simone trying to get her hindclaws into Alex's belly, Alex reaching with his jaws for Simone's neck. Simone struck first, and her kick pitched Alex up and off, deep gouges opening him.

Aiden, with a ferocity that stunned her, got between the hellcat and her injured mate. She hunched her back, causing her fur to rise up all along her spine, and spat a warning. Alex, behind her, groaned and writhed with his hands pressed to his stomach and his blood staining the snow.

She waited for Simone to attack again, knowing she was no match for the older, more experienced, and psychotic female. None of that mattered. She'd defend her mate or die trying. That was the way it worked. That was all that was important.

Simone didn't attack. Simone glanced toward the house and then, with a grimace of grief, hatred, and fear, she spun and fled. The blowing snow swallowed her up in seconds.

Cradling her arm, Aiden fell to her knees beside Alex. He was breathing rapidly through clenched teeth, but the flow of blood was already lessening.

Another shape sailed through the window, through a curtain of smoke and flame. Aiden fell flat as it passed over her, was showered by the snow kicked up in its long, side-skidding landing. A spike of terror pierced her. *Donovan!*

No. Not Donovan.

This changeling was a thickset beast that looked part wolf, and part bear. His coat was grizzled and grey, his muzzle pure white. One hot yellow eye found her and moved on; the other was a socket of scar tissue. Aiden's pulse drummed as she realized this was the same old man she'd seen snoozing in a lawn chair, the one Alex had called Grandfather.

He looked from her to Alex, and then in the direction of Simone's frantic flight. The snow hadn't yet had a chance to fill in her tracks. His hind legs dug deep and propelled him forward in a bound and he was off, vanishing into the night just as she had done.

Alex sat halfway up as if seeing a mirage. He turned his gaze to Aiden in questioning wonder — *tell me I didn't just see that,* he seemed to be silently saying.

Before she could reply, they heard a woman calling out urgently from inside the house.

"Damn it, Jeff, get up, you are *not* allowed to die on me!"

They knew that voice. It was Birdie.

*　*　*

Gideon and Donovan hit like two impacting tectonic plates, both of them buckling under the strain. Birdie, still reeling from the revelation about Mike and Stacey Baker, could only watch as the males fought. No nature-documentary dominance thing here. This was a battle to the death, and its outcome was anyone's ball game.

Simone tried to tip the odds by tearing away from the old-timer and raking her claws at the back of Gideon's leg. She would have hamstrung him and ended the fight then and there, if Jeff hadn't gotten in the way.

His brave effort didn't last long. Screeching, Simone swiped at him twice, once with each hand. Her claws stuttered over ribs like a stretch of bad road and she left a sloppy red letter-X that went from each shoulder to each hip. Even with everything else going on, Birdie heard the puff of air escaping from a punctured lung.

Jeff fell backward, but he snagged double handfuls of Simone's pelt as he went and pulled her over with him. As his back hit the floor, he drove both legs up and out, flipping her. She went head over heels, airborne, spinning past Birdie with an astounded look, and then landed dead-center in the blazing fireplace.

Sparks, burning logs, and a torrent of coals flew out. Simone let loose a wail that hit higher and more intense notes than any scream Birdie had ever managed in her entire film career. Her red fur caught like dry grass, flaring up all around her in a hungry orange nova.

Donovan elbowed Gideon in the face, more desperate than ever to free himself. The carpet and the stuffing of the ruined couch were already igniting as the sparks found tinder. Jeff raised his head long enough to grin a hard, satisfied grin, and then let it fall back to the floor.

Simone, engulfed in flames, lunged out of the fireplace and scattered more embers. She knocked a kerosene lantern off the mantle as she emerged. It hit the floor and detonated like a bomb, runnels of flammable liquid coursing into the seething fire. Already, choking-dark smoke was billowing up, collecting amid the ceiling beams, layering down until it would fill the room. Simone spun to and fro, wild, panicked, and in a surge of sudden decision leaped out the window.

As the glass smashed out, the air rushed in and gave vigorous new life to the fire. The old-timer was by Jeff, hands pressed firmly in the raw hamburger of that red X. Birdie saw air bubbles around his fingers. Sucking chest wound. The sort of thing that would make all the sexy doctors on *ER* be yelling for rib-spreaders and other nasty implements that would have sounded right at home in a torture chamber.

Oblivious to all of this, Gideon and Donovan were deadlocked. Gideon's slightly greater size and determination was matched by Donovan's frenzy over Simone. Muscles quivered. Sparks alighted on them and seared holes in their fur.

Simone appeared in the shard-framed opening of the window, burnt but no longer burning. She was just in time to see Gideon clamp his jaws on Donovan's head. Under that tremendous pressure, Donovan's skull cracked like a walnut.

But in the moment before it did, in the moment before Gideon's fangs punched through to the diseased meat of the brain inside, Donovan thrust his claws with uncanny accuracy and lethal strength into Gideon's unprotected abdomen, up at an angle, coming up through the bottom of the ribcage to seize and crush Gideon's heart.

Both of them went rigid, shuddering in death throes. They collapsed lifelessly in a heap. As they did, their bodies underwent that final change, which was one part of folklore that Ghostman admitted that humanity had gotten right. The final reversion to human form, to protect their race from discovery.

It might have worked before the advent of laboratory testing, tissue samples, DNA analysis . . . but even in the days when doctors used leeches and believed in balancing the humors, Birdie thought they might have wondered at this scene of death anyway. Two huge naked men, dead in bizarre positions.

Simone shrieked again. Birdie saw her tear at her own face. She whirled from the window in horror or denial.

The room was ablaze now, heat baking Birdie in her coat. The perfume bottle, which she'd dropped without knowing when, exploded and added its cheap, fragrant accelerant. The layers of smoke were roiling lower, low enough that some streamed out the broken windows.

The old-timer was shouting at her to get out. She took too deep a breath trying to answer him and went into a coughing fit, the lining of her mouth tasting smoky. Jeff, healing but not fast enough, was having more trouble breathing because he was pulling that smoke straight into his lungs, unfiltered by the bronchial system. Fire was eating its way across the floorboards.

"Help him," the old-timer said. "Get him out."

"What about you?" rasped Birdie. "And I have to find Fergs!"

He didn't stick around to listen. He ran for the same window through which Simone had disappeared, shifting smoothly to his beast-form on the go, never missing a stride. That was a nifty trick that Birdie was willing to bet came only with decades of practice.

Jeff was laboriously getting up, but that was a mistake because the smoke was down to their height and getting lower. He crumpled, wheezing, and then his breath stopped. His eyes rolled helplessly like an animal in a slaughterhouse pen. He clutched at his throat, at his savaged chest.

"Damn it, Jeff, get up, you are *not* allowed to die on me!" Birdie yelled.

Wouldn't you know it, the minute you actually *needed* the stuff you learned in CPR and first aid courses, it all went right out of your head. She clamped her lips over his and blew. Air burbled out of him like bubbles blown through a straw in an extra-thick milkshake. The leak was a pinhole now, not a rip, and without stopping to consider how gross an act it was, she plugged it with her forefinger and blew his lungs full again.

This time, it took. Jeff's chest lurched and hitched, and he inhaled on his own.

The only clear air was down by the floor. The noise of the fire was so loud that Birdie had to tug at him and make crawling motions. He nodded, and with her in the lead they kept low and made their way out of the inferno of the living room.

They got into the kitchen, where the back door still stood open. Blessed fresh air swirled in, bringing dancing white flakes.

A slim, furred shape appeared in front of them. Birdie rocked back on her heels and jammed her taser at it. Hair-trigger reflexes and she almost hit the button before she grasped the significance of a pale blond pelt rather than a red one.

"Birdie, it's me!" Aiden cried in a growling but still familiar voice.

Alex was with her. Neither of them looked in the best of shape, bloodied and alarmingly gaunt, but it was them. Jeff gaped.

"Huh? Alex? What?"

"Now's not the time for explanations, handsome," said Birdie. "Let's beat feet before the whole place goes up like a torch, whaddaya say?"

Between the three of them, they were able to hoist and carry Jeff out of the house. Birdie led them to her car, which was hip-deep in snow. They set Jeff down beside it. Alex lowered himself into a sitting position, probing at the wounds at his waist, which had re-opened in the effort of moving Jeff.

"Stay with them," Aiden said. She sounded slurred and funny with her new teeth but Birdie had no trouble understanding her.

Believing her, that was another story. "What about you?"

"The elder is going to need help against Simone. I may not be much, but I'm better than nothing."

"Aiden, no!" protested Alex. "I'll go."

"You're hurt worse than me . . . and this is all my fault anyway. I've got to do something."

"You're nuts," Jeff coughed, and winced, and lay weakly in the snow. "Good luck."

"I won't let you." Alex grabbed her by the wrist.

Rather than pull away, she covered his hand with hers and looked at him so warmly that Birdie wouldn't have been surprised to see the snow melt away in a five-foot radius. "I love you, Alex."

"Don't go," he begged.

She kissed him on the forehead. This was an Aiden that Birdie had never even imagined, an Aiden she would have scoffed at if anyone had predicted it. This change of theirs was a lot more than physical, all right.

Alex choked on a sob. His head drooped and he shut his eyes tight so he wouldn't have to watch her leave.

"Come back, okay?" Birdie mustered half a grin, best she could do.

"Count on it."

* * *

CHAPTER 5
JANUARY 6, TUESDAY
EVENING

The pain was her entire world. It filled her body, but that would heal. The pain that filled her soul would stay with her for the rest of her life.

Deceived! Betrayed!

It had been a trap all along, a treacherous trap.

Alexander had let himself be captured, that much was obvious. And then sending the girl, alone and so seemingly-innocent, to put her off her guard. When all the while, Gideon, despised Gideon, had been laying his plans.

She shouldn't have expected any better of him. The hypocritical, misbegotten filth! To think she'd ever loved him, ever let him touch her. When he'd gone on to sully her memory by rutting with humans. Rutting by force, and killing, and thinking it didn't count because he used one of his beloved knives instead of his claws, because he'd only killed and not eaten. As if that made him better!

Simone shook with rage as she remembered him, casting her out of the pack. Exiling her. Standing there so proud, so noble . . . so *righteous*. He'd thought that no one would find out his dirty secret. But Donovan had, her precious and darling cub, her virile and dynamic young mate. Donovan had witnessed Gideon's slinking craven act of rape and murder. Donovan had found the other human who'd witnessed it, and brought Ernie to her so they could finish him. Donovan, her love.

Lost to her now.

Lost forever.

She was alone.

There would be no pack.

No! She couldn't let herself believe that. Donovan was gone, yes, murdered, foully slain by his own father . . . the crack and give of his skull, the light snuffed from his eyes . . . these things would haunt Simone for the rest of her life. He had died for her, just as he'd lived for her. In his dying, he had at least taken Gideon with him.

And he'd left her with a cub.

She was sure now. It had only been a few hours, but she was sure. New life, a new start, grew inside of her. A boy cub, perhaps, russet-furred. This one would be hers from the beginning. Devoted. Adoring. Dedicated.

Her skin itched, itched. When she scratched at it, the crisp burnt exterior peeled away in flakes and strips, whisked away by the ceaseless wind. What was revealed beneath was as pink and innocent as the flesh of the cub in her womb. But, perversely, the pain got worse as she healed.

The initial burning, like a bath in lava, like immersion in molten steel, had hurt like no other pain she'd ever experienced. Bright and brief as a shooting star. Once the nerves were deadened, the charred coating of her skin had been numb. Now that those nerves were re-forming, sending re-generated tendrils out along the dead pathways, the agonized cells renewed their cries.

Her hair was a loss, little but an ashy smudge on her bare head. Even her eyebrows, eyelashes, were burnt away. They'd grow back. Until then, she would be ugly, but who would there be to see her? No pack . . . and she'd be fully mended long before the cub was ready to be born.

They had all been against her, all except her dear Donovan. She should have known that they wouldn't be content to leave her in peace. No, Gideon would have his revenge. She wished, bitterly, that he could have survived just a little longer. Long enough to face the shock and recriminations of his pack as they saw the truth of him, and their own folly for having believed in him. He had died too quickly.

Had the rest died? She'd opened Jeffrey like a fish. His corpse was probably being cremated along with Donovan's and Gideon's in the lodge.

Her father's home, in flames . . . and wasn't it fitting? Because *he* was as good as dead, too. He'd died in spirit years before, only his flesh hanging on by force of habit. He'd stood by and done nothing as his daughter, his only cub, was exiled and her children taken from her. No words in her defense. He hadn't even met her eyes, but bowed his head and acquiesced to Gideon's wishes. Gone along with him. Like the rest of them.

Well, they'd paid! They'd all paid. She supposed she hadn't hurt Alexander and his human-born bitch enough, but there was time. She'd be back. Once she had healed, once she'd borne her cub in some safe and far-away place, once it was being raised up strong on manblood and manflesh, chewed in her mouth and delivered into his, then she'd return. She'd find them. Wherever they went.

They might think they could hide from her. How little they knew!

But suddenly, the idea of waiting and biding her time wasn't good enough. She wanted them dead *now*, tonight, the entire pack of them wiped out in one night of fire and blood.

Veering before she entered the woods, Simone approached the stable. The storm had intensified until she could barely see three paces ahead, through the veils and cyclones of wind-whipped snow. It played havoc with the scents as well, and sounds.

Even so, she found the stable without mishap, drawn like a moth to a light by the life force of the horses beating within. To her unique perceptions, honed and made more powerful by the heady alchemy of the forbidden meat, she could sense their lives throbbing, beating, like the drumming of many hearts.

She reached out with her mind. Called to them. Bent them to her will. It was harder with horses than it had been with the cats, because cats were predators and horses were prey. Their nature was to flee the likes of her. Yet she was hot with power, demanding in her summons, and they could not help but obey.

Their whinnies became screams. Hooves battered against wood. Some of them would snap bones, or even die as they hurled themselves against the walls of their confinement. But some would make it.

Dark shapes hove through the spinning white motes. Their eyes were wild, their mouths ringed with foam. A few were bloodied, and stirred Simone's hunger. She ignored it. She seized their minds with her own, in a mental claw no less devastating than the ones at the ends of her fingers.

The horses turned as one, prettily as if they'd been under the crop and guidance of an expert trainer. They broke into a gallop. A single order would be pounding in their brains. To kill. To kill any living thing in the area of the lodge, excepting herself.

The snow swallowed them up. Simone laughed harshly and headed for the forest, bent into the fierce wind with her arm raised over her face.

*   *   *

Her spoor stank of madness.

The smell brought back memories that Malcolm Drachen had banished years ago.

He hadn't wanted to believe that Simone would follow in her mother's tracks, that history would repeat itself so insidiously, so terribly. The scars scrawled into his face burned, a grim souvenir of that night so long ago when his own mate had nearly killed him. As powerful as the healing forces of their bodies were, severed parts could not be replaced and some tissue could never fully mend. She had torn his ear off, practically scalped him, savaged his eye beyond repair.

He felt the vibrations thudding through the ground before he heard, before he saw. It gave him the instant's warning he needed to leap aside as a stallion loomed out of the darkness. It reared and struck out at him, missing but correcting its aim almost immediately.

Malcolm changed course, but here came more horses. Crazed, all of them crazed, seeking to stomp the life out of anything in their path. He nipped at the nearest and made the mare squeal as a patch of her hide ripped away.

But somehow they'd encircled him, snorting and pawing in a manner more suited to bulls than to horses. They charged.

Bracing himself, he watched for an opening and knew he might have to take at least one hoof strike to get through . . .

There!

Quickly, between them, and —

A pair of rear hooves caught him in the side. He was thrown, sky and earth revolving dizzily, and hit hard. Too much like the time he'd gotten close to Olivia, only to have her send a buck after him . . . tossed, gored by those antlers . . . he hadn't been gored this time but the ribs along that side sagged inward and he was a sheet of pain from shoulder to hindquarters.

He lay limp in the snow, his breath steaming around his head. The horses wheeled and came back, nearly prancing in their excitement, each champing for the chance to be the one to stave in his skull.

As they closed in, one of them suddenly faltered and went down, neighing. A pale blur, nearly invisible against the snow, darted behind the lead stallion. Malcolm glimpsed a flash of claws. The stallion's leg buckled. The pale thing sprang onto his back and dug in for a good hold.

If he hadn't already been immobilized by pain, Malcolm would have been immobilized by shock. He had never seen this small female before, but knew as surely as if she'd been wearing a sign that this was the girl, Alex's chosen one. The one over whom such a fuss had been made. He'd had his doubts as to whether any bitten human would be able to transform so completely, or survive the process. But here she was, fighting like a little lioness. Untutored. Lacking the skill even a six-month cub would have. But with gumption, he had to give her that.

The rest of the horses, bound in obedience to Simone, started rearing and kicking at her. Their hooves kept hitting the stallion. He retaliated by biting at them with his strong, square teeth. An all-out war ensued among the horses.

The female launched herself from the stallion's back, leaving ragged slashes. She landed less-than-gracefully beside Malcolm and looked warily up at him with silvery-white eyes brimming with apprehension.

"Well done, cubling," he said, righting himself. Her distraction had given him time to heal. Not all the way, not even enough to be without pain, but he could move.

Her relief was palpable. He surmised that she'd been expecting to be shunned, or attacked outright.

"None of that," he assured her. "We've bigger problems. Step lively!"

She fell in beside him, running well although clearly not entirely accustomed to going on all fours. They left the horses behind, their shrieks as they tore at one another in their frenzy making them sound as if they'd been beset by hornets. Malcolm cast about for the scent, Simone's scent, and found it. Between her sweat and her shed curls of burnt skin and fur, her trail was as easy to follow as if it had been marked with signposts.

All the same, they had to find her soon. The storm was getting worse.

*   *   *

The dropoff caught her by surprise. Simone backpedaled as the snow gave way. Too late.

She pitched headlong down the embankment, loosing a startled cry that cut off sharply as she hit a smooth sheet of ice. Her palm scraped across a ridge of stone that stuck up above the frozen surface of the river, drawing a line of blood.

The ice creaked beneath her. She got onto all fours. She placed each step carefully, testing it, as she picked her way across.

"Simone!"

His voice stabbed her like knives. Simone jumped, rising to her knees and turning with her hair a smoldering ruin.

Malcolm, bearish and grey, stood on the bank looking down at her. A multitude of emotions warred in his single yellow eye, but chief among them were resolution and sorrow. A much smaller form slunk up alongside him, hanging back.

"It is over, Simone. Let it be over."

"Let you kill me, you mean?" she snapped, flexing her claws. "I don't think you can."

"I may not want to, but I can, and I will. Just as I had to kill your mother. I was too lenient with her, and with you. I argued for your exile rather than your death. But I've learned the error of my ways."

"Come and do it, then!" She hurled her weight against a boulder that protruded from the steep slope.

It had perhaps held that precarious angle for years, decades, always seeming about to fall but firmly anchored. When she pushed at it, it came loose with a grinding of earth and rolled-bounced-crashed into the thinnest part of the ice.

Water surged up from the uneven hole, snatching away chunks of frosty blue-white. Gouts splashed high into the bitterly cold air. A network of fractures spread out around the hole and pie-wedges broke off to bob with the sluggish current.

"Cross that, if you can," jeered Simone, fists on her hips as she glared defiantly across the river.

Malcolm backed off. Simone shouted a laugh, which waned as he reappeared at a run. He charged, he leapt, a powerful bound, and it carried him all the way across. He landed a few yards upstream of her, stumbling and whapping his chin on the ground.

He slowly raised his head and she saw her death portended in his eye. No more sorrow. Only grim purpose. It touched her heart with fear and she abruptly knew that he could and he would. He was old, he was maimed and scarred, but he *would* kill her.

The knowledge cut through the veil of her madness and she spun to flee for her life.

Low-hanging branches grabbed at her as if in collusion with her pursuer. She beat them aside and earned stinging welts along her flanks as they sprang back. As the forest grew denser, the snow cover was thinner. Stones and deadwood stripped her paws raw as she ran.

Something was ahead. A shape made of unnaturally straight lines and angles. A cabin, really little more than a hut, its roof sagging beneath a drunkenly fallen tree. A doorframe minus a door gaped like a mouth. Two windows, tarpaper flapping from them, were dark and empty eyes. The cabin had the aspect of a skull from which the flesh had long since decayed.

Simone angled past it. There would be no sanctuary for her in such a flimsy place. One good hit and it would fall in on itself like a house of cards.

She rounded the corner of it and Malcolm was there, slavering, heaving, strings of saliva hanging from his jaws. He stank of overstrain, his muscles trembling from an exertion far beyond him, but his expression showed no sign of it as he slammed into her and sent her rolling.

Before she could regain her footing, he was on her. Digging into the ruff of fur around her neck. Going for the vital throat. Simone struck at him in a wild fury. Her claws pierced deep into his eye and extinguished its yellow-white glow. His blood splattered onto her face, scalding-hot.

Sightless, he fought on. His jaws seized her ruff and pulled, peeling back a swatch of skin and pelt. It hurt but was far from mortal. Simone latched onto the sides of his head with both hands, digging in her claws and meaning to yank off his face as if it were no more than a mask.

His forelimbs encircled her and lifted. Tightened. Her spine crackled in the deadly pressure of the bear hug. She darted her head forward and bit off his ear, spitting out the furry scrap.

He squeezed harder. The dregs of her breath came out in a thin whistle and she could not inhale. Her hands reshaped into a more human configuration, thumbs tipped with thick talons. These, she jammed hard as she could into his eyes.

Malcolm's arms locked. Iron bands. Simone both felt and heard the loud snap as her back broke. She went slack and limp from the waist down.

She dug deeper with her thumbs, met the narrow rind of bone at the back of the sockets, drilled through it. He began to jitter in place, blood pouring out around her hands in freshets. His arms abruptly loosened and she fell. Her legs folded strangely under her, more bones breaking but unfelt in her paralysis.

Her claws came out of his head with twin slurping pops. He staggered back, reflexively raising his hands to his face. His back struck the wall of the cabin and it gave way, dumping him backward. The roof tipped, leaned, but did not quite come down.

A high, whining keen was coming from somewhere. Simone realized that she was making that noise, that pitiful dying whine, and made herself stop. Her upper half was still functioning and she thrust out her arms to grab onto Malcolm's ankles. She pulled herself toward him in short, sliding jerks. He was still moving, still alive.

As she dragged herself beside him, something inside of her let go, a cramping slithery rush that she couldn't fully feel but did fully understand, even before the dark red torrent gushed from between her legs and she scented the death of a cub that hadn't been more than a miniscule cluster of cells.

Screaming in agony at this final loss, she threw herself on Malcolm and tore at his chest. She would have his heart for this, have it while it shuddered its last beat, and shred it between her teeth.

He twisted with shocking strength, one last burst of energy, and brought his jaws to her throat. They closed, fangs meeting around her windpipe, and he wrenched his head. The last thing Simone heard was a thick ripping sound, like someone tearing heavy canvas. Then she knew no more.

*   *   *

Aiden approached timidly on two legs, her hands over her mouth and her eyes enormous as she took in the scene.

She hadn't trusted herself to clear the river, so she'd had to go upstream and cross where the ice was still solid. By the time she'd found the trail and caught up with Malcolm, she'd been too late to do more than witness the final exchange of blows.

Simone slowly shifted to human form, her skin blue-tinged white where it wasn't soaked in blood. She looked smaller somehow, and Aiden was amazed to find that she could feel sorry for her. In death, her face had lost the cruel curve of smile. She was pretty, even beautiful.

Malcolm was still covered in coarse grey fur. As Aiden neared, she saw with shock that his fingers were moving, grasping feebly at nothing. She heard a whispery moan, which turned into a weak cough.

Hardly daring to breathe, she hurried closer and pushed Simone's corpse off of him. Her knees unhinged and she landed at his side, doubting that even a changeling's healing ability could fix him now.

His eyes were gone, blood so dark it looked black pooling in the sockets like dollops of oil. Simone's dying act had been to expose his ribs, so that Aiden could clearly see the irregular seizures of his heart.

The hand that had been grasping rose from the scarlet snow and groped toward her. She wanted to recoil but took it instead.

"I'm here. What can I do?"

He licked his lips and tried to speak, but only produced another of those whispery moans.

"She's dead," Aiden said.

"Over," he said. "Started here . . . ended . . . here. As . . . it . . . should."

The hand she held went stiff, then curled in on itself limply. A single shaky exhalation was followed by only stillness.

Aiden stayed where she was until Malcolm was fully human in appearance. She'd hardly known him, but she wept all the same. For his bravery, and for the brief kindness he'd shown her.

Rising from the bodies, Aiden studied the cabin. She could already hear the stealthy noises of scavengers drawn by the smell of blood, even in the depths of winter and the midst of a storm. She couldn't bury them, couldn't carry them, but she didn't want to leave them here like this.

A few judiciously-placed kicks, and the walls and roof of the old structure came down like jackstraws. It wasn't perfect; an industrious animal could burrow under and get at them, but they were covered.

Once that deed was done, it occurred to her that she had little idea where she was, and the ongoing snowfall would be rapidly filling the tracks. She wanted to say something. But what was there to say?

In the end, she said nothing. She returned to the river easily enough and crossed at the same point. Her fur was caked with snow, the pads of her feet abraded.

Soon she saw the fire, snatches of it through blowing flurries, and used it as a beacon. The horses were gone. The lodge was a skeleton of timbers with flesh of flame, and the tempestuous wind had thrown burning debris all around. Some had landed on the stable, which was catching.

Limping on her sore paws, her legs aching, she circled the blazing structure and saw the minivan, and Birdie's red Volkswagen. Three shadows were outlined by the fire.

She called out, but the wind flung her words back at her. Prompted by some primal instinct, she threw back her head and ululated a silvery howl.

The next thing she knew, Alex was there. He swept her into his arms, speechless, his mouth working wordlessly as his hands framed her face. She huddled against him, pressing into his fire-warmed pelt. He was healed, and as Jeff and Birdie came up to them, she saw that Jeff was too.

"It's over," she said, wiping her eyes. "They're dead, both of them. It's over."

*   *   *

EPILOGUE

The first Saturday in May was blameless blue and picture-perfect, as ideal a Trinity Bay day as anyone could ask for. It was a day just made for a wedding. The town buzzed with excitement, particularly around the Plaza where Georgia Dansbourne had informally deputized two dozen people into setting up chairs, stringing crepe paper, and organizing the refreshments.

The ceremony itself was to take place beneath a white wickerwork bower, not far from the central statue. Most of the guests were already in place, and Damon Blake, in his honored spot as best man, patted Scott James reassuringly on the shoulder.

Scott had come through his ordeal well. Plastic surgery had smoothed away the scars, leaving just the faintest hint of four parallel claw marks. True to character, Scott regarded them more as dueling scars, or badges of honor, than as any sort of disfigurement.

They never did talk much about what had happened in Tom's Market last January. Damon knew that most of the witnesses had convinced themselves that what they'd seen had been nothing more than the work of garden-variety psychopaths with knives. It was easier that way. In Trinity Bay, getting over and moving past bizarre and unexplainable events had become something of an art form in the past few years.

Damon wished he could forget so readily. He had put things together in his mind that would have gotten him committed if he'd breathed a word to any outsiders. Officially, the case was still open but back-burnered. Unofficially, the loose ends nagged at Damon.

Ernie Warrigan's body turning up the way it had, for instance, discovered by an amateur bird-watcher who would probably never get over the shock. The two young women who'd gone missing, and whose homes had been broken into and hastily stripped of personal belongings a few nights later, for another. The detailed lab analysis that had finally come back on the hair samples taken from the Baker house, samples that hadn't been identified as entirely human or as any known type of animal.

And, of course, what he'd seen and experienced that day in the market.

He knew that sometimes it was best to let things go. That there weren't always answers and sometimes a man had to learn to live with his curiosity. His town was safe now, which was what really mattered. His town was safe, and his friend was tying the knot.

The ceremony went flawlessly under the benign spring sun. Theresa served as Dani Kensington's matron of honor, Lora as flower girl in a dress of amber-colored satin that matched her mother's. The James family, most of them big and blond and jovial, cheered as Scott pulled his tall bride's head down so he could reach it for the official man-and-wife kiss.

After, as the formidable Mrs. Dansbourne was presiding over the refreshment table and her daughter Nyx was campaigning for a temporary job to fill in while Scott was on his honeymoon, Damon spotted a late arrival. Chas Vandermere, slim and classy in his tux, wove through the crowd in his direction. Chas had something in his hand that looked like a rolled-up magazine, and his expression was both excited and urgent.

"Come by tomorrow and we'll talk," Damon said to Nyx. He excused himself and went to meet Chas.

"Have you seen this?" Chas asked without preamble.

The thing in his hand was indeed a magazine, a horror and dark fantasy periodical called *Frightastic*. Damon hiked an eyebrow.

"Not my usual reading material," he drawled.

"It arrived in the mail just now," Chas said. "No return address. But I thought you should have a look."

The cover was black, the title in slanted and jagged white letters like bolts of lightning. It was graced with a picture of a rotund man in a dapper white suit, who looked about as scary as an ice cream man. The words slashed in red across the bottom read: *Back From the Dead and Better Than Ever — a Look at Wilfred Ghostman's New Television Project.*

Seeing Damon's quizzical expression, Chas took the magazine back and flipped through ads for slasher memorabilia, horror book clubs, and supernatural-themed video games to the feature story. He wordlessly held it open.

"Horror movie mogul moves to the small screen," Damon read, picking out the boxes sections in larger type than the rest of the text. "*Trace* combines comedy and edge-of-the-seat action with Ghostman's unique horror-shlock stamp and ground-breaking special effects."

Chas tapped the photos. Damon looked. Here was the same rotund little man on a soundstage, huddled around a script with a film crew. Here was a tidy New Englandy-looking town, identified as being someplace in Oregon, turned eerie in the silver-blue moonlight. And here . . .

"Holy smokes," Damon said slowly.

Veteran scream queen Birdie Yale as title character Trace Specter, a psychic debunker who discovers a race of shape-shifters waging their own private war with humanity as the prize, one caption read, beneath a picture of a busty brunette in a fedora and long dark coat. She was shown in a dramatic reaction pose, confronted with a sleek, pale-furred creature that looked like a cross between a cougar and a man.

He turned another page. Now he was looking at an inset article within the body of the main story, a sidebar sort of thing having to do with the incredible transformation sequences and make-up, which Ghostman was apparently keeping so close a secret that most of his crew didn't even know how it was done.

"I reckon I have an idea, though," Damon murmured. "I reckon I do at that."

*　　*　　*

THE AUTHOR

Christine Morgan lives in the Pacific Northwest with her husband, daughter, and trio of cats. She is a graduate of California's Humboldt State University, with a B. A. in Psychology. Her overnight-shift job as a residential counselor in a psychiatric facility allows her ample time to write as well as the occasional flash of inspiration.

She divides her writing time among a variety of genres – horror, fantasy, childrens' fiction, and erotica among them. Her previous books include the *MageLore* and *ElfLore* fantasy trilogies, the Silver Doorway series of children's books, and the other Trinity Bay horror novels, *Black Roses* and *Gifted Children*. She was nominated for an Origins Award for her zombie short story "Dawn of the Living-Impaired," and various others of her works have appeared in anthologies, magazines, and several online forums.

A longtime gamer, Christine can often be found at regional conventions, running games as well as promoting books. She has a fond relationship with the folks at Steve Jackson Games and other names in the gaming industry, all of whom have been incredibly supportive and helpful. In 2003, Christine and Tim released their first role-playing game supplement, the controversial *Naughty and Dice: An Adult Gamer's Guide to Sexual Situations*.

Christine's other interests span a wide gamut – robotic combat, British comedy, documentaries, and reality game shows make up the majority of her television viewing habits; horror, mysteries, and thrillers dominate her bookshelves; and she enjoys cooking and crafts.

Christine welcomes and appreciates feedback from readers. She can be reached by e-mail at christine@sabledrake.com and invites visitors to her websites, www.sabledrake.com and www.christine-morgan.com.

BEFORE TRINITY BAY
WAS VISITED BY THE
CHANGELINGS . . .

IT WAS THE HOME OF
TWO DARKER EVILS . . .

$14.95 • 0-9702189-5-8 • 300 pages

With her marriage over and her career on hold, children's writer Theresa Zane returns to her childhood home of Trinity Bay, California to live with her father. There, in the lush green of the coastal redwood forest, Theresa meets the man of her dreams. Literally.

He is an incubus, able to infiltrate the sleeping minds of women and take on whatever form fulfills their darkest, most hidden fantasies. The strength of Theresa's spirit draws him like moth to flame. He decides that he will not rest until she is his.

The women of Trinity Bay fall prey, one after another, to the power of their dreams. The incubus, draining their life energy, inspires them to acts of violence and suicide, and leaves his victims troubled by the lingering image of a black rose. The same black rose that appears in an heirloom necklace that Theresa Zane finds in her home. The same necklace with a past linked to Seacliff, the mansion on the hill overlooking the town.

A series of brutal, horrific murders all across the country are connected only by one clue – a single black rose left at the scene of each crime. Further investigation into the backgrounds of the men reveal one other thing they have in common, one person they all knew. This lets a Trinity Bay chief of police and two New York City detectives guess who the next targets might be, but how can they be protected against a force that can reach out from beyond the walls of nightmare?

Only Theresa can combat this menace, and she'll need a necklace with a haunted past and the help of three dead girls to do it.

$16.95 • 0-9702189-9-0 • 372 pages

The children of Trinity Bay are like any ordinary American kids. Lora Blake has a way with animals. Toby Edwards is the school brain. Jenny Forrester can talk her parents and friends into going along with anything.

But in the innocent-seeming gifts of these children and others like them, someone has discovered a power of terrifying potential.

A new force inhabits Seacliff, the house on the hill. From the outside, it appears benign – part school, part home, part hospital. Dedicated to healing, helping. But the true work going on at Seacliff is much, much darker.

As the project progresses, it will draw first the children, then their families, and finally an entire town into its shadow.

Gifted Children is Christine Morgan's second Trinity Bay novel. It is set three years after the events in *Black Roses*.

Dork Tower cartoon strip © John Kovalic. All Rights Reserved. Used with permission. http://dorktower.com

Curse of the Shadow Beasts
MageLore Book I

They come from beyond the walls of nightmare, hideous creatures bent on seeking and slaughtering, leaving only death and misery in their wake.

Arien Mirida knows them only too well. He has faced them before and witnessed their evil, and fears that their hunger can never be stopped.

Cat Sabledrake is about to meet the horror, when deadly dream becomes deadlier reality.

$11.95 • 1-56315-188-X • 182 pages

Dark of the Elvenwood
MageLore Book II

They are the Morvalan, elves in the service of a god of destruction. To further their war against humanity, they have joined forces with the minotaur wizard Solarrin. Together, they have hatched a plot to bring about the downfall of the Northlands.

Four reunited companions are all that stand between the Morvalan and success. But as Cat, Arien, Greyquin and Alphonse brave the dangers of the woodlands, a worse peril threatens the very home that they left to save.

$11.95 • 0-9702189-0-7 • 272 pages

Archmage of the Universe
MageLore Book III

He is Solarrin. Once his body was as twisted as his mind. Now inhabiting the form of a minotaur, his physical and magical prowesses are without equal.

The young Highlord is his pawn. The city of Thanis is under his control. His next move will plunge the Northlands into war.

The only ones who will stand a chance against him fled on a foolish quest — to bring his predecessor back from the dead.

$11.95 • 0-9702189-1-5 • 292 pages

Silversilk
ElfLore Book I

Ariana Mirida, sorceress and swordswoman, answers the call to adventure when she travels to her ancestral homeland seeking to clear her father's name. Little does she know how her quest will affect an entire kingdom . . .

$16.95 • 1-930928-66-1 • 340 pages

Knight of the Basilisk
ElfLore Book II

She was not always a warrior-priestess of the dark elven god. Once, she was only Tilanne, granted an unexpected destiny by a dying knight. To attain it, she had to defy convention and give up her dreams. This is her story.

$15.95 • 1-930928-47-5 • 276 pages

Truegold
ElfLore Book III

The future of the elves and the fate of all humanity hangs in the balance. It is a desperate race as the Emerin's rightful king tries to prevent a renegade knight from trading a sacred elven artifact for a poison that is bane to humankind. As they rush toward their final deadly confrontation, the wizards and counts of the Emerin carry on with their own schemes to fill the vacant throne.

$16.95 • 1-930928-92-0 • 276 pages